Praise for Tom Avitabile:

"Frighteningly realistic. Most of Washington really works this way. Homeland Security had better read this one and take corrective action."
– U.S. Ambassador Michael Skol on *The Eighth Day*

"Awesome. I could not go to sleep last night because I couldn't put it down!"
– Donna Hanover, WOR Radio 710 on *The Eighth Day*

"*The Hammer of God* is a tightly plotted, fear-filled and all-too-realistic thriller that is finely written, in fact the best this reviewer has read in a long time. It should be a best seller and will make the reader anxiously awaiting the third and final novel in this thriller trilogy! Great job, Tom Avitabile!"
– Crystal Book Reviews

"Well done and insuring that the reader will grab book three as soon as available."
– Bookbitch on *The Hammer of God*

The God Particle

The God Particle

Tom Avitabile

THE
STORY PLANT

The Story Plant
Studio Digital CT, LLC
P.O. Box 4331
Stamford, CT 06907

Jacket design by Dara Bartosiewicz

Print ISBN-13: 978-1-61188-194-3
E-book ISBN: 978-1-61188-195-0

Visit our website at *www.TheStoryPlant.com*
Visit the author's website at www.TomAvitabile.com

First Story Plant paperback printing: June 2014
Printed in the United States of America
0 9 8 7 6 5 4 3 2 1

Dedication

To all the scientists who have delivered us from the dark ages, and to the men and women of *con*science who have prevented them from returning us there.

And to the submariners of America's Silent Service — past, present and those still on eternal patrol. If I write a thousand books, I will never come close to honoring their courage, sacrifice and grit.

All religions, arts and sciences are branches of the
same tree.
-Albert Einstein

We keep moving forward, opening new doors, and
doing new things, because we're curious and curiosity
keeps leading us down new paths."
-Walt Disney

So a Higgs Boson goes into church.
The priest says, "What are you doing here?"
The Higgs Boson says,
"You can't have mass without me."
-Anonymous

Preface

Once upon a time... that is a refrain one might recall when first seeing the shores of Lake Geneva, dotted with fairytale castles, chateaus, small villages and picture-perfect walks. The calm, croissant-shaped 'lake' is actually a wide, flat portion of the river Rhone. On the French end of the crescent the gentle waves are refocused into a flowing river of crisp Alpine water that resumes its seventeen-year journey to empty into the Mediterranean Sea.

The storybook setting makes this idyllic place a most unlikely point of origin for the smallest particle of God to be used to ignite the ultimate cataclysm: the end of Earth, the solar system, the infinite universes beyond, indeed of all existence — gone in a flash — a flash to be seen only once, upon the death of time itself.

I. RUDE AWAKENING

Twang... Speeong... Pop... Grundle... she couldn't make out the noises through her cottony ears. As on an early school morning with her mother calling up to her room, *Brooke... you'll be late for the bus*, she didn't have the energy to open her eyes. *Ten more minutes, Mom.* She just wanted to lie there and catch a few more minutes of...

A distant cough rose from within her, and upon inhaling, a knife-like slice of acrid air made her choke again. Her right cheek was stinging. Kaarrack... the intensity of that next percussive punch popped her eyes open. They immediately started to burn. She focused on the world, the world around her: sideways, and on fire!

Before her mind could fathom the reality of the situation in which she had awakened, her instinct kicked in and she reared up, her palms scraping against the same sandpaper-rough surface that must have chewed into her cheek. Still disoriented, she sensed a blanket of intense heat enveloping her. As she tried to stand, her head spun and she fell back onto the skillet-hot metal floor. *No, not a floor... a deck!* Fear welled up inside her, forcing her brain to focus on the present. Without consciously deciding to do so, she was up and fighting a shifting equilibrium. *That's right, I am on a boat! There was an explosion.* She grabbed at the pain at the back of her head.

Then a tongue of flame lashed out. The scorching tip caused her to recoil and topple over the side railing that she had fallen near when the blast knocked her down. She fell a few feet and smacked into the salty cold of the sea. The shock of the immersion, the sudden muting of all sound into a watery gauze, and the radiating pain from the salt water digging into her bloodied cheek and hands snapped her into survival mode. She frog-kicked back up to the surface. Gasping for breath, she broke the surface of the ink-black water, which was streaked with orangey glints reflecting off the wave tops. Using her arms proved painful, but she managed to turn herself in the water, toward the heat, and saw she was yards from a burning ship. Around her was fiery flotsam and debris. The main part of the vessel was gone, seemingly bitten off by a huge sea monster that had taken out the wheelhouse and most of the superstructure with one bite. The ship was rolling over away from her. *The bomb must have been on the far side,* she thought. She spotted a chair cushion floating a few feet from her, and holding it beneath her chest and chin she kicked her feet, creating more distance between herself and the still-exploding vessel. Another concussive thud was immediately followed by a flaming piece of wreckage that landed with a splash just ahead of her. She made her way around it.

Her head was sideways on the soggy but buoyant cushion. She had never been so exhausted, even on the survival course at Quantico, where pushing agents to their physical limits for three days was the whole idea. Out of the corner of her eye she saw something rip through the wave tops. She propelled herself upward to see if she could spot it again. There were four of them. Four fins slicing through the water... *Sharks.* She turned; there were more of them, circling her and the wreckage. About ten yards ahead of her one breached the surface, with its powerful jaws locked around the torso of a man. He screamed a blood-curdling scream. The shark's white underbelly flashed in the light of the flames as the creature smacked back down onto the surf, bringing its prey beneath the waves. She heard the man's final scream, then he gurgled as he was dragged below. Suddenly she was aware that the fins were closing in on her. She let the cushion go and kept turning in the water, trying to see which one would close for an attack. A fin heading straight for her was hard to see, as it was just a thin line above the dawn's dim-lit water. She braced herself. As the animal approached she punched down with all her might. She made contact with the nose of the killing machine and it flicked its tail and shimmied off, away from her. The punch cost her dearly. The pain in her arms almost knocked her out. There was another fin about twenty yards out coming around and in. She wouldn't be able to muster that kind of punch again. She tried to position herself in the water to kick this one. Intellectually she knew this was a fight of attrition — she would not stop bleeding and they would not stop coming. She would be shark food as soon as her strength gave out or one blindsided her from the back or beneath. Then she looked to her right and thirty feet off was a capsized Zodiac. She started to swim toward it, but her arms were like lead and the best she could do was thrash around. The shark was coming right at her now. In a panic she looked to her left and saw the cushion bobbing only a few feet away. She screamed with every stroke from the searing pain that shot throughout her body as she swam to it. Brooke placed it under her chest again and kicked like the devil to make it to the upside-down rubber craft before the shark intercepted her. From the corner of her eye she saw the fin approaching as she was just feet from the boat and safety. The shark was closing too fast. She abandoned the cushion and started long strokes; it felt as if her arms were ripping out of their sockets. She was ready to give up and give in to the pain, which was so intense she started to hallucinate. She heard her brother, Harley's, voice, "Don't give up, Brooke. You can do it. Push harder! Come on, Brooke, work through the pain." She yelled out of excruciating pain, "I can't Harley, it hurts so much!"

She heard him insist. "You won't fail Brooke; you will make it. Don't give in." She screamed one more time and her hand touched the craft. She pulled herself up onto the slick bottom just as the shark struck. It took a huge bite out of the edge, a few inches from her dangling right foot. The impact threw her over the other side of the small, overturned boat. She went under and could see, in the dim rising-sun-lit surface, the shark trying to rip the severed piece of the boat free as it wiggled its powerful frame to shake it loose. Its small brain had not figured out yet that it wasn't flesh, but foam-stuffed rubber. She scrambled back onto the hull of the boat one more time, centered herself and held on to the overturned prop of the outboard motor. Now she was the center of attention of at least eight sharks circling her little island.

∞§∞

"Any word from Jakarta?" Agent Joey Palumbo asked as he entered the president's Emergency Operations Center, putting his briefing file down on a nearby console.

"No, sir, just the satellite confirmation of the explosion and fire aboard the Vera Cruz," the satellite communications officer said.

"Air-sea rescue?"

"Scrambled from Diego Garcia, but it's a long trip."

"Why didn't we have assets in place closer?" Joey chided himself.

"Whatever happened, sir, was unexpected," the satellite down-link officer surmised.

"Is the vessel still afloat?" Palumbo asked as he surveyed the screens and console panels of the PEOC. This was not the more famous situation room under the West Wing, but a converted World War II bunker off the East Wing basement of the White House.

"All we know is that it stopped emanating the tracker signal... could be sunk or the tracker may have been discovered," a tech manning a console said.

Palumbo's lean frame hovered over the multi-purpose console, his face locked except for the side-by-side movement of his square jaw as he chewed over his options. Bringing

Brooke Burrell over from the FBI had been his initiative; she was the best and he wasn't going to lose her to the Indian Ocean on her first mission attached to "Quarterback." He set his jaw and he reached for a blue phone. "White House signals... this is Halfback, please voice print confirm... Halfback."

There were some switching sounds and then the voice of a female: "White House interconnect, state your emergency."

"I need to speak to CincPac immediately."

"Connecting."

A few seconds later a squeezed voice shot out of the receiver, after having been encoded, sent up 22,000 miles to Com Sat 7 — a military communications satellite — bounced off a dish in Virginia, then decoded and digitized and finally made analog to finish the trip on the oldest technology it would encounter, the electro-magnetic receiver element of a Bell System phone, circa 1966 that was against Joey's ear. "Commander-In-Chief Pacific Fleet Operations..."

"This is Joey Palumbo from special ops, White House, 'pea-ock,'" Joey used the term for the PEOC to add a little more weight to the call, "do you have any ships at or near eight degrees twenty-nine minutes north at ninety-seven degrees thirty-eight minutes east?"

∞§∞

Brooke's head had cleared a bit as she assessed her situation. The overturned Zodiac she was clinging to was bobbing in the medium chop of sea south of Java. A body, face down, floated by. She recognized a rifle strap slung across its back and tugged it over. When she flipped the body over, half the man's face was gone, along with the center of his chest. A slick and blood-red fish flipped and flapped out from behind the man's lung and squirted back into the water, shedding its crimson covering and returning to its natural silver grey as it descended ahead of the red trail. She undid the sling and retrieved the AK-47. She then pushed the body off

with her foot. Its motion attracted two sharks that immediately descended on the body and tore it in two. Other sharks
started thrashing around the blood slick now marking the
spot. Using the butt of the rifle as an oar of sorts, she started
painfully paddling away from the sinking boat and, she
hoped, from the sharks. The upside-down Zodiac presented
so much drag that she wasn't getting very far, but at least she
was drifting away. The weighted-down end of the craft, with
the overturned motor with its prop and small rudder pointing
up, gave her a foothold against which she steadied herself as
she stretched flat on the pitching raft. She told herself she'd
rest a while and then see if she could right the boat. As she
attempted to relax, all the pain returned, reporting in from
her hands, her face, her knee — *my knee?* She looked down
and there was a gash across her knee spewing blood. With
hurting, bloodied hands, she ripped at the buttons of her
blouse and removed it, then removed her bra. She wrapped
the undergarment around her knee, and cinched it with a
square knot made out of the straps. The under-wired cups
snugly contoured to her knee. She checked that it was secure
and donned the blouse again. It was waterlogged, and the
back was bunched and twisted, but it afforded her some protection against the sun, which was starting to boil off the fog
to the east.

After an hour she gathered her strength, and with her
right foot wedged in the crook between the craft and the
motor shaft, and her other foot high on the propeller, she
tugged at the top of the boat, trying to bend it back while at
the same time applying her weight to the prop for leverage.
She started to yank and buck her body in an attempt to overcome her own weight that was holding it down. After three
hearty attempts, her foot slipped and she slid down and
crashed into the shaft. Had she been a man, she would have
seen stars. As it was, it made her gasp and immediately shot
her mind back to when she had learned to ride her brother's
bike. She scrambled back to her original prone position on

the little rubber continent, of which she was the sole inhabitant. Suddenly the boat was rocked by a collision. She looked around and there were sharks still keeping pace, one having just bumped the still upside-down Zodiac, as if to try to shake loose its prey. It was then she realized she was leaving a blood trail, as her blood was running off the side of the boat. She tightened the straps of the bra around her knee to better stem the flow. Then she splashed water to clean the surface of the boat and break the trail of crimson she was leaving in her wake. She slung the rifle strap around her left arm just above her elbow and the butt on her right shoulder, then drew a bead on the closest fin. When it got as near as she thought it would, she dropped her sights and fired three shots into the body of the shark. It immediately thrashed and slapped in the water. The other sharks converged on the agitation and new blood in the water, and a feeding frenzy began. She drifted away from the school of sharks now busily devouring one of their own. She watched until she could no longer see the fins above the wave caps. Then she rested. She slept with her arm locked around the upright prop.

∞§∞

The USS *Nebraska*, an Ohio-class Trident ballistic missile submarine, was the second ship in the Navy's history to bear that name. Its current skipper, Bret "Mush" Morton was a third-generation Navy man whose submariner grandfather had distinguished himself in major battle actions in these very waters during a stretch from 1942 to 1944. Two years when, on a regular basis, ten boats would leave Pearl Harbor and only four would return. Those odds made that twenty-four-month span in World War II equal to a century of patrol in submarine years.

In this "second century" of sub operations, the big boats like Mush Morton's were relegated to deterrence by guaranteeing the nuclear annihilation of any would-be aggressor.

To insure that mission, they needed to survive. In subs, that meant remaining undetected. Not so easy when prowling the ocean in something almost as long as a fifty-six-story skyscraper is tall, and forty-two feet wide, containing the men, equipment, nuclear weapons and power plants to move the whole eighteen thousand metric tons of the thing at a classified speed exceeding thirty knots. They ran extremely silent and they ran very deep. For that reason, Mush wasn't used to getting flash traffic in the middle of his 'hide and seek' peacetime patrols, and the order he now held in his hands was as sketchy as they come. Simply stated and without the usual naval syntax, he was tasked to steam at flank speed to grid I-7 on the map and look for anything unusual. That was it. No inkling of what he would or should be looking for. As far as he could remember, this would be the first time an SSBN was looking *for* something instead of trying not to be killed *by* something looking for it.

Back at fleet, the rear admiral who was Commander Submarine Force Pacific was not sure either. All they had was a directive from the White House and some mission runner asking for assistance. But ComSubPac was also part of the National Command Authority and this D.C. controller, code-named "Halfback," was invoking the highest level of priority.

∞§∞

Brooke was alternately dipping herself over the side for heat relief and rolling on to the craft to ward off the chill from the Pacific. She had lost feeling in her toes; rubbing them helped get the circulation going somewhat. Dehydration was her big enemy now. She hadn't had anything to drink for twenty hours and had been baking in the sun for half that time. Her mouth was dry, and the occasional salt spray stung her cracked lips. As she had learned in the rugged survival course when she was qualifying to be an FBI agent, her last hope was to capture her urine and filter it through cloth, such as her shirt. She had started unbuckling her pants when she heard a sound. A swoosh of air, about five hundred yards off; something, maybe a whale, had breached the surface. Over the wave caps, she glimpsed a huge grey hulk in the water. Her eyes were salt-burned and she squinted and rolled them wide open in an attempt to squeegee off the stinging salt, but she still couldn't focus. Then she saw a glint; something metallic had reflected the sun's light. *A ship!* Brooke started yelling, but to her surprise, only a squeak came out of her parched throat. She grabbed the rifle strap from around the shaft and lifted the weapon out of the water, where it wouldn't corrode as fast. She shook out the water in the barrel then pointed it in the air and let out three, three-shot bursts. Although deafening to her, from her low angle, the sound quickly dispersed across the wave crests, each robbing the sound of a bit of the acoustic power the gun had generated. The scores of waves between her and the boat had each reduced the sound level to a point that, when it reached the conning tower of the *Nebraska*, was little more than a burble masked by the wave splash against the hull.

With no change in the direction or activity, the hulk continued to pull away from her. She decided to try one last-ditch effort. She switched to full-automatic and tried something she hoped would increase the effective range of the ubiquitous Russian weapon she had studied at Quantico. She emptied the entire magazine as she shot upward, arcing the gun toward the hulk. The rifle couldn't hit the boat with a straight shot, but she hoped that by whipping the rifle and arcing the shots into the air, they would gain distance, like an artillery shell. The mag emptied in fewer than four seconds and along with it her ability to defend herself or signal any other passing ship.

And then there was silence.

Now she was truly alone.

∞§∞

Mush and his exec officer were manning the bridge when five distinct plinks turned the men around. Using the binoculars, they focused on the aft deck of the sub. Three dimples in the hull were highlighted as a bullet rolled around in one of them. "Sir, I think somebody just shot at us."

"Hank, I believe you're right." He leaned into the voice-powered interphone. "Helm, come around one-eighty, I want a fix on a point five hundred yards off our stern and I want to be there two minutes ago."

"Aye, aye. Coming about, sir."

"Stand by for battle surface. Weps, I want the two fifty calibers manned, now. We might have pirates out here."

"Deck guns on the way, sir." The weapons officer said.

"Now who's got the balls to fire on a U.S. Navy warship?" Mush said over the sounding klaxon horn as he scanned the stern, pivoting to keep his sights on a particular patch of water that was rapidly coming around to his prow.

Brooke could see the boat turning now and she made out the conning tower jutting out of the water and its lookouts on the main mast. She tried to fight it, but a small cry welled up inside her. As the relief flowed from her chest in heaves, and tears washed the salt from her eyes, she thanked God. In a minute, she was checking herself; she reached around her back, arching her torso as she attempted to smooth out the crumpled back of her blouse.

"Is that what I think it is?" Mush said, adjusting the focus of his binoculars.

"It's been a long time, but not that long, skipper. That... is a woman! A well-built woman..."

Mush commanded into the interphone, "I want a recovery team on the deck now with blankets, and alert sick bay we got a survivor coming aboard."

From the front hatch on the foredeck of the *Nebraska* four men emerged with grappling poles, heaving lines and stretchers. Each man clipped his lifeline to the receded buckles on the edge of the decking, lest they be inadvertently in need of rescue themselves due to a rogue wave or flailing subject.

Chief Boatswain Murray couldn't believe what he was seeing: a woman in a wet white blouse, hanging on to an overturned Zodiac in the middle of the Pacific. *You couldn't make this stuff up.*

The captain had made his way down to the bow where Mr. Murray was hanging off the edge as he reached down to the woman. The other men stood gaping. She was a stunner, and she was coming onboard in a transparent manner. Mush quickly stepped forward, covered her with a blanket, and got her down onto the stretcher. She coughed out a "thank you." The other men quickly snapped out of it and all helped carry the stretcher below and into sickbay.

Mush looked up at the bridge and shrugged his shoulders to his exec, who returned the shrug, both thinking the same thing — *How do we put this one in the logbook?* Then he ordered, "Weps below, clear the deck, I don't like being exposed like this. Pull the cork, Hank!"

Executive Officer Evans hit the dive alarm and barked over the wailing horn, "Lookouts below! Clear the bridge." He waited for Mush to get below and watched the forward hatch wheel turn, indicating it was watertight sealed; then he lowered himself into the bridge hatch yelling, "Dive. Dive. Dive."

∞§∞

"We got her!" Joey Palumbo blurted out as he barged into Bill Hiccock's White House office.

"Oh, thank God, where was she?"

Joey handed Bill the communiqué with the confirming data. "Floating on a raft in the South Pacific, about three miles from the sinking."

"She okay?"

"She's banged up and bruised but she is alive and we should know more after she gets some rest."

"We got lucky on this one, Joe."

"She's not the best of the best for nothing, Hic," Joey said as he left to make arrangements for Brooke to be ferried back from Midway on a SAM flight direct to Andrews.

Hiccock sat back, his broad shoulders finding the wings of his too-comfortable desk chair, and breathed a sigh of relief. This, his first "op," had almost bitten the dust. Joey was right; Brooke Burrell had distinguished herself many times in her illustrious FBI career for Bill or for an operation Bill was involved with. Bill glanced down at the two platinum five-point stars most people wrongly assumed were paperweights. This woman was a star in her own right, which was the reason he had agreed to this cockamamie "ops" idea when Joey came up with it.

The whole affair started out as a miscue by the modern day descendants of the Barbary Coast Pirates that had plagued the world's shipping lanes two hundred years earlier. Although today they used "Go Fasts," swift, small boats armed only with AK-47s and rocket grenades, their tactics were the same. Board unsuspecting, unarmed, civilian and commercial ships and rip off whatever they could from the crew's personal belongings and wallets, to whatever else was on board they could fence on the open market.

Occasionally there was bloodshed or a kidnapping, but that brought unwanted attention and military responses that hurt their operational ability and profit, so for the most part the attacks were generally scaled to below the point where the international community would make an effort to muster a counter-force. Until recently, the world collectively yawned upon news of another pirate attack.

However, not long ago a group of pirates triggered an international incident, when they took on an innocent-looking Maltese freighter trying to navigate the Strait of Gibraltar, and stumbled onto an illegal shipment of nuclear material supposedly from the Uzbekistan arsenal. The world's intelligence agencies had accumulated enough intelligence over the years to know that a former Russian general, with deep connections to the Moscow black market, had commandeered these nuclear components in the confusion that followed the break-up of the USSR.

Meanwhile, pundits, news agencies, and governments all over the globe speculated in support or denial of the public allegations made by the NATO powers that the barely seaworthy rusting hulk held Russian nuclear contraband destined for some unstable regime with deep pockets and shallow restraint.

The political effect of all this was that American and NATO warships burned millions of gallons of fuel just hanging around the freighter. The most powerful military force on earth was held impotent by the political realities of doing what the U.S. Navy was first commissioned to do by Jefferson in 1801: seek out and kill pirates. Two centuries later, the strongest armada in the world and its allies just lumbered two hundred yards from the rusting, floating violation, while their well-trained SEAL teams were specifically prohibited from donning so much as a bait knife.

The crisis was eventually resolved violently when a Russian destroyer sank the ship after an alleged rocket grenade attack from the pirate-held freighter. Although every intelligence service in the world knew it had been sunk to bury the evidence that Russia couldn't control its nuclear material, the public swallowed the attack story.

There it would have ended, except for something that came across Hiccock's top-secret network a week later. Presidential Science Advisor Doctor William Jennings Hiccock created an intranet network of scientists. He dubbed the network *Scientific Community Involved America's Defense*, or SCIAD for short. Modeling it on the atom, it had two rings. The closer in Element ring had 92 members. These were top-secret scientists cleared for any sensitive information. The second

Compound ring had 300 members with just as prodigious brains but somewhat less-than-squeaky-clean clearances, so they received redacted non-top-secret data. Bill was known as "Nucleus," and all information — speculation, theory and predictions — came to him.

A compound member of the network was approached to see if the Saudi company he worked for was interested in obtaining barium crucibles.

It was a suspicious request, in that it was an early chunk of nuclear technology, more consistent with the Russian method of creating a bomb, as opposed to the American, Chinese, Indian or Pakistani process. Bill immediately realized that the general, who had remarkably evaded any fallout from the freighter affair, was still at it, trying to sell off even more nuclear hardware. It was then that Joey Palumbo, his trusted head of security and a former FBI agent, came up with the plan to set up a buy for the hardware, 'drug-deal' style.

Over the objections of the CIA, which proposed assassinating the general, Hiccock got presidential operational authority to run a mission with the objective of acquiring these crucibles to determine if, in fact, they were from the Uzbekistan stockpile. If they were, it could be a golden chit to play in the international game of poker in which the U.S. and other powers were enmeshed. That was the president's goal and the basis for his buy-in, but for Hiccock it was all about pure, defensive science: *Stop those things from getting into the wrong hands.*

For the delicate role of point person in this shady deal, Joey Palumbo, the former FBI special agent, now assigned to Hiccock's White House Quarterback group, tapped another FBI agent, one who had distinguished herself in many tight spots as an effective operator and one who's loyalty was beyond reproach. Her command of Farsi didn't hurt either. He sold Bill on using Brooke Burrell under double-blind deep covers as the purchasing agent for an interested

Middle-Eastern party willing to spend heavily to gain a membership in to the world's nuclear club.

Two very careful and elaborate backgrounds were established for Brooke. One was thin and meant to be discovered; the other, the foundation cover was solid and thick and hid Brooke's true identity as a U.S. Agent. Her thick cover was Fiona Haran, a high-up arms merchant who was masquerading as her second, thin identity, Roan Perth, an insurance investigator. Brooke had to memorize the details of both identities to cover her real mission of getting the crucibles for America to study while blocking the bad guys from getting their hands on them.

Throughout many meetings in Europe and the Middle East, Brooke, traveling as Roan Perth, was able to arrange a meeting with the general's men. It did not take long for these intermediaries to pierce the thin cover story and land on the thick one: that Roan was, in fact, Fiona Haran. Oddly, that fact actually gave them confidence. Fiona's position as a known arms merchant exclusively working for an oil-backed sect ensured that the money would be ample and good. So they let Fiona believe she was successful in hiding her identity. It also gave the general a negotiating edge; he would decide to reveal her deception or continue playing along depending on what strategic or financial advantage either direction afforded him at the time.

It had all been going well until the op center lost her trail last Wednesday in a Maltese coastal town. They had only picked up her beacon again, in the western edge of the Indian Ocean, an hour before whatever happened, happened. Bill looked down at the communiqué. He reread the line, "Rescued one shipwreck survivor, white Caucasian female, from water." It gave him a momentary chill. *It might not be Brooke.*

∞§∞

Brooke awoke in a bunk looking up at the distinctive architecture of the riveted bulkhead above her. The room smelled of metal, oil and men. She was on a ship. She felt her cheek and found a bandage covering it and a bandage covering the hand she used to inspect it. She looked down and saw she was wearing a blue pajama set. 'USS *Nebraska*' was stenciled across the pocket over her right breast. She remembered her knee and lifted the covers; she instinctively went to bend it and found it hard to move because it was wrapped in a Velcro bandage. There was a gentle whirring sound that came from everywhere; "*Power plant,*" she thought. She became aware of the sound of a click every few seconds. She followed a tube up from her other arm to an IV; the drip controlled by a machine that ticked as it released whatever they were mixing in it and pumping into her.

"Hello," she called out.

A few seconds later, a young blonde-haired man in an ensign's uniform entered. She saw the medical staff insignia on his collar and judged him to be a 'California surfer dude' turned ship's doctor, or at least pharmacist mate.

"Good evening. I'm Ensign Howell and I run the sick bay. Are you in any pain?"

"No. But I am thirsty; got any water around here?"

"Sure thing." Ice cubes banged around the inside of the plastic pitcher as he filled a Styrofoam cup and brought it under her chin. She tried to hold it herself...

"Better let me help till you get those 'boxing gloves' off."

She drank and some dribbled; she used her bandaged hand as a napkin and dabbed her chin.

"How long have I been out?"

"About twelve hours. You were in pretty bad shape when they hauled you in."

"I need to speak to the captain. I must make my report."

"He'll be here in a second; I rang for him when you awoke."

On cue, Mush Morton walked into the compartment. He was a big fellow with a neatly trimmed red beard that flouted regulations, and soft eyes that were anything but regulation. His nose was well-defined, as was his scruffy jaw line, and he wore his skipper's hat tilted back on his head, revealing a tuft of red. His uniform was loosely fitting and yet, despite all these non-regulation features, he still had the immediate effect of electrifying the room with command voltage as he entered.

"Happy with the accommodations? This, believe it or not, is a stateroom on a sub. Held in reserve for visiting brass. You seem like a pretty important VIP so I figured it was appropriate. Need anything?"

"I need to make my report."

"Report to who?"

"Captain, can you excuse your man and close the door."

"Sure. Mr. Howell, give us the room."

The door shut and Mush pulled up a chair alongside the bed.

"I am on a mission, or was, for the President of the United States. I was blown off a ship as I was negotiating to get back some critical material that was stolen."

"That explains the rerouting of a nuclear submarine on deep deterrent patrol. My orders are to take you to Midway so the hospital can get a crack at you and from there you'll jump a Special Air Missions ride to D.C. We'll make Midway by nightfall tomorrow."

"Can I radio my report? You do have secure uplink on this boat, don't you?"

"Yes, we have all the factory installed options on this model — cup holders, twenty-four multiple reentry Trident D5 strategic missiles, heated seats…"

Brooke gave him a confused look. Maybe she was still too groggy for Mush's brand of humor.

"Lady, this is an Ohio-class fleet ballistic missile submarine, a stealth-operating, floating launch pad. I assure you, we've got all the bells and whistles."

"Sorry, Captain, I was a little out of it when you came to my rescue."

"Ma'am, who are you?"

"I guess we missed that part: Brooke Burrell, special agent FBI, attached to the Quarterback Group at the White House."

"Means nothing to me. Is it some super-secret Presidential operations cluster?"

"Something like that."

"How did you wind up on a capsized Kodiak?"

"What's a Kodiak?"

"It's what we call the Russian Zodiac-styled boat you were clinging to."

"Russian!" It was starting to come back together for Brooke. "Captain... this entire boat might be in danger."

"More than usual?"

"I was on a Somali tanker, I was in a cabin... negotiating with an intermediary to an arms merchant when the world exploded."

"Tankers sometimes combust, especially if the crew is untrained in siphoning off built-up gases that collect in holding tanks and..."

Brooke held up her hand. "Wait, let me think..." She started pulling on the threads of her memory that were coming together as she focused. "I ran out to the deck. I was looking over the railing..." Brooke rubbed the bump on the back of her head. "I remember now; just before the explosion. A crewman ran in all agitated about something in the water — oh, what was it?"

"Well, we got surface radar, sonar and a few other gizmos so sensitive that we will know if a whale bumps into a minnow, so we should be safe."

"Whale! That was it! He said a whale had come up to the hull and then something about a mine... a limpert mine?"

"Limpet mine?"

"Yes, that's it."

The captain reached over to the interphone on the bulkhead. "Con, this is the captain. Take her up! Fast. Emergency blow. I want to run the surface all the way to Midway. And double the lookouts."

"What are we looking for, sir?"

"Whales, Mr. Sarin, whales."

"Wow. That was quick." Brooke said as a klaxon sounded three times and a voice came over the P.A. "Secure for emergency blow."

"Better hold on here. We're headed for the roof." Mush said as he gently placed Brooke's hand on the railing of her bunk. The boat took on a deep angle and then she felt the sudden stomach-wrenching feeling similar to the first drop of a rollercoaster, only in reverse. Seeing Brooke's concern and uneasiness, Mush spoke in regular measured tones as if this gut-wrenching rapid ascent was commonplace. "You got me with the limpet mines."

"What?" Brooke said, nervously looking around at the now almost vertical stateroom, as some things slid and collected in the corners.

"Nasty devices that frogmen attach to the side of an enemy's vessel to sink them. I don't know what's going on, but we can't see biologicals with our equipment; just the cavitation they leave in the water when they get spooked by us. But if there is a killer whale out there, armed with limpet mines, our only chance to see it coming is from the surface. In fact," he reached for the interphone again, "Mr. Sarin, raise Diego-Garcia. Tell them we are on a special op for COMSUBPAC and request they scramble a TACAMO for around-the-clock air cover starting immediately. Compose the message; I'll be up to authorize it in a minute."

"Yes sir."

He switched off the box and turned to her. It struck him how good looking she was. Not the frail, dainty features of a model, but the kind of pretty that endures and gets better as it gets older. "You can really see whales better from the air."

"Captain, I have to tell you, I am a little surprised you reacted so strongly to my wild story. I mean, it sounded crazy to me as I was telling it to you."

"I have one hundred fifty-five souls on this ship, Miss Burrell, you make one hundred fifty-six. We are also the fourth largest nuclear power on earth, all by our lonesome. And we cost about one thousand billion dollars when you add up all the special equipment and Trident D5 warheads. So let's just say, erring on the side of caution is better than making a trillion dollar hole in the water."

Brooke took all that in and a warm feeling of safety wrapped around her for the first time since she started on the mission. "Thank you for saving me."

"I was just looking for the son of a gun who shot at my boat."

Brooke was about to say something silly like *"guilty"* or *"I didn't know it was loaded,"* but a sharp pain from her leg froze her brain.

Sensing her sudden discomfort, he unconsciously placed his hand on hers. "You want me to have Howell give you a shot or something?"

"No, it subsided; I need to have my wits about me to write my report." She looked into his eyes and saw genuine concern there. It made her wonder if he was a dad. Owing to her grogginess, she was about to ask him if he had kids, but he spoke before she did.

"I have to get to the con; just let us know if you need anything." He left and closed the door behind him.

I did shoot at his boat. To Brooke he suddenly went from a dad to a teenager with a new car, preening and caring for it, sympathetically hurting with every ding and scratch. *Boys and their toys*, she thought. The last thing she focused on was her freshly laundered bra, on a hanger, under the overhead, as she started to glide off into a light slumber. It didn't last long...

II. WHALE OF A TAIL

Aaaooooga aaaa oooooo ga! The klaxon horn sounded and startled Brooke awake.

On the bridge, Mush swung around with his glasses trained on the rear of the 560-foot-long *Nebraska*, as a plume of white water and orange flame erupted out of the sea. The giant ship shuddered. Then he saw it. A huge gray mass in the water. The huge amount of bubbles told him that the boat's hull had been breached. He screamed into the interphone, "I want weapons free, now!"

He pulled off the binoculars, scrambled down the hatch and came out the access hatch on the deck. He grabbed an AR-22 assault rifle from a sailor emerging from the rear torpedo hatch and ran toward the stern. The massive form was coming in again, maybe with another mine. He started shooting into the body of the thing. Soon more sailors armed with heavy weapons joined in. Thousands of rounds entered the water and most hit the hulk just under the surface; it started to shake. Then Mush noticed something odd — *there's no blood, no wounds.* The bullets went clean in and only air bubbles were coming out. He kept firing. It was working; the thing had slowed its approach to the hull. He turned to the conning tower and yelled to his exec, "Hank! All ahead full now; get us away from this thing. All ahead full!"

A few men lost their footing as the big ship dug a hole in the water and lunged ahead. The grey mass stayed aft of the rudder. A huge tail was the last sight above the water, then nothing. Mush ran to the base of the conning tower and yelled up. "Damage report?"

"Port propulsion plant is flooded, four hurt. Starboard got us out of here. But we are taking on water."

"Close all watertight hatches, get the pumps working in Port Prop." Mush headed toward the rear hatch.

"Aye, aye."

As alarm bells started calling to secure quarters, a midshipman asked, "What the fuck was that, Captain?" Then realizing he was cursing to a superior officer, recanted, "I mean what in the name of ..."

"Carry on, Sailor" Mush snarled as he hefted the gun to the pimply-faced sailor. When the young seaman was out of earshot Mush mumbled to himself, "Just call me fucking Ahab!"

∞§∞

"Attacked? A U.S. nuclear sub was attacked?" President Mitchell couldn't believe his ears.

"We are just getting the details now, sir. But it appears the USS *Nebraska* was on a special op when it was either mined or torpedoed in open water," the secretary of the navy reported.

"Special operation? For who?"

"Why for you, sir," a slight tinge of confusion tightening his brow.

"Slow down. Me?" The president leaned to one side to yell around the SECNAV's body, "Reynolds!!!!"

Chief of Staff Ray Reynolds was entering President Mitchell's office as the Commander-In-Chief was bellowing his name. "I was just coming in, sir. Yes. This is Hiccock's operation. You approved it two weeks ago — to try and get hold of the Russian crucibles."

"Any casualties?" the commander-in-chief asked.

"No fatalities, four crew injured," the SECNAV said.

"How did a nuker get involved?"

The SECNAV went to intercede but Reynolds jumped in. "Boomer, sir, the Navy calls them boomers."

"Whatever; how did a warship get involved and attacked as part of my — Hiccock's plan?"

"We don't know if this has anything to do with that mission, except for the fact that your mission operative was rescued by this boat," the Secretary said.

"So this is Burrell, the agent who went undercover to buy the bomb-making hardware?"

The SECNAV turned to Admiral Shorn who then took over the hastily called briefing. "Yes, it would seem so, but the attack may or may not have anything to do with her mission or the procurement of the nuclear contraband."

"Was she injured?"

"Yes, but before the *Nebraska* recovered her, clinging to a raft in the Indian Ocean. She was not injured further in the attack on the sub though, sir."

"Who attacked us?"

"No way to know yet sir, but it was not a conventional naval attack, of that I am sure."

"How can you know that if you don't know all the details?"

"Because the *Nebraska* is commanded by Bret Morton. He's as fine a Naval man as you're ever going to find."

"Morton... Morton. Is that Mush Morton's kid?"

"Grandson, sir; Dudley "Mush" Morton was one of the best sub drivers in WWII and wrote most of the book on modern submarine warfare on the spot under Japanese fire. The kid's genes got diving planes on them, sir. No conventional warship or threat could get to within 5,000 yards of a boomer and especially one with a Morton in command. I'd stake my last two stars on the fact that this one came out of nowhere or from a new weapon technology we haven't counter-measured yet."

"Okay, I want hourlies on this till that boat is at our base; Admiral you assign someone to brief me."

"I'll do that myself, sir."

The president nodded to the admiral, then turned to Ray. "Get me Hiccock on the double."

"On his way sir; turned him around as he was heading home."

∞§∞

Joey met Bill at the portico off the East Wing of the White House. "The shit's hit the fan, Billy boy. The boat that picked up Brooke got attacked. The SECNAV is in there now with Admiral Shorn."

"Geez, I leave here for ten minutes and ... is anybody hurt?"

"Four crewmen wounded — one is critical. The boat's limping back to Midway, and it's got air cover and a support ship is zeroing in."

"Was Brooke hurt?"

"Not from this attack, but she was pretty beat up when they took her aboard."

"Do we know who did it?"

"No. But they'd either have to be real stupid or really looking to start World War Three."

"You think it's the Russians?"

"It was their junk we were trying to get. Brooke may have stumbled on to something in Malta and been a loose end they weren't willing to let go of."

"Do we have her report?"

"Not yet, what with the attack and all."

∞§∞

Two Navy Stallion helicopters flew in close formation above the crippled *Nebraska* as it made headway on one turbine back to Midway. Two F-18 Hornets, off the deck of the Enterprise, flew Combat Air Patrol ten thousand feet above, alternately topping off their tanks from KC-135 tankers out of Diego Garcia. The entire CAP was under the watchful eye of the TACAMO. The 'Take Command and Move Out' aircraft that was a flying command center for tactical operations. All this because a boomer and her mission were secret and silent; the Navy wasn't comfortable with her exposed on the surface unable to submerge. So this elegant machine, this marvel of U.S. technology packed with the ultra-top secret systems, this battleship of the nuclear age, got the escort befitting her status as America's random player in the still very deadly game of 'who can launch and kill the other guy without getting too bloody a nose.'

In her stateroom, Brooke was writing her report on USS *Nebraska* stationary when Mush knocked on the jamb. "May I come in?"

"Sure."

"Well Miss Burrell, now we are even. If that mine had gone off while we were submerged, none of us would have made it. So we may have saved you, but you saved our boat with that warning about the whale and the limpet."

"I felt the explosion. Is anyone hurt?"

"Four men wounded, one seriously. Bennis got the worst of it. I'm watching him now, but he's a tough sailor. He'll beat it. No whale's going to beach him."

"It sounds so Jules Verne; how can they use a whale like that?"

"Well, whales *are* mammals, and most mammals can be trained. But..."

"But what?"

"There was something fishy about that whale."

"Did you capture it?"

"No, it slipped back under and, as far as we can tell, hasn't resurfaced."

"I heard shots fired."

"We laced into the thing and it stopped advancing for the second strike, but it was odd; not what you'd expect."

"How so?"

"We hit it point blank with heavy weapons fire but there was no blood, no whale blubber, no mournful cry or spouting air hole... fishy!"

"You know a bullet is deflected when it hits the water; maybe all you did was shock and sting it. Maybe they only lodged in the skin but didn't perforate the layer of fat."

"Got to be something like that, 'cause it just sounds crazy, and they're going to think I'm crazy when I report this to fleet."

"We'll if they don't believe you, we'll run a Section Twenty-One B.O.I., and I'll be a witness."

"How do you know about Naval Boards of Inquiries?"

"I was JAG for four years out of Harvard Law."

"Wow, you are full of surprises. So how'd you go from being a Navy adjutant to FBI?"

"I enlisted because my oldest brother Harley — I've got four brothers — died in the first Iraq war."

"I am sorry for your loss."

"Thank you. Yeah, he and his platoon were in a firefight for twelve hours, and right before they were extracted, his corporal took a hit fifty yards from him. He scrambled over the wall they were using as cover and retrieved him. As he was lifting him back over the wall to safety, a sniper got him in the back. He didn't make it back to the forward operating base."

"That must have been quite a loss for you."

"I was devastated; he was always there for me, pushing me to do better, caring about my feelings. He protected me in school when the boys weren't so nice. And I'd swear, Captain, he was with me out there in the ocean."

"Sounds like a great guy; I would have liked to meet him."

"At his funeral, I just made up my mind to enlist. Anyway, out of the Navy with my law degree, I was easy pickins' for the FBI, so I survived Quantico and started up the glass ladder. And now I am floating around the vast Pacific with a character right out of Moby Dick, not to mention the big whale out there as well."

Mush straightened up a bit. "You don't like the cut of my jib?"

"Captain, you look like Hollywood's idea of what a dashing scallywag of a captain should look like."

"In the Johnny Depp or Fred Thompson mold? Please say Depp, please say Depp."

"More like a young Harrison Ford with the beard from *The Fugitive*."

"I can live with that."

She smiled, "Me too."

The obligatory long moment passed between them and then Mush turned his brain back on. "And like, you're *not* some picture mogul's idea of a damsel in distress? Flailing about the ocean, stunning every man-child on the boat with a face that would relegate Helen of Troy to launching a thousand Staten Island ferries?"

"Okay, this is starting to get a little thick in here. Truce, Captain?"

"Thank God you called for it; that's hard to do."

∞§∞

Hiccock was home by eight. He found Janice just putting 18-month-old Richard Ross Hiccock to bed. He was glad that tonight he made it home in time to catch the ritual. Afterward, he decided to put off going through his e-mails in favor of watching his old alma mater try to secure a berth in one of the many new college bowls. So many that now it seemed every team had a shot at being in at least the Corner Grocery Store Bowl. Still, a good ranking meant a school could attract better players, and Stanford was due for a new crop. His own playing time there was still a matter of much focus these days, due to his current stint as the science advisor to the president; mostly because he was the first science advisor anyone had ever heard of. To Bill it was a good trade-off; his grid-iron notoriety got people talking about science again, and his non-traditional route to his post, from college football quarterback to scientist serving the president, was a bit of glitter that gave the average science teacher, fighting for the attention of students, a little more "cool."

He looked across the room to see his Heisman Trophy adorned with Richie's baby duck plush toy stuffed under the outstretched arm. It made him laugh and smile at the wonderful way his life turned out.

Janice came down the stairs and flopped on the couch beside him. "Who's winning?"

"Not us. Richie give you any problem?"

"No, he went right off after you told him that 'touching' bedtime story."

"It's a good story."

"Bill, a one-and-a-half-year-old doesn't even understand most of the words you used in telling him how Thomas Edison discovered the filamajingy."

"Filament! And Edison made up the word, and as made-up words go, it's as good as goo-goo or blankie, so why can't an almost two-year-old know it? It wasn't really a real word. It's like getting one free."

"What?"

Bill noticed for the first time that she and Richie both 'squinched' their faces, a cute combination of squinting and wincing when they were confused by something. "Never mind. I made popcorn, you want some?"

"Where is it?" Janice asked looking around the living room.

"I left it in the microwave."

"So it's not, 'do I want some?' It's more like you want some and you want me to go get it?"

"Well, they scored a touchdown just as the oven dinged."

"I'm going to ding you. Want anything to drink with that?"

"There's a diet Coke in the fridge."

Janice left to go to the kitchen, and when she returned she handed him a bottle of Electrolyte water and some carrot sticks. "Here these are healthier for you and will keep you around long enough to do *my* bidding." Then she saw it — a vase with two-dozen roses in it. "Oh Bill, these are gorgeous. How did you sneak them in here?"

"I hid 'em out in the garage."

"Garage roses! My favorite! What's the occasion?"

"Nothing, I just wanted to get you flowers."

"Really?"

"Really."

"Did I forget that you forgot something?" She wondered aloud as she smelled the bouquet.

"No."

"You didn't cheat on me did you?"

"What!"

"Well, guys usually only bring 'flowers-for-nothing' when they've done something."

"Oh, how little ye knows of me."

"Are you going away on some trip and you want to break it to me gently?"

"No, but that is a good one; I should remember that. No, baby, I just love you and wanted to let you know it."

"So I can breathe?"

"Yes, as many times as you like and for the rest of your life if you want to."

"Ahhh Bill, that's so sweet... thank you."

"Finally!"

With the roses having gone over well, but the Cardinal's march to the Rose Bowl not so well — being detoured by two turnovers — Bill felt he couldn't take the defeat tonight, so he switched off the TV and headed into the den and his e-mails.

There he found a report on the CERN, and he started skimming through it. A half hour later, Janice found him. "You're in here? I thought you went out without telling me."

"Sorry honey, just catching up on black holes and destruction of all matter as we know it."

"Is that going to give you nightmares?"

"I'll just have to hold on to you tighter."

"Then read more, Billy boy, read more. I am going up and getting ready for you."

He closed the report and jotted down a note on the cover, 'Create CERN task force. Use rings and Joey. Skip Burrows, Jason Wallenford?'

Then he turned off the light and headed up the stairs two at a time.

III. UNDERCURRENTS

In the first nanosecond, everything he saw all around him would simply disappear, the instantaneous end of the concept of 'solid.' Everything, every molecule, every atom would suddenly fall apart, its basic ability to hold together dissolved. For a few millionths of a second, it would all be an instant liquid, and in a few millionths of a second more, the concept of liquid would no longer exist, as all that was once matter became a version of plasma. The most minute pieces of existence would suddenly be ripped apart into a gaseous fog, until even that dissipated into nothingness. Within the first seconds the earth would cease to exist. In ten minutes the entire solar system would vanish, then everything in creation, and in time, which itself would be dying, everything that ever existed would become non-matter.

With that apocalyptic thought, The Engineer took one last drag on his *Gitanes Blonde*. Maybe it was the late autumn fresh air flushing his lungs or the bucolic panorama of Lake Geneva surrounding him, but once again he vowed to give up these 'Gypsy women' one day. He snuffed her under the toe of his Italian designer shoe, unaware of the small ritual cough that always punctuated the extinguishing of a cigarette. He walked back to his rented Smart Car to drive to the next surveillance spot he had marked on the map of Switzerland.

∞§∞

Mush took one last drag and flicked the butt off the bridge, twenty-five feet above the waterline, as he scanned the small amount of ocean that lay between the *Nebraska* and the former Midway Naval Base.

Allowed a rare honor, Brooke was "up top" beside him. She noticed that in the Pacific's setting sunlight, his red beard was incandescent. "I heard someone below refer to Big Red. Is that what they call you — Big Red?"

Mush turned and let out a small laugh. "No, Agent Burrell, the boat is Big Red."

Brooke gestured to his head of red farm boy hair under his blue-and-gold peaked cap with the words *Nebraska SSBN 739* and *You sleep. We'll watch* and mused, "You've got to admit, what are the odds?"

"Lady, the only way you get a boat named after you in this man's Navy is to be dead first. And between you and me, that's a big price tag."

"Okay, so help me out here: big black ship..."

"Boat."

"Sorry, boat — nothing red on it that I can see."

Mush turned to her and brought the back of his hand to his mouth as if to block others from hearing him whisper, "University of *Nebraska* ... Cornhuskers?"

"Big Red! Oh, right, of course." Brooke turned both her palms up and weighed two imaginary things. "Football, thermonuclear war, it's a natural match."

"Are you saying we're playing a game out here?"

"No, but I had four brothers and I know what boys like." She turned three hundred sixty degrees and surveyed the ship submersible ballistic missile nuclear, as the Navy lovingly called it. "Yep, this *is* what boys like."

"There *are* women in the Navy, you know?" He said.

"I was one... you know."

"So, you think this is all just the next male evolutionary step after football?"

"My temporary boss was a quarterback in college."

"Click! White House, quarterback, Quarterback Group, Wild Bill Hiccock!"

"That was impressive!" Brooke genuinely was impressed, but she quickly chided herself. After all, everything about her was top secret.

He patted the part of the superstructure they called the sail. "They don't give the keys to one of these things to just anybody, you know?"

"Is that so, Big Red?"

He turned and looked at her, the low amber sun having its effect on her as well. She was looking forward, the wind gently blowing her golden hair. It was then he noticed how the arc of her top lip over her straight bottom lip gave her the look of confidence and perpetual awe, as if she was always seeing something that enticed her. And how, when all that was pointed in his direction, he lapped it up. But now that he saw she gave the same wonder-struck expression to the sea, he felt knocked down a peg.

"You're staring," Brooke said, without deflecting her gaze from the vast blue before them.

"I never did this with a woman."

That caused her to turn with the slightest of smirks.

"I mean, the bridge is a kind of men-only environment," he covered.

"In that case, I am glad we have two lookouts ten feet above us. Otherwise a girl's reputation might get compromised. But thank you for proving my point!"

"I did what now?"

"No women on the bridge — it reinforces my earlier postulate."

"So wait, Agent Burrell, are you saying if women ran things, then boats like this on extended deterrence patrols wouldn't exist?"

"No, not that far, because some side might have foolhardy boys on their boats, and America being caught flat-footed would really be too big a price tag."

He smiled, folded his arms on the edge of the railing and scanned the horizon. She picked up the binoculars and did the same. Minutes passed.

"Are you married?" Brooke asked.

"Yes."

"Oh," she didn't know why, but she wasn't expecting that answer. She adjusted her mindset. "Where's your wife now?"

"You're standing on her."

Brooke tried hard to lasso the smile that busted out of her like a wild horse from the corral. "You start singing 'Brandy' and I am jumping off this boat and taking my chances back in the ocean."

"You mean, 'my life, my lover, my lady is the sea?'" Mush crooned.

"Oh, God, yes! That was my prom song! Because the Homecoming Queen was *Brandy* Hanson."

"I would have bet on you for high school heartbreaker."

"Tomboy! ... 'til I was nineteen, then hormones, phero-mones or something-mones kicked in and suddenly..."

"No more boys being the enemy?"

"Something like that..."

∞§∞

"What would the loading have to be in order to affect the hysteresis dynamics?"

"Loading is not the issue; the issue is power frequency. A half-cycle deviation would result in a six-percent loss in flux and a twenty-five-degree increase in heat output."

"And if there was a ten-cycle shift?"

"The curves are not linear, so at ten cycles either side of the center frequency you would have ninety percent loss of flux and meltdown of the coil."

"How long would the meltdown take?"

"At these operating voltages and given the superconduc-tivity, two seconds to liquefy the structure."

The "Engineer" knew he had just impressed his employer
— *strike that* — his partner, in the great battle that would be
over within two seconds of the first shot.

"Do you have the list of what you need?"

"Yes, but are you certain of the timing of the event?"

"You leave that to me; my unwitting source is impecca-
ble. You focus on your team. With you to guide them, they
will not fail."

"Thank you for your faith in me."

"My faith is in God; He guides you and me."

With that, the man, whom The Engineer only knew as
"The Architect," left and melted into the crowds on the tour-
ist-encrusted Route Suisse, the main road that surrounded
the Swiss end of the lake. The Engineer went in the opposite direction, where he would meet with the woman he had
hand-picked for his team and the main part of this grand
vision.

∞§∞

The old gangplank had a banner on the side that read USS
Tiger Shark. It was a relic and a leftover from when Midway
had a naval facility. At 560 feet, the nearly two-football-field-
long *Nebraska* dwarfed the utility dock, which was now only
used to moor small freighters and supply ships. Mush had
four seamen weighing down each end of the questionable
gangplank just to make sure it was safe. He escorted Brooke
and the stretcher carrying seaman Bennis down to the dock
where the U.S. Park Service Envoy for Midway met them. He
and his car were pressed into service to drive the half mile to
the airstrip where a U.S. Air Force G-4 was waiting to return
Brooke to Washington. Her condition aboard ship having
been upgraded, the hospital check-in wasn't required. She
had been given a set of dress browns befitting an ensign, her
last naval rank. She opted to wear the hat so the salute she

gave the men cramming the deck to say goodbye would be even crisper.

She watched as Mush said goodbye to the injured seaman as he was loaded into the Midway Hospital ambulance. She was taken with how gentle he was as he put his hand on the man's and leaned over, no doubt saying something supportive and encouraging. He snapped a salute as the doors closed and then walked over to Brooke.

"Well, Agent Burrell, I guess you'll be glad to get back to D.C." Mush said, removing his hat for the first time.

Finally seeing his entire mane of red curly hair made her smile. "Captain, thank you so much for the VIP treatment."

"After all you went through, it was the least..."

"I know that space is a luxury on a sub and there is no such thing as an extra stateroom. Thanks for giving me your cabin; it was a magnanimous gesture that I really appreciate."

"If my exec snored, you would have been out of there in a minute!"

Brooke wanted to say something more but thought better of it, and instead she simply said, "Captain, if you ever get to the East Coast, I'm usually free any day that ends in a 'y.'"

"Good, 'cause today ends like that." With that, a yeoman brought the captain's bags to the trunk of the car and placed them inside.

"Where are you going?"

"The exec and crew can get Big Red back to Pearl for repairs. I've been ordered back to Washington to tell them first-hand about Jonah and the whale."

"My offer still stands."

"I already took you up on it."

"No, I mean to be a witness in support."

"Thanks. Hopefully it won't come to that." He said.

"It will be nice to have company on the long plane ride home."

Smiles became the uniform of the day.

∞§∞

"A what?"

"He says a whale!"

"Joey, is this some kind of swab term for a mini-sub or something?"

"Bill, I don't know; I wasn't Navy. But even Brooke reported hearing a warning about a whale."

"I've got five or six guys on the rings who are oceanologists and marine biologists; I'll run it by them."

The "rings" were the organizational center of Bill's SCIAD Network. The name was a double entendre of sorts in that he was the science advisor to the president and his shorthand title in White House memoranda was SciAD. It was his innovation and it brought massive brainpower to all the nasty things that could go click in the night and bring America to its knees. From cyber-attacks, approaching asteroids, nuclear proliferation, and world resource shortages, to medical, biological, and synthetic life, science played big as a National Intelligence asset. Bill's SCIAD rings gave America a fighting chance to counter any technological, man-made, or natural disaster.

"Do you think we can convince Ray to go to bat for us with the Navy?" Joey asked.

"What do we want?"

"A submersible recovery vehicle to plumb the depths of the wreck Brooke got blown off of."

"You think the crucibles are down there?"

"Not me, Brooke." Joey laid the top-secret stamped report down on Bill's desk. "She was on the Vera Cruz to confirm the brokers actually had the crucibles. They were in the hold of that ship!"

"Okay, I'll ask him at the afternoon staff. Anything else?"

"I need tomorrow off."

"Sure. What's up?"

"Going to sign up Joe Jr. to the D.C. Little League."

"How's he adjusting to not being in San Francisco anymore?"

"He's doing fine, makes new friends in an instant. Phyllis? That's another story."

"I'll ask Janice..."

"Bill, Janice doesn't have time to be welcome wagon queen. Phyl's got to get out and meet folks."

"Take it easy on her, okay? It wasn't her idea for you to rip up your roots and plant 'em next to me here in the district."

∞§∞

Brooke had tried on six different outfits in front of her full-length mirror, changing shoes to boots to sling backs to sandals and back to boots. Pearls to chain to choker and back again. Long skirt to short to mid-length to sluttily-high to sensible to pants. Dangles to studs to jackets to feather things. And there was eye shadow, lip liner and four different shades of lipstick on wet wipes and tissues in the trash pail. She tried in vain to cover her scratched cheek and hands with copious amounts of makeup, but abandoned it. *He's already seen me scuffed up.* It was seven thirty, she was meeting Mush at eight, and she was exhausted already! *Just choose a look already and get out.*

In the cab on the way over, she had a panic attack, thinking she should go back and put on the lower cut top. *No, that would be too... desperate.* She took a deep breath and thought, *It is what it is.*

Looking out of the cab window as they passed the National Mall, she tried to control the wild horses she felt inside. Despite her apparent reputation as a girl who must have a lot of admirers, her real life after work was rather boring. In fact, Mush, the submarine captain, had been the cause of an unexpected bit of undercurrent in her lower depths. Although they shared their flight back to Washington, they were well chaperoned by Navy and Air Force personnel attending to their every need... except the one she really needed to address. Through the long night's flight, she hoped he was feeling the same impulse and desire to be alone with her, but she couldn't read him. *Don't make a fool of yourself, girl. He may only want you as a witness for the board of inquiry.* She didn't believe that last bit of propaganda, but she needed a sober thought to avoid gushing like a schoolgirl when she saw him.

She arrived at the little Georgetown bistro at eight o'clock sharp. There was Mush at the bar, looking sharp. His fashion choice was easy: he was in dress blues, a tailored uniform that was crisp and neat. *Did he get a haircut and a beard trim?* She loved the way he looked. When he saw her, he smiled the kind of smile Brooke hoped she'd see on his face every time they met.

"Agent Burrell, you look...stunning!"

"Oh, stop."

"No, really!"

"No, I mean, 'Oh, stop calling me Agent Burrell.' It's Brooke."

"Brooke. I am glad we could see each other tonight."

"Don't you look all dashing in your dress blues."

"Sorry, I came right from the Pentagon."

"Oh." Brooke was a little disappointed he hadn't dressed that way for her.

"Believe me, when you walked through that door, I knew I should have gone back to my hotel and changed into better clothes, because you look fantastic, but I didn't want to be late."

"Good call," the little voice in Brooke's head said, *slow down*, "because I am starving."

He had made a great choice of wine. Not too expensive, yet a label that had been getting a lot of buzz of late. Ordering from the menu, he asked the waiter to prepare the *branzino* a certain way for both of them. The waiter was impressed at the suggestion. Then this master and commander of the fourth largest nuclear power on earth, this captain of one hundred fifty or so souls on a ship of war, this man who was used to having his orders followed without pause or hesitation, did the unexpected and said, "If you think the chef wouldn't mind."

"I don't think there will be a problem, monsieur."

Brooke liked how he was able to slip into civilian mode. Not ordering, but asking, even though he was ordering dinner.

Mush was interested in where and how Brooke grew up. So Brooke did most of the talking during dinner. After he picked up the check, he looked at Brooke — really looked at her. She could see him taking in her hair, her chin, her ears, her lips, and then his eyes fell softly on hers. His mouth curled into a smile of satisfaction and contentment. "Wanna walk a little?"

As they walked the cozy streets of Georgetown, Mush spoke of his plans and ambitions. Brooke was surprised to learn that he wasn't interested in the Admiralty. He liked the sea and the mission; he wanted to do it until he couldn't anymore. Then retire. His passion for the job and his loyalty to duty made him even more attractive to Brooke. That surprised her. She thought she would have liked to hear that he wanted to settle down and explore the land side of life, but she wasn't disappointed at all. They stopped on a corner waiting for "Don't Walk" to change to "Walk." Brooke felt him staring, as he had on the bridge of the *Nebraska*. She didn't look at him but said, "You're staring — again."

"You look as beautiful tonight as on the bridge in the sunset."

She turned to him. His eyes were mesmerizing. She softened her demeanor and wet her lips. He looked at her lips, tilted his commander captain's hat back on his head, raised her chin gently with his hand, and kissed her. They kissed for a long time. People were walking around them. A car honked and they didn't flinch. His arm came around her and he pulled her close; she arched into him and they both held on tight. Eventually they went from their first kiss to a hug. She loved the little sigh that came from deep inside him. They continued walking. They walked and talked for hours. Somehow they found themselves on the Fourteenth Avenue Bridge; they had walked right back to D.C. The sun was rising over the Potomac and they were leaning on the concrete railing looking down at the current sweeping under the bridge. They turned their heads and kissed once more. Mush went to pull her close by her arm but unintentionally grabbed her breast instead; he quickly moved his hand to her arm. Breaking the lip lock long enough to utter, "Sorry."

She found his hand and placed it back on her breast. His touch was gentle but the way he caressed her made a little moan escape her throat as they embraced. That kiss made them both dizzy.

They found a little breakfast place in the Sofitel on Fifteenth, near the White House, that was just firing up the grill for the morning shift. They sat and ordered eggs.

∞§∞

The SCIAD network that Bill created was a super-charged intranet, superimposed across the entire Internet. He logged back onto the network just before the afternoon staff meeting and saw he had three responses. He assumed they were from the marine and ocean experts who were on the rings. They were the most likely to respond to Bill's request for information on any studies or cases where whales attacked or were trained to attack ships.

He was intrigued by one response that struck him as odd. It was from a chemical engineer affiliated with Disney Imagineering, the company that dreams up the cybernetics and animatronics elements for Disney rides and attractions all around the world. Re-reading one particularly chilling part made Bill pick up the phone.

"Brooke, is your bag packed?"

∞§∞

Brooke hung up the phone. "Sorry, I shouldn't have taken that call."

"Gotta go?"

"Yes. It's my boss."

"Quarterback?"

"Yes. He wants me up in New York this morning. I don't want to go. I want to stay with you."

"And I don't want to meet with the Naval Intelligence guys at nine. I want to go back to that bridge and kiss you all over again till the next sunrise."

"We better get the check," Brooke said as a way to uncouple her feelings for Mush from the job she had to complete.

At the curb outside the little breakfast place, Mush said, "I'll flag you a cab."

Brooke took one long last look at Mush. He held his white cap out and let out a whistle that nearly pierced her eardrums. As the cab neared, he took her by the arms and kissed her. "Let's see each other the first chance either one of us gets."

"How long will you be in D.C.?"

"Only today. I leave at five to go back out to Pearl to supervise the repairs."

"Is that where you live?"

"For the foreseeable future, temporary change of station. Our boomer nest is in Bangor, Washington, but the Pentagon wants to flex a little muscle at the Chinese and North Koreans and nothing shows the bad guys you're watching them like a Trident sub on their front porch. Maybe you can come to Hawaii?"

"Yes. I want to." Reflexively she began smoothing his hair. "Be careful."

"Me! You, you're the secret agent here." He reflexively caressed her bruised cheek, taking care not to actually touch the wounds. "I don't want you to risk an eyelash on that beautiful face of yours or do anything to this incredible body until we see each other again. Promise?"

"Just keep those shoulders and arms ready to wrap around me when I see you, Big Red."

They kissed one more time as the horn of the cab lightly beeped.

∞§∞

Conscription is mandatory in Switzerland for men and voluntary for women, so a large percentage of the population has military experience. The responsibility to serve is not easily avoided, due to the yearly training sessions and the fact that almost every home has a closet with an M-16 and a sealed box of ammunition somewhere nearby. The seal is checked on a random basis by agents of the government to make sure the weapon is only used in a national emergency, such as anybody coming after the world's trillions in gold held in the famous Swiss banks.

Raffael Juth grabbed his light coat, barely noticing the M-16 in the back of the closet. He checked that his gloves were in the pocket and headed out the door on his way to work.

He hit the fob of his Audi A6, his latest prized possession. He loved the feel of the car and its hi-tech interface. It matched his position at LHC, where he had risen through the layers as his programming code for the dissemination of retrieved data from core sensors was heralded as a giant step forward for LHC as a whole. What no one knew was that his breakthrough had come from his grandfather. When Raffael was a young boy he helped his grandfather build low field-stone walls. He learned the trick of taking random stones and creating a wall with a flat, level top. The key to the wall, and his program, was the little wedge-stones that balanced and stabilized the big rocks, provided a stable footing for the next layer.

To achieve balance in his program and stabilize the main calculating engine while the live input data was changing, he used a mathematical equivalent of a wedge stone. This little rock of an equation was small enough to fit inside the major algorithm, yet nimble enough to level the output, keeping it stable as new data buttressed and replaced old data on the way to forming a solid wall of numbers that could be relied upon like a fieldstone wall.

The Audi's Bluetooth interface synced to his iPod, and Coldplay rocked the luxury compartment of his trophy-on-wheels. In twenty minutes he'd pass Lake Geneva and be at the complex five minutes later.

∞§∞

The booming bass reverberated ahead, around and behind the Audi as it passed the scenic overlook where The Engineer stood talking to a severe-looking woman with jet-black hair. "Right on time! Like a fine Swiss watch," was his droll observation as he watched the Audi take the curve with ease.

"He's young," the stone-faced woman said with an East German accent.

"Is that a problem, Maya?" The Engineer said, for the first time seeing her as on the younger side of middle age.

"Only that they think themselves invincible and that they will live forever."

"I thought you a professional. Did I underestimate?"

"No. You did not. This is not a problem; let's see the house."

∞§∞

East Hampton Airport is the bus station where the rich and famous park their "buses," namely their G4s, G5s, Hawker 400XPs, Boeing Darts, Citation 10s, and the occasional Cessna high wing. On approach from the air, Brooke looked down on the tons of little white multi-million dollar toys all chocked and tied down, lest a sudden nor'easter come through and pile them all up on one end of the runway. Brooke deplaned the government's Citation 10 down five short built-in stairs in less time than it takes to say "de-planed." She made her way to the interagency motor pool car and driver waiting on the tarmac, that her experience told her had probably been hastily dispatched from the IRS offices in Holtsville, up island.

It took all of five minutes to get to the facility on the outskirts of the airport, blessedly not enough time to strike up a conversation with her driver. Used to driving around tax auditors and low level managers, he was probably dying to ask her about the bruise on her cheek and her chewed up and scraped hands.

At the front desk of Walt Disney Imagineering she was greeted by Todd Yaleman, who was about forty, lanky, and smelled of cigarettes. Next to him was Officer Derrick Barnes, who wore a Town of East Hampton police uniform. Brooke produced her FBI identification and they settled in a small conference room off the main corridor. Even though the room was small, it had all the gizmos: a whiteboard hooked up to a computer, video projector, multiple LCD screens, and a video conferencing rig.

Officer Barnes handed over an old-fashioned paper police file.

She saw his interest in her face and hands. "Skiing accident, you should see the bush." Brooke leafed through it. "Were there any latent prints?"

"We found one set that didn't match the employees. We ran an NCIC but there was no hit."

Brooke found the print slides in the folder and set them aside. "I'll sign a chain of custody and take these back with me and out to Interpol."

"You're saying someone from Europe actually broke in here and took my propulsion plans?" Yaleman said.

"Did you know that EuroDisney in France had a similar break-in, also two years ago?"

"No, I didn't know that. Did they get Claude's work then?"

Brooke took out her Blackberry and flip-fingered through the pages. "Claude Vervant?" She said looking up at the design engineer.

"Yes, he and I worked on it; he on the materials and manufacture over there, while I was working on the fluid dynamics here."

"Well, Mr. Yaleman, what can you show me about the project?"

"Have you seen the movie?"

"*Ishmael's Quest*? No, I'm sorry."

"Well, you and the rest of the world. That's why we never built it. There was no ride potential to a movie that wound with up nobody ever seeing it."

"Aside from the movie, is there anything I can see on the project?"

"We will have to go to the video lab. All I have left are the research and progress tapes."

"Let's go take a look."

∞§∞

Three hours later, Brooke was sitting at a table in World Pie, a bistro in Bridgehampton, one of the picturesque little towns a person encounters on the way back to New York City. She was starved, and the sliced steak salad before her was disappearing at a non-ladylike rate. The government jet that had brought her here went on, and she was to be driven back to New York to check in at her former office on Fifty-Seventh Street. From there she could send the prints to Interpol and also check to see if Yaleman had a criminal record.

Brooke had been the head of the New York office of the FBI until Bill and his QUOG team recruited her. Now she was a prime operator for the Quarterback Operations Group.

As she ate she thought how odd it was that a week ago she had almost died in the Indian Ocean, and now she was in the tony Hamptons. 'Swanky,' her late brother Harley would have called it. Thinking of her brother made her think of Mush. The little reverb that rang throughout her body was a nice feeling. *Wait,* she thought, *don't even go there. He's a sea captain, gone six months out of the year and based in Hawaii for the rest. Well, that part wouldn't be too bad.* She downed her iced tea, paid the bill in cash, and took a receipt.

IV. PIG IN A POKE

Bill looked at the place where the building had been repaired and couldn't tell where the old construction ended and the new replacement façade began. So fine was the workmanship that it made him think it was too good. Maybe they should have left it charred and blackened from the 9/11 attacks, as a reminder to be ever-vigilant, to never be asleep at the switch again, at least not here, not at the focal point of America's military power, the Pentagon,

Inside, Bill and Joey were ushered to a secure teleconference room. Two rear admirals and a civilian contractor were already in the room.

Everyone having been briefed on the meeting in advance, Bill jumped right in. "Can we recover the crucibles?"

"Yes, but it will take a thirty-four days."

"Why not the three weeks we requested?" Joey said.

"The final position of the ship on the ocean floor isn't going to make it easy, because now we know it settled hull up," Rear Admiral Merkel said.

"That and getting in there from a distance without being detected by a satellite, and working in those depths in pressurized hulls and suits, with pre-positioned recharges..." another officer said.

Bill couldn't remember the officer's name, but saw the stars on his shoulder boards. "Please explain, Admiral?"

"From the cover of a freighter specially rigged up for the deep submersible team, the first seven runs to the wreck will be to deposit supply capsules and tools. The eighth trip will bring men and sensors to the site and with the pre-positioned supplies they will have enough oxygen, food and fresh water to work for the two weeks. We anticipate it will take that long to locate, reach, and retrieve the crucibles," Admiral Pensey said.

"How much do you estimate it will cost?" Bill asked.

Merkel nodded to the civilian contractor, who opened a briefing book and quoted, "If the thirty-four-day schedule holds, three hundred eighty-five million, which includes two weeks simulated recovery in Vieques to test and true up the tools and sensors."

"The Navy must have sunk a hundred ships off that Puerto Rican island in gunnery practice, so that will give your men lots of hulls to practice cracking," Joey said.

"Exactly," Merkel said. "Also, it will help acclimate the bodies to pressure and pure O2."

Bill reached into his case and retrieved two sets of documents. "Admiral, I am authorized by the President of the United States, whose seal and signature is duly affixed, to order you to claim under international maritime law, in the name of the United States of America, the ship wreck Vera Cruz, originally registered under the Maltese flag and now classified as adventurae maris or wreckage still at sea. To retrieve from her hold those items hereunder classified by executive order as articles of national security in the highest priority including..." Bill looked up to denote how important this part was. He read on, "but not limited to, nuclear containment crucibles, their crating, documentation, and any other pertinent evidence as to be used at such time in a world court, or court of world opinion, to protect the interests of the United States. The president, as Commander in Chief, and acting under the National Command Authority, on this day declaring these items a clear and present danger to the United States being hereby acknowledged." He grabbed a pen and signed both copies. "I now co-sign these operational orders as your executive officer with the simulated rank of an SES-14."

He slid the orders to the Admiral, who signed them and closed the leather folder. Neither man dwelled on the fact that the paper was essentially a purchase order for three hundred eighty-five million dollars-worth of Navy attention.

"Good luck and Godspeed to you and your men," Bill said as he shook the hands of the two Navy men and the contractor.

"Thank you, Bob." The Admiral dismissed the contractor and waited until he was out of the room before continuing. "Mr. Hiccock, what happened in the South Pacific was very disconcerting to us."

"I can appreciate that, Admiral, but we were also caught off guard," Bill said.

Joey jumped in, "And thank you for the fast and successful recovery of our operative, Agent Burrell."

"That's what we wanted to chat about..." Merkel said.

"Forgive me sir, but I don't think I know what 'chat' means in the context of an Executive Branch, Department of the Navy meeting."

"Of course, Mr. Hiccock. What I mean is, something strange happened out there. One of our finest skippers is now involved in what, for him, could be a devastating career blow; a career killer, in fact, as dicey as if an ace fighter pilot reported a flying saucer."

"The whale!" Joey said.

"If that is what we are in fact dealing with," Bill added.

"What does that mean, Mr. Hiccock?"

"We have the top marine life and cretaceous experts trying to find any research on sea life that could be trained to operate the way Ms. Brooke filed in her report. So far, they all agree it's not likely."

"So if you rule out living creatures, you think it's some machine?"

"Or something machine-like."

"But our subs can hear if a Soviet sub has a bad valve in the officer's head at five miles out. No machine could get that close to one of our missile boats."

"Well, we are looking into some leads now, and as soon as we have anything concrete we'll notify you."

The admiral looked at Hiccock and deliberately paused before speaking his next words. "I have two major areas of concern, sir. One is that I have thirty-seven thousand men at any one time in that ocean. If there is a killer whale or machine or whatever out there, I need to sound the alarm and ramp up my skippers on force protection against such a threat. And second, if there is any information that would be exculpable for Morton, sooner rather than later, it could save a brilliant career."

"Admiral, as to the threat, as soon as we learn of anything that is actionable, you have my word, we'll share it on the double. As for Mush, he saved my agent's life. We owe him a debt that will be hard to repay. Again, if any of our wild-assed assumptions bear fruit, we'll do our best to support our friend."

"And of course, Dr. Hiccock, we never had this 'chat.'"

"What chat is that, sir?"

Outside the Pentagon, Bill turned to Joey, "Tell Brooke to dust off her passport. Let's get her to France and see if we can help out our boomer skipper."

∞§∞

The last time Brooke had been in Paris, she had been with Peter Remo, a sweet older guy who was a friend of Bill Hiccock, and with whom she'd had a brief Parisian encounter a year or so earlier. She had met Peter while on a case, and he had filled a hollow place she hadn't even realized was empty. They had spent a wonderful week in this City of Lights, both ready for the romance of France to saturate their pores. The twenty-year difference in their ages was hardly worth a second glance in this continental cosmopolitan setting where men in their sixties are frequently seen in the company of young women whose age didn't exceed that of the Chivas Regal they sipped.

The brief May-December interlude had dissipated into an impressionist's pastel memory as the pace of their lives ramped back up to American rat-race speed. Still, as she took a deep breath on that early Monday on her little hotel balcony, the memory made Brooke momentarily ache to have someone step behind her, wrap his arms around her and melt away the morning chill. Instead, she did some stretches and deep knee bends and ate a room service breakfast. She was showered, dressed, and in the lobby at eight thirty, when a U.S. Embassy driver picked her up for the drive out to Euro-Disney.

The drive through the French countryside was picturesque, with little farmhouses and big rolls of browning hay on emerald-green fields. *Maybe I should call Peter when I get back.* She immediately discarded the idea; Mush had her sole and total attention now. She wondered if it was because she knew she could have Peter with just a phone call, but Mush was like forbidden fruit. He belonged to the Navy and wasn't kidding when he told her that his main love was the USS *Nebraska*. She wondered if she threatened that relationship in some way. Another woman you could fight, but the other 'she' was the biggest, most expensive, cutting edge, top-secret weapons platform that existed on the planet. Somehow she had to find a way to be the more desirable boy's toy.

Like the Disney facility on Long Island, the Euro Disney Imagineering complex wasn't near the park and its attractions, but in an industrial area. Luckily, both the head of security and the designer she needed to interview spoke English, saving Brooke from brushing off the rusted French of her father.

"How far along had the project gotten?" Brooke asked the head of the project.

"Not far, mademoiselle; we had a working prototype of the propulsion organ, but the chemicals necessary were in violation of the green oath Disney signed with the U. N. agency that gives us a green rating worldwide."

Brooke noted that Yaleman, his American counterpart, omitted the part about the U.N. ban. "So they never went into production?"

"No. Also, it was too expensive for the budget of the rides. However, there was rumor of a live-action sequel to be made. Had we manufactured only two of the units for the movie, we could have amortized the initial cost, but the second film was never made. The Frenchman's eyes momentarily dropped to her legs.

"When did you discover the documents were missing?" Brooke asked as she tugged the hem of her skirt down toward her knees.

"Only when your office called my chief and we dug into the files at your suggestion. Until then, we thought it was just a case of hackers trying to get to our gaming software, or at least, that's how they made it look."

"So they covered their tracks?"

"Very sophisticated, and now we know it had to be a job-inside, as you say."

"How do you know it was an inside job?"

"Our firewall!"

"So you're saying they had to be physically in this facility to — what? Plug into your network, with, like a wire or something?"

"Yes. From outside, not likely."

"With what was taken, could someone have made a full production version?"

"Yes, it was all there."

"In your opinion, could someone do this?"

"The hardest part would be the electro-reactive fluid procurement."

Brooke checked her notes. "And that's what they were cooking in East Hampton?"

∞§∞

Even though he was an ocean away in Washington, D.C., Joey Palumbo had real juice at Interpol, France. As soon as Brooke entered the International Criminal Police Organization's Paris office, she was immediately ushered to a secure teleconference room and Joey was already on the monitor from Washington. Brooke slid into her seat and her image appeared in a multi-partitioned screen.

On the screen in front of her, Joey smiled and asked, "How they treating you, Brooke?"

"Fine, sir."

"What have you found out?"

"We definitely have a potential here for the plans to have found their way into enemy hands. What we need to do on a worldwide basis is look for any thefts, purchases or intel on the various forms of..." she glanced down at her notes, "... electro-static, electro-dynamic, electro-reactive or electro-kinetic fluids. I've uploaded all the keywords to our Washington Bureau, and Interpol is distributing them to the rest of the jurisdictions. Also, Bill's science network may be of use here."

"Very good, Agent Burrell. Anything else?"

"There was a red flag in the file of the French Disney designer; we're running that down now."

"Okay, let me know if that comes to anything."

"Aye, sir!"

"Bonsoir, agent..."

"Adieu, boss."

V. BAITING THE HOOK

"Ewwww! I am going back up to the house and leave you two he-men to the great outdoors," Janice said as she got up from the dock and brushed off the seat of her jeans.

"Okay fella, it's you and me left to provide for the women folk," Bill said to his progeny as the little boy giggled at the wiggly worm dancing on the end of the hook.

It was one of those moments that define a man's life: the transmission of values from one generation to the next. Although in this case Bill intellectually knew it was a warm-up for the same scene to be repeated when little Richie reached five and would be able to appreciate it more, still it was instinctively emanating from him and he couldn't control it if he wanted to.

The reel whizzed as he gave the line a little whip into the water. Richie watched as the hook and sinker disappeared into the murky depths of the lake Bill had swum in since he was six years old. Bill had many great memories here at the summer cabin his dad and uncle used to own together, till Uncle Bill died in `78.

With Richie nestled under his arm, his legs dangling off the dock, he bobbed his pole gently. Richie's hair had the smell of baby shampoo, and Bill found himself breathing deeper than usual. Richie's hand grabbed the reel and started cranking it, more to hear the sound, Bill guessed, than to reel in an imagined fish. At intervals, Bill released the lock and let it free-spin back down, then clicked it on again so Richie could continue ratcheting. The pole dipped and Bill instinctively pulled up. The reel started to click and let line out. "Richie, you caught a fish, son. You caught a fish!" Bill put his hand over his son's and reeled the fish in. Soon a silvery flittering image appeared near the surface. He unhooked his arm from around Richie and, keeping the rod between them, coaxed the boy to turn it more. "C'mon Richie, reel it in, keep turning boy." At that point little Richie started laughing and stopped turning the reel. That made Bill laugh, "C'mon Rich, reel it in, do like daddy." Click, click, click went the reel, but little Richie was laughing too hard.

Bill lifted the line out of the water and a found a silver blue pike female hooked at the end. "Whoa! Looky there Rich... a fish! You caught a big fish!"

The little boy looked at his daddy, then at the fish and back to his daddy and said, "Fishy."

Bill was flabbergasted. "What did you say? What is this?"

The little boy with his mother's big beautiful eyes just looked at his daddy and banged on the reel. The fish worked itself free and swam off.

"What was that? What did you just catch?" Bill tried to elicit the word again, but all the little boy did was laugh. Bill picked him up and went running back to the house.

"Janice! Jaaaaanice — Janice!" Bill called out as the screen door to the cabin slammed behind them.

"What? What happened — did you catch a big fish?" Janice asked as she came from the kitchen in her mommy voice that Bill had not known she possessed until Richie emerged on the scene.

"Janice, he said it."

"Said what?" she said, looking at her son as if marveling at him for the first time.

"He said, 'fishy'!"

"You did! You caught a fishy with Daddy?"

"Come on Richie, tell Mommy what you caught."

It went on like that for two minutes until they both realized it was approaching child abuse.

"Well, I'll finish making lunch. Why don't you wash the worm goo off both your hands." Janice went back to the kitchen.

"Come on, champ, let's go wash up," Bill said as he hefted the boy up and carried him to the bathroom.

"Fishy."

"Jaaaaaanice!"

∞§∞

"You've got to be shitting me," Joey said. "I can understand piracy on the high seas or even going up against the U.S. Navy, but the bad guys must have balls to bring on the disdain of Greenpeace and the greenies who use ecological blackmail to knuckle companies into bleeding money to save the whales. Hey, that's funny!"

"Joey, you've got to work on your political skills. You sound so...retro," Bill observed as he took back Brooke's briefing paper from him.

"C'mon, you don't see the irony in a bunch of save-the-whale types being responsible for creating the killer whale of all time?"

"How do you make that connection?"

"First this movie, *Ishmael's Quest*, was the continuing stories of Moby Dick, but in this version Moby turns into a good guy or good whale... not a dick!"

"Are you here all week, Shecky?"

"Some college professor did a paper on the public's lack of caring about the plight of whales. He cited *Moby Dick*, still to this day, as the main cause for the callousness over the fate of the cretaceous."

"Stop being cute, just tell me the facts."

"Fact: a percentage of the proceeds of the movie was going to a whale protection group. The first movie, it's animated, and it bombs. The die-hard save-the-whale heads vow to try again, but this time with a live action film. You know with actors and some CGI..."

"Joey, I got it. Are you finished?"

"So they plan on making this mechanical whale for the film, you know, so no real whales were hurt in the making... Disney doesn't build it because the chemicals are on a banned list they corporately signed an oath never to use. They shit-can the sequel. The plans sit until these bastards throw caution to the wind, environmentally speaking, steal the blue prints, and build the thing."

"I still don't follow, but even more important, I don't care. Can you tell me who built it and how we can catch them? Or at least prove it's a real entity to get Red Beard off the hook." Bill pulled out the page that had the different fluid names.

"Hey, that's funny too! Red Beard... Pirate... Hook?"

"You are in a rare mood, buddy boy. Did you get laid last night?"

"As a matter of fact..."

"Good, I am happy for you, and I feel for Phyllis. Now, stop giggling like a kid and be the cop I owed a job to."

"Okay, but I already did all that."

"You hard-on, when were you going to tell me?"

"Just before you shoved this report that I already read in my face."

"Okay cut the crap; what do we got?"

"The propulsion bladders were of rubber, made by a subsidiary of Michelin out of Libya. The specs were right out of the WDI plans. The electro-reactive fluid came from a chemical tanker presumably pirated off the Somali coast. The ship's owner, the Marnee Line, claimed the pirates let seawater into the hold and ruined the load of P784. It made a claim and received 1.2 million of the insured value of this very rare gunk. Of course, it's possible the bad guys took all they needed first, then flooded it."

"And the sixty-four thousand dollar question is — " Bill announced in a game show host styled voice.

"Who are the bad guys? Hold on to your girdle, Mabel — UNESCO."

"As in the United Nations?"

"The terrorists in Turtle Bay, that's correct."

"What the hell?"

"The rotating head of UNESCO was the Somali ambassador. During his reign, his half-brother, T.R. Maguambi, used the UN's credit card to finance the whole op and opened accounts in Geneva that would endow their little terrorist Orca for years to come."

"How much are we talking about here?"

"Near as we can tell, one hundred million in the various Swiss accounts."

"How could this happen?"

"At the UN only the big things like global warming, nuclear proliferation and human rights are watched by the Security Council, which is us, France, Germany, Russia and China; the relatively good guys. The rest are all thugs and thieves trying to use the UN as a big bat to bash in the brains of century-old enemies."

"That's a rather cynical view, Joseph."

"Bill, if they didn't have metal detectors at the doors up there, these tribes and clans would be stabbing one another during every vote."

"So Maguambi takes advantage of the chaos in the General Assembly and funds his personal pirate program."

"Why not? The last Secretary General's son hit the mother lode on "oil for food" right under everyone's nose. They're still trying to find the millions squirreled away around the world."

"How do we shut him down?"

"Right outside is the guy who can help us build the case."

"Case? That sounds like court, cops, plea-bargaining and years. I want these guys stopped, yesterday."

"Ah, Billy boy, now, now, here's where that nagging little crinkly piece of old yellowed paper pisses all over your righteous indignation. The Constitution says you can't just wipe 'em out without proof."

"Wrong! Maritime Law clearly says you find a pirate, you can hang a pirate." Bill stuck out his tongue as the school yard decorum continued.

"Wanna take this to the judge? You are going to lose. That only covers at sea and in the act. Here you have a diplomatic figure from a sovereign nation who may or may not be implicated in an illegal conspiracy to commit piracy on the high seas."

"I hate you..."

"Really off your game if it ain't science, aren't you Bill?"

Bill gave him the finger by holding up three and asking Joey to "Read between the lines! Now, who's outside?"

"Percival Cutney, from Lloyds of London."

"An insurance investigator?"

"From London!"

"Okay, bring him in." Bill got up and moved over to the small conference table in the right corner of his office.

He remained standing until Joey entered with the insurance man.

"William Hiccock, this is Percival Cutney from Lloyds of London."

"Nice to meet you; do you go by Percy?"

"No, I prefer Percival, Professor Hiccock."

"Of course, Mr. Cutney. But while we are being so formal, it's Doctor Hiccock, I am no longer a research professor at M.I.T." Bill already felt like this guy had judged him a cardboard cutout bureaucrat. Percival was impeccably dressed in a Crombie topcoat and Savile Row bespoke grey suit, and sported a thin, tightly furled umbrella, fully coifed hair, and a tan that seemed air-brushed onto his skin. He had blue-green eyes and uncharacteristically perfect teeth, caps most likely. Bill noticed he wore a Notre Dame ring, which was a bit of an oddity — he'd expected to see an Oxford ring. He also sported an odd sort of wedding ring, seemingly made to resemble barbed wire. *That's one way to keep a marriage together,* Bill mused to himself. "Mr. Palumbo tells me you have corroborating evidence in the piracy affair."

"Yes. May I have a glass of water?"

"Er... sure." Bill went back over to the credenza behind his desk and poured a glass of water from the pitcher. He placed it in front of Percival and sat.

Percival reached into his vest pocket and produced a vial of clear liquid, unstopped it and poured it into the glass, and then removed a double-A battery from the same pocket and dropped it into the glass. He then flicked the glass toward Bill.

Bill immediately reacted, pushing back from the expected mini-deluge, but instead the water with the battery in it clunked onto the table as a solid. Although shaped in the form of the tumbler as if it were ice, it was not cold at all. Bill gave a little smirk, then leaned in and touched the solid water with the end of his pen.

"It's a solid as long as there is a voltage from the battery," Percival said.

"Electro-reactive fluidics," Joey added.

"Yes, except the pirates have stolen something even more rare — electro-expansive fluids."

"So, in the presence of a voltage, the liquid expands." Bill picked up the solid water and looked through it.

"Yes, and that's the breakthrough that has Maguambi rolling in ill-gotten gains." Percival opened his folio and placed a stack of papers on Bill's table. "Here are some of the extortion letters our shipping clients have received in the past months. In every instance, the carrier is threatened with attack from an entity no ship can defend against."

The whale! Bill thought.

"We think there is only one of these entities. It is our policy to pay the relatively small sum to the pirates, rather than to pay out on a loss of ship and life claim. But it has to stop. We are being bled dry."

"So that's why you are sharing these letters with us?"

"If you stop them, you stop our bleeding. Besides, there is a rumor this machine has attacked one of your Naval vessels."

Rather than confirming or denying the attack, Bill grabbed the stack of letters, "I can use these in a court of law?"

"In a U.S. court, yes."

"What about the International Court of Justice in The Hague?" Joey asked.

"The UN may not be totally objective in this case," Percival said as he sat back, his little show over.

Joey gave Bill a look that said, "*See*? I told you."

"In any event, your agent was definitely attacked at least once by the machine, then."

Joey stiffened, "What are you talking about?"

"Bad form? So sorry. We understand your agent was aboard the Vera Cruz."

It was all Joey could do to control the shade of red he knew his ears were turning. He also deliberately didn't look at Bill, so as not to give the statement any weight.

Bill deftly moved off topic back to an earlier point. "Why do you think the world court wouldn't...?"

"Maguambi is running the table, and there is no state interested in bringing up proceedings against him. Therefore he has carte blanche, I am afraid."

"So to be clear here, Mr. Cutney, neither I nor the United States government is offering you or your company any quid pro quo for the information you offered to us today. Are you satisfied with that?"

"If you stop this menace on the high seas, as I know you will, that will be recompense enough."

Joey added, "You'd be willing to sign a release to that effect, Mr. Cutney?"

"Have your counsel draw it up and I will sign for Lloyds. I am at the St. Regis till the day past tomorrow. Well, that being my only business here today, I'll bid you gentlemen farewell and good hunting." Percival was up and leaving so quickly that Bill had just enough time to buzz Cheryl, who was surprised to meet him at the door to escort him out of the White House.

"He's a little thin for Santa Claus, ya think?" Bill said as he probed the solid water not soaking into the blotter in front of him.

"And five hands shy of a gift horse, but I'll take it." Joey turned deadly serious. "How did old Saint Nick know about Brooke?"

Bill threw it back to his head of security and operations. "I thought we were supposed to be Ultra on this."

"We are!"

"No, I'd say having a complete stranger come in here and let on that he knows our biggest secret ever, kind of indicates we are not," Bill said in a manner more suited to a kindergarten teacher.

"I'll do some digging into Percy's lineage."

"That's Percival to you, Joey!"

"Sorry old chap, right you are."

Joey left Bill staring at the battery and thinking about the ramifications of the other liquid, if it existed, which not only became solid in the presence of so low a voltage, but also actually expanded. It would truly be 'electric ice.' The liquid would act just like water being frozen, becoming a solid and expanding at the same time but only at the flick of a switch. His mind immediately raced through all the possibilities, a new source of hydraulics for everything from earth movers to reclining chairs — hydrodynamics, new piston engines, miniature air conditioners, manufacturing and shaping machines, black box recorders, black box shipping containers that would solidify against any shocks, vacuum pumps, and nano-technology. In spite of the endless possibilities, someone had developed the technology as a weapon, a weird weapon; one that was right out of a classic novel.

∞§∞

It had happened; Bill and Janice had become one of "those couples" — the ones who bring their eighteen-month-old out to dinner, to be subjected to the wary scrutiny of suspicious couples to determine if the tyke could be the type to explode in a spine shrinking, shrill scream at a moment's notice. Or worse, fling spaghetti and meatballs or strained peas all over their Saturday night date clothes. It wasn't too long ago that Bill and Janice had been the "on guard singles," scrupulously avoiding a close encounter of the third grade or below. But parenthood had defeated or deafened those senses, giving them immunity to certain wailing frequencies emanating at full force from developing lungs.

Happily for all concerned, Richard Ross Hiccock was an inquisitive little boy who, for the most part, amused himself. He would from time to time burble out a giggly laugh if something moved or dripped or slid or just sat there long enough for him to try to get it to do something by letting out this laugh. So tonight it was a good night at Mimmo's Villa Napoli.

"Tiramisu or cheesecake?" Bill offered to Janice as the waiter hovered with the dessert tray.

"How about cheesecake with chocolate ice cream?" Janice said with eyes lighting up. This combination, discovered during her cravings with little Richie, had stayed with her.

"Fine," Bill said with the smallest of smiles because he knew it came from that time as well. "With two forks please." He picked up his napkin and wiped his lips. "Excuse me honey, gotta hit the room of men."

As Bill walked through the restaurant, he was unaware of the man who watched his every step.

In the men's room, the daily Naples' newspaper was thumbtacked to the wall above the urinals so a man had something to look at other than looking down. Bill was stumbling over Noticas de Oggi and the Campangola Region

Soccer results, so he didn't pay attention to the man entering the restroom. When the man didn't appear at the urinal next to him he casually turned to see where he was. The man was leaning against the sink, his hands behind him, propped on the corner edge of the vanity's Corinthian top.

Bill finished up and turned to him, "What? Was I in your favorite spot?"

"Dr. Hiccock?"

"Who wants to know?"

"Russ Klaven, USN, retired."

"Retired as what?"

"Commander, Office of Naval Intelligence."

"Okay, so why did you follow me into the head, Russ?"

"Sorry, but I wanted to speak to you alone."

"I got an office, pal. Call and make an appointment, I am with my family right now..." Bill crumpled the paper towel and made a three-pointer right into the wicker waste basket in the corner.

"You can either hear me out right now, or forget we ever met, in which case you are going to spend a lot of time, money and resources finding out what I can tell you tonight for free."

"Can we not do this in a bathroom?" Bill suggested.

After excusing himself from the cheesecake and suffering the mild scorn of a wife upstaged, Bill walked with Russ to an empty corner of the parking lot. Russ took out a pack of Lucky Strikes and lit one, exhaling a long drag into the crisp mid-Atlantic night's air. "How much did Merkel get from you?"

"I'm sorry, didn't you say you were retired?"

"I also said Naval Intelligence. You never rotate out of that."

"Then look, you must have been around the block enough to know that I can't talk to you, or the vice president, for that matter, about anything real or imagined, so why are you trying to get me to talk?"

"Okay, don't talk. Listen." He took another drag from the cigarette, then continued, "I was the guy who designed, built, and ran the DSRV during the Cold War. When we started, we couldn't catch a fish in a butterfly net. But soon we were retrieving missile parts and, hell, whole submarines, from ten, fifteen, twenty thousand feet. We were snagging Soviet nose cones from spent rockets and ICBMs, whole codebooks and decoder machines from sunken *Akula-* and Victor-class, red missile boats. Christ, we even tapped the Russian under-sea telephone lines and listened in to everything from data bursts to lovesick sailors trying to sweet talk their girlfriends to wait till they got home from the sea and not to fuck the guy from the vodka factory. We got a shitload of stuff."

"Okay, well thank you for your service. What's all that got to do with me?"

"You are about to be taken by scrambled eggs who don't give a shit about you or your project. They just need funding for the shit they really want to do that Congress won't authorize."

Bill recognized 'scrambled eggs' as the term given to the yellow filigree embroidered on the visors of flag officer's hats. Still, he remained silent; for all he knew this could be some sort of security test dreamed up by the CIA to tarnish him and take over many of his projects and budgets.

Russ took him in and decided to go on. "Okay, keep not talking, but hear what I am telling you. There are two special ops subs that can crack your buried treasure from miles off — in two weeks. They are already bought and paid for, and their operational expenses are, I bet, one quarter the cost Merkel and the rest gave you."

"How do you know these boats are still on line?"

"I retired last week."

"Look, Commander, I hope you're doing what you are doing out of patriotism and not some beef you have with Navy brass. In recognition of your service and your rank, I am going to make believe all that happened tonight was I shook twice and flushed once. Have a good retirement."

As Bill walked back to the restaurant, Klaven called out, "Try the *Halibut*!"

∞§∞

At the White House the next day, Peter Remo stopped dead in his tracks when he attempted to walk into Bill's office. The scene in front of him made him smile. A sound engineer pressing headphones to his ears sat at a rolling cart, which held a mixer and a digital recorder. Seated across from Bill was a woman with a stopwatch and a big book full of what seemed like script pages. Seated next to her was a man with his chin resting between his thumb and forefinger listening intently to every syllable coming from Bill. In front of Bill was a microphone with something that looked like a fly swatter made out of panty hose material between the mic and his face. Right below was a small easel with loose pages on it and around him there were stands holding thick, heavy blankets, Pete surmised these were sound deadening blankets to ward off the roomy sound only a microphone could hear.

Bill was smiling as he talked, the director sitting across from him having recommended it because a smile affects the tone of voice, making the speaker sound more energetic and happy. "In our next show, can Tiffany and Diego outsmart a robot mouse controlled by the freeze-dried brain of a real mouse?" Bill finished the line and looked to the director.

The director gave an okay sign, then held up his hand, waited, and pointed at Bill.

"Come on now, Diego, say cheese!" Bill added, as if taunting the boy who wasn't there.

"Cut, circle it. Okay, that's a wrap. Thank you, Bill, We'll see you in four weeks."

"Bye Mo, Jenny, take care," Bill addressed them as they bugged out in an instant. Bob, the sound guy, stayed behind and took down the sound blankets and stands.

"Peter! You're early."

"Radio star?"

"TV actually. I do a PBS show for kids called *Science Beat,* and a Science And Technology Policy Review once a month for U.S. Information Agency. We are hoping CNN picks it up."

"So which was this?"

"The PBS show. I shot the opening and did a series of wraparounds on camera a few months back. These were the audio tracks for the coming attractions." Bill rifled through his desk and came up with a DVD. He walked over to the TV and popped it in. "Tell you what Pete, you check out this DVD of the show. I am going to hit the men's room."

Peter watched the opening of *Science Beat.* There was Bill on the fifty-yard line of his alma mater. As he cocked his arm back to throw a pass, his body changed into a computer graphic of the musculoskeletal system as he propelled the ball. The ball was shown in a perfect spiral (what else?), bulleting through the air. Around the spiraling ball were vector lines and parabolic arcs, as well as math formulas on lift and drag. Then the panning camera caught the big Jumbotron in the stadium and zoomed into the screen until the pixels were as big as baseballs. Peter could see the alternations of the pixels from red to blue to green that create a picture, shooting down the cable to the camera, as well as the splitting of the image across a chip that digitized the picture. After going through the lens, flipping and shrinking through the focal point, the picture was right side up as it came out of the last lens element. The subject of the picture was a woman in the stands wearing an iPod. Her earphones became one half of the cutaway showing the diaphragm of the earbud on the opposite side of the eardrum. The vibration off the earbud sympathetically vibrated the eardrum and the signal was transmitted through the tympanic bone into the brain as impulses. On the screen, her brain began to spin and transformed back into the football. When a wide receiver caught the football in the end zone, he looked down and saw he had caught a brain, not the ball. At the end, a graphic announced "*Science Beat* with Professor 'Wild' Bill Hiccock." A series of credits ran over drawings by da Vinci and Michelangelo, ending in a computer-aided design of an airplane on a huge screen. The CAD drawing of the plane started to materialize as the SR-71 Blackbird at the Smithsonian Air and Space Museum, as Bill appeared standing on the wing of the fastest supersonic spy plane in history.

He held a rock in his hand as he spoke to a circling camera giving a three-hundred-sixty-degree view of the plane and the museum. "Today we are going to see how a rock in a river led to the development of the fastest commercial aircraft in the world, as Roscoe Banks takes us on a trip that goes back three hundred forty-five years and proceeds at supersonic speed to land in a secret Air Force base during the Cold War." The image of Bill standing on the wing digitized into a stream of dots and was replaced by Roscoe standing near a river as people dressed in Middle Ages attire beat clothes against rocks to clean them.

Just then Bill re-entered, "Well, what do you think?"

"Don't quit your day job."

"Hey pal, education is my day job. All this cloak and dagger crap is extracurricular."

VI. I LOVE THE NIGHT LIFE

There are many reasons men don't wear leather pants anymore, but in the after-hours clubs of Switzerland, the diffused euro-sexual gender ambiguity was in full view. In this case, the view was that of Raffael Juth's simulated-cowhide-covered butt. The observer was Hanna Strum, an attractive woman whose long curly blonde locks dangled and played peek-a-boo with her pushed up breasts that 'Victoria' was not trying to keep secret. Raffey, of course, exhibited all the male characteristics of trying not to stare while staring that tickled Hanna at a level she dared not let on. After he caught her looking a few times, he drummed up the courage to walk over to her breasts and ask if she'd like to dance. She made sure not to look at him approaching; however, another woman watching would have noticed the subtle "girls up" pose she morphed into.

"Hi, I am Raffael," he said as he bobbed and weaved a little to place his face in her line of sight as she scanned the room.

"Hi." She gave him a quick glance then continued her not-interested investigation of the gyrating room.

"I was wondering if you would like to share a dance with me?"

"You were?" She said without looking at him.

"Yes, unless you are here with someone?"

"Would that matter to you?" She said, finally locking eyes with him.

"It would be a pre-condition of which I was not aware and therefore acceptable to me as your preference."

"I don't understand a word you just said. What are you some kind of word nerd?" She turned her attention back to the dancers on the floor.

"No, I assure you, words are not my craft."

"No kidding."

"I am more of a theoretical physicist."

"If I dance with you, will you talk like a normal person?"

"Most assuredly — eh, yeah. Sure."

"You're learning," she said as she offered her hand.

She sounded like she was from the U.S., but there was something else, something Germanic mixed in. Raffey couldn't discern it over the throbbing bass of the music.

They hit the floor as the DJ changed to a popular house music cut that any American would have known was five years old, but the crowd let out a collective "whoo" as the first slamming drum beats were instantly recognized. Hanna's hand flew from Raffey's fingers as she became a writhing, flame-like entity, wavering to the seductive beat. Raffey maintained his two-step, stiffly choreographed routine, one that most girls let pass for some kind of dance. In her throbbing bass-induced dance trance, Hanna was in a world of her own. Raffey was drawn to her indifference, as if she were beckoning him to her boudoir with a come-hither finger gesture. He was hooked.

∞§∞

"The report you requested is in from the Navy."

"Are they still at four hundred million for the recovery?"

"Here's where you got to love the government, even though I was at the meeting. See here where it says, Ultra Secret Eyes Only. That's the part that says, not for me to know and for you to find out," Joey said as he spun the thirty-two-page finding across Hiccock's desk.

"Raise your right hand."

"What?"

"Raise — your — right — hand!"

Joey did.

"Repeat after me, 'I am a big jerk.'"

"I am just like you. So help me God," Joey ad-libbed.

"Good! You're cleared to see this — go to the summary page and tell me the number."

"Recovering crucibles from the bottom of the Indian Ocean...deep sea trials...target acquisition and plotting soundings and imaging...here it is, total estimated costs four hundred two million dollars. Wait. Didn't they say three hundred eight-five at the meeting? Now it's four hundred and two? What did they do, add tax?"

"Sounds cheap at half the price," Bill noted sarcastically as he reached to take the page back.

"Wait, you agreed to this number or something close. You having buyer's remorse?"

"I don't know," Bill said flipping through the report.

"So what's wrong? They're not making you pay for this personally are they?"

"Nah, but a funny thing happened at Mimmo's the other night."

"Indigestion?"

"A guy cornered me in the men's room."

"I don't want to hear the rest of this. Maybe you should take it up with the White House shrink."

"Listen, shit for brains, the guy was an ex-spook. Somehow, he knew all about the meeting I had with the Navy brass. He said some things that were, at best, disturbing."

"Now that I am cleared for this restaurant review, you gonna tell me the rest of the story?" Joey plopped down into one of the two tufted, plush leather chairs in front of Bill's desk.

Hiccock wrote down the man's name, rank and the notation 'Nav Intel,' then tore off the page from the pad and handed it to Joey. "Read the Navy's report, then see what you can dig up on this guy."

"If he is an ex-spook the shovel will have to go pretty deep," Joey said, tapping the report.

"Keep it tight, but use sources we can trust. Don't tell them why or who wants to know in case you are on a two-way street."

"Got it. People we can trust but only one way — that's going to bruise a few egos."

∞§∞

Hanna's gyrations weren't attracting Raffey's eyes alone. Prince El-Habry Salaam, nephew of the Saudi King, was unwinding in the VIP section of the club. His father had sent him to study banking in Switzerland so he could better administer the Royal Family's billions. Across the velvet ropes, Hanna's undulations made him don his hated glasses, which he never wore in public, in order to see if she was the vision she appeared to be. Upon more focused inspection, he nodded to Abrim, his head of security. Abrim knew the drill.

As Raffey and Hanna were in the middle of their fifth dance, the six-foot-three-inch guard of the Prince appeared and, in English with a hint of Arabic accent, asked for forgiveness. "Pardon the intrusion, but my employer wishes for you to join him." He pointed in the direction of the roped off area.

Hanna shot a quick glance at the thin, dark-skinned man wearing dark glasses in a dimly lit corner of the club. "No, thank you."

Abrim pushed, "He is a prince of the Royal Family Saud. His intentions, I assure you, are the most honorable."

"Not interested." Then she turned away and danced even more seductively.

Raffey moved in close, "Who was he?"

"An errand boy. Want to get a drink?"

Raffey smiled and led her to the bar. It being three deep, he decided to get the drinks while Hanna found a small table.

She removed her right shoe and rubbed a complaining instep. When she sat back up, Abrim was there.

"You again?"

"With apologies."

"Look, why doesn't he just come over here himself?"

"He is a Prince. He could not be seen making an overture to a... a... "

"Commoner? Is that the term you are looking for?"

Abrim just half smiled.

"Well, my father always called me Princess when I was a little girl, so what's he so high and mighty about?"

"The Prince has a great interest in you and would be happy to pay you for your time."

"Oh he would, would he?"

"Yes. Ten thousand dollars, U.S.?"

"Fuck off!"

Abrim imperceptibly twitched his hand, the result of the conflicting instinct to strike this infidel bitch, and the training that the social dictates of these Western countries demanded, which immediately stopped him. He just nodded and walked away.

"What did she say, Abrim?" the Prince asked.

"She declined your offer."

"No, I mean what exactly did she say?"

"A crude woman, I'd rather not repeat it."

"What did she say exactly?"

"She said, "Fuck off!"

He turned to admire his new interest, "Brilliant. She is full of spirit. One to be tamed."

Abrim just rolled his eyes.

Raffey came back with the drinks. "I saw him from the bar; he came over again. What did he want this time?"

"He didn't want anything, he was sent by someone with no balls. At least you had the courage to approach me yourself. Let's get out of here."

"But our drinks..."

Hanna reached down and grabbed Raffey between the legs, "You'd better have a set." Then she walked off. Raffey followed like an obedient dog.

∞§∞

Brooke was finishing her room-service breakfast while reviewing her notes and trying to find patterns in the international web of petty crime even the local police didn't pay much attention to, and only then for insurance requirements. Yet, something was in there she couldn't quite see as yet. She had taken statements from Disney employees at both the Long Island and French facilities — managers, artists, engineers. She checked past employee histories, even janitorial staff. Like this one, Davis Honsberry, a Nigerian who had locked up the night of the break-in in Easthampton. *Wait a minute.* She put down her coffee cup. *The janitor on duty the night of the French break-in was...was...* She rifled through her notes and circled the name Jean Claude Vastow — a Nigerian.

Her suspicions were confirmed when she opened a PDF with the personnel roster for both Disney facitilities and found that both had suddenly left their jobs the day after each break-in. She reasoned that their getaways were clean because no one had suspected an immigrant janitor of a high-tech robbery. She packed up her laptop and left.

Her next stop was to U.S. Immigration and its French counterpart. It took half a day to find out that, although their passports claimed Nigerian citizenship, in each case the port of departure prior to entry to the United States was Sudan. *Pirates.*

Her next call was to the African desk at the CIA. It took some sweet talk, but she managed to get a small investigation going into any connection between these two Nigerians, whatever their real names were, and the outlaw regime of Theodore Roosevelt Maguambi. Named after the U.S. president, and using his half-brother's United Nations clout to wrangle funds, Maguambi went on to bribe and murder his way into power. Now he had unleashed on an indifferent world the second coming of the Barbary pirates. But unlike the 1801 solution ordered by Thomas Jefferson, "Find them and hang them," which solved the problem once and for all, today's more civilized approach was to pay off the pirates and hope they went away. They didn't — and the ransoms enlarged their war chests and created more acts of high seas piracy.

The cop in Brooke knew she needed to connect the robberies at Disney to the pirates and then maybe to the attack on the Vera Cruz and the *Nebraska*. *Mush.* That was it, today's Mush moment, as she had started to call them — times when her mind wandered to Mush and she got all — mushy. These episodes made her doubt she had matured at all. Silly schoolgirl crushes were supposed to have been drummed out of her at Harvard Law, and if not, surely in basic training, JAG School, and then Quantico on her way to becoming number one in the Bureau's New York office. Now she worked at the White House. If they only knew that late at night, when it was just her and the moon shadows on the wall, she was just a teenage girl with insecurities intact. Somehow they always evaporated with the morning light. The real issue she dealt with whenever she met men, certain men, was that as soon as they found out she was an agent, they viewed her as "butch" and crossed her off their list of potential love interests; but not Mush. The fact that she worked in a man's world never affected the way he looked at her. *I wonder where, and under what ocean, he is now?*

∞§∞

Joey Palumbo hadn't been on a carrier since he visited the Intrepid Museum back in New York. The USS Ronald Reagan was massive, twice the length of the old Fighting "I," and a city unto itself. Eight minutes after getting an escort to lead him down to the CIC, he was finally face to face with the man he had come seven thousand miles out to sea to meet. He had traveled the last four hundred of those miles in the backseat of an EC3 Hawkeye, which hit the carrier deck at one hundred miles an hour and was jolted to an arresting-wire stop just forty feet later. He was still rubbing the welts the four-point seat belt had made in his chest as his body kept moving at one hundred while the plane lurched to a stop.

"Hi, Brick."

"Palumbo! This has got to be real important to get you out of San Francisco."

"Is there someplace we can talk alone?"

Sensing that the issue was really serious, he extended his hand and they left the Combat Information Center and found a small stateroom in officer country a few feet down the hall. Two LTs were about to bunk in it. When they saw him they snapped to attention.

"At ease, men. Give us the room for a minute."

Joey waited for them to pile out and then shut the door. "I ain't in SF anymore, Brick. I'm now at the White House. I am here on a very urgent and sensitive matter."

"White House, huh; so that's how you get the frequent flyer mileage to fly out to the Mediterranean tail-hook class."

"I can't give you any details, but I need you to tell me everything you know about Commander Russ Klaven."

"Clay? Is that why you are here? Joey I served with him..."

"Yeah I know, ten years ago. It took forty hours of computer time to match databases with someone I knew who also worked with Klaven. Your name came out of that hat."

"You know he was Naval Intelligence, right?"

"I pulled his service jacket. What I want, is to know about him, the man?"

"I need more than that."

"I told you I can't discuss the details." Joey started to feel concerned; he hadn't come all this way to make some kind of deal.

"No, I mean, I need to see some contravening orders to my oath of secrecy before I put myself in Leavenworth."

"Fair enough." Joey opened his portfolio and took out an order from the White House, endorsed by the Secretary of the Navy. He slid it under Brick's nose. "Will this do?"

"The president? Yeah, I'd say so. All the same, I'm keeping this just in case," Brick said as he folded the "get-out-of-the-brig-free-card" and slid it into his day-uniform shirt pocket.

"I understand. Now, about Klaven."

"Man, he was the brains of the outfit."

For the next hour Joey learned all about the man who had confronted Hiccock in the rest room of Mimmo's.

∞§∞

Outside the club, Raffey took out his ticket stub for the valet; Hanna stuffed it back in his pocket. "My place is just on the corner. You can pick up your car in the morning."

Raffey liked the sound of that, especially the "in the morning" part.

As they walked off down the street arm in arm, Abrim emerged from the club and watched.

In the hallway of the flophouse hotel, Hanna fumbled with the key as Raffey started kissing her neck. She laughed and shook him off to better focus on the lock and key. Once inside she went straight to the cabinet and pulled down a bottle of vodka. "The bathroom is through there. I'll fix us a drink."

"That's okay; I don't need to use the bathroom." He plopped down on the couch and started to unbutton his shirt. Because her back was to him he didn't see the slight mask of frustration wash across her face. He grabbed the remote for the TV and turned it on. Behind him a man emerged from the bathroom with a rolled towel between his two fists. As Raffey yawned, the man brought the towel down across Raffey's mouth. Startled, the young man started to scream, but the towel heavily muffled it. Hanna was tapping the air out of a syringe when the doorbell rang.

She and her accomplice were stunned. "Hold him." She put down the syringe and went to the door. "Who is it?"

"It is Abrim. I have a message from the Prince."

"*Scheisse*. It's the goon from the club," she said in a whisper to the man who was trying to stop Raffey from making any noise.

"Get rid of him." He whispered loudly.

"Go away — I am not interested," she yelled to the door.

"The Prince has asked me to tell you he will pay fifty thousand dollars if you'll just agree to have dinner with him tomorrow night."

"Fine, I will. I will be at the club tomorrow at eight. You can pick me up there. Now go away."

Abrim didn't know whether to believe her or not. But he didn't really care. He had done his "pimping" for the night. He could report back that he had made the offer and she accepted. If she didn't show up, it would only make the Prince more smitten and he'd up the sum to one hundred thousand. He turned to walk off.

Raffey had started to kick and caught the coffee table in front of the couch. It swung his body sideways and his next kick toppled the ginger jar lamp on the end table. It hit the floor with a terrible crash. In his attempt to stop him, the man had loosened the grip on the towel and Raffey's scream accompanied the crash.

Abrim stopped dead in his tracks when he heard the calamity and went back and pounded on the door, "Is everything all right in there?"

The man behind the couch punched Raffey in the face as hard as he could and Raffey slid down to the floor like a sack of hammers. Rubbing his fist, the goon nodded to Hanna to open the door and let the man inside. He stepped to the right of the door and snapped open a stiletto-type knife. Hanna saw the shiny blade and knew at once what she had to do.

"No, please help me, he's passed out," she said as she opened the door. Abrim saw Raffey barely moving on the floor. "Could you just help me get him on the couch to sleep it off?"

Abrim was no more than four feet into the apartment when the blade entered his lung between the sixth and seventh vertebrae. The killer's hand came down on the man's mouth at that same instant to stifle the scream. But Abrim was a big hulk, and even though fatally wounded he shook off his attacker like a rag doll. Hanna grabbed the vodka bottle and hit him hard on his temple. The bottle shattered and he went down on his back. She thrust the broken end of the bottle into Abrim's neck, severing both his carotid arteries, which sprayed blood all over her. The man held his hand over Abrim's mouth. In ten seconds his legs kicked one last time. He was dead.

When Hanna rose to wipe the blood from her face, she saw that Raffey was gone. The window to the fire escape was open. She turned to her partner, and cursed in German, "*Verdammte Scheiße!* You idiot."

Raffey, choking, spitting blood, and gasping for air, was hobbling with a limp from jumping the last six feet off the fire ladder. He bounced off cars and storefronts as he staggered down the empty 3 a.m. Genève streets.

∞§∞

At seven thirty, Hiccock powered up his SCIAD terminal at his desk. At the top of the list was a report from a leading synthetic materials chemist. Bill read with great interest that electric ice, Bill's pet name for the electroexpansive fluid of the kind Percival had flung at him, was non-existent in the commercial chemical field. The writer had never heard of or even considered the possibility of such an invention, but theorized that in order to have that kind of molecular slowing coefficient, some sort of nuclear agent must be employed.

Even at Bill's elevated level of scientific knowledge, in his mind he substituted the words 'chemical reaction' for 'molecular slowing coefficient,' and 'radioactive' for 'nuclear.' Percival had walked through the entire White House security system's radiation, biological, and chemical detectors. Had it been a radioactive or chemical catalyst, the clear liquid in a plastic vial would have had Percival in irons. The rest of the chemist's report actually questioned whether Bill had seen what he reported seeing. It wasn't that the report's author doubted Bill's word, rather that he had been the victim of a trick or sleight of hand. Bill considered this for a moment but dismissed it, because Joey had seen the same thing, but from an angle behind Percival. As a cop, he would have noticed a 'switcheroony' or up-the-sleeve move. Bill wrote back a quick, terse thank you and a mention he'd have to check on his recollection.

Bill was scanning the rest of the SCIAD traffic when Cheryl came in with her morning cup and his. "Cheryl, Percival Cutney's at the St. Regis — I need to talk to him, now."

∞§∞

The Stallion helicopter was winding up on the aft deck helipad of the USS Ronald Reagan as Joey and Brick hit the flight deck from the main bridge stairway. The Mediterranean Sea was rocking and roiling and Joey was glad his transportation was taking off and not trying to land on the pitching deck. As they neared the chopper, they raised their voices.

"See ya next time we make port in Virginia, Joey."

"Drinks are on me, Brick."

Joey climbed into the hatch of the Navy's workhorse, and a seaman handed him a helmet, secured his seat restraint and plugged in the helmet headset. The pilot came over the helmet as the engines revved and the bird lifted up and tilted toward Europe.

"Mr. Palumbo, welcome aboard. The *gipper* got us to within one hundred twenty nautical miles of RAF Station Eastchurch, so we'll be airborne for about forty-eight minutes. There's water and some snacks in the armrest. Let us know if you need to use the head; I'll have someone hold you tight while you aim it out the door."

"Thanks. I won't be drinking any water then."

Navy humor, Joe thought as he watched the thousand-foot plus Nimitz-class carrier shrink down to the size of a discarded cigar in the water before the craning of his neck was stopped by his helmet.

He opened his iPad and continued making notes on Commander Klaven. His headphones crackled. "Mr. Palumbo, I have an encrypted radio message coming through for you."

"Okay."

"Joey, it's Bill. Change of plans."

"What's up?" Joey yelled over the engine noise.

"Percival is gone. I need you to pick up his trail in Paris."

"Paris? I'm heading for RAF Station Eastchurch, Dover."

"Not anymore you're not. I am re-routing you to France. I'll have more info waiting for you with a state department driver when you land. Good luck."

Joey looked forward, as if he could see the pilot, "Hey, Lieutenant, do you have enough gas in this thing to make France?"

VII. NO ESCAPE

Not accustomed to being awakened at 3 a.m., The Engineer knew the call would be bad news. A minute after he hung up, he placed a call to a number he had stored in his head. "There's been a complication."

"What is the nature of this complication?" The Architect said.

"The target has escaped."

"This is not good. I thought the team you hired was good at its craft."

"They are the best!"

"This woman, this psychotic killer who was released from the Stasi when the Berlin wall fell, she is to be trusted, this animal who kills for pleasure?"

That last reference rattled The Engineer. He had recruited Maya because her homicidal tendencies were necessary to make the threat credible.

"She asks no questions and is only too happy to kill for money. The real nature of our mission is safe with her."

"Except, we have lost our prime subject."

"It was an unforeseen circumstance, but the leverage part of the mission has gone well. We will soon have all corrected."

"I never believed in your heavy-handed tactics, but I assumed you knew what you were doing. I shall not make that error again."

"You may rest assured there will be no further problems."

"For your sake." And then he ended the connection.

∞§∞

Raffey made it home on the tram. In the hallway mirror, he touched his swollen black and blue cheek and winced. Blood had dried and caked down his neck from his cut lip. He reached for the phone to call the police and stopped halfway. He was a major team member on a scientific enterprise of massive import. He needed to be mindful of his budding reputation Even in liberal-minded Switzerland, being rolled by a hooker and her pimp would not look good on his record and would surely get him demoted or expelled from the project.

Then where would he go? What kind of work could he find? He placed the phone down quietly so as not to disturb his sister and her sleeping daughter upstairs.

∞§∞

"Hanna" had removed the blonde wig and let her black hair fall from the wig cap. They rolled up to Raffey's house just as he entered the front door.

"Well, Maya, he is predictable," her partner said from the backseat. She knew the house well, having been there only hours before. "*Das ist gut,*" she said.

∞§∞

Holding ice on his lip, Raffey went upstairs and gingerly closed the bathroom door before turning on the light, trying not to disturb his niece and her mother. He opened the medicine chest and found the iodine and gauze. *Tape*, he thought as he moved a box of tampons to see if the roll was behind it. A bottle of witch hazel fell off the shelf and crashed loudly on the edge of the toilet. He stiffened, waiting to hear his sister call out — nothing. He opened the door. "Sorry," he said in a whisper. He strained to hear any response. When there was none, he ventured into the hall. "Leena?" He approached her bedroom door and found it half open. He opened it all the way and the light from the bathroom splashed across the bed. It was still made, and had not been slept in. He walked to his niece's room figuring that since the child had been having bad dreams of late, maybe his sister slept with her.

Again, both beds neat. He returned to Leena's room and turned on the light. Not a sign of her. He went down to the kitchen and found the electric teakettle was on but all the water had steamed out. He pulled the plug. Walking into the living room, he turned on the light and was shocked to see the place in a shambles. He ran to the front door, opened the closet nearby, and pulled out his home guard rifle. He fumbled with the magazine and landed it in the breach. He was shaking like a leaf, not knowing what to do next when the phone in the kitchen rang.

"Your sister and her daughter are fine and they will continue to be unharmed as long as you do what we say. If you deviate from the plan or alert the authorities or anyone else, Leena will watch her daughter die slowly and horribly. Do you understand?"

"Hanna?" Raffey recognized the voice and immediately went into a spiral of confusion.

"*Verstehen*? Do you understand? Do you understand? Raffael!"

He snapped out of his momentary paralysis. "Yes, please don't hurt them."

"That is solely up to you. Go outside, get in the blue car. Bring nothing. We already have your papers and personal items."

∞§∞

In the sedan, Hanna closed her cell phone. Next to her, Leena was crumpled in the passenger seat. Hanna's partner was sitting next to Kirsi in the backseat. Both were unconscious, having been injected with a fast-acting anesthetic.

"We give him two minutes. If he doesn't come out..." She pulled a gruesome-looking folding knife from her belt and clicked it open. She reached around and handed it to Hans in the back seat. "...chop off one of the little girl's fingers and I'll bring it to him."

∞§∞

In the house, tears started to well up in Raffey's eyes. What had he done? What was going on? Why would a hooker do this? He tried to clear his mind, then had an irrational thought. He got up and parted the curtains in the living room window that looked out on the street. There was a blue car he hadn't noticed before. With shaking hands he brought the rifle up to his chin and tried to aim at the car. He flipped the selector switch to burst as he had been trained to do. He tried to catch his breath, tears now rolled down the wood stock of the semi-automatic weapon. As if in a spasm, his finger jerked on the trigger.

Maya asked, "What is that?" The man with the knife turned to look up.

Raffey jumped back, the rifle hitting the floor — he had forgotten the safety. His whole body now shook. Then he thought for a moment. She must have accomplices. Shooting whoever was in the car would surely mean a death sentence to Leena and Kirsi.

"Whatever it was is gone now. How long do we give him?" Hans asked, as he positioned Kirsi's hand in his, extending one of her fingers to be clear of the others.

"He's coming out now," Maya said with a slight tinge of disappointment.

Raffey approached the car, half expecting to be shot as he neared. The rear door opened and he got in.

"Shut the door. Turn your back to me," a voice said, and he complied.

He thought he caught a glimpse of his niece in the back-seat but it was too dark. "Please just don't hurt my nie..."

That was as far as he got as the injection directly into his neck put him under.

∞§∞

A young government man in a three-piece suit watched as the Navy helicopter flared and did a perfect three-point landing dead on the circle at the Brétigny-sur-Orge Airport helipad. Joey emerged quickly and half-jogged toward him and the State Department vehicle.

As he stretched out his hand he said, "Joey Palumbo."

"Yardley Haines, State Department."

Joey got in the back. Yardley went around to the other side and also got in the back. When he closed the door, he tapped the driver's seat and the car took off for the seventeen-mile ride north to Paris.

Yardley handed Joey a red-lined folder. "Ever hear of this Percival Cutney?" he asked as he scanned the papers within.

"No, not that I would. He is a subject of the UK; I have been stationed in Paris for the last nine years."

"That's it. I knew I had heard your name before."

"Yes, I worked with your Quarterback team on the Peter Remo killing a while back."

Joey couldn't remember at that moment what part of the operation code-named Hammer of God had been declassified, so he chose not to inform Yardley that Peter was alive and well. That the murdered man had been a poor schmuck who had stolen Peter's jacket. "Yes. You did good work on that. What happened with Lloyds of London?"

"I'm afraid they are denying all knowledge of Percy."

"He most stringently prefers Percival."

"Yes, of course."

"The douche bag."

Yardley smiled — here was a guy from back home.

"So, where do we go to get a lead on him?"

"We've cross-checked the White House scan of his ID and, using facial recognition, have him entering the UK through Gatwick yesterday, traveling under the name Percival Smyth."

"Traveling to where?"

"Paris, we think."

"Think?"

"We think he's "chunneling" over this morning."

"So that's why I am here."

"You were already airborne when we learned this, and Quarterback had the copter vectored to here. We have men at the train depot and his picture is everywhere as a person of interest in the UK bank scandal."

"Cute—covering your bases with the cross-channel rivalry?"

"There are many die-hard French civil servant soccer fans who hate Manchester United and would pull out all the stops to embarrass the English. We should know more in an hour when the train arrives."

"I'd like to be there."

"That is where we are heading. We should be there thirty minutes before the train."

"Good, then I have time to take a piss without risking my life."

Yardley didn't bother to ask.

∞§∞

Cheryl poked her head into Bill's office and announced, "Agent Burrell on line two."

"Brooke, how is France?"

"Lonely place to be working while others are here for love. But it forces me to focus on how crummy my love life is."

Her TMI response reminded Hiccock of how women respond differently to work and life. A guy would have said, "Like a foreign film where everybody speaks a funny language," or something else 'shrug of the shoulder' neutral, but a woman sees and hears things differently. And that was why he was glad Brooke was on the case.

"Maybe when this is over you can catch some R&R there."

"Been there, done that, got the black French nightie."

Bill just went with it, "Well all-righty then... let's get down to the case. What have you found out?"

"The two break-ins are definitely connected, and while each on its own means nothing, the patterns are obvious. It seems to point to a Nigerian connection."

"Maguambi?"

"Ding-ding-ding, you win the kewpie doll. How'd you find out?"

"Somewhere there's a leak. A Percival Cutney, a.k.a. Percival Smyth, came in here and knew all about you, the Vera Cruz, the crucibles, and the whale thing."

"That's not comforting. Is he foreign intel?"

"We are trying to track him down now. In fact, Joey is in Paris as we speak, on his trail."

"You think this Percy guy is a Maguambi operative?"

"Could be, but he seems more MI-5ish. And you'll piss him off if you call him Percy — he prefers Percival."

"Well isn't that precious. I tell you what, I will meet up with Joey and make my report and maybe we can double team old Percy while I am here."

"Sounds good; be careful."

"Bill, can I ask you something?"

"Yeah, what?"

"When you talk to Joey, do you ever tell him to 'be careful?'"

"Yeah... I think I do, especially when he's out there doing something for me. So, I'll tell you what I always tell him. 'Be careful... and wear a cup if you scrimmage.'"

"Thanks, Quarterback."

∞§∞

Raffey awoke in a cold concrete room, strapped to a bed. He strained to look around. A woman and man entered the room. It took a second and then he realized it was Hanna in black hair. "Hanna, why did you do this to me and my family?"

"Shut up and listen. Blindfold him."

Hans tied a strip of cloth around Raffey's head and made sure his eyes were covered.

Raffey sensed someone else had entered the room. He smelled cigarette smoke and started to think they were going to beat him. His body tensed. Then the new voice talked.

"You are Raffael Juth?"

"Yes. Where are my sister and niece?"

A switch of metal, like an old car-radio antenna, whipped down on his legs and stung him so hard he whimpered.

"You will only answer my questions and not deviate from that or she will hit you again, only next time across your face. Do you understand?"

"Yes."

"Good, now, you work at the LHC?"

"Yes, I work at the Large Hadron Collider. I am attached through CERN."

"You will follow our instructions to the absolute smallest detail or we will make your family suffer and curse your name as they die."

"What can you possibly want with me?"

The whip came down across his face, aggravating his already sore cheek. He screamed.

"You are supposed to be smart, yet you can't follow the simplest instruction not to speak except in response to my questions," the man calmly said.

"Are you ready to obey or should we amputate one of little Kirsi's limbs?" Maya added.

"No, no, don't do that. I will listen; anything you say."

"Good, now maybe we can proceed without interruption." The man coughed as he ground his cigarette into the carpet of the hotel room. "So you are familiar with the high voltage distribution circuitry that powers the magnets in the machine?"

"Yes."

"I want you to program an aberration into the frequency regulator module. At our direction you will pre-program this variant to occur at the time we choose. You will do this and it will work or Leena will watch her baby be dismembered slowly. Do you believe we will do this?'

"Yes."

"Do you plan to carry out our wishes?"

"Yes."

"Then they shall be spared."

There were no more questions, and Raffey sensed that he was alone in the room.

Outside the room in an abandoned warehouse, the man reached into the pocket of his car coat and retrieved a pack of Gitanes, placing one between his lips. It wagged as he spoke. "Has he asked for proof of life?"

"No."

"Surprising," was all that The Engineer said as he lit his cigarette and left without saying another word.

∞§∞

"The conductor on the train is French ex-paratrooper and my former brother-in-law, so I e-mailed him the picture from the ID. He says your man is in the fifth car, first row of seats," Marc Dupré, the rather rotund director of the French Intelligence service said matter-of-factly.

"You have an ex-brother-in-law on the train who was a paratrooper?" Joey Palumbo said.

"Oui. From my first wife, but we still like each other." He turned as the horn of the train announced its entrance into the grand station at Paris.

Joey watched as a few dozen people departed the train. Percy, whatever his name was, was indeed in the fifth car from the engine. Dupré approached him and in a very gallant way extended his arm as if to say follow me, although Joey thought he probably said something like, "s'il vous plaît." And judging from the non-confrontational look on Smyth's face, he had probably called him Percival to boot.

As he approached, Joey could see the recognition on Percy's face as he matched Joey's to the White House.

"Hey, Percy, good to see ya! Let's have a chat, shall we?" Joey said in a grand gesture as he opened the door of his state department car. The only response Percival gave to the slight of excessive familiarity was a tired facial expression. The car had reached the end of the parking lot when two Paris police cars came to a stop in front of the Intelligence Agency's car. Joey was out in a flash. "What is the meaning of this?"

The tall, thin sergeant of the Surté simply said, "You must hand over your prisoner to us."

"First off, he is not a prisoner and second, Director Dupré is my liaison and he is right over there."

"Sergeant, what is this about?" Dupré yelled as he trotted up to the cop car.

"I have a warrant of protection from the court, signed by all three magistrates with their seal affixed below."

Dupré pulled out his reading glasses and scanned the document. "Mr. Palumbo, my friend, I am sorry, but a judicial order is sacrosanct. I must ask you to let Monsieur Smyth go with these officers, please."

"Where will they take him?" Yardley stepped forward.

"That is for the judge to decide, but for now we must comply."

Joey thought about handcuffing himself to the limey bastard and throwing his own key in the nearby sewer. That way, wherever Percy went Joey went, but he figured they'd just produce a hacksaw and it would all be for show. "Yardley, I want the ambassador notified and a formal complaint filed before we get to your office."

"Yes, sir," Yardley said as he dialed the number.

The cops reminded Percy to watch his head. As he was loaded into the backseat, he looked at Joey and said, "Better luck next time, old bean."

"You know, you are really starting to bug me, Percy!"

With that the two cop cars sped into Paris traffic. Joey turned to Dupré, "Okay, now explain this bullshit to me."

"Unlike America, the courts here are the judicial system. They have unequaled power and it is absolute. I am sorry, my friend."

"Not as sorry as the president of the United States is going to be when he hears about this."

∞§∞

Joey was right. The president didn't like it when his hand-picked team, headed by Bill, didn't get what it wanted. He made sure the secretary of state understood how steamed he was. That prompted the phone call Bill made to Joey on the secure scramble link. "I just got off the phone with the secretary of state. He says he'll have the French ambassador in front of him within the hour. But he also said this can go on a while because it is a Metropolitan Paris matter, not national."

"But what about Dupré? He's a fed, or whatever the frogs call their national cops." Joey mouthed the word 'sorry' to the French-born attaché in the US Embassy standing in front of him.

"If he couldn't stop the judge's orders on the streets, I don't think he'll have much luck up the chain, but I'll check. Oh by the way, Brooke is in town, Paris, I mean. She is going to call you."

"Okay, maybe between the two of us we can find this English twerp."

"Hey Joey, that's it."

"What is?"

"If he's English, we can get Downing street involved. That should get attention."

"The more, the merrier. Meanwhile, Klaven seems to come up clean and a real officer and gentleman. He did some wild shit back in the Cold War. This guy tapped the Russian phone line to their missile bases. He used a decommissioned sub like the one they have in New York."

"Sub in New York?"

"Yeah, I was on it ten years ago. The USS Growler — it's right next to the Intrepid. Anyway her sister ship in the Pegasus missile system, the USS *Halibut*, was fitted with a DSRV and they clipped a bug onto an undersea cable."

"Joey, wait! What did you say?"

"DSRV, Deep Submersible Recovery Vehicle?"

"No, the name of the sister sub was what, again?"

"Halibut."

"Son-of-a-bitch. 'Try the Halibut,' he said to me at Mimmo's that night, and I said to myself, 'What a dumb ass, they don't even have that on the menu.'"

"Fish stories aside, as far as I can tell, he is the real deal and you should have a talk with him. I'll have the details encrypted and sent to you from the Embassy."

"I'll set up a meet for tomorrow. How's Paris?"

"Like one of those movies they'd make you watch in Film Appreciation 101."

"Oh, and Joey, I do tell you to be careful from time to time, don't I?"

"Did you watch a chick flick or something last night?"

∞§∞

Bill's car picked him up promptly at 6:45 a.m., as it did every morning, for the thirty-minute drive to the White House. Allowing five minutes to stop at the Starbucks on Wisconsin Avenue for his and his driver's morning jolt always got him to his desk by 7:30. The driver pulled up to the loading zone and left Bill in the car, secure that the White House tag in the windshield would stop any D.C. cop from harassing him. Bill was leafing through the morning rundown when he was startled by an intruder who climbed into the back seat with him.

"You wanted to see me?"

"In my office, Klaven! God, do you always sneak up on people like..."

"Hands up, out of the car now!" Bill's driver said, holding a Glock pointed at Klaven through the rear window.

"Bill, call off your dog."

"Do you promise to stop scaring the crap out of me?"

"Oh, grow up and tell him to stand down before he shoots a patriot."

"It's okay, Warren. I know this man — he's just a little unconventional. In fact, Warren, if you wouldn't mind, get him a Venti... er, black?"

"With two sugars."

"With two sugars, if you would!"

Warren holstered his weapon and announced to the shocked citizens that it was all a misunderstanding and to go about their business.

"Mr. Hiccock, I can't be seen as part of this. I still monitor and try to keep the powers-that-be honest."

"You do what now?"

"Look, from what I gather, you ain't a political pussy. My sources tell me you are someone who acts, and you've seen your share."

"I am a bureaucrat and a science geek."

"Cut the crap, son. There's a quarter trillion dollars-worth of warship deep in the Pacific Trench that begs to differ."

"That's extremely classified, sir, and you are in violation of the Secrets Act just bringing it up."

"Are you going to stop treating me like I am some outsider? What you and Mitchell did was historic, heroic and demonstrated the utmost measure of devotion. That's why I selected you."

"You selected? Okay, I don't know what or how much you know about the USS Princeton but..."

"Don't forget that business up in New York and the first nuclear attack on U.S. soil. The way I hear it, you're not there, and New York is a glowing graveyard for seventy-eight years. Instead we got a concrete containment dome encasing a botched H-bomb."

"Can we get back to, '*you* selected me?'"

"Throw in the HCN complex 33 bio attack thwarted, and that escapade in the lead mine out West; oh, and saving the entire San Joaquin Valley, and I'd say I know what I am talking about and who I am talking to."

"You know, when you put it that way, I should ask for a raise. Who the fuck are you?"

"One of many who took an oath to defend this nation. Being out of the service doesn't reduce that honor and obligation."

"I don't know whether to let you out of this car or turn you in."

"Relax, if you haven't gotten the message yet, I am a big fan. Besides, you got the Bridgestone seal of approval."

That name hit Hiccock like a ton of bricks. Master Sergeant Richard Bridgestone was a one-of-a-kind army of one. Bill had enlisted his special skills and secured unprecedented presidential authority for him to cut and tear his way across America and the globe searching for a suitcase nuke. Bridge had also saved the life of Bill's wife as well as the lives of his mom and dad. In fact, Bill had named his son, Richard Ross

Hiccock, after Richard Bridgestone and his partner, Ross, who had been killed in the Hammer of God affair. "Now I get it. Well, if you are a friend of Bridge, you are beyond reproach — and you are my friend. What can I do for you?"

"It's what I can do for you. That mission you want the Navy to undertake? I designed it in 1965."

"Yeah, the USS *Halibut* and the DSRV. Very impressive! But not as out-of-the-park as raising the entire Soviet *Akula* class sub that went down — and right under the Commies' noses!"

"Now I am the one who is humbled, Mr. Hiccock."

"Please call me Bill."

"My friends call me Clay. So how did you find out about that *Akula*?"

"Let's just say, I know some people as well."

Just then Warren came back, balancing a cardboard tray with the coffees. Bill rolled down the window and handed Clay his and took his own. "Warren, wanna give us five minutes?" He then rolled up the window.

"Anyway, recovering the evidence you want, adjusted for today's dollars, will be a one hundred million dollar operation, tops!"

"So you were right when you said they were soaking me to fund something else, what else?"

"Political campaigns."

"Whoa."

∞§∞

Joey and Brooke had set up shop in a small conference room at the US Embassy in Paris. In most spots on Earth, the US Embassy is the ultra-class way to go. However, having to eat, sleep, and work in the building, with Paris right outside the gate, was like a prison sentence, but they muddled through. Brooke worked out in the compound's gym for ninety minutes every other day. Her training had always stressed peak physical conditioning, and surviving her ordeal in the Indian Ocean was a testament to that commitment. Even the guys from the Embassy's diplomatic security detail weren't as dedicated in their routines.

When it came time to leave the compound, Brooke opted for shopping the Champs Elysées, while Joey wanted to go to the great Cathedral at Notre Dame. "Aren't you part French?" Joey prodded Brooke.

"Yes, on my father's side. Mom is Irish."

"So were you brought up Catholic?"

"Yes, but I haven't been to church in years."

"Wanna join me?"

"I really had my heart set on seeing the shops and all the fashions I can't afford to buy."

"Well, good hunting."

"Have fun...genuflecting."

∞§∞

As the cab pulled up to the huge edifice of the Cathedral, Joey's thoughts returned to the first time he had walked into the Immaculate Conception Church. To the nine-year-old Joey, it was the biggest church in the world. Now here in the great Cathedral, those feelings returned. He was spellbound by the Church at a young age. It was something about the ritual, the reverence and the comfort he saw in the faces of the people attending Mass, that made him want to get more involved. As soon as he could, he became an altar boy. It made his mother deliriously happy; his dad wasn't quite so enchanted. For five years, Joey had helped with the celebration of Mass, then weddings and funerals. At first, the funerals were hard to take, but as he saw how the families needed to cry, grieve, and celebrate the lives of those they had lost, he began to appreciate the role he and faith played in helping people get through life. He would later in life define it as 'divine serenity.'

When one of the brothers of the Church asked Joey if he thought of becoming a priest, even at fifteen he knew it wasn't a good fit for him. He liked the result but wasn't into the process. He liked the helping part, but the study, the theology, was boring to him. What loomed as his largest objection, however, was the uncertainty as to where he might be sent. It could be to St. Pat's on Fifth Avenue or to a small tent in Zimbabwe; you just didn't know.

A broad grin appeared across his face at the thought that if the Sisters of Immaculate Conception school in the Bronx could see him now, entering Notre Dame, "Our Lady of Paris," they would drop to their knees because it would surely be a sign of the end of days.

He dabbed his finger in the font of holy water and crossed himself. Even though he had never been in here before, he felt at home. At that moment it hit him — that's why the ritual, the icons, the Stations of the Cross, the altars, and every other element were the same here as in any Bronx church. Although more splendid and more ornate, still they were familiar. It meant that anywhere in the world a practicing Catholic went, he or she could always find home, or at least something that felt safe and familiar. When Latin was more prevalent, Joe imagined that it must have been easy to be able to communicate at some level with a parish priest in Latin, even if he was Chinese and you were in China and couldn't speak a word of Mandarin to him or anyone else.

His footsteps echoed off the marble and stone that had made the reading of the scriptures reverberate in the time before microphones. He found a pew about halfway to the altar and bent down on one knee, crossed himself, and sat. Looking up and all around the nave, he took a deep breath. He remembered preparing the incense for mass — the combination of myrrh and other ingredients creating the distinctive smell that meant you were in God's house. He put his hands together and said a few prayers, along the way praying for his son, his wife, his parents, his sister, and then for his country, and asked for guidance in the work he and Bill did.

He crossed himself and decided to move closer to the altar to get a better look. A young priest was setting up for a service. He nodded to Joey, who responded with a nod and the word, "Father," to the man, who was probably five years younger than he.

"American?" the priest asked.

"Yes."

"Me too. I'm from Philadelphia."

"New York."

"Frank Mercada."

"Joey Palumbo. Nice to meet you."

"First time here?"

"Yes, first time."

Father Mercada looked up to the eight-hundred-year-old architecture. "Magnificent isn't it."

"Gloria in excelsis Deo."

"Theologian?"

"Nah, I was an altar boy as a kid."

"Me too. I just kind of stayed with it. Now..." He looked up again to the ceiling of the apse.

"So how did you go from Philly to here?" Joey said.

"You never know where they are going to send you."

Joey smiled.

"So you used to prep for mass?"

"Five years."

"Want to see the rest of the church?"

"I don't want to take you away from what you are doing," Joey said, in a way that kind of meant "sure" which surprised even him.

"I've got two hours; besides, I was a little bored anyway."

They spent the next half hour walking through the cathedral and then under it, as Mercada showed him the catacombs and ruins of the ancient Roman baths on which the cathedral was built. At one point they crossed into an area that had an old door with huge wrought iron hasps and hinges from the Middle Ages. It was definitely locked.

Of course Joey asked, "Those two big wrought iron rings on the door look like a ring of thorns. Is that where they keep the crown?"

"The Crown of Thorns? No, that's upstairs; I'll show you later."

"Then what's in there?"

"I don't know. I have never been in there."

That earned Father Mercada a quizzical look from Joey.

He responded by way of explanation, "When I first got here there was a deacon, who has since left, and he referred to it once as the Knight's Chamber."

"As in night and day or the Sir Galahad variety?"

"Definitely the k-night."

"See, that is exactly why I couldn't do this; become a priest. I made the right choice, all right," Joey said stretching his palm, face up and gesturing toward the ancient portal.

"What do you mean?"

"I couldn't sleep a wink or eat until I got on the other side of that door. It would be killing me. You, you my friend, have the acceptance and great forbearance that I lacked."

"And I, my friend, also don't have the key; thus the forbearance comes easy. So what did you do instead?"

"I became a cop and then an FBI agent, and now I work at the White House."

"Well, I'd also say you definitely made the right choice."

∞§∞

"Dean Robert McNally on two," Cheryl announced as Bill was finishing up an opinion paper on 'Privatization of Aerospace Initiatives.'

"Thank you for returning my call, Dean McNally. I was surprised to learn that you have no record of a Percival Cutney or Smyth as having attended Notre Dame."

"Mr. Hiccock, I even e-mailed the picture you sent to retired and relocated teachers and professors and almost no one seems to remember him."

"Forgive me, Dean, but as a scientific discipline, 'almost' is statistically not 100 percent."

"Well, there was one professor, Professor Cecil Hughes who misidentified him as Parnell Sicard. And although there is similar likeness from our year book photo, it is impossible that it could be him."

"Why is that, Dean?"

"Because Parnell died in the Mideast back in 1983."

"Can you send me that photo? Oh, and Dean, what did Hughes teach?"

"Theology."

"Thanks, Dean McNally, you've been very helpful."

VIII. ANCESTRAL KAI

Looking out from the bridge of the Shobi Maru, her captain, Kasogi Toshihira, worried about the front moving in across the part of the Pacific he was traversing with sixty-five hundred new Toyota Tundras and Tacomas in the hold of his vast floating parking lot. The wide expanse of calm, for the moment, blue ocean spread out before him like a soft carpet. The bottom of his vista was dotted with the early morning ritual run of the three Imperial Marines of the Japanese Defense Force keeping their regimen and their physical prowess in peak condition. Since the re-emergence of pirates, the Japanese government posted the JDF Marines on cargo ships that were the main artery of the economic lifeblood for the island nation.

As he watched the soldiers effortlessly perform synchronized push-ups, he thought how surprising it was that attacks on car carriers were as rare as they were, especially a ship configured like his — RORO, or Roll On Roll Off. It was a ship type that required no loading and unloading equipment or any special port. All that was needed, other than the metal ramps that were part of the ship's equipment, were drivers.

An entire boat could be unloaded in a matter of hours. The Marine detachment was on his ship because the remnants of SEATO, the South East Asian Treaty Organization, the counterpart of NATO, had determined that this particular cargo of pick-up trucks had a paramilitary value, it being the platform of choice for insurgents and rebels. These amateurs cobbled Russian and Chinese missile launchers and anti-aircraft guns to the truck beds. The world's TV news reports were peppered with these hastily assembled weapon systems, which prominently displayed the large red Toyota logo across their tailgates.

Kasogi's grandfather had sailed these waters for the Imperial Navy during the war against American and English imperialists. He was the commander of the great battleship *Musashi*, a Yamamoto-class battlewagon that was the sister ship to the glorious Yamamoto. It was a somewhat more esthetic improvement in terms of her sleeker lines and more proportioned profile, which made her name *Musashi*, meaning elegant or splendid, a fitting touch. Now, because his grandfather and the Empire had lost that war, the Navy was reduced to a coastal defense role, and Kasogi was shuttling cars to America instead of following in the path that surely would have led to command of an aircraft carrier or fleet, if Japan had been allowed to have offensive weapons.

"Captain, contact five thousand yards astern."

Kasogi quickly snapped out of his retrospective frame of mind. "Commercial traffic?"

"Small signature, wait, three targets closing at thirty knots," the radar operator twenty feet to right in the wheelhouse reported. Before the natural acoustic echo of the seaman's voice faded off in the cavernous bridge, Kasogi hit the recently installed large red button, which sounded a klaxon. The Marines immediately broke their pace and scrambled at a flat-out run to their weapons lockers. The muted sound of all watertight doors being closed and sealed followed. The radio shack started transmitting an advisory back to the shipping company that a potential attack was under way.

From over the mast atop the bridge, the best weapon Kasogi had was buffeted by the air as the American-made Cobra attack helicopter roared into a big loop and tilted its main rotor in a beeline to the three blips now forty-five hundred yards in his wake. This additional weapon was a part of the aviation branch of the Japan Air Self-Defense Forces. Even though he was merchant marine, he was at least in ceremonial command of the kai (sea) and kuu (air) troops. Kasogi took a position on the starboard thruster control station right off the bridge, where he could see the stern of his ship. The Marines had taken up positions aft, training their Squad Automatic Weapons and one portable Gatling gun at a target they couldn't yet see. Only four times before, twice without the Marines and armaments, had his ship prepared for an attack. Luckily, each time it had been a false alarm. Even so, on one of those very days, a Greek freighter, not ten miles from his ship, had been taken and her cargo and crew held for nearly a year until a ransom was negotiated and paid.

Kasogi thought of his son's tenth birthday, now six weeks away. He was planning to be at the celebration, not held in a makeshift prison in some God-awful desert prison camp. He found himself urging the copter to get there already and report. A few seconds later, the radio crackled, "Fishing boats, changing course to the west. Repeat — fishing boats, changing course to the west."

Kasogi took his first deep breath since the initial report of the targets seven minutes ago. It was like a shot of whiskey finding its way to every nerve ending in his body. His shoulders resumed the erect posture of an officer befitting his rank and his next breaths were deeper and sweeter than any he could remember that week.

∞§∞

On the way back to the hulking car carrier's improvised helipad, Lieutenant Pilot Koji Takahashi smiled as from his noisy perch two hundred feet above the calm Pacific Ocean he saw the dark grey outline of a huge whale underwater, right behind the Shobi Maru, probably feasting on plankton stirred up by the huge props of the forty-two hundred metric ton displaced hole in the ocean. He snapped a picture with his iPhone and then keyed his mic to inform the captain of the good luck omen that was playing and feasting off the tail of his ship.

IX. THESE BOOTS ARE MADE FOR TALKING

Nine hundred euro is only one thousand three hundred fifty dollars, and they were the best Louboutin boots she had ever seen. She'd cut down on the Starbucks and skip a few dinners out, and in four months or so, she wouldn't even feel the pinch in her pocketbook — the new one — the French one, the four-hundred-euro one, that anybody who had seen both would agree, went perfectly with the coveted red-soled, knee-high snake-skin-print boots that were actually her size! The normally twenty-five hundred-dollar boots were a deal and a steal. *Maybe seven months*, Brooke thought as she turned the corner toward her hotel. Her phone rang.

"Brooke, its Bill; are you near a computer?"

"Two minutes away from the embassy."

"Get on SCIAD and call me once you are on."

"Bill, what's up?"

"Not over the phone."

When Brooke got to the conference room, Joey was already there. The TV was on and CNN international was showing file footage of a big cargo ship. Superimposed on the screen was a still of a reporter relaying information over a phone to the CNN anchor. The lower third title on the screen read, "Toyota ship attacked."

Bill was on the speakerphone as Brooke used her portable retinal scan device to log on to Bill's private super-encrypted SCIAD network.

"Okay, I'm on."

"Good, Brooke. Joey, I think this has a connection to what happened to Brooke in the Indian Ocean and what you are tracking down now."

"Bill, the news is saying the pirates somehow got a bomb aboard the ship." Joey said.

"I just sent you a video that the State Department, at my request, has asked the Japanese Defense Forces to hold tight."

Brooke hit the video icon and a QuickTime movie popped on the screen. It was a voice print pattern that wiggled and modulated as the sound of a voice in Japanese was dialed down low in the background. A zipper of English words traveled past as an interpreter voiced them in synchronization. The voice being heard was identified in a graphic as: JDF PILOT. "Captain Toshihira, you have luck on your aft quarter. There is a magnificent whale surfing in your wake."

The graphic identifying the speaker changed from JDF PILOT to: SHIP CAPTAIN, "May he stay clear of those commercial fishermen."

The video ended. Brooke looked back at the TV. "So the media doesn't have this?"

"No, and we are going to keep it that way," Bill said.

"You're thinking this is Brooke's whale?"

"You guys tell me."

"So the pirates didn't get a bomb on the boat, the whale attached it to the boat? Is that your thinking?" Brooke asked as she watched the endless replay of stock footage of the giant car-carrying ship on CNN.

"Unless you believe in coincidence. I am informed there was a small detachment of JDF marines in addition to the helo stationed on that ship."

"Is that standard procedure now for cargo ships, Bill?" Joey asked as he jotted down something.

"Only this one — it was carrying Toyota pickups."

"Oh." Joey nodded.

"Wanna clue me in?" Brooke prompted with her hand.

"Those trucks are the ones the ragtag guys in battles all around the world use for 'shoot and scoot' attacks. Somebody could make a lot of money selling them to outlaw forces."

"So that's why they didn't sink the ship." Brooke re-ran the voice print video.

"The captain was radioed and told that the bombs were placed above and below the waterline and if he didn't surrender they would remotely blow the submerged bombs." Bill said.

"Bill, what happened to the chopper?" Joey said.

"He landed before they knew of the bombs. Once he learned they were going to surrender, he literally had the thing pushed off the deck and into the ocean. Smart move, too."

"Scratch one heavy weapons platform for the pirates to use in their next attack."

"The captain and crew and the JDF guys gave up three days ago, the ship was reported missing two days ago, and then presumed lost yesterday. Today the pirates called with the ransom demands for the ship and crew, but not the cargo," Bill said over the speakerphone.

"Sure, the trucks are already halfway to the killing zones."

"So they steamed to a port within three days of their last known location?" Brooke said.

Bill posted a map on the SCIAD screen that had the range/search overlay, "JDF and the seventh fleet tactical air units are doing the fan-outs now."

Brooke paused the playback, "The captain mentioned fishing boats?"

"As far as Naval intelligence has it, they were just that." Bill said.

"So command control and communications were all centered in the whale?" Joey said.

"Unless the pirates have a satellite."

When the conversation ended, Joey noticed the box on the end of the table. "Mind?"

"No, go ahead; tell me what you think."

"Nice boots; you get 'em on sale?"

"Yeah."

"How you gonna chase down bad guys in five-inch heels?

"These babies aren't for chasing bad guys, they're for catching bad boys."

∞§∞

The crew of the Shobi Maru had been herded off the ship, blindfolded and roped together, and driven in the beds of trucks for four hours over rough roads. The last hour or so was off-road but on soft terrain. On the first morning, Kasogi scanned the terrain surrounding the camp and mentally classified it as scrub desert. That was a good sign, because any vegetation meant some water somewhere, if they were to escape. The three JDF marines and the helicopter pilot had been separated from him and his crew sometime in the night. They were warriors, which meant they might have been summarily executed or were being held elsewhere.

Kasogi Toshihira was mindful that he was still in command of his crew, albeit they were all now the prisoners of the pirates. To that end, he woke everyone at an early hour, stressed exercise, and encouraged story and tale telling to pass the hours. Ostensibly this was to keep up the morale of men who, without having signed up for it, were suddenly prisoners of war. But he also knew that if an opportunity presented itself to escape, his authority would be crucial in moving everyone in the direction of freedom, and their physical strength would be sorely tested if they made it beyond the fence line into the bush.

Therefore, he was trying to negotiate with the seeming leader of these pirates, a skinny twenty-two-year-old kid who never separated from his AK-47, even when he prayed five times a day. The bone of contention was the quality of the food, which was disgusting and laced with various insects.

Although the pirates didn't eat much better, he staged the mild protest for his crew's benefit. He had to keep them hopeful, disciplined and regarding him as still in command.

After much hand gesturing and trying to translate Japanese to Sudanese with some English and French thrown in, the kid was nodding, but Kasogi didn't know what that meant. Two hours later, the slop they called a meal was delivered. However, a separate plate was handed to him. To his surprise, there was a higher quality of a food-like substance on his plate than on the tin plates of the others. *So the kid thought I was lobbying for myself,* Kasogi thought as he looked down at this relative feast and saw a way to keep the unity of the group even tighter.

He rose and went over to a group of oilers and engine mechanics. One of them, Oshi, had kept doing jumping jacks after he had called rest. He took the obscene plate from Oshi's hands and replaced it with his. "You have shown great respect for me and our men. You deserve this today."

The men quickly got the notion.

As he walked away, he felt that the pirate kid had handed him the key to ensuring that all his men would survive this ordeal. He looked up at the night sky and from the three dots of stars that make up Orion's Belt he "dead reckoned" he was in mid- to southern Africa.

∞§∞

"As-salaam-alaikum," the nomadic tribesman said to the official, who was inspecting his documents as if he had never seen papers before. He watched the twitching of the official's nose as the man stepped away from the vehicle, putting more distance between himself and the huge stinking pile of dung in the bed of the rusted truck. Meanwhile, the driver, a shabby denizen of the desert, whose olfactory senses had been already bludgeoned by the reeking pile in his truck, looked up. Here, at an outpost in the middle of nowhere, the night sky was un-obliterated by man-made light, allowing him to imagine the shepherds of legend who created astronomy by connecting those dots in the sky into pictures of archers, crabs, lions, and water carriers. He mentally tried to connect those pinholes in the deep black blanket into what a modern day shepherd such as himself might imagine; a coffee cup, an iPad, and a Prius, if you left off the right wheel. He mused about these things because, as he had found in the past, getting your mind off your actual mission during intense moments like this was the best way to not unconsciously tip off your enemy, who might not even know he was your enemy.

"Where are you headed?" the uniformed man asked.

The nomad's hand cleared the way to the belt-slung knife under his overcoat as he answered in the dialect of the Bedouin, "Wherever the next flock is in need of shepherding or shearing. I work for ranchers and those who live off the animals. I follow the animals."

"Well, you have a problem."

His right hand was an inch from the handle of the knife. "What could that be?" He shifted his weight to give him more leverage with which to slash the throat and stab the heart of this checkpoint jackal.

"There are no goats within a hundred miles of this place."

"That is Allah's will, praise unto him."

The sweaty cop looked into the Bedouin's eyes. The silence lasted past the point of comfort.

"You may go."

"His blessings upon you." With that, the herder got back into his dilapidated Daihatsu Grand Max pickup and rumbled off in a cloud of dust and sand.

At a distance of three miles beyond the checkpoint, the pickup made a hard left and rumbled on the uneven desert surface. Twenty minutes later, with the lights off, the herder left the vehicle and walked to the top of a rise. Peering over the top, he produced a night vision scope. He panned the valley down below until he spied the outline of a makeshift camp. He noted a few guards and something a little odd. About twenty men were out in the night air, exercising! They couldn't be other guards or soldiers — in that they were shabbily dressed and somewhat emaciated, they must be the crew. Sgt. Bridgestone calculated that the chances of his plan succeeding had just increased 200 percent.

X. STRANGERS ON A TRAM

Raffael was doing his best to handle his nerves each day knowing that his sister and her daughter were in the hands of these evil people. He knew he was being watched around the clock and he heeded the warning not to contact any authority. However, the pressure was taking its toll. He understood that what the kidnappers wanted him to do would destroy the super hadron collider, a multi-billion dollar project that was the pride of the European Union and the premiere example of international cooperation in big science. Yet, how could any price be put on the lives of his innocent niece and sister?

Upon returning home to his empty house in the evening, his hand shook as he fumbled to get the key into the lock. With his overcoat still on, he poured wine into a glass. Every night now he drank to calm his nerves. He had shunned all his friends, shutdown and erased all trace of his Facebook and Twitter accounts, and avoided any contact with anybody, as instructed. Whenever the kidnappers were going to have him do their bidding, he hoped it was soon; he couldn't take this much longer. The cell phone they had given him rang.

"You took the tram today," Maya's flat voice stated.

"Yes, I hadn't slept at all last night; I didn't want to drive and have an accident."

"There was a man in a brown coat; was he a policeman?"

"Who? What — a policeman? What man?"

"Do we have to send you Kirsi's right eye to help you remember?"

"No, no, I tell you! I spoke to no one!" His mind raced, *who is she talking about?* He replayed the tram ride. Then he remembered the man who stood next to him for a time; he had a Bluetooth earpiece and was chatting to someone. "Wait, there was a man next to me talking on his phone, but not to me; it was a small earpiece; you couldn't see it? I didn't speak to him at all."

There was a long pause. The sweat beaded on Raffey's forehead. These animals on the phone acted swiftly and with no mercy. *How could I have been so stupid to take a public tram?* "Please believe me, I didn't speak to anyone; I wouldn't; he wasn't talking to me! I wouldn't do anything to hurt them." More silence. Then the line went dead. "No! No! I didn't do anything wrong. Don't hurt them — please," Raffey cried out as he strangled the phone in his right hand. He crumpled to the floor and whimpered, imagining the horror he had just brought down on little Kirsi.

Then the cell phone rang again. He fumbled with it to open it. "Please, please..."

"We will allow this one breach. But now the punishment doubles — if you disobey us, both eyes." She hung up.

Raffey screamed and began to shake uncontrollably.

∞§∞

Being former FBI has its cachet, and still being an active FBI agent had perks, so Brooke, the current, and Joey, the former, stood before Paul Dumond, the chief of Station Interpol, Paris. His office looked as though it had been painted a semi-gloss putty color twenty years ago. It gave the place the same dismal funk as a South Bronx precinct house.

"We think we have found your mystery man. His name is Parnell Sicard, a.k.a. Percival Smyth, Percival Cutney and Percival Wallace. He is dead, 1983 Beirut. He was a Jesuit missionary trying to help the Christian sect in Lebanon when he died in the Hobart Towers blast."

"Well, now we got a problem because, as I said, "Percy" was very much alive when the Surté snatched him right out from under me at the train station," Joey said.

"Ah yes, that 'incident' officially never happened."

"Wanna run that by me again?" Joey leaned onto his desk, his palms nearly missing an old spike onto which an inch of phone message slips were shish-kebabbed.

"I mean, there is no record, no radio calls and no judge's decree on file."

"Wait a minute; the director of French intelligence was there with Mr. Palumbo. Surely he has corroborated his story," Brooke said.

"We have spoken with Director Dupré. He maintains the documents were authentic and he had no choice but to comply. Since there was no outstanding warrant to the contrary, he could not detain Sicard, especially with the clarity of the judge's orders."

"Can you at least tell me which judge signed the order?"

Even for a French guy, the look on his face said, 'Oops, I didn't think of that' as he reached for the phone and told his secretary to contact Dupré.

Seven minutes had passed. Joey was looking out a nicotine-tinged windowpane at the comings and goings of the Parisians on the street. He realized that few were actually coming or going, as most were sitting at sidewalk tables, on benches or steps. Everyone was smoking and drinking coffee. *This whole friggin' country is one big Starbucks.*

The phone rang; it was Dupré. Dumond put him on the speakerphone. "I believe it was Magistrate Vaval."

"This is Joey Palumbo; what was the cause of the order?"

"The order read 'person of interest' in a Grand Inquiry."

"Agent Brooke Burrell, FBI here. May I ask, inquiry into what?" She looked down at the phone as she talked.

"Ah, bonjour mademoiselle, that only the judge can say."

"It's like your Grand Jury, only a lot more secretive. Our liable laws and privacy statutes demand that all inquiries into possible wrongdoing be held in the closest confidence until, and only if, there is an indictment," Dumond said, shaking his head in apology.

"That explains why there is no record of a file." Brooke said.

"I work directly for the president of the United States. Do you think the judge will tell me?" Joey said.

Both Dupré on the phone and Dumond in the office said simultaneously, "You can try!"

It took all of two hours, but the American ambassador to France, the French charge d'affair, a handful of French diplomats and Joey were huddled in the judge's outer chamber. His clerk emerged and announced that the judge would see only the ambassador. Joey thought better of protesting as the ambassador was well briefed and a good negotiator.

Ten minutes ticked by as Joey sat in the judge's anteroom, which smelled of steam heat and plaster. His eyes kept falling on the visages of past magistrates, frozen on canvas in the somber hues of cracked oils, each one looking fouler than the last. It was as if their game face was scorn — a way of letting the Jean Q. Publis know his place in their legal system.

The ambassador exited and nodded for Joey to follow. As was good practice in foreign government buildings, they both walked in silence.

It wasn't until they were in the ambassador's limousine that the man spoke. "Well, that cost me."

"He charged you for the information?" Joey asked.

"In not so many words. He knows my brother is the dean of admissions at Harvard and, well, the judge has a niece — "

"Oh, dear God."

"So he asked me to call my brother right from his office."

"Okay, can we get to Cutney, eh, Smyth, damn it, Sicard? Who is he and why did the judge pull him from me?"

"He would not say."

"Whoa, I thought you were good at this? You got the girl into Harvard and walked away with Stu?"

"I'm sorry, Stu?"

"Stu Gatz!"

The Ambassador wasn't familiar with the slang Italian term meaning 'nothing,' whose actual translation was "testicles." When the old men at the barbershop would say a deal didn't work or fell through, or they didn't win the amorous attention of a lady, they would ceremoniously grab their crotch and say, "Stugatz." It was sometimes shortened to I got or didn't get 'Stu.' Although not in the lexicon of the diplomat, he got the gist of it by its usage. "Now, I did get some information. It seems Sicard was called in for questioning about a long-abandoned case."

"So in other words, the judge just dug up some reason to get him away from me?"

"This is the case file." His aide handed him his portfolio. "This is what I got for the phone call."

Joey perused the files. They were in French, but he was enough of a cop to recognize the universal appearance of a police death investigation report. Joey handed the pages to the ambassador's aide, "Here, I cut French in high school."

The aide scanned it quickly and translated. "On or about August 20, 1997, Franciscan Friar Wilhelm Gregory, known local transient address 324 of the Sofitel on 14 rue Beaujon was found deceased in a stairwell at said address. The coroner ruled the cause of death was asphyxiation arising out of a blunt force trauma to the larynx. Probably as a result of a fall down the hotel's concrete exit stairway. The body found slumped face down with the head hanging over the metal railing of the landing. No suspicious forensic evidence was found."

"Is there an investigating officer's signature?"

The aide flipped through the pages, "Yes, here it is; Sergeant Dupré, fourth prefecture, Paris."

"Wasn't there a Director Dupré somewhere in all this?" The ambassador recalled.

"Yes, he was my liaison when Sicard gave me the slip."

"Do you think it's the same Dupré?"

"If he is, I am going to be really pissed."

XI. THE GOLDEN GOAT

Brooke had traced a branch of her family tree to the small mountain town of Èze, in Monaco, on the French Riviera. She had also traced the path of the electrolytic fluid to a shipping company in Nice, a few kilometers down along the coast. On the way back from her investigation of the manifests of three ships, one of which she had come to suspect handled the P784 fluid that propelled the "whale," she would divert to the mountain-top hamlet and look up a cousin she had met only once in America.

The Marnee Line was a small company that operated only three ships, older freighters that regularly traversed the Mediterranean. The vessels carried mostly specialty cargoes, things like Italian leather goods to Libya or Egyptian cloth to Naples or French tires to Tunisia. This was cargo that didn't travel by or wasn't containerized freight. The company was definitely a dying remnant of the merchant mariner past. Still, this method of shipping offered direct, three-days or fewer, point-to-point delivery without losing time in the big containerized hubs. In addition, the line offered some degree of anonymity because there weren't enough EU customs agents to cover the hundreds of thousands of containers, much less three small ships. Then there was the fact that one of the ships, which they barely used now, was a tanker/freighter. It had a cargo hold and a tank hold. It was rumored once to have brought Burgundy wine to the then-dictator of Libya, and returned with thirty thousand gallons of diesel oil in return. Although the market price of the wine per gallon was greater than the fuel, it was during the worldwide shortage in the late 70s, which, to the shipping company, made that 'vintage' of fuel worth its weight in champagne!

Brooke's fairly decent Americanized French served her well enough that she was getting along nicely with the woman who was part bookkeeper and part cargo facilitator. Brooke was keenly interested in a shipment of "automotive fluid" that went to Saint-Eugene, Algeria. "There is a Saint-Eugene in a Muslim country?"

"Before it was Muslim."

"Right, I see. Where did the cargo come from?"

The woman opened up three filing cabinets and scoured through densely packed manila folders, their tabs bent and folded. Soon she selected one and fought to liberate the folder from the vice-like grip of too many in one drawer. "Here we go," the woman said with exertion, then she flipped open the file and quickly scanned it. "The origin point of the load was Marseilles."

That was a relief for Brooke, because in Marseilles they had heard of computers. And the bookkeeper actually had a shipping order number, which the boat crew used to identify the cargo they were to load. She thanked the woman and then planted one more question as innocently as she could. "Wasn't the wine spoiled by the remnants of oil in the tanker?"

The woman laughed, "No, no, my dear, the wine was in the dry hold in casks but the oil came back in the tanks."

"Oh, I thought maybe that was the reason for the insurance claim your company filed."

"Pardon?" Suddenly there was concern on her face.

"Or was it pirates? Oh, yes, that was it. Your boat was attacked by pirates and you settled a claim for damages at sea."

As she watched for her reaction, Brooke could see the wheels turning in the woman's head. Brooke knew the chain-smoking, emaciated gal (Monday through) Friday was covering for her boss, who had probably made the whole story up and cashed in on the 1.2 million of insurance money for the P784 liquid that Joey had discovered found its way to the terrorists.

"I know nothing of this. It may have been before my time here," she said as she snuffed out her third cigarette since Brooke arrived.

Brooke let her off the hook because, after all, she wasn't there as an insurance investigator. "Perhaps I am mistaken." Thank you, you have been most generous with your time. Adieu."

As Brooke left the offices on the seamier edge of the otherwise beautiful Nice waterfront, she took a deep breath to clear her lungs from the smoky little office. She saw the last light of day in the deepening red sky and looked forward to dinner with her cousin, Mathilde, in Èze.

∞§∞

The French Rivera is legendary as the playground of the rich and famous. Its combination of sun, sea, air and bio-rhythmic waves ease the compression on the human nervous system. It makes everyone, from a rich Arab sheik to a plumber, breathe easy and see the world as a beautiful place. This night, the air had a warm softness, with the aroma of baker's ovens and chef's stoves preparing dinner for the restaurants of the Château de La Chèvre d'Or.

The entire hotel was nestled high atop the highest peak in Èze Village, and the delightful odors wafted up to Brooke's still-higher room. As she sipped crisp white wine on her terrace, she could see airplanes landing at the airport in Nice on her right, and the lights from the multi-million-dollar yachts steaming into Monte Carlo to her left. Her cousin, Mathilde, who was the manager at the hotel, had saved her the best room and sent along an incredible bottle of '09 Le Montrachet white burgundy. The little cheese and baguette plate was heavenly, and as she pinched off and popped a perfect grape into her mouth, she thought of the last time she had seen Mathilde. It was Easter and they were both twelve. Brooke's Uncle Danny brought Mathilde and his family to America on vacation. In that week, Brooke and Mathilde became the best of friends. When it came time for her to go back to France they promised to be pen pals for life. Soon, Brooke began plastering her room with the aero stamped red-and-blue-striped airmail envelopes from each letter she received. They communicated by mail for years, well into their late teens. Then, as they were both distracted by life, letters became less frequent and eventually trickled down to none.

They hadn't seen one another in almost twenty-five years. Recently, like millions of other people on Earth, they discovered Facebook and now they were "friends." In a few minutes, a quarter-century of separation would end, as Mathilde was coming to her room for a glass of wine before a dinner being prepared especially for them by the hotel's executive chef.

"Alo, Brooke?" came from inside the room, and Brooke sprang from her chaise on the terrace. The two cousins squealed and hugged as they had when they were twelve.

"I can see now what you meant when you said that you work "close to God," Brooke said as they walked out on the terrace under the deep purple and orange hues of the Mediterranean's last breath of sunset.

"Sometimes this whole hotel is inside a cloud."

"You look great," Brooke said. She did; Mathilde was perpetually thin but curvy. She had always looked good in the pictures they sent each other as kids. Now her hair was relaxed, long and wavy. Her green eyes had always been surprising in how they lit up.

Mathilde did a little prance as she flared out her skirt. "You like? There is a designer who always comes to the hotel. She gave me four of her samples. This is my favorite."

"Like it was made for you!"

"I think maybe so, because she is a little, you know, into the *femmes*, and she is always giving me big tips. I think maybe she made it for me."

"Whatever works," Brooke said, shaking her head as she poured her alter ego a glass from the four-hundred-dollar bottle. "A toast! To cousins who are like sisters."

"To my sister who happens to be my cousin!" Mathilde said.

To Brooke, who grew up with four brothers, that notion tickled her heart; she realized she did have a sister.

They sat on the two chaises and spent the next half-hour catching up on family — who had gotten married, had babies, and who had died. When Brooke told her that Harley had been killed in action, Mathilde crossed herself and uttered a little prayer in French for the cousin she only remembered as a boy. Brooke was glad she had held that bit of news off Facebook and until she was face to face with her cousin. They sat for a long minute, then Mathilde took a deep breath, smiled and scanned the horizon that encircled her world. "You like the room? I am sorry I was in town when you checked in, but you were early!"

"No problem; I'm here and that's all that counts." Brooke looked over the edge of the patio down at the sea. "I can't believe there is a spot like this, this high up, with such a breathtaking view. I felt so sorry for the bellman, carrying my stuff up the little path. It must be a half-mile from the front desk, uphill."

"That is why they are all young and very well built. I make sure of that."

The girls laughed again as the women regressed to a giddier time.

"What is the name of the one who brought me up here, red hair, blue eyes, wide shoulders?"

"Ah, Benji. He is from the farms to the north. Sweet and dumb. Just the way I like them."

"Mathilde, in America that could be considered sexual harassment by a superior."

"Brooke, if I have sex with them, it is superior."

"You don't really — do you?"

"We are way up on a mountain. Sometimes it gets quiet and sometimes the only thing to do is sip wine and let nature take its course."

"Yes, but how do you face them the next day? How do you go back to telling them what to do?"

"What go back? I am telling them exactly what to do the night before — sweet and dumb."

"Whatever works." Brooke toasted again.

By the time the Mediterranean was snuggly wrapped in a deep blue blanket of stars and a blue-white moon, they had killed off the whole bottle of expensive wine and decided to head down to the restaurant. The chef, who Brooke compared to Gérard Depardieu, *didn't they all look like him?*, came out and greeted them. He actually did the French thing and kissed Brooke's hand. Well, the true French way, more like he blew a kiss onto her hand. He then spun a wonderful tale of what he had prepared, why, and where his ingredients had come from, making special notice of the fact that he went to an out-of-the-way market that morning for the morel mushrooms that were a leading ingredient of his creation for them that evening. He had a twinkle in his eye and a boyish smile that said to Brooke, *"Don't worry about your food; cooking is the way I make love to women, and I do it every day."*

As he returned to the kitchen, Brooke lifted her Cosmo and proposed another toast. "To you, who really knows how to make a girl feel welcome."

Mathilde took a long sip. "I am so excited to see you. What has it been, twenty-four years? And as soon as I see you, it is like we live on the same street for all these years. You know, I got this job because of you."

"Me? How did I manage that?"

"Your letters helped keep my English good. I followed what was going on in America because I knew you and you were there. This hotel caters to many Americans. I always am telling my guests from New York, I have a cousin there, she is a big cop."

"That must make them nervous."

"No, I tell them, you are with bureau of federal investigation."

"Actually, not so much anymore. Now, I work more at the White House."

"The White House, like Clinton?"

"Well, that was a few years back, but yes, that's the place."

"He was so sexy. I went to see him speak in Paris once. He make the room all...all...swoon."

"He was never my type, but I understand the attraction."

"There were thousands of French girls who would have cued up to be his Lupinsky."

"Lewinsky, but I get your point."

"So, what is it that you do for, who is it? Michelle?"

"It's Mitchell."

"Yes, I am sorry, but no Clinton that one."

"No, no he's more the father figure. Not a sex symbol."

"Too bad, it would make your job more intriguing," Mathilde said as she snapped a breadstick in half and chomped down on one end.

"Mathilde, you make me feel like I have never had sex before in my life."

"If you are not having sex four, five times a week, then you aren't having sex."

"Come on, don't give me that; you really do it almost every day?"

"Look around; you are in France, and the most playful part. One of the chambermaids, she is huge and she has pimples on her face. A man has to search to find her pussy and yet she is making love more than me."

"You are terrible — "

"It is true; everyone here is always making the love."

"Well, it might be sex but I wouldn't necessarily call it making love."

"Ah, you speak like it has grown back and you are once again a virgin."

"Might as well. I am so busy all the time."

"But look at you. You are beautiful and you have a great body. I would kill to have your tits; don't you meet men?"

"Yes, but half the time I am trying to put them in jail and the other half, they are afraid I will. I travel a lot and at the end of the day, I just don't have it in me."

"That is the problem, you don't have it in you — enough!"

Brooke laughed, but that one landed a stomach punch from the inside out. "Hey, I got an idea; let's talk about something else. How is your father? My dear Uncle Daniel."

The conversation took a small detour as the courses came out. But Mathilde eventually started discussing the men in her life.

"... and I call him the choker. All he wants to do is choke me with his penis — very rough, but after, he is so gentle and attentive; he gives me many orgasms."

Brooke kept looking around, but no one seemed fazed by Mathilde's now totally explicit recitation of each and every man with whom she had sex, her little nicknames for them, and the size and ability of their manhood.

"... he, of course, wants to do the anal thing... but with him, I don't so much..."

As her cousin went on with a litany of various ways men had entered her and she them, Brooke drifted off into an internal soliloquy of remorse over her own pathetic love life. A few months ago she was blown off a ship and almost died in the ocean. Two years prior, she had nearly been killed in a foiled terrorist plot to launch a poisonous gas cloud over New York City. A brave retired detective had saved her life and the lives of millions in the metropolitan area by sacrificing his own. In another case, she had stared down a mastermind terrorist, the scariest man she'd ever met, and got him to blink first, which led to the unraveling of a nuclear bomb plot. But she had relegated her joy, her happiness, to somewhere after doing the laundry on her to-do list.

Mathilde was now painfully describing her soreness from a well-hung guy who must have been her Wednesday booty call, *or was she up to Friday?* Brooke had lost count.

"Brooke, Brooke. Are you somewhere else? Did you hear what I said about his — what's wrong?"

"Nothing, I was just thinking—never mind."

"No, I have been talking all the time. What is on your head?"

"You got me thinking; here you are living a life where you have sex more than I work out, and it just...just makes you think, that's all."

"Who is he?"

Brooke didn't bother to play cute with a, 'Why, whomever do you mean?' ploy. Mathilde had broken many barriers tonight. "I met him briefly. He saved my life actually."

"Ooo this is good! Go on."

"He is unbelievable; he is the captain of a ship."

"A big one?"

"Yes, it's a submarine..."

"No, his cock, does he have a big one?"

"You are unbelievable! When did you turn into such a sex fiend?"

"Right after I started getting my period. I was in school — "

Brooke held up her hand, "Hey wait, we are talking about me now."

"Yes, yes, I'm sorry; I will tell you about Claude and Jeremy later."

Brooke was about to speak when what Mathilde said finally registered, "TWO? At what, thirteen?" The she stopped herself and held up her hand, "Ah no, I don't want to hear this now — back to me." Brooke shook off the image of a thirteen-year-old Mathilde kissing two boys under the stairwell between history and math. "Anyway he's got the most trusting eyes, he's big and strong, and he just bristles with maleness."

As she spoke, Brooke realized she sounded like the girl in the hall in high school who was all 'dreamy' over some jock, but never so much as kissed him. Here, Mathilde was ready to open the Happy Hooker Ranch and she was still damp over some guy she barely knew and never slept with. *Pathetic* was the word that kept bouncing off her brain. But still, she kept talking like an infatuated teen. "He is one of a handful of men on the planet who is trusted to command a weapon with the power to destroy dozens of cities and millions of people. Getting close to that kind of power is intoxicating. I tried to deny that but I can't. He is a rare breed; the Navy makes sure of that and I can't stop thinking about him."

"Go to him and fuck him," Mathilde said as if she were suggesting bringing him a cup of coffee.

Brooke wanted to say something — some objection to Mathilde's crude suggestion. But she couldn't. She tried, but no words came out. Was it that simple? Had she miscalculated? Then it hit her. "But what if that isn't enough?" she said, leaning over the table so as not to broadcast her fear to the entire restaurant.

"If he has a small zizi, better to find out now."

"No, no, you lunatic, not his thing. What if just 'doing it' isn't enough? What if I want him more, want to be with him, want to make him my world? Where would I go? What part of my world would I have to give up to keep him?"

"My beautiful cousin, you think too much with your head."

"You obviously don't have that problem?" Brooke couldn't bring back the words; she was sorry before she finished the sentence. "Oh, I didn't mean that, Mathilde."

"But it's true; my heart and my pussy are two separate things. I want that kind of relationship you are looking for but it doesn't always happen. In the meantime, I have fun. I have needs and I make sure they are meeting."

"Well, just the same, it was an awful thing for me to say." The moment hung. "Do you really? Do you really want that too?"

Mathilde gestured to their barely eaten appetizers. "It is like food; you want to have a fabulous dinner in the best place in the world with the best wine and the best service. This does not mean you don't also eat a hamburger when you are hungry?"

"I guess that's a healthy way to look at it if you make it a veggie burger."

"Veggie? Oh yes, no meat! That is your problem, no meat!"

They both laughed, and with that, the tension shattered and the night became beautiful again to Brooke. They lingered on till one in the morning, then strolled back up the steep hill, formerly the province of mountain goats, hence the name Chèvre d'Or — Golden Goat. They hugged at the room's door.

"Oh, it was great seeing you, Mathilde. I love your life. You are happy and doing what you want."

"Brooke, don't listen to me too much, I work in a hotel and people are always coming here to find romance. It is all around me all the time. You — you are out in the world, exciting job, FBI, now the Clinton Girl. Don't let my silly affairs sway you. Your captain will come to you; he may be one-in-a-million, but you, my cousin, are one-in-a-billion. *Bonne chance.*

"*Bonne chance*, Mathilde." Brooke went into her room and out onto the terrace to view the lights twinkling all the way to Nice. A lone airliner was silently lifting into the night sky. She looked out over the sea and imagined that beneath those waves was a trillion-dollar boy's toy. Her Mush giving orders and thinking of her. Her head was floating; she had drunk more tonight than in a month. She flopped down on the chaise, and with the moon bright overhead and knowing there was no one higher than her perch who could see, her fingers wandered and she visited with Mush once again.

∞§∞

Joey was scanning the London Times, the first English language daily paper available at the embassy each morning, as he sat on the veranda and sipped his espresso. He read about the latest sex scandal to capture the attention of the British. Under the scathing headline, "Saudi Royal Sex Scandal," he read about the bodyguard of an Arabian prince who had been found dead in Switzerland. Seems the security man had taken to a hooker in a dance club and had been seen following her out of the club. His body had been found in a cheap hotel and the police were assuming he and the prostitute's pimp had an altercation, during which he was stabbed to death. The article ended with a statement from the royal family. "We regret the death of our trusted and loyal aide. His dalliance into this regrettable incident is not in the tradition or countenance of the Prince or the Royal Family. May Allah have mercy."

Joey had done some protective service detail as a New York City cop during the General Assembly, and knew the children of the royals were holy terrors. His cop's sense told him there was no way the prince wasn't somehow involved in this. In fact, back in the seventies, one of the biggest, loudest playboy "princes" was the son of a big Arab construction tycoon, who burned up the cobblestone streets in lower Manhattan with his Ferrari and held sway over ten of the hottest clubs and their precious female constituents. This privileged offspring *started* his day at 7 p.m. and ended it in some after-hours shindig in a series of hotel suites about sunrise. He was a playboy of the first order. His name was Osama Bin Laden.

Just then an embassy staff member knocked on the doorframe that led to the veranda at the ambassador's residence. "Mr. Palumbo, there is a Director Dupré at reception."

Joey found the director in the library. "Thank you for coming on such short notice. How did you get in here?"

"My brother-in-law works here as your community information officer."

Joey couldn't find the words so he smiled and said, "In August 1997, were you involved in an investigation of the death of a priest at the Sofitel? I have the file and it is signed by a Sergeant Dupré, who I assume isn't another brother-in-law."

"No, yes, that is me. As I remember, I found no evidence of foul play. How, may I ask, did you come into possession of that police file?"

"It is the underlying case the judge used to snag Sicard from us at the station."

Joey had read a lot of expressions on the faces of a lot of criminals, bosses, and women. Dupré's read as genuinely surprised. Joey decided to push a few buttons. "Director, you set me up. You were in on this whole charade."

"Yes, I could see why you would think that. May I see the file?"

Joey handed him the folder. "You are not denying it then?"

"I am not denying that you think it. I want to see if I should apologize or thank you."

Joey looked at the French cop wondering what his angle was. Dupré studied all the papers, the reports, and the little stamps and signatures. After a few minutes he said, "Would you like to come with me?"

"Where?"

"To find out who this Sicard is."

Ten minutes later, they were at the back door of a mosque. The director reached down, unstrapped a small .32 caliber pistol from his leg and handed it to Joey. "Just in case." He then unsnapped the strap on his service Glock and left his jacket buttons opened.

Joey stuffed the .32 into his waist and let his coat hang free as well. The director knocked on the door. Soon it was opened by a man in imam's garb.

"Ah my friend, perhaps you have a minute to chat," Dupré said sweetly as he flashed his French tin.

"Of course," the man of Allah responded to the man of the law.

"Are we alone?"

"Yes. Who is this man?"

"He is working with me; he is here to observe."

"What can I help you with?"

"I was thinking the other day of when I interviewed you years ago in the case of Friar Gregory; you remember that unfortunate affair?"

"Yes. Very tragic."

"Indeed. Back then you were working as a counterman at the hotel. You said there was no one who inquired or came to see the priest prior to his being found dead."

"If that is what I said then, that is what happened."

Suddenly, Dupré pushed his forearm across the man's chest and dropped him back across a table, knocking over a vase and some artifacts, which crashed on the floor, reverberating throughout the entire old stone church-turned-mosque. Dupré pulled his gun and stuck it in the man's chest.

Joey was observing this interesting interrogation technique when he heard hurried footsteps approaching the room, Dupré cocked his head toward the door and Joey pulled the .32 cal. When five men burst in he waved it at them saying only, "Uh, uh, uuuh!"

Dupré pulled out a picture of Sicard. "You never told me about this man."

"I never..."

"Don't even think of lying, and don't waste our time. Now, who is this man?" Dupré emphasized his request with a jab of the 9mm to the rib cage.

"He is one of you. No?" The man said, scared out of his wits.

"I ask the questions. How do you know him?"

"He's a killer, an assassin."

"Who was he to kill?"

"Why, don't you know?"

"Refresh my memory, *si vous plez*."

"The Pope."

Joey tightened the grip on his pistol and felt a chill run down his spine.

Five minutes later they emerged from the side of the mosque, got in Dupré's car and sped away.

"I'm going to go out on a limb here and guess what I saw back there wasn't recommended Metro police procedure."

"Here, as director of intelligence, I have more — latitude."

"So now Sicard is an assassin. Hired by whom to kill the Pope?"

"Time to dig; how's your French?"

"Sucks, but I have an associate who is part French. She'll be in Paris early this afternoon."

"I'll start without her; join me at my headquarters at two p.m."

XII. QUIET LITTLE WEEKEND

Bill had hoped for good weather. This little family outing was going to be a real once in a lifetime experience. President Mitchell had offered him Camp David. It was the perk of all perks. He felt odd, loading up the Escalade as if they were going to the beach, but instead going to a historic place where world leaders hobnobbed. Little Richard Ross Hiccock would ride the 'horseys' and fish in the lake where presidents and their families played.

Janice was looking forward to it as well. Bill planned to spend a lot of time with Richie, and she was looking forward to some downtime and a chance to get back to writing more of her book on brain disorders. Janice came out of the house with Richie and a little bag of stuff. Bill snapped his fingers and ran back inside the house; a second later he emerged, locked the front door, and got in the front seat. "I almost forgot my Nikon. I want to have some good pictures of this."

On the drive to Fredrick, Maryland, they chatted about whether or not to change the pool service, if they should get a bigger TV for the family room, and if they should invite both sets of parents to the house for the holidays. All in all, a pretty mundane conversation to have on the way to an ultra-class resort with a detachment of US marines as a personal protection force.

Bill's secure phone rang. He couldn't find it. Janice started moving around the things in the front seat, and then looked in the back. Richie had it and was waving it around as it rang.

She answered it and then handed it to Bill saying with an air of resignation, "Hold for POTUS." She knew a call from the President of the United States couldn't be good. She only heard Bill's end.

"Yes sir. Of course, sir, I completely understand. No, not at all. Of course. Thank you, sir." He ended the call and placed the phone in his shirt pocket.

"So..."

"Last week a particle physicist had a breakthrough."

"Okay, and the president called you — why?"

"He wants me to meet with this guy."

"When?"

"Tomorrow."

"Oh, Bill; we were counting on this weekend."

"We are still having our weekend. The president is flying this guy in and he's going to come to Camp David. It should only be a few hours. I'm sorry, but it is his place, you know."

"Well, I guess that's not too bad."

"So then you're not disappointed?"

"I should make like I am so I can get you to do my bidding."

"Your wish is my command."

"I got plans for you, big boy."

Bill knew that tone and that look. This was going to be a good weekend!

As soon as Bill went past the gate his immediate thought was, *it easy to see why FDR first called this place Shangri-La.* It was a beautiful patch of Maryland countryside. The grounds were, as he expected, meticulously kept. It was Navy neat, with the Seabees assigned to run it and the Marines assigned to protect it. Little Richie ran from the car and took to the place like he was visiting Grampy and Granny Alice. While watching him run down the path toward the horses in the paddock, Janice gave him one of those looks a wife gives to her husband that says, "You did good."

After dinner they did what most families might do on a weekend night — they watched a movie. Only here it was in a private movie theater and it was a clean release print of Dumbo. Richie sat between his mommy and daddy and was entranced by the color and the sound. Bill and Janice held hands across the back of the seats until their hands went numb. Janice liked having wine with her movie, and Bill enjoyed the president's favorite, kettle corn.

Bill put Richie to bed. Tomorrow they would ride the horses and maybe fly a kite. It took all of five minutes and Richie was deep in the land of nod. Janice was already in the bedroom, reading the guest book. "Oh my God! Menachem Begin slept in this very room. Alan Dulles. Margaret Thatcher. Cynthia Nixon Cox. Sure that makes sense. Amy Carter! John D. Rockefeller. Bob Hope! This is so incredible.

Bill looked over her shoulder, grabbed the pen, and scribed, *Mr. and Mrs. William Hiccock*, and the date. He closed the book and said, "Now let's make a little history of our own!"

Like kids, they jumped on the bed and practiced a kind of diplomacy that would surely cure all the ills of the world.

∞§∞

Having anything one could imagine for breakfast was a reality check that one was indeed in a most exalted place. Chocolate chip pancakes with a face made of cherries and whipped cream was set before Richie by the Navy steward. Janice had her 'firm', not runny Eggs Benedict done perfectly; Bill had the breakfast of astronauts, steak and eggs. At nine thirty, the horses were brought around. Being the parents of an eighteen-month-old, they were suddenly challenged with what to do with him?

Janice sighed, "I guess you can ride first; I'll stay with Richie and go later."

"That's no fun; it's about being together," Bill said.

As they puzzled with the minor dilemma, one of the Marine guards quietly stepped away.

"Well, maybe we'll ride some other time." The resignation in Bill's voice registered.

"No, Bill. You go, honey."

Bill's attention was suddenly totally taken by the Marine who reappeared leading a pony.

"Sir, I couldn't help overhearing. I got a little guy of my own and this will work just fine if your boy can sit up by himself."

"He's a virtual genius at sitting up on his own, isn't he, Daddy?" Janice said, her whole day starting to take shape.

"Corporal...?"

"Bradley, sir."

"Thank you, Bradley. How does this work?"

"Well, if you don't mind an easy walk on the trail, I'd be happy to lead the little cowboy here."

"Oh, we couldn't ask you to do that." Janice said.

"Like I said, I got a little fella, just about his age, and I miss 'im. So you'd be doing me a favor."

"Corporal, you've got the detail."

Bill lifted Richie into the safety saddle on the miniature stallion, strapped him in, and then mounted his own horse. They rode at a walk through the beautiful trails and breathtaking routes that cut through the rolling hills and scenic valleys. Richie was given to outbursts of laughter as Mommy or Daddy's horse would raise his tail and do what horses did when they raised their tail. His laughter settled into both parents like warm honey. They could see Corporal Bradley was trying to hide his bittersweet delight, no doubt imagining his own son laughing.

Taking it all in, Bill was prompted to say, "Bradley, if we ever get to come back to this unbelievable place, I'll ask the boss if you can bring your son. The boys can play together and ride together. What's your son's name?"

"Darelle, and if you can get the president to okay that, you got a play date, sir!"

Lunch was as unbelievable as breakfast. Janice had mused about white truffles, and magically, linguini with shaved white truffles appeared. Bill finished off the best French dip roast beef he had ever had, and looked at his watch. It was quarter of two and the professor was due at two. He excused himself from the front porch table where the stewards had set up their lunch, leaving Janice and Richie reading a storybook.

In the visitor's guest office, Bill fired up the computer and went onto his SCIAD network and had three flagged e-mails from particle physicists on the rings. He read all three e-mails and was actually three minutes late to the helipad where the Sikorsky and Dr. Roland Landau, professor of atomic science at University of California at Berkley was waiting.

"Sorry. I was up at the main house doing a little research, Professor."

"No problem; thank you for seeing me on such short notice," Professor Landau said.

He was a tall, thin man with a white mustache and thick grey-white hair and steel-blue eyes. His broad shoulders and the way he carried himself told Bill he had probably played ball as a youth.

They made their way up to the main house into one of the meeting rooms and Bill closed the door. "Professor, your claim is, to say the least, astounding."

"Yes, I am aware that I traversed very hallowed ground to reach my conclusion, but I think the peer review will show my methods are coherent and my hypothesis on firm footing." The older man's soft friendly eyes belied the fact that his brain was rapier sharp.

"What will you call this potential discovery?" Hiccock asked.

"There is no better name than that of our quest for all these decades — the God Particle."

"Well, the Higgs Boson branch of particle physicists will be miffed, but I must say, if your protocol bears fruit, it is an appropriate moniker."

"We may be on the precipice of an entirely new branch of science and understanding that will catapult man's grasp of creation a thousand-thousand years. But please, Dr. Hiccock, don't misunderstand me. I stand on the shoulders of the great Peter Higgs and his theoretical discovery of the boson. I feel my work is consistent with his findings and further advances that breakthrough work."

Bill took in the professor; last week he had never heard his name, but soon he could be as well-known and revered as Einstein.

"I'm sorry, Professor, but I am still stuck on the fact that, until recently, I've never heard of you."

"Of course, that's understandable. Right after July 2012, when they found the resonance of the Higgs boson, I applied for a small research grant and was given unprecedented access to the data generated at Cern. It was during my analysis that I found the key to the next level of exploration."

"May I ask?"

"I recognized anomalies in the decay of the particle that could be proof that the Higgs is not a fundamental particle."

"Whoa. That's an astounding thesis, Doctor."

"If my postulate is correct, then extreme agitation would reveal properties that could open a whole new branch of particle physics."

"So you want to use the next power level of the LHC to find evidence of a Techni-Force?"

"Yes, if the Higgs boson is not a fundamental particle, but in fact, made up of Techni-Quarks, then we might be able to shake them loose."

"Or split it."

"Well, if, as I believe, the Higgs is a product of super-symmetry, then a dark-matter companion to the particle may exist. So we wouldn't be splitting it as much as shining a light on it to see it's dark matter shadow, if you will."

"That could tie together the Standard Model with the inconvenient paradoxes of the 2012 discovery." Bill's mind reeled with the possibilities, "I see now why you got the grant, Professor."

"It all happened very fast from there. I presented to the board at LHC, and they approved my protocol to diagnose the particle under extreme force destabilization."

"That's quite a feat, reviewing terra-bytes of data and seeing something every other scientist in the world missed."

"It was, I assure you, pure luck meeting blind chance."

The humility he displayed made Bill feel bad about the rain he was about to sprinkle on the man's parade. "I am duty-bound by all that I know of science to ask the following question, Professor."

"I know your next question; I wish I knew with scientific certainty that the risk can be contained. I can only tell you that at the foothills of the atomic age, there were many learned and weighty thinkers who predicted that an atomic chain reaction, once initiated, could not be stopped and that everything, all of Earth, would be consumed in atomic fire. They were resolute and certain of their math, their findings and their beliefs. Yet, almost eighty years of atomic energy and research later, we are all still here, as is the Earth."

Bill was well aware of the atomic controversy of the late 30s and early 40s, but the atomic bomb ended all that when it only evaporated the Nevada Salt Flats and left the rest of the Earth intact. Still, he knew that if he had been advising President Truman at that time, he would have warned against detonating the "gadget" in the atmosphere. "Do you have insight into the controlling method to arrest the possible calamitous outcome, as barium rods are used to control an otherwise very unstoppable nuclear chain reaction?"

"At this time no. But I believe that discovery is at hand. In fact, the latest data from the LHC at CERN may be indicative of suppressing plasma."

"Professor, the president has asked me to advise him on this. I feel it is the most crucial scientific decision since the Manhattan project. I cannot be a proponent of further active research, or an attempt at agitating, splitting or illuminating the particle without simultaneously developing

the safeguards, because this time the critics may be right."
Bill didn't have to remind Landau that along with the critics
being right, it would also be the end of all existence if the God
Particle didn't like being dissected.

"I fully understand. I do not envy your position, Dr.
Hiccock, but providence and fate have chosen you. May your
judgment be guided by divine intervention and inscrutable
logic."

"Professor, I believe you have just uttered the first scientific prayer."

∞§∞

The car was at the reception desk promptly at 6 a.m.
Having said their goodbyes the night before, Brooke didn't
awaken Mathilde to say goodbye, and she surmised they
would see more of each other now. The car was to take her to
the train terminal in Nice, where she would board the Côte
d'Azur. As Brooke walked behind the young hotel bellman
who was pushing the cart with her luggage on it, she couldn't
stop thinking about what Mathilde said about him and his
butt. She found herself staring as he held the cart back from
rolling down the steep path to the hotel's entrance area. She
couldn't get rid of the image her cousin had planted in her
mind the night before about what he liked to have done to
him in the back while she was pleasuring him from the front.
She literally had to shake her head to wash the riveting images
that formed in her mind anyway. "Here you go, Benji, thank
you," she said in French as she handed him more than twice
what would have been considered a great tip. As she got in
the car, he shut the door. His crotch was now eye level with
her through the rear seat window. She laughed to herself, and
when he turned around to answer someone who called out
to him she found herself staring at his now infamous butt. All
she could say to herself was, *God bless you, Mathilde.*

At 9 a.m. she was in the Office of the Ports in Marseilles, to track the shipment of P784 from its point of embarkation.

Here the computer age sped things along quite nicely. The shipment originated from the Picardie region in Northern France and had been shipped by rail to the port, where it was loaded on the rusting tanker/freighter destined to Saint-Eugene in Algeria. By 11 a.m. Brooke was aboard the TGV to Paris. From the high-speed train she requested the embassy to find out about the Picardie Company that made the chemical. They, in turn, notified her that upon her return to Paris a meeting had been scheduled for her with Joey and Director Dupré.

∞§∞

"...so then when Mitchell was elected, somehow they got my name and he offered me the post."

"May I just say, Dr. Hiccock, that your tenure has been a much needed boost to science and technology."

"You are too kind, Professor, but all I do is cheerlead for the team, a team with star players on it like yourself."

"Yes, but if you'll allow me an analogy, you are the star quarterback of that team."

Bill was genuinely touched that this giant of science knew of his gridiron past. "Tell me, are my suspicions correct that you played some organized ball at one point, as well?"

"Yes, I was picked up by the White Sox in '58. But I never made it out of the farm system, then my wife died, and I knew I'd never remarry, so I used every dollar I had saved for tuition and went back to school. There I found my new game in atomic physics."

"Ah, I guess sports has played a role in both our lives."

Then his mood turned serious. "May I ask something that may be rather indelicate?"

"Sure. Feel free."

"There is a rumor that you have a private science network. If that were true, how would one such as myself be afforded membership in such an indispensable enterprise? I believe I have suitable enough credentials, but I will leave that assessment to your judgment."

"Professor, may I be blunt?"

"Science is blunt."

"Although at first I didn't recognize your name, I see now that that was my oversight. This is the first time I have focused on you or your work. In fact, I used that very network to garner information on you this morning. My network, Scientific Community Involved in America's Defense..."

"Yes, that's it, SCIAD!"

"Exactly, well that was the outgrowth of several threats and attacks against our country, which in many cases, I am happy to say, have been thwarted by a strong scientific analysis and investigation. I would be happy to consider you as an "outer ring" member. My assistant, Cheryl, will be in touch next week when I return to Washington after this little vacation."

"Yes, thank you. And I do apologize that the timing of our meeting necessitated interrupting your family time."

"Thank you for coming here and making it less intrusive."

"Well, I'd best be going."

"Allow me to walk you to the helipad."

"That won't be necessary; go enjoy your vacation."

"We are not scheduled to ride until four, so I have ten minutes."

As they walked back down the path to the heliport, the professor asked for clarification, "What are the outer rings?"

"Forgive me a little scientific bravado, but I have organized SCIAD in the model of an atom's electron shell. The inner rings K, L, M, and N hold Class One security clearance. They are cleared by the president to see raw, top-secret intel. The second group of rings, O, P, Q, comprise people who may not want, or would not do well under, the federal scrutiny that Class One would involve. Yet, their scientific opinion and acumen is of great service to our nation."

"And am I correct in assuming that the nucleus would be you?"

"In fact, that is my screen name in the network."

"Well, again, I would be honored to contribute in any ring."

"Thank you, and good luck, Professor."

With that, Landau was met by a Marine Guard who took his briefcase and escorted him up the steps of the helicopter. The older Sikorsky unit might have served as Marine One in the past, but was now assigned to ferry missions of lower level personnel to and from the White House to Andrews or Camp David.

Little Richie came crashing into the back of Bill's legs as he watched the professor board. "Hey, you! Trying to chop-block me?" Bill said as he reached around and threw Richie a few feet up and caught him, bringing him in close in his arms. "Let's watch the helicopter go."

They stood and watched as the door closed, the turbo fans spun up, and the green and white hulk rose at a slight angle, then started turning toward Washington.

Instinctively, Richie waved bye-bye and said, "Bye-bye! Bye-bye!" Bill just kissed his cheek.

Suddenly there was a hot flash that smashed into the side of Bill's head. Richie's face glowed orange as Bill's central nervous system kicked in, turning him to shield his son just as the first shockwave hit with a deafening explosion. The force knocked them both to the ground. Bill was able to use his elbows to prevent crushing his son beneath his weight. From the corner of his eye, he saw the orange plume of fire and black smoke rising up as the hulk of the copter spun out of control and exploded on impact into a shattered mass of metal and parts. Flaming debris landed twenty feet from them. He put his head down and covered his son with his body and his mind. It took a few seconds for Bill's hearing to return, and then he heard the sounds of Marines and Seabees trying to take control of a situation that was out of control. A voice said, "Dr. Hiccock, come with me, sir. Now."

Bill got up, cradled his son's head, and trotted back to the house with a Marine in front and one behind. A few feet from where they were blown down, a six-foot part of the chopper's rotor blade impaled the ground and jutted out like a twisted knife. Once in the main structure, the doctor on call and the paramedics checked Bill and his son for wounds and concussions. The two Marines who had been helping on the helipad were rushed in. One was bleeding; the other was out cold.

"Is my son okay?" Bill demanded.

"He seems to be fine."

"Then I'll take care of him; help those men over there."

Just then Janice came in and grabbed her son. "Are you okay; did you get cut?" She started immediately feeling his body and looking for wounds. All she found was singed hair on his head. Bill had taken the brunt of the heat, and one whole side of his hair was severely singed. The paramedic had applied a salve to the first-degree burn on his face.

The captain of the Marine detachment came in and ordered a report from the medical staff.

"Civilians are shaken but sustained no injuries. Lance Corporal Leeds has multiple lacerations and blunt trauma, but he'll make it. Sergeant Rhodes was knocked out but coming around with no apparent physical trauma."

"We are in lock-down, people. Evacuate the civilians to the safe room." He approached the Hiccocks. "Sir, your family will be safe in an interior room. I'll post a guard. Come with us now."

"Captain, if that helicopter was attacked, it could have the most serious national security consequences. I am a member of the Nat Sec Comm. Does the safe room have commo capacity?"

"Yes sir, it is designed for the commander-in-chief to carry out military and national emergency command and control, sir. This way."

Bill carried Richie and held Janice's arm as they entered the secured conference room, which was blast proof and gas proof. Four Seabee techs entered with them and one Marine in full battle gear with loaded arms and his own radio gear. Then the giant blast door shut and the clunking mechanical sounds indicated it was sealed.

Bill knew the Navy insignias well enough to decipher that he had two ensigns, a lieutenant, and a captain with him. "Captain, do we know what brought the chopper down? Was it mechanical failure or an attack?"

"Playing back helipad surveillance camera video now, sir." He shuttled the tape (they still used tape here) fast forward until Landau was on board, then slowly advanced until the chopper lifted out of the frame. "The camera is fixed and didn't follow the chopper up, but no one got near the bird sir. No one placed anything on it."

The video continued showing an empty helipad, but then Bill saw something. "What was that?"

"Going back." The captain jogged the tape slowly in reverse. As the frame lines rolled, a brief streak appeared over two frames of the video.

"Do you make that out to be what I think it is, Captain?"

"Seems like a missile, sir, just over the tree line on a trajectory up. And here, a few frames later, the helipad is lit by the flash and now debris is falling. I'd say it looks like a surface to air missile, sir."

"Are there any other camera angles, Captain?"

"Lieutenant?" He turned to an officer who was at a series of screens that held multiple video-camera feeds.

"Checking the roof security cam now sir. Yes. There in the upper right; it appears to be coming from the lake."

"Scramble perimeter defense, stop and inspect all lake traffic immediately. Set up fifteen and twenty-five mile perimeter checkpoints, and I want those up immediately, ensign."

"Aye-aye sir," the third Navy man in the room said.

"Dr. Hiccock, who was the passenger?"

"It's Bill, and he was a man who may have held a secret as great as the universe itself." Bill turned to the ensign on the communication console. "I need the president, immediately."

"White House Interconnect, this is Camp David, secure command and control. I have ultra-flash level comm for Phantom. Repeat this is an ultra-flash level comm for Phantom," the ensign barked.

Bill noticed he used the president's Secret Service call name, 'Phantom.' He was probably airborne right now on a seventeen-hour flight to Bangkok for the Asian Rim Summit, which was the reason Bill and Janice had gotten the invite to Camp David.

The loudspeaker in the room came on, "Air Force One operator, hold for POTUS... This is Mitchell."

"Can he hear me?"

"Yes, I can hear you; who is this? Bill, is that you? What's got you calling me? Not enough towels in the guest bathroom?"

"Sorry, sir. Professor Landau is dead. Right now it looks like an attack; a missile attack on his helicopter as he was leaving the Camp just seven minutes ago now."

"Dear God, are you and your family okay?"

"Yes sir, just a little shaken up, but thanks for asking."

"Who's in command where you are, Bill?"

"Captain Weld here sir, first Seabees, I am comm. Marine Captain Holliday is detachment OD, but he is outside the secure con, sir."

"Any casualties, son?"

"Two wounded, expected to survive, on the ground. The chopper had a crew of three, sir. I am afraid they are all lost."

"May God have mercy on their souls, Captain." The president spoke to people on the plane, "Ray, get FBI and NSA patched in ASAP!" and then returned to the phone. "Have a nice relaxing time in the country, I said, Bill. Any thoughts on what happened?"

"Someone who doesn't want the professor to continue his experiments found out he was here and had the where-withal to stage an attack."

"Who are we looking for, Bill?"

"Long list of activist groups who don't like particle research and feel it is dangerous."

"Black-holers, Bill?"

"Essentially, yes. They come in two forms. The scientifi-cally motivated, who may or may not understand the inherent risks in fiddling with the glue that holds all creation together, and the deist, motivated by the belief that big science is med-dling in God's handiwork."

"Any of those groups have missiles last time you checked?"

"That is the random element here, sir. Who would have had that kind of armament at the ready, waiting for this opportunity, which I myself didn't know about until yester-day afternoon when you called me?" Bill heard someone speaking to the president and he mumbled something back.

"Bill, they tell me I have FBI, Sec State, Sec Home, and NSA now on the line."

The president then recapped the situation. "Gentlemen, we have an attack on American soil on a scientist who was involved in controversial research. The press is no doubt going to be all over this in a matter of minutes. I need your assessment and suggestions as to how we handle this. Bill, tell 'em what you know and what happened."

Bill repeated the events of the last ten minutes while they asked questions and made observations. At the end, the president summarized the conference call. "So the wreckage is on federal land and within the security perimeter of the compound, therefore, we control the crash site. The majority of you think mechanical error is the best positioning, and I agree. It preserves our investigatory options and keeps public

panic to a minimum. The professor is a known particle physicist, but his finding is relatively recent and has only been circulated among the peer groups, so it is not generally known.
Bill will use his influence to keep a lid on it within the scientific community. Have I left anything out? Good. Then you
all have your tasks. We will reconvene at — Ray when are we
wheels down in Thailand? Okay let's say 6:30 DC time. Thank
you ladies and gentlemen, that is all."

Almost on cue, one of the media monitors in the room,
the one tuned to CNN, showed they had interrupted their
programming for a news flash. Bill asked that the sound be
turned up.

"... getting reports of smoke, a thick column of black
smoke originating, we believe, on the grounds of the presidential retreat known as Camp David. I believe we have amateur video — let's see, can we put that up? Here it is. As you
can see from this exclusive amateur video obtained by CNN,
there does seem to be black smoke rising from — and we
can't be sure from this video — but what we believe to be the
grounds at Camp David. Now, my producers are telling me
to point out that the president is not at Camp David, or even
in the country, for that matter, because as our Washington
Bureau Chief Candy Crowley pointed out, he is at this moment
mid-Pacific on his way to the Bangkok summit. Whether this
is a fire, a forest fire or something else, we'll just have to wait
and see. But what we can say for certain is that smoke has
been seen rising from the general area of Camp David. Stay
tuned to CNN for more coverage of this breaking news."

"If you suffer from erectile dysfunction..." The tech
switched off the sound when they rolled a Viagra commercial.

"White House on one, sir."

"How do I pick up...oh," Bill said, as a Seabee picked up
the receiver, punched the line switch and handed the receiver
to him. "Hello. Hi, Brent." Brent Cummings was the assistant
press secretary, who was handling the situation because the
press secretary was flying on 'One' with the president. "Yes,

you were on the call, Brent; that's the way the president wants to handle it. Oh, I see your point. Hey, here's a thought. The professor was interested in joining my group; maybe that's why he was here. What group? Eh, um — the 2020 conference. Yeah, I never heard of it either, I just made it up. It's a way to see clearly what the scientific challenges for America and the world will look like in the year 2020, but it also means perfect vision. You know, I like it. I'll have my office draw up the press release that I was *going* to release when I got back from the Camp on Monday. Good. Let me know."

Bill hung up and went over to his wife and son. "How we doing, big guy?"

"It boom!" Janice held her son a bit tighter.

"Yes, it did but its okay. Everything's okay. Later, Mommy and I will take you to the movies again, would you like that?" He tickled his arm a little. "Yaay! Dumbo!" Bill said as he kissed Janice and walked away, thanking God for the innocence of children, which could shield them from the kind of horror that had just befallen them.

"Bill, look," Janice said, "CNN."

Bill looked up in time to see a video of himself, Janice and Richie taken at the Easter Egg Roll on the White House lawn this year. "Turn up the sound."

"...advisor, his wife Dr. Janice Hiccock and their son were scheduled to be at Camp David this weekend according to our White House correspondent, Miles Whitaker. Miles..."

The scene switched to what the networks call the portico shot. It is a standby position outside the White House where all the major networks have a camera, a tent-like covering, and an assigned reporter and producer ready to go live at a moment's notice. Miles was framed by the columns and large lantern on chains that hung in the vestibule of the mansion.

"Linda, on Friday the press office here at the White House released its weekend news schedule, and on it, down at the bottom, one line simply reads, 'At the president's invitation, White House Science Advisor William Hiccock will be staying at Camp David with his family.' Now, once again, at this time we don't know for sure if the smoke we are seeing has anything to do with the compound. There's word that a press conference is being held in fifteen minutes to address not just this matter but also a pre-release of the president's remarks on the upcoming Bangkok summit. Back to you Linda."

"Thanks, Miles. Let's hope that the Hiccock family and the staff at Camp David are safe and sound. Moving on to international news, the body of Saudi security man Abrim..."

The tech cut the sound. Bill looked at Janice. "So much for a quiet little weekend getaway."

"The worst part is now we have to explain why we didn't invite our friends. Oh, God, Bill. We should call your folks and my mom before they see this."

"Lieutenant, is there a phone my wife can use? Honey, it's a non-sec line, so just tell them we are fine. Nothing else, okay?"

∞§∞

Joey was in the director of French Intelligence's office awaiting Brooke's arrival when he and Dupré saw CNN International's coverage of the Camp David story. He had immediately called Bill's cell but didn't get through because of the secure room Bill was in, so he called through the White House switchboard.

∞§∞

"White House interconnect for you Dr. Hiccock, on one."

This time Bill beat the Seabee to the phone. "Hiccock. Joey, you heard."

"Are you guys okay?"

"Yeah, Richie and I were looking right at it when it exploded. He's okay but I am going to need a trim — and some more medicated cream." He said the last part out loud to the room hoping someone would appear with a tube.

"What happened?"

"Looks like a surface to air missile killed a professor I was meeting with."

"Huh?"

"When he was leaving by helo, he had just lifted off and wham. This could be a new science war, Joey. Somebody trying to change scientific policy by force."

"Does anything normal ever happen around you? Should I come back to DC?"

"No, not at the moment. Besides, what you are doing there is also important."

"Well, I'll brief you on that when you have the time. I just wanted to make sure I wasn't looking for another job."

"Thanks Joey, you are all heart."

"Hug Janice and Richie for me, and hey, be careful."

Bill laughed at Joey admonishing him with his own words.

∞§∞

The Fox News anchor was stalling for time as the screen was split into two, with the picture-in-picture focused on the White House pressroom podium. The "heads up" to the networks noted only that there would be a statement about Camp David at the now-moved-up afternoon briefing. The assembled press corps bristled a little as the assistant press secretary and a Navy commander entered the room, followed by a phalanx of aides. They knew something was up and started dialing their personal cells. This created a cacophony, which caused Brent to wait until he had their attention. Seeing this in the Fox control room, the director cued the anchor over his earpiece to say, "We now go live to the White House press briefing room for more on this breaking story."

The pool cameraman and the pool producer both wagged a finger at Brent and he started by reading a prepared statement as his aides handed out printed copies.

"Good afternoon. It is with great sadness that I report to you today that a Marine helicopter on a routine assignment at Camp David in Maryland crashed earlier this afternoon. All persons onboard the aircraft perished. The dead include Navy Lieutenant Commander Niles Markey, Marine Aviation Captain Jesse Higgins, and Warrant Officer Peter Klug. The sole passenger, Doctor Roland Landau, was also pronounced dead at the scene. The next of kin have been notified and the president has spoken to family members to offer his condolences and prayers during this difficult time. The circumstances surrounding this crash, which appear to be related to mechanical failure, will be further covered by Commander Bowman, who will take the podium shortly. That is the end of my prepared statements. I will take limited questions because, at this time, we do not have all the facts. Miles."

CNN had broken the story, so Miles Chafee got the first question. "We have a report that the president's science advisor was at Camp David when this occurred. Is that why Professor — " He looked down and checked his reporter's notebook, "Landau was also there?"

"Yes, Miles, I am glad you reminded me. First off, let me say that Dr. Hiccock and his family are fine and have not been affected by these events. As the commander will speak to later, the aircraft went down outside the compound proper, and at no time was anyone in the compound in danger. As to Professor Landau's visit, and there will be a follow-up information packet on this within the hour coming from the office of Science and Technology that Dr. Hiccock heads up, I believe that Dr. Landau was there to accept a position in the '2020 Committee' or '2020 Initiative.' I'm sorry I don't have the exact title."

He turned to an aide to the right of the podium and then repeated out loud what the staffer read from his jotted down notes. "The '2020 conference?' Thank you, Jeff. As I said, that information is coming, but essentially, it is a new program that was to be announced Monday, focusing on the scientific challenges facing America and the world as we approach the next decade. Professor Landau was accepting the chairmanship of this commission and would have been heading up the recruitment of leading scientists and technological innovators around the world. And again, although the loss of every life is to be mourned, Dr. Landau's untimely demise is certainly a great loss to the scientific community."

Brent switched his focus and bodily direction to the other side of the room and called on the reporter from CBS. "Harold."

∞§∞

"Was this aircraft a Sikorsky from the president's fleet or was it — "

The sound switched off as a hand put down the remote and scratched at a scraggily beard. "They didn't mention the missile."

"Of course they didn't. They need to show control. They also didn't mention the research. They are hoping the story dies with Dr. Landau," was the calm and measured response.

"We should have waited a little longer till the helicopter was over public land. Then there would be evidence of our attack and the world would be forced to find out what these monsters are doing." The man's stress was evident in the rising pitch of the voice.

"It happened the way it happened. But we still have a card to play."

With that he picked up a cell phone and dialed. "Hello, CNN, I want the editor on the helicopter crash. He will want to talk to me. Tell him it was not an accident. I will hold."

His fingers tapped the phone. At that moment, there was a knock on the mobile-home door. Both men in the trailer jumped.

"United States Marines. Please come out of your trailer; this is an investigation. Repeat, please come out of your trailer."

The nervous man not on the phone whispered, "What do we do?"

"Hold them off while I speak to the world."

"How am I supposed to do that?"

The man on the phone reached under his chair and produced a MAC 5 machine gun. "Distract them for only a minute more."

"They will kill me!"

"We will all die if they continue this research. Now go; I am sure I will be right behind you."

"Is there no other way?"

"Be brave. Give me a minute more."

The shaky hands of the man about to take on the US Marines fiddled with the latch and pushed through the flimsy metal door. He screamed as he opened fire, spraying bullets toward everything that moved.

∞§∞

"Dr. Hiccock, I have an after-action report from Perimeter Squad Two."

"Who is this?"

"Sergeant Holmes. We just engaged an individual who attacked us with a machine gun. We lost a man in the fight. Three wounded. However, there was another man in a trailer. As near as we can tell he caught a round in the right temple as he was attempting a call. I think he was calling CNN."

"Why do you think that?"

"I picked up the phone and CNN was on hold. A man answered and said, 'National Desk.'"

"Did you say anything?"

"No, sir. I hung up."

"Good work, Sergeant. I am sorry about your man. Where are you now?"

"By the north ridge line."

Bill turned to the leader of the men in the room. "Captain, I need to get out there."

"Sir, you are a civilian…"

"Hold up; I am an SES 14, which is the simulated rank of major general, Captain. This is a matter of national security and I am the ranking national security officer on the scene."

Five minutes later, a Humvee carrying Bill and two armed Marines pulled up to the trailer as a military ambulance evacuated the wounded. The body was being covered with a blanket by the medics. Bill was shocked and saddened to see them cover Corporal Bradley, the soldier who had brought the pony for Richie. Bill closed his eyes and thought of man's little boy and how much Bradley loved him. Fear suddenly arose from Bill's inside. He had been in tough situations before and he'd reluctantly seen a lot of action. Before he was a father he had almost bought the farm on a few occasions, but this was the first time he felt like he had skin in the game. He now sensed a hesitation and an anxiety about even being out here so soon after gunplay. Richard Ross Hiccock wasn't going to grow up without a dad. Then he thought about Bradley again. Bill found strength in Bradley's courage and sacrifice. He breathed deeply and trudged ahead thinking, *Everyone in harm's way has a little Richie at home. You ain't that special; now get over yourself!*

Sergeant Holmes was ordering his men to fan out and search for the rocket launcher. He approached Bill. "You must be Hiccock."

"Must have been a hell of a fight."

"Fast and unnecessary. A good man, killed. Three wounded. Two scabs dead. I screwed up. I didn't expect unfriendlies."

"Sergeant, we aren't in Fallujah. This is the Maryland countryside; who would expect…"

"He came out blasting."

"Sergeant. Not your fault; now where's the other guy?"

"In the trailer, sir.

Bill entered the trailer and was shocked. It wasn't the dead body with the blood pooled under its head. It was what the body was wearing — a priest's collar.

"Don't touch anything," a voice said.

Bill turned around and saw a man in a suit holding a badge. "Barkley, Naval Criminal Investigations. I am impounding this crime scene."

"Bill Hiccock, White House. We need to find out who this guy is working with and if there are more of them out there ready to attack other installations."

"The Secret Service has every sensitive spot in lockdown by now."

"I am not talking about government. These guys want to attack science."

"Wanna run that by me again?"

"This attack was based on their objection to scientific policy. As egg-headed as that might sound, they shot down one of the president's helicopters to kill a scientist. What else are they prepared to do, where else are they planning to hit or hitting right now?" Bill's face turned to stone as a thought locked up his entire central nervous system. He blurted, "I gotta go."

Bill ran to the Humvee. "Sergeant, I need to get back to the house quick."

Bill jumped into the Humvee, which sped back to the main house. Bill jumped out, ran inside and fired-up the SCIAD computer. He typed as fast as he could...

> Warning, all SCIAD members and your institutions. Probability of an attack on science and/or technology properties: high. Take measures to protect yourselves, your work and your families. This is not a drill. Repeat, this is not a drill.

He was just about to hit *Send* when he thought again. *The president wanted this contained.* He deleted the messages to the outer rings and only included the top secret cleared inner ring. He added the words TOP SECRET to the message line and added the word "Quietly" in front of "take measures to protect..."

Then he ran back to the communications center. The Marine outside challenged him for ID and then the big fifty-ton door swung open.

"Get me the president." He kissed Janice and patted Richie's head.

"Air Force One on line two."

"Mr. Pres...I'll hold." He turned to Richie, "You rode very well today, son. I bet you could be a cowboy. We are going to be riding a lot more this summer ... Mr. President. Sir, I believe you should quietly raise the threat level to all government science and technology installations. We may have found the attackers and they might be fringe religious groups. I'll have a report drawn up and to you within the hour. Yes sir, I'd like to err on the side of caution. I will, sir."

He hung up and turned to the communications officer. "Get me the director of the FBI and use the words 'Quarterback priority.'" He spun around to the leader. "Captain, I need to know what the fellow from Navy CIS finds out as soon as he has any information, especially who the shooters were and if they found any more of them. Same for your perimeter patrols. If they find that launch tube I want it tracked and identified stat."

∞§∞

"Put it in the power rotation and get me Graphics. Tell Henson I want a four-second theme music cue for the bumper. I want four staff writers on this now. Who was this professor guy and see if there is an angle on budget cuts affecting helicopter maintenance? Oh, and get me the safety records for this kind of chopper. Get to it, people." The CNN national desk editor hung up the phone on the inter-office conference call and looked up at a staff researcher. "What?"

"I overheard the call that came in claiming it wasn't an accident."

"Whoever it was hung up; probably some nut case. We've gotten twenty-five calls already, claiming everything from the Tea Party to aliens. Why are you standing around? See if the pilots had any drinking or drug issues." He pulled out the budget to see how he could pay for all the stuff he had just ordered, and mumbled to himself, "Why does a story this good have to happen on a Saturday when the A-Teams are off?"

∞§∞

"... Aviation Captain Jesse Higgins and Warrant Officer Peter Klug. The sole passenger, Doctor Roland Landau, was also pronounced dead at the scene. The next of kin have..."

The Architect put down the science journal he was engrossed in and reached for the remote, not believing what he had just heard from the Swiss National news that was on as background noise. He rewound the DVR feature on his hotel room's TV and replayed the entire White House helicopter crash news conference that had broken, unbeknownst to him, an hour and a half before.

He was stunned. He had been monitoring Landau and twenty other particle physicists and scientists for a year. Once Landau got his grant from LHC, he turned up his surveillance by having the professor's house electronically bugged, as well as his computer at the school. It paid off. As soon as the Landau Protocols were being considered, he had the opportunity he had prayed for. It was an odd twist of faith that this man, his main source, died in an accident.

The Architect immediately assessed the damage. He concluded, that the professor's death didn't impact his master plan, because he had already gotten the most crucial strategic information from him: the exact day and time of the event.

∞§∞

Cheryl was driven to Camp David by uniformed Secret Service. Five more of Hiccock's staff were scheduled to arrive within the half-hour. The president and Bill both decided to let Bill run the operation from Camp David, away from the press and the limelight. Cheryl entered, gave Janice a kiss, and then kissed little Richie, who was playing with a toy truck on the conference room table.

Bill was on the secure teleconference. Cheryl immediately recognized the face of the director of the FBI on the screen. Bill seemed to be just finishing up. "That's why I want a separate task force, and the president and I agree to run the whole op from here, away from the White House. If this leaks out, there could be world-wide panic and chaos."

"Okay Bill. Neil Cutter, my assistant director, will coordinate." The head of the bureau paused, and when he spoke again his tone had changed, "Bill, is this God Particle thing real? I mean, are they fooling around with the apocalypse?"

Bill was taken aback by the question. He decided he should recalibrate his thinking on the impact of this, if even the notion gave the director of the FBI the chills. "Director, so far, and until I see proof, this all remains in the realm of particle theory, a speculation on the standard model. But the existence of this particle, or Higgs' Boson for that matter, is purely an assumption which may be only one of many possible explanations for why everything holds together."

"Some day when there's time…"

"Yeah, we'll go over the nuclear physics involved. Let's talk again at six?"

Both screens shifted to the Camp David logo. Bill jotted some notes on his iPad, then turned and saw Cheryl. "Good, you're here. Sorry to blow your weekend. Get me Kronos fast!"

"Kronos," was the self-adopted name for Vincent DeMayo, a former hacker for the mob whom Bill had sprung from Elmira prison by presidential pardon during the Eighth

Day Affair. His digital genius with computers had helped Bill thwart the greatest cyber-attack on American soil and saved millions of lives.

Cheryl burrowed in right away. She commandeered an area of the room and started logging in and moving phones, and somehow found a headset. She had it on and was calling Kronos as she synced her Blackberry to the system in front of her. Between her laptop and Blackberry she brought the entire operation with her. Then Bill recalled he had 'stolen' her from the White House chief of staff . She knew this place and the drill. She turned to Bill and said, "Kronos on c.o. four."

Bill looked at his phone for anything with a number four.

"The flashing light, boss," Cheryl gently said.

"Kronos. I need you to do something extremely important."

Kronos was at a skate park with a helmet on and a skateboard under his arm. He was definitely the oldest guy there, and in the opinion of many, a 'cool coot,' a local skater term for, 'old guy whose skills are pretty decent.'

"Is this legal?"

"A, since when have you ever cared about that, and, B, I don't know, but it's going to be covered under a presidential directive in five minutes. It will authorize us to sweep something from the Web. We need it not to have ever existed and I need it gone yesterday."

"No big whoop, as long as it hasn't been hash-tagged yet."

"I'll make believe I know what you just said and assume you will do this. When you get to your computer, Cheryl will fill you in."

"Hey Bill, everything okay? You sound tense, man."

"Nah, I am having a relaxing day in the country."

XIII. SIRROCO: THE DESERT WIND

The good shepherd Bridgestone took in the routine of the prisoners through two days of observation. He was able to identify the leader of the captives by his taking charge of the exercises. The next step was easy. All the captives were Asian. All the guards were African. He had counted seven guards. During the exercise periods, all the prisoners were together and the guards all neatly at the perimeter and very visible. Although he could have called in a small squad of SEALs from a carrier strike group one hundred twenty nautical miles off, instead he went to his pickup and dragged the manure covered top plate off. He took out a Gepard GM6 .50 caliber, heavy sniper rifle. He'd have to spot the targets himself, but the distance, terrain, direction of wind, and the towels he'd wrap around the barrel would ensure that the last guard to die wouldn't have heard the previous six shots. 'One shot one kill' was the sniper's motto, more because of the exposure of his position that a second shot would bring than any concern about ammunition.

Soon the morning exercises would begin. He used the uplink radio to notify the carrier to spin up the rescue choppers. He figured five Stallions could handle the head count. They were forty-five minutes out. That should be more than enough time.

∞§∞

Captain Kasogi roused his men, giving them their five-minute heads-up before the morning exercise routine. The early chill was burning off, on its way to being a scorcher of a day here in the desert. He had noticed that the supply truck, which came every three days, never showed yesterday. That meant little or no food for his men today. To that end he would cut the exercise time in half. The little award system he initiated, which the men were now calling The Captain's Table, had about half the crew competing to earn the "culinary" prize by crisply doing their exercises and showing camaraderie.

As the men assembled in the middle of the ramshackle camp, the guards took positions around the group. Kasogi smiled as he addressed his men, "Later today, our resident poet, Yosi, has written a poem and he will honor us with a reading of his fine work. I hear this one has a very steamy verse about a woman of questionable choices."

The men responded in half-hearted laughter. Kasogi was happy that he had Yosi. His men of the sea were not prone to poetry, but in this God-forsaken place it gave them a point of distraction, a trace of normalcy. Kasogi knew that the captors would win if his men surrendered their spirit. The guards seemed unfazed by his strategy, possibly not understanding its true value. If rescue — when rescue came, or an escape opportunity presented itself, the window of success would be narrow. Men who were fit and spirited, men who had not succumbed to their captors, stood the greatest chance of survival.

Kasogi stretched out his arms. "Okay, we start with fifty jumping jacks. Ready, begin."

Suddenly there was gunfire. All the men hit the ground covering their heads. From the dirt, Kasogi tried to see what was happening. The head guard was laughing, lowering his gun from shooting in the air as he walked over to Kasogi and said in half-baked French, "No exercise! We unload truck!" Kasogi stood and saw the plume of dust heading toward camp. The food truck, which was supposed to have arrived yesterday afternoon, was finally coming. Kasogi addressed his men, "It's okay, the truck is coming to be unloaded. We'll exercise this evening."

∞§∞

It really sucks when your plan goes to hell, Bridgestone thought, as he keyed his radio. "Kingmaker, this is Sirocco, abort, abort. Target parameters have changed. Will update." The satellite radio hit the sand with the force of frustration. He watched the truck approach through his sniper scope. He watched for thirty minutes as the prisoners unloaded the truck; then something bad happened.

Yosi, the radioman/poet, was heaving an extra-heavy crate onto his slight frame when he became unbalanced and the crate smashed onto the floor. Unfortunately, it was the guards' eggs and only a few survived. The sight of "the good food" in ruins on the dirt made one guard lash out, and he struck Yosi in the face with the butt of his rifle. Yosi's bloody teeth immediately splattered on the egg-covered ground as he went down. An oiler from the engine room, a huge hulk of a man, hammered the guard with a punch from his fist and Kasogi heard the guard's jaw snap. For his effort, the oiler was immediately perforated with several bullets, which he absorbed with groans and gasps until his body hit the ground with a thud. All the prisoners scrambled and the guards started screaming. One of Kasogi's men was shot in the back when a guard decided he was running too far away.

Through his scope, Bridgestone could see the guards were all pointing their weapons toward the prisoners. Starting with the ones at the perimeter, he squeezed the trigger and the head of a guard popped and fell back. Next target, a full chest hit; next shot, center mass — a huge exit wound visible as the impact spun the man around; three rounds, three seconds, three down. He then trained his weapon on a guard beating a prisoner and caught him in the right eye just as he was about to smash in the skull of the prisoner.

∞§∞

Kasogi saw the guard go down. His confusion lasted a few seconds as he looked around and saw through the melee that four guards were lying dead. *Someone is shooting them. From where?* He quickly decided it didn't matter; this was the moment. He ran toward the nearest dead guard and picked up his rifle. He aimed it at the first guard he saw and let out a burst that rippled across the man's chest. He turned and found the next guard. He fired and missed and the guard turned...

∞§∞

Bridge could see the prisoners were starting to fight back and he realized the leader was now shooting as well. He saw the man miss and get the attention of his target. Bridge quickly re-aimed and fired, but the guard was spinning and Bridge's round only glanced his shoulder.

∞§∞

Kasogi was frozen as the guard had turned and aimed his AK-47 at him. He instinctively went to crouch low, when the guard suddenly went into a spasm, sending a burst of gunfire into the air as his shoulder exploded. Kasogi took advantage and shot him again. One of the Kasogi's men had slammed a rifle into one of the remaining guards, who was down with a broken sternum. There were only two guards and a truck driver left. Four prisoners now had rifles and the remaining captors knew they were going to be killed, so they started firing into the mass of Kasogi's men.

∞§∞

Bridge couldn't draw a bead on the shooter farthest away, but the one firing from behind a stack of crates was in the clear. Bridge took him out with a shot to his back, which went right through his heart. The prisoners were now training their fire on the one remaining armed guard, who was out of Bridge's line of fire. He grabbed his Mac 5 and webbing with the extra magazines and grenades clipped on and started running toward the camp.

With the exception of the wounded and dead prisoners still in the open, the survivors had all found cover. The four with weapons were taking pot shots at the remaining guard's position but getting nowhere.

Bridge had circled around and come to the side of the camp opposite the holdout shooter. He grabbed a grenade from his webbing, placed it at the bottom of a fencepost and ducked for cover. The explosion tore a hole in the fence and he scrambled through. The prisoners turned in the direction of the blast and were about to fire when Kasogi yelled to his men to hold their fire and get down. They buried their heads as the "desert man" man scurried up to their position.

"*Konichiwa*," the desert dweller said, then added, still in Japanese, "I am here to get you out." He took out a grenade and pulled the pin, then tossed it to the lone guard's position. A second later, the threat was neutralized. He turned to the leader of the prisoners and asked, "Where's the driver?"

∞§∞

The Combat Information Center of the aircraft carrier Carl Vinson was restarting the operation to extract the operative, Sirocco, from the Sudanese desert. Only minutes before, it had been aborted, but now was back on. The report stated, four dead, six wounded.

∞§∞

"I am Captain Kasogi Toshihira. My men and I are in your debt." He bowed as he met the man who had come out of the desert like the wind.

"Thank you for holding your fire as I approached, Captain Toshihira" Bridge said not offering his own name.

"You are the sniper?"

"Yes, and I have helicopters on the way to take you and your men to safety. Is this everyone?"

"Of my crew, yes. But there were three Marines and a pilot and we haven't seen them."

"Where is the driver?"

"He's over there."

Bridge went over to the driver, who was in a state of shock, but clearly not a combatant. It took a couple of minutes, but Bridge discovered that he reported to no one and there were no reinforcements for the guards. The scared man told of another place where he delivered supplies, where there were two guards and four men, Japanese, in uniforms, who were never unchained, in a shack. He went back to the captain.

"I don't think anyone else is coming, but just in case, Captain, have four of your best men serve as lookouts in all directions. The choppers will be here in thirty-five minutes. I will order a small detachment to rescue the Marines; they are being held about four kilometers up the road."

XIV. PAPAL ENVOY

Bill had turned the communications center at Camp David into a working operations center. Nearly one hundred people had been mustered to help him find out who was behind the shoot-down and if it was part of a bigger plot, or just some lone nuts. The nagging thing was the priest. *Priests don't kill. Yet —*

"Joey Palumbo on the screen," Cheryl said.

Bill sat down in front of the secure teleconference screens. Joey was coming from the Sec Con at the US Embassy in Paris. "What's up, Joey?"

"I got to tell ya, Bill, I think I should be there right now. Can you fill me in on what you know so far?"

"Well, we got a dead priest, Father Cleary, and his accomplice. As far as we know right now, he's out of a Boston church and the other guy is from Vermont. No military past for either of them to account for the missile launcher or how they got it."

Cheryl, working a keyboard next to Bill, hit a few keys and the dossiers of both men appeared on a second screen. She also flash-trafficked them to the Embassy Signals Department under encryption.

Bill could see Joey's eyes divert to the screen to his right as he thought out loud. "Irish priest out of Boston; Cheryl, who from my staff is there?" Joey said.

"Hal!" She called out to Hal Unger, Joey's assistant, bent over next to her to get into the picture.

Joey saw him. "Hal, good. Check with Boston P.D., Interpol, and Scotland Yard. You are looking for any connection to the

IRA or any paramilitary group, for either of these guys that could access a tube launcher. Also get a track on the tube and tell me who made it and who had it last."

Hal left and Bill continued, "As you probably know by now, Dr. Landau was a leading researcher into the God Particle. So the priest thing is a little unsettling. I have two major theologians on the way right now, along with a papal envoy to the State Department."

"Cheryl, have Hal also check Earth Liberation Front and other environmental terrorism groups. Remember that ELF nut up in New York who was pissed off at Brookhaven National Labs?"

"Yeah, our first 'black-holer,'" Bill said. "Joey, you know what? Since you are in Europe, see if you can cop-talk to someone in security at CERN. Maybe they have a threat file."

"Good thinking. Anything else?"

"No, not at this time."

"How's little Richie handling all this?"

"He's running around with one of his toy helicopters going, boom, boom, boom."

"I guess that's good he isn't holding it in."

"I hope so. Be safe, Joey."

"You too, boss."

As the screen switched to black, Bill rolled back on his chair and re-ran the entire day's events unconsciously rubbing his seared cheek. Was he missing something or not considering some essential aspect of what could be a new wave of attacks on America and American science?

The phone rang.

"Hiccock."

"Bad news, boss."

"Kronos, I am not accepting any more bad news today; quota's filled."

"I contained as much as I could about Landau and the experiments he was advocating but a small thumbnail article got out. I'll send it to you on SCIAD, but essentially it announces the start of what they are calling the Landau Protocols next week at CERN. I took it down, but not before the blog page got 326 hits."

"Keep scrubbing the Web for any of the keywords and include this new term, 'the Landau Protocols.'"

"Already done, Hic. I'll keep you updated."

Bill knew that nothing, outside of theoretical science, was ever 100 percent, but he would have loved it if this Landau business had been totally contained. He would have to wait and see if anyone connected Landau's death to the upcoming experiments.

∞§∞

As the late afternoon sun was setting behind the blue-green hills, Bill could hear Richie and Janice laughing as they played in the pool when he passed them. The president's Camp David office was rustic and had none of the intimidation of the Oval Office, which was purposefully designed without corners to disorient visiting heads of state and favor no domestic direction as to North, South, East or West. Here the soft tan leather chairs and brown and white cowhide rug made Bill think of it as an office more befitting a rich rancher or oilman.

Cheryl led the three members of the clergy in for the meeting. After the introductory pleasantries, which included Bill's request for confidentiality regarding the discussion, he got down to the heart of the matter, asking if there was any theological basis for organized resistance to particle research. Their opinions and positions narrowly steered clear of any culpability for the recent attack. Yet, Bill sensed that they didn't necessarily mourn the death of a man who was about to open the Pandora's Box that held the God Particle.

However, nothing they said was as intriguing to Bill as what the papal envoy was wearing. For the rest of the meeting Bill's thoughts were distracted by the envoy. At the end, he thanked them all for the president of the United States, reminding them of their agreement to secrecy. As they were leaving, he innocently asked the papal envoy to remain.

The bishop acquiesced. "Of course, Dr. Hiccock."

When they were alone, Bill went out on a diplomatic limb. "Your Eminence, I am not a diplomat, but would you mind speaking off the record with me?"

"It has been my experience that nothing in Washington is ever off the record."

"Does here in the Maryland countryside count?" Bill tried a smile, but the Prince of the Church wasn't cutting him any slack, so he moved on. "I advise the president of the United States, and normally I need nothing more than my scientific acumen and research, but this matter crosses a boundary between science and faith. I need your counsel on the part where I am not an expert, and I am afraid there may not be time to hash this out through normal diplomatic channels, so I ask you once again. Will you go off record with me? If you like we can draw up a non-disclosure agreement to bind both of us."

The bishop considered Bill's offer. "Are you a Catholic?"

"Not as observant as I should be, but yes."

"Then your affirmation of privacy will be all that I require, my son."

"Thank you, Your Eminence. Now again, I am not a diplomat, so please excuse me if I am a little blunt. What would the possibility be of getting a Vatican statement in favor of the research?"

The man of religion weighed the question. He tapped his fingers for a few seconds and adjusted his position in the seat. "So you feel that a papal decree will defuse some of the animus being directed toward this research?"

Bill pulled up a picture on his iPad and handed it over to the bishop. "This is why I am asking."

The bishop's eyes widened as he saw the disturbing image of the dead priest in the trailer. "Have you identified this man?"

"Unfortunately, he's one of yours."

"Does the press have this?"

"No, sir. And they never will."

"Unless I don't cooperate?" the bishop said in a matter-of-fact way.

Bill was stunned; he never meant to imply this as a threat. He was about to say, *no, no, no, that's not it,* and then he thought again.

"We are not interested in casting any suspicions on the Church. I am, however, not sure if Father Cleary acted alone or is part of a larger conspiracy. I want to make sure that there is no gray area in Church doctrine where his possible cohorts might hide."

"What you are asking for would be a departure from past practices. We don't often find ourselves bolstering the — science."

"Father, that right there! You were trying to find another word, a word more politically correct than the one you were going to use — enemy!"

"I cede your point. Bias is difficult to spot, even in one's own view of the world."

"We can go back on the record now, Your Eminence."

"Very well."

"If I were to recommend to the president that our State Department initiate talks with the Vatican, the result of which would be to create a statement which would denounce anti-scientific violence, would the Vatican be disposed to agree?"

"Absolutely not."

Bill was thrown a bit. Had he misjudged the man?

"I do believe there may be some meeting of the minds as to whether or not this kind of research is in concert with Vaticanum Secundum."

"I see. The statement you are proposing doesn't recognize violence, yet the scope is limited by Vatican II, which doesn't lock the Pope into a corner. I think we could live with that."

"And you said you weren't a diplomat?"

Bill smiled; his mind was running at one hundred miles per hour because none of this was the reason he had held the bishop over. Although he had broken some diplomatic ground that could be helpful, when the bishop stood to leave, Bill felt the pressure. He purposely overreached as he accepted the Bishop's proffered hand. "Ouch, what the — " Bill retrieved his hand with a little shake.

"Sorry, my ring."

"No, my fault. That's some ring, Your Eminence." Bill continued his little play-acting by rubbing his hand.

"Yes, it can be a little dangerous."

"What is the significance of it?" Bill marveled at the ring, which looked like barbed wire, and felt like it as well.

"It is the last remnant of a very old order. I'm afraid I am rather sentimental."

"What order is that, er, was that?"

The Vatican envoy's sixth sense kicked in. "Why do you want to know?"

"I'm sorry. If it's a secret fraternity or something, I didn't mean to — "

"No, it is an antique. Rings such as this were worn by the Knights of the Sepulchre."

"So they are no more?"

"Pope Gregory disbanded them in the late 1800s."

"Well, forgive the vernacular to a man of God, but that's one hell of a ring!"

The stern patrician took the mild expletive with small exception, but noted nonetheless, "Go to church more, Dr. Hiccock."

"Thank you. Yes of course, Your Eminence."

∞§∞

"The Knights of the Order of the Holy Sepulchre of Jerusalem. Founded in the Holy Land, 1099 A.D. during the First Crusade by Godfrey I, de Bouillon, Duke of Lorraine, as a Sovereign French Military Religious Order."

"Military?" Bill noted to Marilou Delacruz, a researcher from the State Department who had been hastily ordered to Camp David as a new member of the "Camp David Task Force."

"Yes, their *raison d'être* was Class One artifact protection."

" — and Class One means?"

"Any artifact that has actually touched the body of Christ."

"Like the Shroud of Turin."

"Yes, but in their case, specifically the Ring of Thorns."

"You mean the Crown of Thorns?"

"Yes, ring or crown, either translation from the original Aramaic is correct."

Bill snapped his fingers, "That explains the ring! It wasn't barbed wire, it was the Crown of Thorns." The implication sunk in and Bill exploded out of the chair, leaving Marilou in the office.

Being in her first few hours with Wild Bill Hiccock, she just shrugged and figured that's why he was called that.

Two seconds later, Bill called out to her, "Marilou, could you come with me, please?"

A minute later, they were back in the secure conference room. Marilou sat next to Bill as the techs hooked them back up to the Embassy in Paris. While they were waiting, Bill engaged in small talk. "How long have you been at State?"

"Six years, sir."

"It's Bill. I want you to speak your mind here, no pulling punches. This ain't diplomacy, it's science. And it's even more blunt than science, it's about national security."

"Yes, sir — Bill, I understand."

"By the way, are you Catholic?"

"Yes, my father was a deacon at an R.C. church back in the Philippines before they came to America and had me. I went to Catholic school and graduated from Fordham in international treaty law."

"Listen closely, and if you want to add anything just do it, don't hold back." Bill said with a smile he had learned was a reliable personnel management tool.

Joey's and Brooke's images popped up on the monitors. Joey said, in an affected accent, "*Bonjour!*"

"Hi Brooke, Joe, this is Marilou. She is on loan from State and an expert on theological history. She has been briefed up a little bit, but she's catching it on the fly as we go."

"Welcome to the team, Marilou," Joey said.

Bill handed a yellow pad to the tech and as he placed it under a camera on a copy stand, the image appeared on a monitor next to the one with Joey and Brooke on it.

In Paris, it was on the monitor next to the one displaying the faces of Bill and Marilou. Joey immediately recognized the pencil drawing. "That's the knockers!"

"Wait, that's a kind of 'police sketch' of the ring that both Sicard and the bishop had on. What are you talking about knockers, Joe?"

"In the cellar of the Great Cathedral of Notre Dame, there are two big rings like that on these old wooden doors."

"Can you..." Bill was interrupted.

"Excuse me, but Notre Dame is where they hold the Crown of Thorns; first placed there by Saint Louis in 1239 A.D. Currently on the first Friday of the month and every Friday during Lent, they hold the Veneration of the Crown of Thorns." Marilou sheepishly looked over to Bill to see if he had meant it when he told her to speak up. Bill's smile was her signal that it was okay.

"Joey, I am starting to get a funny feeling here. Marilou, tell him about the Knights."

"The Knights of the Order of the Holy Sepulchre of Jerusalem were the guardians of the rings, or crown."

"The Knight's Chamber!" Brooke said, looking at Joey.

"What is that?" Bill asked from three thousand miles away.

"Brooke is talking about what a local priest told me they called the room behind the doors with the rings.

"And if Sicard wears the ring of the Knights and they have a chamber here at the Cathedral in Paris and now he is here..."

"Holy Shit!" Bill said. "Sorry Marilou."

"It's okay."

"Hey, what am I, chopped liver?" Brooke mildly protested.

"My apologies all around, but we could be in the middle of a lot of holy sh... stuff!"

"So we are now thinking that this man, Sicard, is a modern-day Knight of the Sepulchre?" Joey asked.

"It all seems to fit," Brooke said.

"Joey, I think you and Brooke should visit the church again and see what you can dig up. Joey? Hello." Bill was trying to break through whatever pensive fog Joey was suddenly in.

"Sorry Bill, it's just that this is getting kinda weird. I am an RCH away from placing Sicard at the murder scene of a Franciscan brother. Actually, they'd have called him a friar here in Paris back in '97."

"RCH?" Marilou asked.

"Er...that's a ...um," Joey fumbled.

Marilou looked at Bill.

"I...ah...it's a phrase meaning small amount...very small...a smidge." Bill attempted to describe it by making the smallest of space between his thumb and forefinger.

The fertile mind of the Mensa student, herself an RCH away from her doctorate, tried to detangle the code. "Real close...real close happening...real close to happening?"

"That's close enough," Joey quickly dismissed.

"Works for me," Bill was quick to add.

Brooke was laughing and felt that she as a female had the cred to explain the term, woman to woman. "Marilou, RCH stands for..."

As she described the term, born out of the construction trades as a reference to a tight fit between two things that were not just a hair's width apart, but a pubic hair — a red, female, pubic hair apart. Only she used the street vernacular c-word for vagina, which made both Bill and Joey wince.

For her part, the prim and proper Marilou Delacruz, daughter of the Filipino deacon, simply said, "That's charmingly colloquial."

∞§∞

Aboard the Carl Vinson, Bridgestone was kept separate from the Japanese crew he had rescued. However, the Japanese captain and he were in the Commander of the CVN's quarters, meeting with a CIA officer.

"Captain Toshihira, you have expressed deep gratitude and appreciation for the United States' efforts to release you and your men. Speaking for the president of the United States, we are glad you are safe. Now I must ask you to help us save future crews and captives of pirates and terrorists around the world," the CIA officer said.

"Of course, I would consider it my duty."

"Good, because you will have to stick to a story that erases any involvement by this man. He is a valuable asset and as such his identity cannot be revealed."

Kasogi looked at Bridgestone in a way that said he understood.

"The story from this point forward is that the guards all fell sick because of contamination of their food, which was separate and apart from the food served you and your crew. When they were weak, you and your men overpowered them, used their radio equipment to send out a Mayday and this ship responded and air evacuated you out. You and your men will be heroes and will make much money writing your memoirs, but no one must ever know the actual story. Do you feel you can do this and order your crew to do the same?"

"This is not the military. I can order, but they are Merchant Marine. I cannot guarantee."

"Understood, but in our debriefing of your crew, in all the confusion of the rescue many were unaware of this man's role. Those who remembered him only know he was a nomadic tribesman who helped. In fact, much of the crew credits you with securing the first weapon and firing. So the story is almost complete."

Toshihira nodded, as he understood how far along the story was. "I will do as you ask; I will take our secret to my grave."

"May that be a long, long time from now," Bridge said, and then left the quarters.

Once they were alone, the intelligence agent asked, "Now, tell me about the whale."

∞§∞

Brooke and Joey were in Director Dupré's office rifling through stacks of police files, looking for any shred of evidence tying Sicard to the dead priest, or to the Knights.

"This is interesting. I can't find anything on the victim, Friar Gregory, for two years prior to his death."

"We could have a case of assumed identity here." Brooke said.

"Director Dupré, can you have your people obtain a picture of the priest prior to 1995?" Joey said.

"Agent Burrell, my staff is at your disposal. If you don't mind, dial seven-seven and ask Roland to do the search." Dupré turned to Joey. "If we are dealing with assumed identity, it can turn our investigation one hundred eighty degrees."

Brooke opened one of the old files and pulled out the coroner's picture of the victim. She went to the computer. "Roland is fast: he just e-mailed me a 1992 driver's license photo of Friar Gregory." Brooke held up the paper photo against the screen image. "Fasten your seatbelts, gentlemen. We are about to make a screaming u-turn!"

Both Joey and Dupré concurred that the dead man was not Friar Gregory. Brooke put it into words. "So it seems like this imposter could be the assassin, and Sicard was the assassin's assassin."

"And since it was a dead priest with ID on him, and the Pope was in town..." Joey started.

"And there was no trace of foul play or evidence of anything other than an accidental crushing of his larynx possibly by a fall..." Brooke added.

"Then of course, I didn't order a DNA confirmation of the priest's identity because I concluded it was a non-crime," Dupré confessed.

"That's what I would have thought also, given what you didn't know then," Joey said, then added, "This guy Percy must be a really well-trained operative to be able to cover his tracks so perfectly and not reveal his true mission."

"Sure, and if we don't follow Sicard to Paris and Joey doesn't dig up this case file, then the phony dead priest decomposes in the ground and no one is the wiser," Brooke concluded as she printed out the grainy license photo and pinned it on the corkboard they were using to see the bigger picture that was emerging.

"I will do what I should have done before and run the coroner's fingerprints of the dead imposter through our files as well as Interpol."

"Brooke, include the bureau on it too. There's no telling where this guy came from." Joey said.

"Will do. We should pull in your friend from the mosque. If Sicard killed the phony priest to stop him from killing the Pope, maybe he knows more about the plot than he let on," Brooke said as she picked up the phone to call the bureau in Washington and get the prints run through the FBI and the NCIC national fingerprint databases.

∞§∞

"Hello Joseph!"

"Joey."

"Yes, of course, how are you Joey?" Father Mercado reached down and shook Joey's hand from the altar of the grand cathedral.

"I am doing well, and you?"

"No complaints. What brings you here today? You aren't thinking of joining up are you?"

"Father, I need..."

"Joey, in the confessional or during the celebration, calling me Father is cool, but when it's just you and me talking, please call me Frank. It makes me feel like I'm home."

Joey laughed a little, "Okay, Frank. What I need is to pick your brain a little more about the Knight's Chamber and a few other things."

"Hold on, if you are here as a cop, then we can go back to Father Mercado."

"How about as a concerned citizen and Catholic?"

"This sounds serious."

"It is, my friend, and I would like you to help me on background so that I can understand things a little better."

"Give me a minute. Let's go down the street to a place on the corner. I don't want to do this in here."

"I totally understand," Joey nodded.

The challenge of sitting in a sidewalk café on the streets of Paris with a priest is that when the inevitable French girls prance down the street without the benefit of supporting undergarments, the undulating motion instinctively attracts the eye of the male. There were many 'bouncing Bettys' passing by, and Joey had to focus in on the fact that he was talking to a priest and didn't want to be obvious.

"Frank, I have to ask you if you can hold what we discuss here between us. Almost like it was confession. I don't want to put you in a dilemma, but I need to insist on discretion before I proceed."

"I will agree if there is no compulsion for me to answer something which I don't feel comfortable with."

Joey let those words sink in and tried to imagine what would trigger that but decided he'd find out soon enough. "Agreed." Joey opened a file on his iPad and showed the Paris morgue picture of Franciscan Friar Gregory, who was found dead in a stairwell of the Sofitel in '97.

"I assume he's not sleeping in this picture?"

"No, he is deceased, but it's the manner of his death that intrigues me." Joey flipped to the next image, the front page of *LeMonde*, the French paper of record, chronicling the arrival of the Pope in Paris back in 1997. "Now I know you weren't here then, but that Franciscan priest died the day before the Pope arrived."

"Actually, I was here. Not as a priest, but the Pope was here on his 'reach out to youth' initiative. A few friends and I came here to participate. How did the priest die?"

"Probably murdered, and he isn't a priest, but someone we believe was here to assassinate the Pope."

Frank now understood the weight of Joey's inquiry. "You know, Joey, the Pope was one of the reasons I answered the calling. He spoke to me and millions around the world. Who would want to kill him?"

"Frank, unfortunately, it is a long list."

"Yes, I guess I am a little tunnel-visioned there, but okay, who killed the would-be killer?"

"That's what I am trying to find out."

"How do you think I can help you figure that out?"

Joey fingered the next image onto the screen. It was Marilou's police-style sketch of the ring Sicard and the bishop wore. "Ever see this?"

"Looks like the Ring of Thorns."

"Exactly. Remember when I asked you about the room under the church?"

194 *The God Particle*

"Wow. You said you couldn't sleep a wink until you got inside. You weren't kidding, were you?"

"Well, the door knockers on the doors of the Knight's Chamber and the rings worn by the Knights of the Sepulchre are exactly the same."

"Knights. Okay I got that part but I don't follow what..."

"We believe the man who killed that assassin was wearing this ring. He is the same man I came here to Paris to find. I nearly had him, and then the French law pulled him away from me."

"So a Knight of the Sepulchre saved the Pope's life by killing his would-be assassin."

"That's our working theory thus far, so I ask you, do you know of this group or this man?" He brought up Sicard's picture.

Frank took the iPad and tilted it to avoid the glare. "You know, I think I have seen this guy."

"Remember where? When?"

Joe could see Frank thinking, "Joey, if this man saved the life of the Pope, even though I don't agree with his method, he is a hero to me. Why would I help you incarcerate him?"

"I can see your point. But I am not interested in arresting him. He is only sought as a person of interest in a completely different affair with the most critical national security implications, which I am currently trying to stop. What happened here in Paris in '97 is out of my jurisdiction. I have no interest in that."

Joey's mind immediately filled with the phrase "sin of omission," because, although what he was saying was true, he didn't bother to mention that his co-investigator, Director Dupré, would see it differently and surely stop at nothing to press for the prosecution of the murderer he had let slip through his fingers.

"Joey, I am a priest. I take confession and celebrate Mass. I am not an informer."

"Frank, I can't go into what this is all about, but this man has knowledge of threats and methods that makes him someone valuable to talk to."

"Joey, I have seen the movies. 'Talk to' can mean rendition, handing him over to some god-forsaken dungeon in some dictatorship that isn't queasy about little things like human rights."

"Whoa, Frank, don't hang that crap on me. I work for the science advisor to the president, not Attila the Hun. You are a priest, but you are also an American. I need you to remember that. Sicard might help us thwart an attack, an attack using scientific means, that could be worse than one hundred 9/11s."

"Do I have your word then Joey, as a man, and as a Catholic to a priest, that if I help you, Sicard will not suddenly disappear?"

Joey didn't know if he could guarantee that. After all, he didn't know the depth of complicity Sicard might have had in Maguambi's whale tale. "Frank, I cannot grant a pardon. I mean, I don't know how clean Sicard is, but I can promise you this: if his involvement is purely academic and he hasn't compromised any national security secrets, then yeah, he talks and then he walks, free as a bird."

∞§∞

Frank took a minute. He looked across the street at the citizens and tourists going about their day. He focused on a young girl and her mother, who reminded him of his sister and his niece, back in Philly, back in the USA. Joey was in some way protecting them as well. "Okay, I have seen him at the church. He takes a special confession; he goes to only one particular priest, never to any of the rest of us.."

"The priest that takes the confession, what's his name?"

"Monsignor. Monsignor Mancuso."

"When can I speak to him?"

"Tomorrow."

∞§∞

Joey sat back, took a sip of espresso and looked across the street at the chocolate shop with the pink awning. *Maybe I should get some for Phyllis?* It was the first normal thought he'd had in a long time. Now that he had connected Sicard to the Monsignor, it was only a matter of time until the rest of the pieces fell together, not only in the whale case, but possibly in the shoot-down of the chopper as well. *Maybe a big, like two-pound, box of chocolates.*

∞§∞

A full company of Marines was now bivouacked in the woods surrounding Camp David. All two hundred men had one purpose: stop any shoulder-launched missile from inter-rupting any future helicopter flights. All of which made Bill feel better as he boarded the chopper on the charred and scarred tarmac of the helipad for a quick visit to the CIA in Alexandria.

The hastily arranged conference included the head of Homeland, director of National Intelligence, the DCI of the CIA and the general in charge of DIA. It was the Defense Intelligence Agency that had the skin in the game with the attack of the USS *Nebraska*. Everyone else was there because the Commander-In-Chief was involved and none of them could risk being on his bad side. After all, the president could cut their funding and they would all be looking for new jobs.

Bill relayed what he knew and reported on what he thought. The various heads all offered their agencies' services and promised operational plans to Hiccock by 5 p.m. Bill had circulated the picture of Sicard to all in attendance, to be fil-tered through their networks of spooks and sources in the hope it would ring some bells.

As he was leaving the meeting, a man approached him and said, "Excuse me, sir. You dropped this," and handed Bill a folded piece of paper.

"Bill said, "Thank you," and continued walking as he unfolded the paper. It had three words: Washington Monument — Klaven. He turned, but the man was gone. Bill turned to his secret service man, Moskowitz, and said, "Steve, hold the chopper. I need a car to get me to the National Mall ASAP."

"Yes, sir." Steve called control and ordered a service car.

∞§∞

As they approached the Mall, Bill had a heart-to-heart with Steve. "I need you to give me at least five hundred yards here."

"I can't agree to that, sir. You are my responsibility."

"Steve, I get all that, but I have to meet with someone who doesn't like to be known — by anyone. He won't meet me if he senses any kind of surveillance."

"I am qualified at fifty yards. I can give you that, but if he sneezes wrong, I will drop him."

"I guess I'll take fifty, when you put it that way."

Bill left the car and walked from the World War II Memorial across Seventeenth to the base of the monument.

A young boy walked up to him and handed him a throw-away phone. "A man gave me five dollars to give this to you."

"Thanks, kid." Five seconds later, the phone rang, "Clay? Where are you?"

"The monument is on high ground. I saw you and your nursemaid from three hundred yards off."

"I'm sorry about that; it's his job and I can't stop him."

"There's a bench next to a trash can with an umbrella in it."

Bill walked for a minute and sat on the bench. The phone rang again. "Taped under the bench." Bill retrieved a yellow envelope and opened it. He was shocked to see a picture of Sicard and a CIA dossier.

"You keep surprising me!" Bill said, shaking his head.

"As far as the company is concerned, this guy went rogue back in 2001."

"So, his death in Lebanon in 1996 was actually his graduation to the spook house?" Bill reviewed the dossier.

"Yes, but then *we* lost him. I understand you are looking for him. Can I ask why?"

"Because he walked into my office last week and knew things only the president and I should know — and of course, you."

"He may have been turned." Klaven spoke into his phone thirty-five feet away from Bill's back.

"Wait, you said rogue? You mean the Russians or Chinese?"

"There are other ways for an operative to turn."

"Look, Clay, why not save me a whole lot of time and a few mini-heart attacks with you jumping out at me from every bush, and just tell me who he is, what he's doing and who he's working for."

"Sorry, Bill, I just don't know that."

"Stunning confession from you, Mr. Ultra Spook."

"No need to get petty, here. How did you make out with the scrambled eggs?"

"After I did a little homework, they suddenly backed off from the big number and came in at about one hundred twenty mil."

"Oh, I would have loved to hear that discussion at Navy."

"Hey, Clay, thanks for all your help. Do you need anything from me?"

"I'll take a chit, payable someday!"

"Your credit is always good here."

"Take care, SciAD!"

"You too, Clay."

∞§∞

Bill looked at his watch and decided to use the car to go home and get a few things he and Janice needed during their extended stay at Camp David. He informed Steve of this new plan and asked him to hold the chopper a little longer at the CIA.

Bill entered his house and went to the bedroom. He started going through the list of things he and Janice had talked about wanting. He couldn't remember if it was her red outfit or the coral one, but the phone rang as he was reaching for it to call her.

"Hello?"

"Bling!"

Bill knew the code word instantly. It was Bridgestone. He and Ross had used it during the Hammer of God operation to positively identify themselves and confirm that what followed was not being transmitted under duress.

"Well, hello my friend. I just kinda met with an old Navy buddy of yours."

"We'll have to finish that one on a secure line, Dr. Hiccock."

"Right you are. What can I do for you?"

"A little bird told me you had a sudden interest in whales."

Two minutes later, Bill was on his secure phone to the U.S. Embassy in Paris. "Brooke, I need you back in Washington tomorrow."

"What's up, boss?"

"We might be able to clear the Navy captain who saved your life."

Brooke's face lit up. She started packing as she called Joey in his room, but he wasn't there so she left a message.

∞§∞

The residence of the Cardinal of Paris was opulent. Although the man himself was in Rome, his staff was more than attentive to Joey and Father Mercado. The Monsignor had picked this spot for its privacy.

Joey noticed the now familiar 'ring of thorns' on the finger of the septuagenarian's liver-spotted hand. "Thank you for seeing me on such short notice, Monsignor."

"I won't know if I can help you in your quest until I know what your intention is."

"First off, I am not interested in anything of a criminal or illegal nature, if any were to exist. I am here to speak to Mr. Sicard because he has come into some information that could greatly aid the United States and all free nations of the world in the fight against tyranny."

"Are you a Catholic, Mr. Palumbo?"

"Yes."

"Are you an American or a Catholic first?"

"With respect, they are two separate things. One is who I am and the other is what I believe."

"So, you are not a man of ideals?"

"Politically, my ideals are those of the Bill of Rights, the Constitution, and the Republic. Spiritually, my ideals are those of Jesus and the Holy Roman Church. Again, I see them as separate."

"Is not America a Christian country?"

"It is based on Judeo-Christian ethics, but there is no national religion. God is apart from any one religion, but he is recognized as the grantor of certain rights, which no man or government can take away."

"Do you believe that Jesus is the Son of God?" As he leaned forward, the cross dangling from his neck hit the table's edge.

"Again, with respect, I already went through Confirmation. I don't see how this will be relevant to why I am here." Joey was restraining his annoyance.

"There are loyalties that go beyond politics or nationalism," the old man said.

"There is no loyalty that trumps the law." Joey was resolute.

"But you believe in God's law. So, if man's law contradicts God's law, what side are you going to align with?"

"In my country, because we acknowledge that there is a God and affirm that our basic rights come from him, our laws strive to be consistent with God. Therefore I see no conflict. Again, I didn't come here to have a theological discussion in the abstract. Do you plan to help me find Sicard or not?"

"Abortion is legal in America. How do you reconcile that with the law of God?"

"I don't see what that has to do with..."

"Indulge me, please," the Monseigneur said, as sweetly as a grandfather asking for another piece of cherry pie.

Joey resisted the urge to utter, *Oy.* "Okay, abortion is legal because of judicial fiat. It is not in our constitution and the whole issue is still a matter of much debate. In time, America may go another way. But yes, in that instance it is not God's law. But it is the will of the people and God gave the people not only will, but the gift to exercise that will."

"Everything you said then is irrelevant because you can arrest a priest who obstructs an abortion."

"Look, where are you going with this? Am I wasting my time here?"

"I will not help you. I find you to be not of a proper Catholic mind."

Joey went where he didn't want to go. "If that's your final answer, then I am going to have to ask you where you got that ring."

The Monsignor glanced down but remained silent.

"The Knights of the Sepulchre; you wear the ring and so does Sicard. Therefore, I will consider you a hostile witness, and I thank you for wasting my time. I'll show myself out, come on, Frank. "

The Monsignor turned as Joey was walking out. "How do you know of the Knights?"

"I think we are finished here. And based on your lack of cooperation, I intend to make sure the Knights are finished as well."

Joey had reached the street before Father Mercado caught up with him. "That was really intense."

Joey stopped and turned. "Look, Frank. Maybe you didn't get what just happened in there, but a technical state of war now exists between the United States and the Knights; and you are in the wrong uniform."

"That's a little dramatic, isn't it?"

"I am going to rain a shit-storm of American law down on him, the Knights, and the Pope if I have to. That man went too far in questioning my faith when he's the one hiding something that could get people killed. So, you better unhook from me, Frank, or get splattered with the mess I am going to make."

Joey stormed off down the street leaving Frank shocked. His mind reeled with the dilemma he faced. He also thought the Monsignor had been out of line, but to say that out loud would surely mean he'd wind up in some dirt-floored hovel, teaching scripture to Aborigines a thousand miles from a telephone. He would have had no problem with that assignment when he was a young priest, but after Paris — it gave him pause. Frank watched Joey turn the corner; then looked back at the residence, then back to the corner, and finally capitulated to his religion and walked back to the residence.

Joey's cell phone rang. It was Bill. "Joey, I got a little present waiting for you when you get back to the embassy."

∞§∞

Joey entered the Secure Conference room at the American embassy in Paris, which had become his and Brooke's de facto office.

Brooke was shaking her head as she reviewed the scanned documents on the large monitor in front of her. "Joey, between us we got forty years of investigative experience. How does Hiccock the science guy do this? Look at what he sent us."

Joey's jaw dropped, because on the screen was the CIA dossier on Sicard. "Son of a bitch, he was a spook?"

"'Was' being the operative word. Looks like he went rogue after the Beirut bombings."

As the images scrolled, it was clear he was no Lloyds of London insurance salesman. "This guy has black ops methods and training. Where did Bill get this?"

"Someone named Clay. Do you know him?"

Joey smiled. "I only know his reputation, and I can see it wasn't exaggerated. Brooke, can you boil all this down into some usable intel?"

"Actually, Joey, I was ordered back to Washington. I delayed my flight when this came in."

"What's back in Washington?"

"Naval Board of Inquiry into Mush...Captain Morton's whale episode."

"Going to put on your old JAG insignia?"

"No, but I am a witness and I can bird-dog the defense and make sure they aren't missing something. How did it go with the Monsignor?"

"Infuriating. We could be on the verge of a diplomatic war between the Vatican and Uncle Sam."

"He wouldn't give up Sicard?"

"He wouldn't give up the ghost," Joey said, noting that the document now on the screen was a scan of Parnell Sicard's death certificate.

∞§∞

Maybe it was because he was also an American, or maybe because of the way the Monsignor insulted Joey, but Father Frank Mercado of the Paris Diocese was a little less enamored with his immediate superior. Halfway back to the residence, he turned and went to back to his church instead. As he sat in the Great Cathedral he prayed to Saint Sophia for wisdom.

Afterward, he walked down the Left Bank of the River Seine. He watched long, low-slung dinner boats glide under bridges adorned with gold-clad statuettes. Tourists breezed along the cobblestones, while above the beam of light from atop the Eiffel Tower arced across the night sky. He liked Joey. He didn't see him as a cop, but more as a kid in the church. Frank liked the way Joey was reverential to the church, yet respectful in his career choice away from the calling to service for his country. It made him wonder how the monsignor could be opposed to a man like Joey. In theology, Frank had learned that without faith as a counterbalance, people are motivated by what they fear. It was obvious Joey's fear was for his country. But the Monsignor's fear must have been more personal, and that should not be. The pious shepherd should fear nothing of his personal existence; only that of the flock! Yet...

The sound of people singing "Happy Birthday" rolled over the water and echoed off the stone walls of the river walk as a *bateau* slipped along the river. The half American and half heavily French accented strains, the latter obviously from the local waiters, who learned all the major language salutations of one's anniversary of birth, made Frank smile. Especially when they sang *Happy Birthday dear, Fra-ank, Happy Birthday to you.* That was the trouble with single syllable names. You have to force them to be two syllables in order to fit the music of the American "Happy Birthday." To-om, Fra-ank, Mi-ike, Su-ue. Through the curved dinner boat's sightseeing windows, he could see a candle-festooned cake being presented to a middle-aged man who, as he had done fifty or so times before, took a deep breath and blew out the candles. Although Frank couldn't hear it, he knew somebody said, *Make a wish.*

As Frank continued his contemplative walk through the Parisian night, the little refresher on America made him dwell on his birthdays and life in Philly, which became the cornerstone of a plan he would invoke tomorrow after Friday confessions.

XV. BLOOD TRUCE

Brooke had gotten permission from the East Coast inspector general to wear her uniform during the board of inquiry. This surprised her, as she was also a witness and she wondered if her uniform, with JAG insignia, would be prejudicial to the prosecution. However, she had gotten her wish and if the IG and prosecutor didn't have a problem, then it was moot.

As she walked into the BOI chamber the old rush returned. The prep for a case, the razor's edge on which a favorable decision balanced, the satisfaction of diligent research and inspiration of a strategy that ultimately wins the day, recharged her jurisprudence battery! In a little more than an hour the proceeding would begin. She picked out in her mind her seat in the gallery, where she was sure to have a direct line of sight to Mush as he sat at the defense table. She took one last look and headed for the attorneys' room.

She did a double-take as she entered the room, there he was, clean shaven in a service dress khaki uniform, hat on the table, trimmed beard, and eyes that actually seemed illuminated to her.

He smiled broadly when he turned and saw her. He stood and extended his hand. "Lieutenant Burrell, nice to see you again," his voice said, while his eyes screamed, *Girl, I've missed you.*

The look in his eyes relieved Brooke's apprehension about seeing him again and replaced it with the prickly energy of intense attraction, amplified by separation. In that one gesture, she knew her place with him was good. Now she could relax and really drill down into the case. The lead JAG officer for the defense was forty-two-year old Captain Lance Porter, who had intellectually gotten over the absurdity of a whale attack and now specifically concerned himself with preserving the career and reputation of the latest in a long line of naval heroes of the Morton clan.

Brooke broke into the conversation. "Captain Porter, I am here personally because I have a witness who could offer exculpatory evidence in Captain Morton's defense."

As expected, Porter bristled at the unexpected. "I wasn't aware of any such witness and none has been listed with the prosecution."

"I apologize for the lack of procedure, but the witness just became available and is testifying out of a top secret mission under the direct orders of the president." Brooke said.

"I see. I'll have my staff call in the prosecutor and the IG and we'll get him to testify in closed session. When is he expected?"

"Right now; he's outside."

Mush was surprised to see a Japanese merchant captain enter the room with a U.S. Navy translator.

Brooke explained the circumstances under which Captain Kasogi Toshihira came to lose his ship to pirates, his whale story and subsequent rescue by special forces, which must never be named.

Porter was dubious. "What evidence of the whale does the captain present?"

Brooke opened her briefcase and removed the print of a picture taken from the iPhone the helicopter pilot had used to pop his good-luck-shot of the whale frolicking in the wake of the huge vehicle transport. "The JDF helicopter pilot assigned to Captain Toshihira's ship took ball-camera shots of the whale, but those were lost when his aircraft was scuttled to avoid letting it fall into enemy hands. He did, however, manage to text this picture to his son, who is studying whales in school, before the ship was attacked."

Mush looked at the photo, then spoke to Toshihira, then looked at the translator. "You were attacked in the Indian Ocean?"

Toshihira didn't wait for translation, "Yes, south of Java."

That being roughly the same area of both Brooke's attack and the attack on the *Nebraska*, Mush looked to his lawyer, Porter. "That's where the Pacific meets the Indian Ocean, Lance. And not too far from our encounter."

The windfall of collaborating evidence was immediately apparent to Porter, who understood that suddenly the positive outcome of this board as it related to Mush was a certainty. More importantly, the information would quickly advance into a strategic initiative to ward off a new threat by a new weapon. "Excuse me, but I think I want the IG and prosecution in here now."

It took an hour and essentially the whole BOI took place in the lawyers' room. The IG made a pro tem decision that Mush be cleared of all charges and his record reflect that he had acted in the highest traditions of the US Navy. Then the IG called Naval Intelligence and asked them to debrief both Morton and Toshihira so that tactics and defenses might be established and communicated to all commands and ships at sea. There were handshakes all around, and soon only Mush and Kasogi were left in the room awaiting the Navy intelligence guys.

"Your English is very good!"

Kasogi nodded, "Thank you. I get most things, but certain phrases I don't understand. That's why the translator was here."

"How long have you been at sea?"

"Twenty years. And you?"

"About the same."

"Not the same. I am merchant, you are submarine!"

"True, but as merchant you are just as important to your country as I am to America."

"You are very kind, but you command an SSBN. I simply pilot a floating parking garage."

"And those missiles and boats cost my country trillions, but your boat makes money for Japan."

"I was to be a warrior, not a truck driver."

"How do you know that?"

"My grandfather; he was commander of the battleship *Musashi* during the war against the American and English Imperialists. He personally served with Yamamoto and on many occasions had the honor of bowing before the Emperor."

"You are the grandson of Rear Admiral Inoguchi Toshihira! The *Musashi* was a noble ship of the Imperial Navy. I always liked her lines better than the Yamamoto."

Kasogi was impressed. "You study the war? You know of my grandfather, and of the *Musashi*?"

"Yes, I did a paper on the War in the Pacific at Naval War College. I too had a grandfather who fought in World War Two."

That caused a light bulb to go on in Kasogi's head. "Morton — you are descended from Dudley Morton, the Commander of the Wahoo?"

It was now Mush's turn to be impressed. "Yes. I never got to meet him, so studying sub tactics and the war was a way for me to understand him, and why and how he died."

"As I remember, he was lost at sea?"

"He was on his nickel patrol, went out, just never came back."

"I am sorry, nickel?" Kasogi said.

"I apologize; slang for his fifth war patrol. In the Sea of Japan he sank four enemy, uh, Japanese ships, before the Wahoo was sunk on October 11, 1943, in La Pérouse Strait; she went down with all hands. My granddad received his fourth Navy Cross, posthumously of course, for that patrol."

"I am sorry. My grandfather died almost exactly a year later, when the *Musashi* was sunk by aircraft; over one thousand men died. They posthumously promoted him to vice admiral."

"Many men, boys actually, from both our countries died. Many didn't have the chance to have children or grandchildren," Mush said as he looked down at the table.

"Yes, we owe much to our forefathers."

"Amen, Captain Toshihira."

Mush was well aware that he was sitting across from the grandson of a man who would not have hesitated to kill his grandfather, and he knew his granddad would have risked all to put two or three fish into the Jap battlewagon. Given the same situation, if he and Kasogi had met in battle, one of them would surely be dead. Yet here they were, speaking as brothers, in reverence of men whose blood and dedication they shared, understanding the ideals by which their antecedents gloriously lived and died, long before they were born. As Mush wiped the thought of Kasogi as a "Jap" captain from his mind, he could only conclude, *War perverts humanity.*

The moment hung almost as a silent prayer; then Kasogi the 'truck driver' noted, "Still I envy you to be the commander of a nuclear submarine."

Mush finally relented. "Yeah, it's a pretty sweet command."

Brooke entered the room, and the energy shifted from the two offspring of mortal enemies brought together by a new, common enemy. "The Intelligence guys will be here in twenty minutes."

"Where is the bathroom?" Kasogi asked.

"Left, then a left," Mush said.

Kasogi exited and Brooke looked at Mush. "How have you been, Mush?"

"Better now! I seem to have gotten a clean bill of mental health and I am five feet from you."

Brooke closed the door. "That's too far." She walked toward him as he stood. They embraced and did what could best be described as a Hollywood kiss. Every sleepless night, every longing sigh over the memory of each other's faces, bodies, and smells was squeezed out from between them, leaving them both enwined in each other's contours. After the longest kiss of her life, Brooke rested her head on the shoulder-board of his dress khakis and breathed deeply. "How long do we have?"

"Depends if he drank a lot or..."

"No, silly, I mean us."

"A week."

"Mmmmm a week! I can work with that." She nestled in tighter.

She pulled and back touched his jaw, "You shaved! I like it."

"Yeah, no sense giving the judges something to bitch about."

They hazarded one more kiss and then reluctantly separated, lest they shock Toshihira upon his return, which happened seconds after they released one another.

∞§∞

After Bill spoke with Joey, he started to consider things he had never dwelled on before. He always thought church was a local thing. Although he was aware of the Pope and Rome, somehow he had never really connected the Pontiff to the local priests, other than as a figurehead. Now a new and somewhat more sinister, if that was the right word, configuration was forming. To that end he asked Marilou to enlighten him on what was becoming the opposing team.

"So Marilou, I want you to take the position of a zealot, a fanatic. I want you to help me understand what I might be dealing with here."

"I understand."

"Good. Okay, first question: why would the Knights be operational instead of just ceremonial?"

"The artifacts could be considered the riches of the Church, with their monetary value unfathomable, but their spiritual significance at the heart of Christianity. Rome would go to war to keep them."

"Actual war?"

"Yes. The Church is very capable of this. Look at the history: the Inquisition, the brutal Holy Wars, death on a grand scale.

"But those conflicts and victories all pre-date the modern era and the current Pope."

"True, but the power to declare holy war still resides in the Papacy today."

"The world is much different now," Bill said.

"Only to you newcomers. We have a long lineage that dwarfs any modern government. The papal realm preceded British royalty by almost nine hundred years. Even the office of president of the US has only been on the world's stage for some two hundred-plus years. Popes go back almost twenty centuries, to 33 AD."

"So then, to Rome we are just the upstarts; they never conceded world control. They just let the world be, as long as it didn't bother them," Bill said.

"Again, I am speaking in the role of a zealot, but the reason the Roman ruins and remnants of the Caesars have never been touched, left right where they fell, is because the Church wants all who see them never to forget that they won and the pagans, with their mighty edifices, lost."

"Thanks Marilou, you've given me a lot to think about."

∞§∞

At 7 p.m., Brooke was getting dressed. At 8 p.m., Brooke was still getting dressed. She and Mush were only two floors apart at the Washington Marriot.

The phone rang. "Should I swing by and pick you up?"

Brooke was nowhere near ready, and in fact she was in the middle of her fourth outfit change. She was about to say, "Give me a half-hour more," when she caught sight of herself in the mirror. She still had the new boots on, but had removed her dress. Looking at herself she said, "Yes, I'm ready. Come get me."

She ran to the bathroom and checked her makeup. She gave the hair one more brush, checked her teeth for lipstick smear, gave herself one more look over, and headed for the door. On the way she tenuously reached for the hotel robe. As she held it in her hand, she considered it and then placed it back on the bed. At three steps from the door, she turned to retrieve it. There was a knock, she started to put it on, but then carried it to the door. She thought to check the peephole lest she give some poor bellboy a very wrong message. Even distorted by the fisheye lens of the peephole, Mush looked good. She breathed in and went for it.

∞§∞

Mush had his hat in his hand and was fingering the brim. When the door swung open, he was walloped with a thud of invisible energy that literally knocked the air out of him. The hat hit the floor. It took a half a second, but he managed to shut his mouth and put his eyes back in their sockets. Standing before him was the object of many nights of desire. His circuits overloaded as he took her in, in her lacy black bra, panties, and tall boots with giant heels. She was pure sex. The epitome of every male fantasy he had ever dared dabble in. Her physique was cut but not bulky, her curves were perfect and the shape of her legs and tapered thighs just invited him to explore — but instead he stepped into the room, shut the door with his foot, grabbed the robe, and draped it around her. "We need to talk."

∞§∞

Brooke's heart immediately stopped. *Oh, God, he is married. Shit!* Then just as fast and to her amazement, *I don't care I want him, now!* Although she had just been embarrassed to the depth of her soul, his eyes were soft and kind, and devoid of any negativity. They actually soothed her, even though in her mind she was melting down. *How could I have been so stupid? I blew this.*

He grabbed her by her robe covered shoulders and in a slow motion she focused on his lips as he started to speak.

"Brooke, I can't believe I am about to say this. It could be grounds for kicking me out of this man's Navy."

Oh no, he's pulling rank? Fraternization? "What do you mean?"

"There ain't a sailor on earth who would stop what we both want to have happen right now. But..."

"But what, Mush?"

"Have you thought this through? You are not just some girl. I can't and I don't want to be casual with you. Things that start fast don't last."

Brooke started to speak, "I ..."

He placed his finger on her lips. "This is hard enough, let me get it out before I give in. Brooke, I am sworn to duty, a job that takes me away half the year. I am stationed seven thousand miles away. The Navy has spent tens of millions training me, nearly half of that on evaluating me before they let me cruise around the ocean with twenty-four ICBMs. My hitch isn't up for five years, Brooke. I have been able to do it for the last twenty because I didn't know anyone like you. I still don't really know you — "

Brooke had an impulse to jump in, he was distancing himself, committing self-quarantine as if she were a disease infecting his life. She was on the verge of feeling awful, her stomach started churning; she felt the blood warming her ears. She held her tongue. She thought he had finished.

" — except that I can't stop seeing you everywhere on the boat. I swear, sometimes when I am in my bunk, I can still smell you. Being a love-bitten, horny teenager isn't a good career move for a fleet-boat captain with nuclear-release authority, you know what I mean? "

She melted into his arms. He held her. "Oh, Mush. We are both committed, but how many chances like this are we going to get in this life to have everything we want in one person."

"Brooke, intellectually, I was hoping you would agree with me..."

Ice started to form around his tone. Brooke was suddenly aware she was clinging to him like the lifeboat in the ocean. He placed his hands on her shoulders and separated them enough to see her eyes, "...but, God, how I was praying you felt the same as I do."

They kissed, a long, deep kiss. Neither pulled away; they just kept adjusting their embrace, getting closer and closer, contouring into each other more and more. It seemed like it lasted for five full minutes until each started to involuntarily laugh through the kiss. Finally, they came up for air.

"Aren't we supposed to be above this? Isn't this too normal for our jobs?" Mush said.

"You mean, if we weren't working for the government..."

"We'd be on a beach somewhere..."

"A secluded beach..." She said as she pulled him in for another long, deep kiss.

∞§∞

In the morning, the hotel's housekeeper was confused. Her rules of engagement were clear and based on whether the dangling doorknob card requested privacy or maid service. She didn't know what this meant. Sometime during the night, a passerby had hung the captain's hat over the doorknob to the room. She was about to knock when a passing Air Force major advised her, "I wouldn't disturb the man, miss."

∞§∞

Raffey had lost fifteen pounds from his already wiry frame and he was beginning to look emaciated. The hopelessness of his reality reared up into a shuddering series of anxiety attacks, as he found no safe harbor for his thoughts. There was no good side, no peaceful thought upon which he could land safely, and he fought hard not to spasm again. His best defense was the avoidance of thought. That avoidance was easier when his mind focused on work. At the lab, with its many distractions, he had fewer episodes; every hour though, he focused on what it was they were going to ask him to do. His worst nightmare was that the people who took his sister and niece didn't have a political or religious rationale in their desire to cause a calamity at the site, but simply wanted to start Armageddon; the destruction of everything, for some unfathomable reason.

He was tortured with conflicting emotions, one moment wanting to flee and keep running ahead of the screams and horrors they would inflict on his sister Leena and his niece Kirsi and another moment he would decide to play along and help them destroy the machine. Today his mind quickly went to the third extreme. If they were in it to destroy creation, then everyone, everything, was dead, including Leena and Kirsi. So what was the point? Suddenly the path became more clear. He now had a decision point, and his logical, organized, engineering mind was able to crystallize a plan of action. If they were just interested in disabling the machine, he'd play along. If their goal was the end of all, then he'd kill himself, and seal the fate of his loved ones. But the math worked. Three dead in exchange for all that ever existed or would exist, for all of for-ever! It was as if someone had opened a window in a stifling room. He suddenly inhaled and exhaled as a free man. He had his operational model.

XVI. BEANTOWN BUST

Bill was taking a Special Air Missions flight from Dulles to Logan so he could be there when the ATF busted the South of Roxbury branch of the Knights of the Sepulchre.

The State Department was totally against this raid; their thinking was that the Vatican should be notified prior. Bill vetoed that idea and had to pull rank by invoking his presidentially bestowed authority as head of all of the Homeland Security departments. It also didn't hurt that the President had backed Hiccock's position, agreeing that the Vatican might be compromised by zealots with sympathy for the late Father Cleary's cause.

The operation had been green-lighted by Bill only twenty-four hours before. Here is where countless exercises by ATF in conjunction with state and local police paid off. Giving him "off the shelf" options with which to fill in the operational gaps in the hastily hatched plan.

The location was the Dublin Pub, a tourist trap, long forgotten by the Boston Convention and Visitor's bureau and apparently a few health inspectors. No doubt, its Teflon shield was buttressed by the expatriate Irish community's deep inroads into Boston politics. For that reason, Bill insisted on a cover story to be used to all local and state resources employed in the raid. One block away was a check-cashing store. Bill quickly got the IRS, through Treasury, to claim that the honest business was a money-laundering ring to Bolivian drug lords. The BPD and Massachusetts State cops were not told that the actual target was the Dublin Pub. In fact, until the evening roll call, nobody in Boston knew there was even a raid planned for the check-cashing joint.

As he waited in an up-armored SUV three blocks from the pub, he wished he had Joey by his side. This field stuff was Joey's happy place. Bill's mind went back to last weekend and the corporal who had been glad to take little Richie under his wing in an effort to stave off the separation anxiety he was feeling over his own son. The fact that Corporal Bradley was dead only an hour later still stung Bill.

He looked at the Secret Service agents and members of the FBI HRT as they prepped and went over the takedown details for the twentieth and final time. *Do any of these agents or Hostage Rescue Team members have kids? Of course they do*, he thought as he reached around and patted the Glock he'd been carrying for a few months now. Although his protective detail hated the idea of another gun in the mix, a gun carried by an amateur to boot, he had promised only to carry it in situations like this. If President Mitchell decided to show up on a whim, either his head of detail or Bill's own, would ask that he surrender his weapon until the president was no longer in the area. That was okay with him. So although it rubbed most security types the wrong way and was against their instincts, Hiccock was strapped.

Bill had never felt the macho impulse for a gun. However, along with the resolve that no one was going to force his son to grow up without a dad came the need for Bill to have a chance to vote against it — fifteen votes with a full magazine!

The agent in charge appeared at the rear window of the war wagon Bill was sitting in. Bill lowered his bulletproof window.

"We go in one minute, sir! You are requested to stay at least two hundred feet back from the operation, sir."

"Agent Simms."

"Yes sir?"

"You married, got kids?"

"Er... yes, two girls..."

"Be careful, okay?"

Simms didn't know how to respond; he didn't expect that kind of sentiment from a superior. "We are all going to get home tonight, sir. Good men, well trained and well-armed." He left to lead the assault.

Boston Public Works employees and phone men stood at key points in the circuitry, with a federal agent on a walkie-talkie ready to cue them when to pull the plug and ditch the phones. A vehicle with a special transmitter similar to those used in Iraq to block cell-phone-activated bombs would start blocking all cell phone signals on cue.

As Bill's vehicle rolled up to his safe perch seventy-five yards from the pub, he watched as the two-man assault teams started from each end of the block, sweeping all civilians and securing all building entrances and in general making sure no members of the public could be caught in the line of fire. Also locking down the street insured that none of the citizens would tip off the men who, if the confidential informant to FBI was right, were having a meeting inside the pub to plan their next moves.

As the lead men advanced, local BPD took their places securing those doorways and civilians. The lead guys with the battering rams hit the doors of the pub hard. Five helmeted men went through the door, shouting commands. Forty-five seconds later, agents in suits went in. To Bill, this was a good sign. These were the guys who would collect the evidence and interrogate the people inside, and they would have only gone in once the bar was secure and everybody safe. They would set up a legal triage so the next move could be planned instantaneously.

Bill opened his door and stepped out into the damp night air coming off the bay. His driver had already exited and run to the doorway. Then Bill saw a third floor window open and a leg jut out, followed by a man, who causiously traversed the adjoining roof.

Bill watched, but the man never appeared at the narrow alleyway to jump across to the next roof. Bill surmised that he must have slipped down the stairway of the adjacent building. Bill ran down the alleyway next to the building, figuring the man wouldn't leave by the front door being guarded by BPD. Bill made it to the back of the building in time to see the man jumping the last eight feet from the rear fire escape ladder. Suddenly it was as if Bill were watching a movie. The Glock was in his hand and he was yelling, "Freeze!"

The man got up and was turning toward Bill.

"Freeze! Goddammit!"

But the man kept turning.

Then Bill's ear stung as someone yelled, "Freeze!" He turned while wincing to see his Secret Service man, Moskowitz, in a full military-like crouch stance, his service weapon cupped in his upturned right palm. Bill turned back to the man he was chasing who was crouched and squeezing off a round. Moskowitz's fired before that bullet hit him full in the chest. Both men went down. The secret service agent's shot found center mass and crumpled the suspect. Bill ran to the downed man and kicked away the weapon. He ran back to Moskowitz. Bill was surprised he was conscious and helped him sit up. Bill saw the small hole in his shirt, but there was no blood. *Kevlar vest,* he thought.

"You okay?"

"I'm good; stop him!"

"He's not going..." Bill turned and saw the man wobble to his feet and head for the gun. Bill took off as if he were escaping the pocket from defensive linemen, went low, and field tackled the guy. This time he pinned him down and called for help. "Hey, somebody give me a hand here!"

A BPD sergeant showed up, placed his knee on the man's back, and slapped a pair of cuffs on him. Bill went back to Moskowitz. "Looks like everybody's wearing a vest but me."

"What the hell were you doing, Hiccock?"

"I saw the guy running and no one was going after him, so..."

"There's an army of cops and Feds here; you were only here to observe," he wheezed as he tried to catch his breath. "Hell, I turn my back for a second and there you go playing High Noon with a thug." He winced through the pain that the punch of the bullet had transmitted through his vest.

"I guess 'sorry' is kind of weak, huh?"

Two EMTs came running. One checked Moskowitz while the other went to the man in the alley.

∞§∞

An hour after the take-down, Bill found himself playing the role of referee in a jurisdictional dispute in which he held all the cards: those that identified him as oversight chairman of the FBI, Secret Service, CIA, NSA, and DHS. All under the order of the president, who felt he and his authority had been ill-served by these agencies in the two previous affairs where Bill's instincts had proved to be superior to that of the heads of the agencies. Since they all worked for the Executive Branch, President Mitchell rearranged the administration's furniture, putting Bill's seat closer to his and ordering all the agencies to answer to him before Mitchell got their attention. So here he was, a professorial academic, holder of three degrees in science, no political agenda and no favor bank credits or debts to repay, in the back of a Boston pub deciding who got to interrogate the seven men rounded up in the Boston pub raid.

The Secret Service wanted first crack because the helicopter that one of the group's alleged members blew up was in their bailiwick. The FBI persuasively argued that this was domestic terrorism and totally within their mandate. Owing to the need for secrecy and to contain the entire affair because of its religious sensitivity, he decided on the Secret Service. Having made the decision, he briefed the special agent in charge and in no uncertain terms told him of the need for quick, actionable intelligence under a blanket of secrecy.

222   *The God Particle*

∞§∞

In the U.S. Embassy in Paris, when Joey received the first reports and got the gist of the Boston operation, his blood pressure began to rise. First was a feeling that he should have been there. His best friend was involved in a shootout while he was sitting behind a desk in France. Second was the upward pressure that was being exerted on him from the Bureau's Boston office due to Bill's decision to make Treasury the lead agency over the FBI. It was still Joey's alma mater, albeit one that had jettisoned him from its active-duty ranks for his display of loyalty to Bill during the Eighth Day affair. Yet he was still a product of Quantico and the Bureau was in his blood, so it was with a sympathetic ear that Joey listened as the special agent in charge of the Boston office relayed to him that Joey's new boss, Bill, had given them the cold shoulder on the investigation into the chopper shoot-down. Joey listened, but steered clear of agreement with the SAC of the Boston office, but commiserated nonetheless.

Now, Joey was about to meet with Father Mercado, so he put the Boston op behind him and wondered why Frank the priest had asked for this meeting.

One of the embassy staff led in the priest, who, to Joey, seemed overwhelmed.

"Father Mercado, it's good to see you. Are you okay?"

"I must have gone through five security checks."

"Sorry about that; I should have escorted you in myself. My apologies."

"Mr. Palumbo..."

"Joey!"

"Joey, I know you are a government representative and your allegiance is to Uncle Sam, but I need you to talk to your superiors."

"My superiors? They pay me to listen, not talk."

"You know, back in Philly, and I'm sure it was like this in the Bronx, when the baseball cards came out, we'd flip 'em and the winner would take all the cards. But if the next card up was a Pete Rose, you panicked, because you could trade the whole rest of the team for one Pete Rose card."

"I once had five Mickey Mantles and later three Reggie Jacksons! I was the king of 213th Street."

"So if a Mantle came up, would you flip it? No, too big of a risk, right?"

"Yeah, sure, but where's this going, Frank?"

"I am no scientist; heck I'm in the anti-science uniform," he pulled at his black shirt, "but the stakes here are the highest ever. If your science men are wrong, then everything, all creation, is gone. The Church is not willing to take that big of a risk with God's creation. Why is your government willing to flip all the cards?"

"Frank, I can't answer that. But my friend, my boss, Hiccock, he is as good a man as I have ever met. I don't think he'd walk us all off a cliff to oblivion. I know he would seek every assurance that each step was safe."

"Joey, your man Hiccock may be a virtuous and inscrutable man, but in the end he is just a man. Fallible and unaware of God's plan, as are we all. And the same is true of whomever he would get these assurances from. Joey, your greatest military commanders, all the armies and planes and bombs you could ever amass, can be wiped out by one tsunami. An earthquake can render a nuclear plant a radioactive catastrophe. All of the accomplishments of man pale in comparison to God's power and that which he gave to the earth, the planets and the universe."

"No argument from me."

"Then you have to realize the United States government is talking about allowing a small group of people to take a flip on all the cards that exist. Every living thing on earth is at the mercy of this decision, with no ability to object or even understand the power that might be unleashed. Is it right for just a few people to sign the potential death warrant of seven billion people, not to mention the untold trillions yet to be born?"

Out of reflex, Joey was about to speak, but didn't know how to respond. The priest made some sense. What gave the president, Bill, and an egghead scientist the right to risk the lives of every living thing on earth on a scientific bet?

∞§∞

Bill's G5 was late leaving Logan. He had delayed the flight so he could transport the two leaders of the Boston cell to D.C., to give the FBI, CIA and NSA a crack at them. It was a small sign of contrition from Bill, after the blistering phone call he had gotten from his friend, Joey. When Bill interviewed the leaders on the plane, he came to understand that they were convinced the government was acting in direct opposition to God. Unfortunately, he was not able to discern where their counterpart who blew up the chopper got the shoulder-fired missile, but suspected the various agencies would connect the dots in short order.

He was met at the airport by a replacement driver, since Steve Moskowitz was being held for observation at Massachusetts General overnight. Although the bullet had been stopped by his Kevlar vest, a blood clot arising from the deep bruising caused by the impact of the bullet was always a concern. Bill remained silent for the forty-minute trip through Maclean, past the CIA to his home. As he emerged from the car, he took a long moment to just look at his house. It looked like a postcard, with the bluish cast on the house from the moonlight, the reddish glow from the downstairs den light filtering through the sheer curtains, and the whole scene set against a starry night backdrop. He walked toward the front door, grabbed Richie's toy fire engine off the lawn, and brought it into the house.

He tiptoed in well after 11 p.m. and went right to Richie's room. He placed the toy on top of the Star Wars toy chest and stood looking at his sleeping son. In the crack of hallway light coming through the door ajar, he studied the little boy's features. He had never realized how long his eyelashes were; how he had the beginnings of a well-defined jaw line emerging from baby fat. He got real close, stroked his son's head, and spoke in low tones. "You father did something really stupid today, son. I acted without thinking. I didn't think of you or your mom. I'm sorry. I'm sorry, son." He lingered a bit longer, then bent over and kissed the boy's forehead, breathing in a hint of baby powder. He backed away and silently closed the door.

∞§∞

Joey didn't sleep all night, as he couldn't heal the rip down the middle of his brain between his duty to country and his obligation to humanity. The rift was freshly revealed because up until now he hadn't doubted for a minute that his duty and humanity were one and the same. Suddenly, science was emerging as the perpetrator-in-waiting of a potential crime, and he worked for science guy number one. But Bill was also his best friend. They had grown up together, and Bill had saved his bacon when Joe's sense of right and wrong got him on the bad side of the FBI director. Plus a million other things that friends consciously and unconsciously do for one another. No matter how much he turned and tried to rinse his brain, the dilemma was inescapable. He finally found peace at 4:30 a.m. when he remembered that the first thing he had done upon entering the Cathedral at Notre Dame was to pray for, among other things, guidance in the work he and Bill were doing. Next thing he knew there was Father Frank Mercado preparing mass and engaging him on the priesthood and choices in life. Could it be? The tantalizing nature of the situation also brought calm and allowed him to settle on a plan.

∞§∞

There was a stain on her uniform skirt. *Damn it*. She went to the hall closet and pulled out a duffle bag that had rested undisturbed in the corner of the closet for nine years. The smell of mothballs brought thoughts of her mom front and center. If her mother were here now, she'd know. She'd break right through Brooke's gung-ho attitude and disarm her with soft words like, "What's the worry on your mind, dear?" Brooke knew she would reflexively answer, "Nothing." But Mom would go right by that, right to the heart of the matter, as she always could. Brooke heard the internal dialogue in her head as she gave in to the only person she could never defend against. Her mom knew her and still saw her as a ten year old, as though she never survived high school, college, her training at Quantico, and the Survive, Evade, Resist, Escape course at Fort Bragg.

"*I am not crazy about going back to the Indian Ocean, okay?*"

"*I know, dear,*" she could hear her mom say. "*You are afraid.*"

"*No, Mom, I'm not...*"

She couldn't lie to her mother, even when her mother wasn't there.

She was afraid. In a recurring nightmare, the sharks were out there, circling, waiting for her, the one that got away.

She unhooked the clip and opened the top of the bag. She pulled out all her old dress shirts and dug down deeper through the khaki slacks and finally got to three skirts. She examined them quickly, eliminated the one with the pull, and weighed the two she now held in her hands. The one in her right seemed fresher; she placed the other in the suitcase next to the Navy regulation shoes. She closed it, hauled it off the bed, and rested it by the front door. On a hanger on the hook over the door, she hung the newly dug out skirt next to her uniform blouse with her cap resting on top.

It had been a while since she deployed on a Navy ship. *I'll be on a Navy ship. I won't be alone — like last time.* She found reassurance in that last thought, then struck the entire conversation from her mind as she decided to open the suitcase again to hit the shoes with the shine cloth one more time and run an iron over the skirt. *Be Neat, Be Clean, Be Navy.*

XVII. LITTLE CHICK

Brooke had never been too bothered by seasickness, but tonight was woozily different. She had choppered out to a U.S. sub tender in the Indian Ocean and then transferred by launch to a commercial fishing trawler. Although sailing under a Japanese flag, it was actually a U.S. Naval command and control ship, under the helm of Commander A.E. Randell.

Below deck in the operations hub of the boat, a whole lot of equipment including sonar, radar, satellite, and something called VLF was being used to track the progress of an ancient atomic-powered submarine. It was one of the first and was now deeper than deep and dispatching a deep-sea submersible to the site of the ship Brooke had been blown off of two months before. There were live video streams from the submersible on one of the screens in the hub. "Commander, how sure are we that we are in the right area?" Brooke said.

"The *Halibut*'s magnetometers have indicated a high deviation in this sector, and as best as can be reckoned from maritime logs, no recent shipwrecks besides yours happened here. Of course, it could be some non-recorded wreck or from a time before they kept such records." Commander Randell said.

"That blip on the radar?"

"That's target designate 'Lana.' We know all about her; she's a Russian trawler not unlike us. We figure it's a good sign, 'cause it means the Russians think this is the area also."

"How do you know the Russian captain isn't saying the same thing about you?"

"That's the rub. You live and die by what you think the enemy knows about you, until somebody fires a torpedo up your a... rudder. That's when you'll know he said *exactly* what I said. Besides, the Russians have been using trawlers since the '50s. We aren't known for using a boat like this, and because we have more sensitive equipment, we can be far enough off so as not to raise suspicion."

Brooke didn't look convinced. The commander turned to his chief, "Wags, show me the EE of the trawler."

Brooke watched as a cloud suddenly appeared over the blip of the trawler.

"That cloud is a representation of the boat's electronics emission, the sum total of every piece of equipment that is using electricity, plus the transmitters and receivers operating at this moment. Now, Wags, scan us."

Brooke watched as the scale expanded on the scope and the blip was joined by a new blip, which she knew was the "fishing" boat she was on. There was a small set of lines hardly noticeable.

"Our cloud is consistent with a standard ship-to-shore radio, loran radar, fish finders, and crew personal equipment like iPods, a TV or computers."

"Impressive; how do you do that?"

"PFM. The specifics are classified, but in broad strokes, every emission from this room is first shielded by Mu metal, which is a little like lead to Superman; you can't see the majority of EE through it. Then we have EE monitor/transducers on this ship. They send out exact, but oppositely phased, signals of our emissions, in effect canceling out each and every wavelength that might escape from this room."

Brooke was aware that the Navy term PFM stood for "pure fucking magic," and after his explanation she agreed it was. "So that is what the Russians see electronically when they look at us?"

"As far as they know, a bunch of Japanese fisherman on this here boat are watching sumo wrestling right now."

∞§∞

Deep below the Indian Ocean, eighty-five hundred yards off from the Russian trawler and fifteen thousand yards from the U.S. control ship, the crew of the submarine USS *Halibut*, not one of whom was close to the age of the boat in which they were submerged, were focused on the "vid" feed from the Deep Sea Recovery Vehicle as it plumbed through eighteen thousand feet, a depth which could have crushed the Chrysler building, to slowly descend onto the magnetic anomaly on the floor of the ocean another two thousand feet below.

Like her sister ship Growler in the 1950s Pegasus missile system, *Halibut* had two giant structures on her bow that were originally hangers that held two cruise missile type nuclear tipped rockets. From the bridge, the pregnant bulge on her foredeck resembled a large double-barrel shotgun with two giant cue balls sticking out of the end — the curved shape pressure doors. These hangers now housed the DSRV and its support equipment. It made the perfect delivery platform to silently and secretly deliver the ability to plumb the deepest depths, in many cases right under the nose of the Russians or any other adversary.

This was the *Halibut*'s final trip to this site. Although the Navy was betting with Hiccock's money, it was still something of a big gamble. Of course, they had gotten far less money than they had wanted, since Hiccock suddenly balked at the cost estimate for the mission. It was as if he had seen their books and realized the Navy had inserted a 300 percent mark-up in the cost. With pressure from the president, the SECNAV magically found a sharper pencil in that ring of the Pentagon and the mission had been ordered.

The risk was that the *Halibut* had already made five stealth trips. The first had been a magnetometer search of the one thousand square miles in which the probable debris field of the Vera Cruz could be located. Then four trips to drop off, like parachute drops, pre-positioned supplies and equipment which the DSRV needed to retrieve the nuclear crucibles the president wanted as evidence in the world court. If however, their guess that this anomaly was the Vera Cruz proved to be wrong, all the equipment and supplies would never be retrieved. Two of the units, with classified equipment, would be destroyed by a remote signal to onboard bombs. For its part, the supposedly decommissioned *Halibut* was nearly undetectable. Originally, the hull was laid as a diesel electric sub in 1955, but she had been outfitted in dry dock, before her maiden voyage, with a nuclear plant to enable Russ Klaven to use her for the most secret of cold-war missions. Refinements and noise cancelling modifications were added as the technology advanced. Combined with her smaller size, it made her quieter than a fish's sneeze. In war games with American and NATO forces, the *Halibut* slipped effortlessly in and out of sonar nets and lines of air-dropped sonar buoys from Orion sub hunter-killer aircraft. Its level of silent stealth rivaled that of the vaunted boomers, which were fifty years younger and $1.9 billion more expensive. *Halibut* had been officially scuttled in 1994, but in reality it was the hull of a never-finished sub that had been taken from mothballs and in the dead of night, and with much fanfare, scuttled in her place. Thus, the USS *Halibut*, thanks to Clay Klaven, added one more notch to her decades of stealthy service with the greatest cover story of all: she didn't even exist.

∞§∞

The descent of the DSRV was necessarily slow and cautious. Inside the command and control center of the fishing boat, Brooke watched the various screens and was starting to come to terms with the realization that this was the last page of the final chapter of a mission that had been written into her life. A mission that started as curiosity over the whereabouts of a Russian general turned black market czar. It was

Brooke, whose antenna went up when she looked deeper, who had gotten the assignment from Bill with the blessing of the president. It had led to her meeting Mush. Being around a sub mission and back in the Indian Ocean made thoughts of him come at even greater frequency than usual. Right now she was on a make believe fishing boat, playing hi-tech hide and seek with a similarly configured, make-believe Russian trawler, and she found the game fully engaging. Of course, Mush played "catch me, kill me" every second he was on patrol against at least three nations who would love to hear of an "accidental" sinking of a U.S. Ballistic Sub, especially if one of those nations caused the accident.

"DSRV, now minus one thousand feet," a seaman called out.

Brooke looked up, observed the blip representing the DSRV that was now one thousand feet above the sea floor, then went back to her line of thought. Her career had gone well ,and this mission would be a big feather in her cap. Maybe she should think about leaving at the top of her game. She could put this all behind her and sleep well at night, knowing she served her country with distinction and valor. She could do the Hawaii move. Maybe hire on as a local cop, no, as corporate security — as a consultant. *There must be corporations in Hawaii.* Then she'd have time for a life with Mush when he was home from patrol. And maybe in a few years, he'd take a desk job at Pearl or Bangor, Washington. *Oooo, Groton, Connecticut, that could be great! Good schools. I wouldn't be too old by then, maybe a kid or two.*

A sigh escaped from Brooke, and it got the attention of the commander. "You okay, Agent Burrell?" Randell said.

"Sorry, just got lost there a second; where are we?" Brooke tugged at her uniform skirt. The commander had given her permission to wear her uniform below deck, but said she'd have to change into "civvies" if she went anywhere on-deck or into the superstructure. Normally, she opted to be in uniform when she was on a Navy ship. It helped her avoid unwanted attention from seamen who had been away from their wives or girlfriends for many months. Today, not so much; this particular vessel was a super-secret spy ship, operated on deck by U.S. Japanese-American sailors in civilian clothes. The daily uniform for everyone onboard was always civilian, so now she stuck out like a Girl Scout at a Sunday picnic.

"Little Chick passing through minus five hundred feet. It won't be long until we know," the Commander commented.

Brooke found herself looking at a green dot — a new green dot — "Commander..."

"Wags? What the hell is that?"

∞§∞

At that moment on the *Halibut,* the sonar man pressed the headphones closer to his head and ordered quiet. "Sir... there's something..."

The Russian sub had come through a thermal layer close to the *Halibut.* The temperature anomaly had effectively masked the sound signature of each sub to the other as well as to the control ship. Neither ship was aware of the other until they were practically on top of one another.

A huge wallop rocked the *Halibut.* The angle indicator bubble disappeared behind the edges of the scale as the boat pitched nearly ninety degrees. Fortunately, the pitch and yaw and subsequent righting had slammed most watertight doors within the ship closed. They weren't sealed, but they were at least shut.

The *Halibut's* captain shook off the ringing in his head, caused by its impact with the edge of the chart table at full force. As the boat righted herself, and he tried to ascertain what had happened, there was a loud bang. Immediately, the boat rose violently up, the hull popped and groaned, and everyone was slammed to the floor.

∞§∞

Aboard the modified *Akula* class Russian sub, Captain Vashilli was killed instantly when the conning tower was crushed and peeled back as easily as the top of a sardine tin, the result of the top of his sub slamming into the bottom of the forward hull of the older, heavier American sub. The tons of water pressure at that depth caused the entire Russian boat to implode as its pressure hull was violently breached and everything inside was instantly crushed. The huge explosive release of air had lifted the *Halibut* above it two hundred feet in only a few seconds.

∞§∞

The crew of the *Halibut* was reeling; each had been sledge hammered by the impact and floored by the rapid ascent from the explosive air. For the *Halibut,* it was the luck of the accident that the Russian sub's conning tower, her weakest part, had hit her low and forward. The *Halibut* absorbed the impact of the top of the Russian sub's conning tower across the full breadth of the hanger-reinforced hull. The crack in the forward part of the *Halibut*'s hull occurred over several seconds. That allowing the lone occupant of the forward torpedo room, Ensign Jack Hargroves, to 'dog it down' — turning the hatch wheel and securing the seal of the already slammed shut door. This valiant action prevented the flood that entered the torpedo room and drowned him from flooding the rest of the ship.

Halibut's sonar man got to his senses and put on his headset. He reported what he heard: "Sir, I got a popping, crackling sound in my cans, consistent with a hull breach."

∞§∞

The cold, dead hulk of what had been a noble Russian boat slipped deeper and deeper into the murky black. The two-man crew in the DSRV was jarred by the implosion of the sub, but had no idea what had happened. Their calls to *Halibut* went unanswered, causing them to think they were suddenly alone. "Henhouse, this is Little Chick, do you copy?"

∞§∞

Onboard the *Halibut,* the captain learned that his forward torpedo room was flooded, but sealed by a heroic selfless act. He made a mental note that if they survived this, he'd recommend Hargroves for the Medal of Honor, posthumously. He ordered the ballast adjusted to right the boat under the dead weight of the flooded bow. The few leaks that popped up were being handled by chocks, wedges, and leak collars. He agreed with his chief of boat that they were watertight and seaworthy, although unable to make full forward speed.

∞§∞

Down in the DSRV Little Chick, the crew members clicked into their four-point seat restraints and rotated to nearly vertical in an attempt to use their strong lights to see above them. As if they had turned on the high beams in a blizzard, the visibility got worse because the plankton and other organisms reflected light right back to the crew through the three-foot-thick polycarbonate front window of the DSRV. Still, being human, they invested a few more seconds in this futile endeavor than logic would have dictated. But it was enough time for the lights to catch a glimpse of an enormous black mass plunging downward toward them. The pilot of the submersible pulled back on the hand grips, and the machine did a sort of back flip as he gunned the small motors and tried, in an upside down orientation, to gain distance between them and whatever it was that was coming.

∞§∞

"Henhouse, this is McDonald. Henhouse, this is McDonald. Henhouse, what is your situation?" Brooke watched as the commander of the surface control ship she was on kept clicking the transmit switch and showing just the slightest bit of frustration over not being able to raise the sub and find out what had happened.

Then the magnetometer operator reported, "Sir, I recalibrated the Maggie and there is a mass concentration sinking fast at Chicken Coop One."

The commander had two simultaneous thoughts. One: code-naming the operation after reading a nursery rhyme to his four-year-old daughter, when this retrieval looked like a lark, had been a mistake. Two: that the *Halibut* had sunk. He turned to his first officer. "What do you think, Hal?"

Hal lifted the peak of his Yankee's cap, which had a small metal insignia of his rank in the middle of the interlocking N-Y (his only concession to being an officer aboard this U.S. Navy spy ship), and said, "Is *Halibut*'s VLF carrier still intact?"

"Good point; Wags?"

"Checking — yes sir, Henhouse is still broadcasting VLF."

"Triangulate for position. Radio, try hailing 'em again," the commander said.

"Henhouse, this is McDonald, what is your situation?"

The wave of relief swept through the boat as they heard, "McDonald, this is Henhouse. We have suffered a breech but we are contained and all watertight seals are holding. One fatality."

"Any idea what hit you?"

"Whatever it was came out of nowhere. I'm guessing you didn't experience any event?"

"No. Why?"

"That rules out a seaquake or tsunami."

"Ben, we got a Maggie reading that something big just went down in your area. We thought it was you."

"My sonar man said something before the bang. Said there was something in the water and then reported sounds consistent with a hull breaking up."

Brooke got it right away, "Time to recalibrate your equipment, commander. Someone just snuck up on us."

"And obviously he couldn't see the *Halibut* either," the commander countered. Brooke noticed he had switched into a mental state that could best be described as deep contemplation.

A few seconds later, he hit the switch on his mike. "Henhouse, can you continue your mission?"

That surprised Brooke.

"McDonald, assessing status of Little Chick now," *Halibut*'s captain reported.

"Henhouse, advise when you know."

Brooke got up and walked closer to the commander. "You really intend to continue as if nothing happened?"

"If we have operational ability, then yes."

"Okay, fill me in here. The thing sinking to the bottom, that's a sub right?"

"Probably."

"There are men on that sub and you don't know if it's an American or NATO sub."

"Whoever they are, at this depth they are all dead."

"Yes, but what if it sunk from the surface? Then there would be survivors."

"First off we'd have seen a surface ship from fifteen miles off, and second, what do you propose we do about that? We are on a dark mission here. Survivors would compromise our mission and this boat's secrecy."

"Look, I was alone up there when the Vera Cruz sank, and I am here right now, alive, because someone didn't give me up for dead."

"Agent Burrell, you are here to advise and observe. I am the mission runner, and as long as there is a chance we can complete our mission and maintain operational integrity, we go. And that, Lieutenant Burrell, is an order, my order."

Brooke's blood started to overheat. She was about to pull rank as a White House operative, but she thought of Mush. His command. How as master and captain of a ship, the one essential was that his authority could not be undermined. So she flipped on her brain's safety switch and said, "Yes sir," and returned to her seat. She saw a second thought slam into the commander's head. "Has there been any nuclear signature?"

"Reviewing now — there is a slight level but far less than a crippled nuke would put out. It could be natural background radiation in this part of the ocean floor, sir, but definitely not any indication of rupture of a containment vessel. So, sir, if it was a sub, the reactor scrambled and for now it is contained."

"Okay, but I want you on that monitor. If it raises one rad, I want to know about it and we all get the hell out of here." He then turned to Brooke, the slightest attitude of contrition visible on his furrowed brow.

∞§∞

On the *Halibut*, the captain was trying to raise the DSRV, "Little Chick...Little Chick."

∞§∞

The DSRV, caught in the tremendous eddy of the sinking sub, was lifted up and arced around like a Ferris wheel going in reverse, its tiny motors no match for the swirling water rushing to fill the hole where the giant hull was falling. It was only the skill of the driver and his adroit manipulation of the handgrips that directed the attitude of the motors, allowing the tiny craft to just miss the descending bow of the crippled craft. As it slid by, the DSRV's lights briefly illuminated the bow and the name *Vladivostok*. The wreck plummeted through their position, two hundred fifty feet above the ocean floor. Then the currents quieted and they were finally able to take stock of their situation.

∞§∞

"Henhouse, this is Little Chick."

"Good to hear you, Chick. What is your situation?"

"A little shook up, but still watertight and we have maneuverability; batteries are good, air supply nominal."

"Did you see whatever that was?"

"Affirmative. Russian *Akula* class sub, read *Vladivostok*. Deep sixed."

The captain's eyebrows rose at that bit of data.

The guys in the DSRV continued, "Henhouse, do we abort?"

"Hold for orders, Little Chick." The captain switched the frequency on his overhead panel and hit the transmit switch, "McDonald, this is Henhouse; Little Chick is good to go. I recommend proceeding unless you got a big picture reason to abort?"

∞§∞

With that, Commander Randell turned to his radar and sonar techs, "What is the trawler doing?"

"Still in place, no increased EE, sir. It looks like he's unaware of any calamity."

This confused the commander. Surely they were listening and the implosion of the *Akula* was a giant noise in the water. "Sonar, where's the thermal layer?"

Wherever warmer water lies atop cooler water, a sonic wall of sorts is created. Therefore, it was possible the trawler never heard the implosion. The sonar man affirmed that the position of the temperature gradient could have shielded the Russian spook ship from the acoustic waves. He knew it was just a matter of minutes before the Russian trawler would try to make contact or try to ascertain the *Akula*'s situation. It meant there was a window of opportunity to complete the mission. "Little Chick, let's keep dancing."

"Affirmative."

∞§∞

The *Akula* landed upside down three hundred yards east of the shipwrecked hull, which was suspected to be the target ship. The DSRV buzzed down and hovered at fifty feet above the wreck. They radioed back to Henhouse confirmation that they were indeed above the Vera Cruz.

∞§∞

The news was met on the control ship with a slight cheer. Brooke, however, was processing all the data she had absorbed. The cop in her took over the meeting going on in her head. "Commander, what was the *Akula* doing here? Why is that trawler here? Why would the Russians be as interested in this wreck as we are?"

"It's possible they want those crucibles back."

"Doubtful; they are old tech to them. No, the only value they have is the value they have to us — evidentiary." Brooke's mind reached for a criminal motivation to the Russian behavior she had just observed. Returning to the scene of the crime was axiomatic. However there was one reason that would compel a perpetrator to return. "Commander, call off the DSRV!"

The commander turned with a look that said, "Why would I do that?" as he said those exact words.

"That sub was here to destroy the evidence."

"Well, he's not going to be doing anything but becoming a reef."

"How do you know they haven't set charges or..."

∞§∞

The driver of the DSRV nearly jumped out of his harness as another DSRV entered his field of view. "Henhouse, we got company. Holy shit, another DSRV!"

∞§∞

"Little Chick, this is Henhouse; they must be from the *Akula*!" He threw the switch to relay the news to Brooke's spy ship, "McDonald, we got more company."

∞§∞

"Son of a bitch," the Commander on board the American control ship uttered. "Have they seen your Little Chick yet?"

"No, sir."

"Tell 'em to go dark, play possum, and let's see what happens."

"Roger that."

Brooke couldn't help but interject. "Commander, that Russian DSRV is now an orphan. They could alert the trawler."

"Not likely, for the same reason we cannot speak directly to ours; because they don't carry powerful RF so as not to waste battery. For all the trawler knows right now, the *Akula* went off the air."

"The men in the Russian DSRV had to hear the implosion; they are on the same side of the thermal layer," Brooke said.

"So what are you saying?"

"That they're as dog-headed as you, and are out to complete their mission if they can still breathe."

"And you think their mission is seek and destroy?"

"Why else haven't they tried to surface after their "Henhouse" sank?"

Brooke could see the commander was an agile thinker as he judged her words purely on their merit and seemingly with no baggage left over from the tug of war they'd been playing for the last few minutes.

He keyed his mike, "Henhouse, can you disable the other DSRV?"

∞§∞

Aboard Little Chick, the two-man crew looked at each other as they heard the request. They immediately engaged their thrusters and advanced toward the Russian submersible, ready to attack with nothing more than claws — and balls. They switched on their HD video feed but not their lights, so as to not give away their approach. The Russian's lights were on and the Little Chick crew could see they were carrying a five-foot wide container that was roughly the shape of a beer cooler in the arms of their machine.

∞§∞

Brooke was watching the feed along with everybody else aboard the 'fishing boat.' "Commander, that's a bomb right?"

"Yes, it definitely could be."

She turned to the seaman watching the radiation monitor. "Sailor, could the small trace of radiation you're getting be from that device?"

The commander turned, "Agent Burrell, are you suggesting that that's a tactical nuke?"

"It makes sense. Small yield, immediate obliteration of the evidence plus a hot debris field for years to come, thwarting anyone from picking through the rubble."

"I better get our guys out of there..."

"Hold it, Commander, not so fast," Brooke said in a voice usually reserved for "Freeze."

The commander's first instinct was to tell her in no uncertain terms that he didn't take orders from her. But Brooke had anticipated his objections.

"Commander, I am responsible to the President of the United States for the ultimate outcome of this mission. So far, events have taken us off our game plan, which was how you charted your course. Now we are in uncharted waters and nuclear weapons are in play. I am going to do you a favor and relieve you of responsibility for what happens next."

"Meaning what?"

"Meaning under the authority granted me by the Commander-in-Chief, I order you to do nothing and let the Russians plant the device."

"You want what now? A minute ago you were all, 'let's abort,' and now you are all gung ho. With all due respect ma'am, you want to rethink what you are suggesting here?" the commander said, with a slight tinge of patronage.

"Stop the attack." Brooke was dead serious.

"Henhouse, have Little Chick immediately break off the attack and hold for further orders." He turned to Brooke with an expression that asked, *"What now?"*

The crew was riveted; this woman had balls.

"Okay, here's how I see it. If the Russians are on a suicide mission then our guys are already dead. They'll never get away in time. But either those guys in the Russian craft don't know their sub is dead, or they plan to surface and make it to the trawler."

"Once they are on the surface, they could cell phone the trawler," the sonar man said, then quickly pulled back when his commander glared at him.

"Exactly, sailor, so I am going to bet that they are going to plant the bomb and then either trigger it remotely or set a timer to get them clear. Either way, that's our chance to tie this up and cover all our tracks." Brooke said.

The commander kept an open mind and said, "Go on, I'm listening."

∞§∞

"You want us to what?" was the Little Chick's response to Henhouse. Then they proceeded to watch from the inky black as the Russian unit planted the bomb atop the hull of the Vera Cruz, then turned and began the long, slow ascent to the surface, presumably to alert the trawler of its fallen mother ship and the success of its mission.

As the machine was swallowed up in the jet-black cold, Little Chick moved in. Making for the bomb, they gingerly closed their own articulated arms around it turned in the direction of the *Akula*. Six minutes later they were back at the Vera Cruz. They used their beacon locator to find a prepositioned tool locker. The GPS Auto Nav took them right to it, some fifty yards from the hull. They retrieved the diamond-tipped self-powered cutting saw.

The huge thirty-six-inch saw blade sliced through the hull of the ship at exactly the spot along the hull where the forward hold was. They made a ten-by-ten-foot square hole in the steel plate between the steel ribs of the hull. The metal started to bend as they made the last cut. They stopped just short of freeing the piece for fear it would fall onto the crucibles. Just as in the rehearsals on the shipwreck off of Puerto Rico, the weight of the newly cut plate hinged down under its own weight like a trap door. They freed the saw, let it fall to the ocean floor, and then headed for locker two. There they retrieved a grappling-hook-like device into which they slid the machine's arms, then headed back to the Vera Cruz.

∞§∞

"How much longer, Commander?"

"So far they are on track for our best time trial off Vieques, so just ten more minutes to ascend back to Henhouse."

"It's amazing, Commander, after all that's happened and all that the crew has been through, they are still so focused and so on schedule."

"Good men, good training, and good luck, ma'am."

"I don't know if you could call colliding into an *Akula* luck, but I'll give you the other two."

∞§∞

Their first try to snare a crate with the grapple claw almost killed the mission. Like a carnival midway claw machine, the crate "kewpie doll" dangling on the end of the claw broke free and wedged itself between the load and the bulkhead. The DSRV bounced up and down on the crooked crate to dislodge it.

On the second try, the grapple hit pay dirt and they worked the controls and retrieved a crate, which fit the same size and shape outline as a crucible shipping crate. They rested it atop the hull, maneuvered around and turned their craft's Halogen lights on the stenciled crate.

∞§∞

"We are getting a feed now, ma'am," the video operator announced.

Brooke opened her iPad, pressed her right thumb onto a green square on the screen which scanned her fingerprint, and typed in the file name for the Vera Cruz manifest.

The Vid-Op read the numbers. "One, four, five, two, nine, Cyrillic E, C, P.

Brooke read down the list, "Roger that. We got one."

A cheer went up in the compartment as the commander ordered, "Henhouse, get Little Chick and her Egg back to the barn on the double."

"Aye aye, sir," was the response.

∞§∞

Thirty minutes later, Little Chick was nestled safely in the Henhouse hanger as she sailed as fast and as far from Chicken Coop One as the flooded bow would allow.

∞§∞

Aboard the faux fishing boat, Brooke reported to Hiccock on the mission over secure satellite link. Bill had patched in Kronos, his high tech ace-in-the-hole, who asked the commander if the trawler was still emanating Electromagnetic Emissions. He then informed Brooke and the commander that the trawler would have all electronic equipment switched off right before the blast. He recommended that Brooke's vessel also shut off everything at the breakers, everything that could be unplugged, unplugged, and all power switches off. Otherwise, the electromagnetic pulse that a small yield nuke might emit would fry everything plugged in. With that, all agreed to shut down their link and all non-essential equipment on the boat, the last being the EE monitor.

Twelve minutes later the sailor monitoring the Russian trawler's EE reported, "Target Lana's gone dark, sir."

The commander immediately barked, "Kill the electronics at the breakers. Everybody brace yourselves." Less than a minute later, they felt a crescendoing rumble that rose in seconds to full-blast shock wave, followed by the low, raspy sound of the blast.

The commander turned to Brooke and said, "Smart play, Agent Burrell."

"Nicely executed, Commander."

"Archie."

"Archie."

Brooke's gambit killed two birds with one nuclear blast — provided by the Russians. The *Akula* — and any clue that the U.S. was now holding the evidence — was vaporized. The world would believe, and the Russians would not deny, that the *Akula* suffered a nuclear event, exploded, and went down with all hands. Even the Russian DSRV ops could only report that they heard a bang and the *Akula* went dark, well before they finished their mission. Brooke guessed they would, of course, be summarily executed to contain the story, then awarded the Hero of the Russian Federation medal posthumously.

All in all, a neatly tied, no-loose-ends finish to what was shaping up to be a busted play in the depths of the Indian Ocean. In fact, the first time the Russians would even realize they had lost the game would be when the Secretary of State presented the actual crucible, with its serial number intact, to the World Court in The Hague.

XVIII. FREE AGENT

A week later, with the Russian Crucible Affair wrapped up in a tight bow by Brooke, Hiccock was able to focus on the many elements stemming from the murder of Professor Landau. Top of the list was the discovery that a priest had brought down the helicopter. Next, that he, Bill, had obtained the Vatican's joint statement designed to lower the temperature of rhetoric on the research programs the U.S. was a vested partner in.

The third item on the list still nagged at him. Parnell Sicard had known of his entire secret mission's particulars, and now Joey had connected him with the Vatican. As a Catholic, Bill had never thought he'd have to choose loyalties between his country and his religion. And what did electric ice have to do with any of this? He'd review all of this with his team. He looked at his watch, and right on time, Cheryl entered with the velvet blue box.

"Everyone's outside," Cheryl said as she also handed him a folder.

"The boss?" Hiccock asked as he flipped it opened and checked that all was in order.

"No, the president is in Ohio. You got the Veep."

"Okay. In here?"

"Yes, the Roosevelt Room has Boy Scouts in it."

"Fire up the monitor and let's start."

Cheryl turned on the video conference monitor that connected the White House to Joey's set-up in the Paris Embassy, then went outside and returned seconds later with the vice president, the heads of the FBI, CIA, NSA, ONI and the woman of the hour, Brooke.

Bill spoke first. "It is necessary from time to time to acknowledge the extraordinary accomplishments of patriots who risk it all to protect, defend and preserve our American way of life, and insure that the good America does for the rest of the world remains uninterrupted. Mr. Vice President, if you will, sir."

"Someone once said the job of the vice president is to break the tie in the senate and to inquire as to the health of the president every day. My job today however, is a great pleasure and a defining moment for me as much as it is for you, Agent Burrell. In the 'house' here, we know FBI stands for Fidelity, Bravery, and Integrity. We are here because you have exceeded those noble standards. Before I read your official commendation, the president has asked me to relay this personal message: he is sorry his schedule didn't allow him to be here, but he requests your company tomorrow morning for coffee at oh-seven-hundred hours in the residence."

On the monitor, they saw Joey's eyes widen as a toothy white smile escaped his "standing at attention" demeanor. Face time with the president was an incredible coup.

The Veep read from the scroll, which would be locked away in a vault as soon as the ceremony ended. "As Commander-in-Chief, I do hereby commend the actions and recognize the valor of Special Agent Brooke Burrell, attached to the White House Quarterback Operations group, by awarding the Medal of Valor for extreme bravery in the execution of her duties, and for her successful capture of invaluable evidence for the United States at extreme risk and peril to her person. Her actions to complete the mission at all costs represent the finest traditions of the service and law enforcement. I express the heartfelt gratitude of millions of Americans who will never know of Agent Burrell's sacrifice and commitment, but whose security today is more assured due to her unselfish actions. Signed this day, by James Mitchell, President of the United States."

The vice president looked to Bill, who opened the velvet box and extended it for the vice president to remove the medal, which was on a ribbon to avoid the uncomfortable act of pinning it on the chest of a woman, and slipped it over her head. He shook her hand and said, "Thank you."

He stepped back and said, "Gentlemen." On cue all the others in the room snapped a sharp salute to the recipient. A man from the White House library entered. He took the medal on the ribbon, placed it back in the box and sealed it. He then wrote out a receipt for "property" and handed it to Brooke. The medal, awarded in secret for an act of extreme bravery on a secret mission, would go in the vault of the Mitchell presidential library, ostensibly to be opened in seventy-five years. Until then, all Brooke had was a commendation in her file and the receipt for her grandkids to claim in three quarters of a century.

Joey chimed in from Paris. "Brooke, congratulations on getting the recognition I always knew you deserved."

"Thanks Joey."

"Take care." Then Joey leaned forward and the screen reverted to the State Department logo.

As the room cleared, Bill asked Brooke to remain. "You are an outstanding member of the team, Brooke. The meaning of this will only be known to a few, so here." He handed her a red velvet pouch.

She opened it and found a five-pointed star, exactly like the two on Bill's desk. She gasped and clutched it to her chest, now understanding the meaning of the "paperweights" on his desk. When she choked up, Bill thought she had been overcome by emotion, but that wasn't it.

"You okay?"

"Bill, I've been doing a lot of thinking. Getting blown into the ocean makes you start to see things a little differently. I never thought I would ever say this, but I think it's getting to the time I should do something else."

"Whoa. Sounds serious, Brooke, but you've earned the right. What do you want, Brooke?"

"I want a shot at some kind of normalcy in my life. I want a home and someone to live there with me who would care if I got blown off a ship. I want what most everyone else takes for granted."

Bill listened and understood. Brooke had paid her dues many times over. After some silence he spoke from his heart. "When I met Janice, nothing else mattered. Not school, football, the NFL or my doctorate. I just knew what I wanted, and I wanted her."

"You were lucky she wasn't a thousand feet under the ocean six months a year."

"I won't deny I was lucky, but I was also stupid."

"What are you saying, that it was wrong for you to want her, or me Mush?"

"No, no, not at all, I was stupid to allow those very things I didn't care about then to get between us later."

"But you two are like Mr. and Mrs. America. With a kid right out of central casting."

"Yeah, but Brooke, I stumbled big time, and then got super lucky when she gave me a second chance to marry her... again."

"So what are you saying?"

"I guess I am saying that it's not only about you wanting him and the life, but that you continue making that life your number one priority. Otherwise, like me, you'll wind up just putting off all those same things that are stopping you from doing it now till later. And that could screw up a good thing. So, as much as you want him, you have to also *not* want the life you are currently living; otherwise it will creep back in and screw it all up."

"Okay, I think I got that."

"Brooke, I don't mean to pry, but as the head of the team, I'd like to know if you have expressed your plans to Joey?"

"No, these feelings are very recent and I wasn't really sure till just now."

"Do you want to tell him or would you like me to?"

"No, I owe it to him to hear it from me." Brooke sat silent as the circumstances sunk in.

Bill broke the silence, "So when do you want to resign?"

Brooke had a reflexive and reflective moment. "Wow. Just hearing the word 'resign' makes this suddenly so real."

"I didn't mean to rush you; take your time. Think it all over, twice if you have to. You've earned carte blanche with me and I am sure I speak for Joey as well when I say, we care about you and your happiness foremost."

As hard as she tried not to, the waterworks started. Bill handed her a tissue and just sat in silence with her for a few minutes more.

∞§∞

Later that afternoon, Bill had a moment to reflect on Brooke and her tremendous accomplishments, and as a self-check once again affirmed to himself that she had earned her right to do whatever she wanted with her career. However, the whole notion of his team changing brought a long simmering issue up to the front burner. Cheryl. He buzzed for her.

Cheryl entered the office in her usually cheerful demeanor. "Yes, boss!"

"Sit a minute, will ya."

"Okay, sure, what's up?"

"A while back, you correctly asked for some kind of game plan for continuity of our department. I am sorry it took me so long to focus on it, but I have decided to make you my deputy, or second in command or whatever term is governmentally appropriate."

To her credit, Cheryl didn't react personally but as a team member, "Thank you. I think this decision will insure uninterrupted flow of command and control during any kind of situation, and I am honored that you put your faith in me."

"You've earned my trust and my respect."

Cheryl allowed herself a small smile of satisfaction. "Shall I draw up the contingency protocol?"

"Actually, I thought you'd have it ready and in your top drawer."

"Actually it is; I just need to fill in the blank of who you appoint." This time, a broadside smile found freedom.

"So how'd I do?" Bill asked returning the smile.

"You did real good, boss!"

"Thanks, it means a lot to me."

"Anything else?"

"Yeah, hold this tight till it's announced, but Brooke will be leaving us."

Cheryl recoiled at the news. "That genuinely shocks me, sir."

"I must say I didn't expect it either, but as I told her, she's earned the right to do what she wants."

"Oh, God, Joey's going to freak out, unless he already knows?"

"Brooke wants to tell him, so until then it's just us. Soon after though, I want you to coordinate with Joey to find a replacement for her... er, strike that, for her position."

That simple catch reaffirmed to Cheryl why she liked working with Bill. He understood the difference between the rare individual Brooke was and the slot she filled in his Quarterback group. "Will do." Cheryl got up and left. Besides the two surprise announcements from Bill, she also understood how losing Brooke had forced him to decide about her.

∞§∞

Brooke walked the streets of Washington, aimless and with no sense of urgency, a totally alien state for her. Her head spun with ideas, plans, uncertainties and certitudes. She stopped at the little breakfast joint where she and Mush had eaten. She opened her phone and dialed Mush's cell.

"Hi, Bret here, I'm going to be out of reach for a while, you can leave a message, but I probably won't get right back to you," his voice-mail greeting said.

As the phone beeped, Brooke's eyes shut. She knew the vague message was Bret's way of not compromising national security, yet letting all those who had his number know that the Gold crew had gone deep for the next seventy to ninety days. She ended the call, satisfied to just hear his voice.

Suddenly she felt cold. Then her own voice-mail beeped with a new message alert.

"Brooke, it's Mush, I tried to reach you but your phone wasn't connecting. Our patrol got moved up and we are shoving off in four hours. I hope we get a chance to talk before we go. If not, I just wanted you to know that you've become a part of me. And I can't even imagine what my life was like before you came flailing onboard my boat. I love you, Brooke, and I am going to do a lot of thinking on this patrol. Well, that's it. I hope you get this. See ya soon, baby."

It was turning out to be a bang-up day for Brooke's tear ducts; they were getting more of a workout today than they had in years.

XIX. SWISS ROULETTE

Raffey was managing the stress by drinking tons of tea. He had become convinced that chamomile tea had near nuclear powers in settling his nerves arising from the unfathomable dilemma he was in. As psychosomatic as his remedy may have been, it served him and allowed him to do his job without his jittery nerves raising suspicions, save for the frequent trips to the loo. On one trip, he passed a secretary who was playing a game of online roulette. Ten minutes later he was searching for an older program which he co-wrote as a member of the development team. He found it; Roulette Demo X-5.3/v2.2. Suddenly, he no longer needed tea. He recompiled the source code and copied the original onto a flash drive. He also took a copy of the older systems folder. He had everything he needed to do this at home tonight.

∞§∞

Joey had taken an overnight flight from Paris to D.C. to catch Bill in the morning. He had rehearsed his speech many times at thirty-five thousand feet above the pitch-black Atlantic. In many ways, this would be the most important conversation he'd ever had with his lifelong friend, and although he was about to put himself on thin ice, he was ready for the risk.

He arrived at the White House at 7:20 a.m. Bill and his driver would be pulling into the portico in five minutes. Joey went straight to his office and printed out the pages he had e-mailed himself from France.

Cheryl caught sight of him first. "Joey? This is a surprise! Does Bill know you are in this morning?"

"No Cheryl, I kind of jumped on a plane last night. Phyllis doesn't even know yet."

"Wow. Have you spoken with Brooke yet?"

"No, no I haven't; what's up?"

"I'll let her fill you in."

"Look can you give me a half hour with Bill, first thing?"

"Yeah, I think so. He's got a light morning till eleven."

"Thanks, buzz me when he's in?"

"You got it."

Joey pulled the pages from the printer and arranged them in the order he wanted them. A few minutes later, he was entering Bill's office.

"Hey buddy, when did you get in?" Bill said, surprised in mid-sip of his coffee.

"About an hour ago."

"How come you didn't tell me you were coming? I mean, Paris is still important."

"I'm going right back."

"Okay, this is confusing. You could have been here yesterday for Brooke's ceremony."

"I had leads to follow. Then I decided at the last minute to hop a seat back because, Bill, I needed to talk to you, man to man."

"Okay, shoot!"

"Are you sure about this God Particle thing?"

"What do you mean, sure? It's a theory, so no, I am not."

"I mean are you sure we aren't playing with the end of everything here?"

"Joey, what's gotten into you?"

"This ain't about me, Bill, it's about everyone, everything, everywhere."

"You turning into a black-holer?"

"No, but how much risk is there?"

"Under strict protocol with proper safeguards, little to none."

"So what you are telling me is that *everything* has to work at 100 percent, the safeguards have to be 100 percent effective to get what — a level of assurance of only 'little to none?'"

"In the breaking of every scientific boundary, a certain amount of uncertainty..."

"Bill, we're not talking about 'Oops, I dropped the test tube; oh look, anthrax!' Correct me if I am wrong here, but we are talking lights out forever."

"Joey..."

"Bill, why do we have to even go there? I mean, what's so goddamn important about breaking this boundary, when the cost might be everything that ever was, is, and could be — including my son and Richie? What value could possibly be worth that risk?"

"Look, it's my job and it's your job."

"My job? My job is to protect: protect my family, my country, and now my universe. So I am doing my job. What are you doing?"

"Hey, have you noticed it ain't just us? The Europeans are the lead on this. I keep our interest in the game. As long as we have input, we can affect the work."

"Can we bomb the fucking machine?"

"Joey, take it easy. Talk like that, especially in this office, is unwise."

"Oh, but possibly making everything disappear is somehow wiser?"

"Where is this coming from?"

"I started thinking, Billy, started thinking about what we are trying to do here, stopping the guys who want to stop this machine from possibly taking us all out!"

"No, Joey, you are too good of a cop to let that get in the way. It has to be something else. Who have you been talking to?

"Are you saying I ain't smart enough to come to this myself?"

"You should be smarter than the apocalyptic conspiracy crap you have been spewing this morning."

"What happened to you Billy? You always were a robot, but I always saw a soul in you, although you tried hard to hide it, first from Janice and now from me."

"My personal beliefs don't enter into it. I am the goddamn science advisor to the whole freaking United States. I represent science, not hearsay, not rumors, not scary stories. Quantify, qualify using qualitative analysis, otherwise it's just a supposition. That's what I owe my kid, my wife, my country, my world and you. And I don't need you coming in here and accusing me of being some sort of criminal."

"Look, I always follow any order you give me, but if I think it is immoral or unethical, you are going to hear from me. And I think you are not thinking this through, Billy. I think you might be a little too pumped up on being the 'goddamn science advisor to the whole freaking United States' to stop and think about what you are enabling here."

"Enough! Look Joey, this ain't a debate and your concerns are duly noted. Now can you please get back to finding Parnell Sicard?"

"Don't blow me off! I'm not just some low-level flunky here. I am the one who you need to get this guy, who just may be trying to stop them, by the way, from possibly destroying everything. And what I want to know is, why? Why, Bill, are we protecting this Landau Protocol, this whole evil enterprise?"

"EVIL! Are you out of your mind? What's evil got to do with it? The church pulled that shit on Copernicus. They tarred and feathered him as evil just because he said the Earth orbits the Sun. Evil has no scientific weight. Only objectivity and evidence rule the day around here."

"Right or wrong, Copernicus didn't have any power. He couldn't have destroyed everything in God's creation in a flash."

"Listen, pal, as of now you are off this case and as of now you are on sabbatical. Take a few days, a few weeks, hell, take a fucking year; just get your fucking head on straight before you come back to work."

"Fine with me; I just hope we have that long."

"Get out, just get out!" Bill pointed his fingers toward the door.

Joey threw his papers down on Bill's desk and stormed out. He blew by Cheryl without a word. She had never seen him like that. *That couldn't be about Brooke*, she thought. She looked back to Bill's office and something told her to give him a few minutes.

∞§∞

Joey walked out onto Pennsylvania Avenue and hailed a cab. "Airport — no, take me to the FBI." Looking out the window he replayed what had just happened. He wasn't going back to Paris; he wasn't going to work tomorrow. He was on leave. Bill could be such an asshole. As he watched a group of first graders cross the street, all tethered together, led by their teacher in front and a parent taking up the rear, he thought about his little family. He changed his destination one more time as he gave the driver his home address. Bill could stop him from working for Quarterback, but he couldn't stop him from protecting all that he loved.

Joey Palumbo and his wife, Phyllis, had an agreement about Joey's work. She knew that sometimes there were things he could not share due to the security of whatever operation he was involved with through the years. Even so, she was shocked when Joey's keys rattled in the door as he called out, "Phyl? Phyl, honey, I'm home!" Little Joe got there first, "Dad! When did you get home?"

"Just now!"

"Hello, stranger," Phyl said, smoothing her hair.

Joey looked at her and opened his arms as she filled them.

"Why didn't you call? I look terrible."

"You look great, babe."

They kissed, and after a quick breakfast Joe left for school and the morning quiet, interrupted only by raucous calls of blue jays, hung there for a minute. Phyllis looked over to him. "Can you tell me about it?"

"I am going to be home for a while, but everything else is fine."

"Okay. I won't ask. Are you going to work today?"

"I thought I'd work from home today."

"Okay, now I really won't ask." Phyllis got up and cleared the dishes.

XX. PARIS BY NIGHT

Inspector Dupré was confused. Neither Palumbo nor Burrell was returning his phone calls. He had left messages at the Embassy but he knew those weren't worth the recycled paper they were written on. He had a solid lead on Parnell Sicard, mostly because of the intelligence that had come from this Quarterback in Washington.

No matter; the cop in him wanted to ferret out this man because he felt responsible for the possible lapse in justice over the killing of the Franciscan Friar. To Dupré, it had become personal. He was also aware that Sicard was being protected by someone up high in the French government. The Americans would have added a little more lift to his efforts to get his hands on Sicard, but they weren't essential, not with the plan he had devised. His intercom buzzed. "Yes..."

"We are ready in five minutes, Inspector."

"Very well, I am coming down." He took out his desk key, opened the always-locked bottom drawer, and took out his .32 caliber pistol and slid it into his ankle holster, then clipped his service weapon's hip holster to his belt and slid something else in his waist band. As he came around his desk, his immediate superior entered with a tall American.

"Marc, here is someone I would like to introduce you to."

Dupré zoomed past them, not stopping to even shake hands. "Hello, nice to meet you, but I am on my way out."

He was almost out the door when his boss said, "Pity, I thought you'd like to meet Quarterback."

Dupré stopped dead in his tracks, turned around, and extended his hand. "Pardon, I am running late; in fact, to pick up someone you have met! Would you like to come along?"

"Sure. Bill Hiccock..."

"Marc Dupré, pleasure to meet you."

On the way down in the elevator, Dupré turned to Bill. "May I ask why you are here?"

"I see Sicard as the key to my investigation and I am a little light on personnel right now, so I jumped the next flight out of D.C." Bill had reviewed the files and reports. Joey had written that this inspector was an honest guy and a good cop. He also knew how much Dupré knew and how much he'd been cleared to know.

"Then our talk with Monsieur Sicard should be quite interesting."

"I am looking forward to it."

As they emerged from the elevator into the garage, there were three SUV-type vehicles idling. Dupré opened the door of one vehicle for Bill and he, as soon as the door shut, the convoy was off and out of the underground garage. On the street they were joined by two motorcycle cops who ostensibly were there to block cross traffic ahead, then fall behind, race to the front, and do it all again at every major intersection.

Bill took notice. "This is very impressive. Are you responding to some sort of threat?"

"No, we are trying to get there before the courts, police, or whoever is protecting Sicard knows we are coming. That's how we lost him last time."

"I see. How good is your information?"

"Actually, because of the files you forwarded, we were able to connect with a retired French operative who worked intimately with your CIA. He identified a former safe house, which he believed Sicard would still use. One of my men positively identified Sicard as being in the house..." he looked at his watch, "...some thirteen minutes ago."

With military precision, the two vehicles stopped in front of the house while the third circled around back. The two motorcycles sealed the street at either end. The men were out of the vehicles with heavy armor, helmets and automatic weapons. Two cops held the battering ram. Then they all froze in position as Dupré simply walked up to the door and rang the bell.

"Alo," came over the intercom.

"Monsieur Sicard, may I have a word please?"

There was a moment's hesitation. Bill waited for something theatrical to happen, like machine guns suddenly popping out of the second floor windows or an escape helicopter launching from the roof. Instead, the buzzer clicked and Dupré just walked in. A minute later, Dupré came back to the door, pointed to Bill, and waved for him to come in. As Bill crossed the street, he was keenly aware of the eight rifles trained on the house he was about to enter and the fact that all he had was a leather portfolio as a shield. *How did I get in the middle of this again?*

Inside, Dupré led Bill to stuffy library that smelled of dust and aged books. Sicard was seated across the room and did not get up to greet him. He did, however, give an exasperated look, as seeing Bill genuinely surprised him.

"Percy! Oh, I'm sorry, Parnell. Or is there another name you'd like to go by today?"

Parnell Sicard, also known as Percival Cutney, Percival Smyth, and a few other 'noms de ruse', sat silently.

"Doctor Hiccock is here as an interested party, but I am here in a more proactive role."

Bill could see the subtle facial changes as Parnell suddenly recognized Inspector Dupré.

"You remember me? 1997? The Pope?"

"I wish to be represented by a lawyer," Parnell said, looking straight ahead.

"That would only be necessary if you were under arrest." Dupré lit a cigarette. He offered one to Parnell.

He didn't respond to the offer but instead said, "Then I don't have to talk to you and I am free to leave."

"No." Inspector Dupré pulled a gun and pointed it at Parnell.

Bill resisted the instinct to object, because he had no power in France. He hoped this was a ploy, but immediately thought that Parnell was too well trained to be rattled. Then Bill's thoughts turned ugly. *What if Dupré had lost it? What if the only blemish on his long distinguished career, the bobbling of a potential Papal assassination, had affected his brain? What if he was going to settle that score with this smug operator in one shot?*

"If you shoot me, you'll have to shoot your witness here as well," Parnell calmly said, nodding to Hiccock.

"Too melodramatic." Dupré tossed the gun into Parnell's lap. "Remember that gun?"

"No."

"Look closely at the side of the grip. You see those scratches? Please point the gun at Mr. Hiccock."

"Is that so you can shoot me, claiming I was going to shoot him?" Parnell said, leaving the gun in his lap.

Dupré pulled out his service weapon now and urged, "Please, indulge me."

Parnell gripped the gun and pointed it at Bill.

Bill tensed; he was about to duck behind the chair when Dupré motioned for Bill to check the gun in Parnell's hand.

"Tell me that thing ain't loaded," Bill said.

"Doctor, the second Sicard picked up the gun he knew it was too light to be loaded. Please look at his grip." Dupré prodded again with his gun as a pointer.

Cautiously, Bill approached the gun from the side and put his hand over the slide as Parnell held it, still aimed at the spot he had left. He looked closely at the grip, and there, spanning the knurled wood of the grip and onto the nickel-plated metal of the gun body, were small scratches around the area where Parnell's ring on his ring finger encompassed the grip.

"It's scratched by the ring."

"What does that prove?" Parnell said indignantly.

"Ah, this weapon was found at the Sofitel in a hamper, one week after the death of the Franciscan, Friar Gregory. At that time it was brought to my attention. You had already wiped it clean of fingerprints, but those scratches puzzled me."

"And since the death of Gregory was ruled accidental by fall with no gun play, it seemed like a separate issue." Bill was catching on but still mindful of the gun in Parnell's hand.

"Yes. It was delivered to me because I was chief investigator at the last crime at that location. I deemed it unconnected and sent it to the evidence locker, after having its ballistics categorized, in case a bullet surfaced in some cold case," Dupré said as he retrieved the gun from Parnell with a handkerchief. "Thanks for the new set of prints, in case a bullet ever shows up."

"I still don't have to talk to you."

"I know you are expecting a squad car to intercede and some judge to whisk you away again, but — " Dupré pulled out his portable radio and said, "Are the suspects in custody yet?"

"Affirmative; we are looking for evidence now," the scratchy reply buzzed out.

"Please take your time, do everything twice and then check it again," Dupré said into the radio.

"Yes, sir."

Dupré snapped the radio back to the belt clip under his jacket and sat in the chair across from Parnell. He motioned for Bill to sit as well. "Did you know that right next door there is a man who was once associated with the Algerian separatists? Of course, it's all circumstantial evidence, and in a few hours he will be cleared of all suspicions, but for now, all that your judge, or anybody else for that matter, knows is that this is a national security raid on a possible terrorist safe house next door. Your name and even this address is not in any official report. So my friend, let's relax and just chat without fear of interruption, shall we?"

Bill finally took a breath. It was the same diversionary tactic he had used in the Boston op. Of course, he had no way of knowing that the 'separatist' next door who was being detained for twenty minutes and then released was a rug merchant who was actually only guilty of separating Dupré's brother-in-law from his money for a supposedly genuine Turkish rug which turned out, regrettably, to have been made in China.

"What you think you know, I can neither confirm nor deny," Parnell said.

"Think? I don't think, I now know, my friend, that you are a member of a secret order that protects the Pope." Dupré held up his left hand and tapped the inside of his ring finger with the tip of his thumb as he spoke. "You got wind of a plot to assassinate the Pope here in Paris. You found out that an extreme radical Muslim sect had a hit man posing as a Franciscan priest here to take part in the Youth Day ceremonies. You dispatched the killer with blunt force trauma to the throat, possibly with a pipe, then positioned the body over the edge of the staircase's metal railing to seem as though he had slipped, crushing his larynx, and died unable to cry out for help. Spilling a cup of coffee on the step just above him and pouring some on the soles of his shoes was brilliant. You then discarded your backup weapon in a clothes hamper in the basement so you could leave light."

"Assuming you might be right, how do you come to the conclusion that it was radical extremists?"

"A local Imam. He was persuaded to tell me everything that he didn't tell me the first time I interrogated him when he was the deskman at the Sofitel. Although he didn't know of the plot, he led me to a small fish in the plan, who years later had gotten on the bad side of the radical Blind Sheik. It was the Sheik who put out the fatwa and ordered the Pope's assassination, and this minnow had somehow angered him. Once we offered him protection from the Sheik, the little guppy started talking and we couldn't shut him up."

"Look, for what it's worth, I am a Catholic, and I am thankful you thwarted the plot," Bill said.

"And I am pleased that a case I misjudged has been rectified," Dupré said, as his physical stance relaxed from a purely defensive one.

"So, if I say you are both welcome, can I go now?"

"The Inspector has his answers; now I need mine." Bill turned to Dupré and said, "Inspector, could you let us chat in private, please."

Dupré reached around his back and produced a pair of handcuffs. He closed one end around the steam pipe next to Parnell's chair and held out the open cuff. "If you would be so kind."

Parnell reluctantly offered his wrist.

"Is that necessary?" Bill asked looking at the cuffs.

"I don't want a hostage situation, Mr. Hiccock. Once I leave, this very capable fellow might find a way to change the dynamics of the situation. He gently tossed the key up and snatched it from the air. "I'll be right outside with the key."

Bill watched him leave, then turned to Parnell. "Sorry about that but it is his jurisdiction and you and I both know a man with your training and skill is not going to be thwarted by a handcuff."

Bill watched and confirmed that this man was good at liar's poker. He didn't take the bait. Bill decided to be straight with him. "Parnell, since you disappeared I did a lot of digging. You were CIA, and then after Beirut you went off grid."

Being well-trained, Sicard did not betray his shock or denial when his greatest secret was exposed.

"Only a few in the spook house totally bought your faked death. And they do not rule out the possibility that you were turned. But I looked at your record, and to me you don't come up as someone who would work for the Chi-coms, the Russians, or the North Koreans. Then a little bird, as in full bird colonel, opened my eyes. A greater cause doesn't have to be political, hence the ring. And you proved that by saving the Pope."

Bill's inference that a 'colonel told him' was a deliberate attempt to protect his line to Klaven and the Navy. "Look, I understand that religious patriotism can trump national-ism. I get that. And personally, I don't care about any of that. Except I know I got you nailed, and your effectiveness as a stealth operative is now in my hands. I squawk, and you are done as an operative both to the Pope and to the order."

For the first time since Bill started talking, Parnell stopped focusing on a spot on the wall and turned to him.

Bill upped the stakes. "Knights of the Sepulchre. I know all about them, the Monsignor and that judge, who got you sprung from Dupré the first time, is also one of you. You and they will be exposed and rendered ineffective if you don't answer my questions honestly and without hesitation. Do you understand me?"

Parnell weighed the proposition. He looked at Hiccock.

"Look, Parnell. Don't underestimate me. I run a top-se-cret operations cluster at the White House. You knew that when you came to me. So you know where my loyalties lie. I will not hesitate to destroy the five-hundred-year old order, or you, if you get in my way." Bill could see he was running this over in his mind. "Just tell me what you know of the elec-tro-dynamic fluid you brought to me and how or who is using it to attack ships."

"I gave you the lead. It's up to you to connect the dots, Doctor." Parnell dropped the affluent Euro-trash accent and spoke like an American for the first time. It was a small nod to Bill's information being correct.

"Here's the last chunk for you to bite into. I have nego-tiated with the Vatican to back off on their opposition to the Super Collider. So I now have juice with the robes in Rome."

"The ring?"

Bill nodded, "Yes the ring of thorns, the knights, I will blow the cover on all of it..."

"No, no, the ring, CERN!"

It was a ten-ton bucket of ice water that hit Bill in the back. "Holy shit!" The collider at CERN was a seventeen-mile 'ring' 574 feet deep in the ground. It was used to separate matter down to its basic elements. The next threshold would be to pierce the attraction force or "glue" that holds the sub-atomic parts of atoms together. "Are you telling me the knights have something to do with the supercollider ring?"

"Dr. Hiccock, we are the Knights of the Ring of Thorns. We think it a prophecy and our destiny to defend against this 'ring of science' that is the greatest threat to creation there could ever be."

"You sound like my partner, ex-partner."

"He's right. You're wrong." Parnell summed up as he relaxed his body language.

"I tell you what wrong is; killing this man and almost me and my son." Bill held up a picture of Roland Landau from his folio. He switched to the bloody photo of the dead priest from the trailer. "And this guy, one of yours, shooting surface to air missiles in the Maryland countryside."

Bill noticed a slight show of surprise rippled across Parnell's face. "You know this priest, don't you?"

"He was a knight but left the order. He felt we weren't aggressive enough."

"Well, he got aggressive, all right. Let's put the collider ring to the side for a moment. Tell me about electric ice."

At first Parnell was confused, but then he reasoned it out. "Yes, I can see how it is like ice. We first got on the trail because of someone we know only as The Engineer. We were trying to find out who he is, but so far we haven't."

"Why were you after The Engineer?"

"We think he's one of the leaders of a plot to blow up the collider at a critical moment and destroy not only the machine, but everything else."

"So how does 'ice' come into it?"

"At first the plot seemed to involve infecting the supply truck of helium coolant with the same substance I showed you. We think their plan was to have the liquid helium cooling system crush the rings when they reached the speed in the rings to smash the protons."

Bill digested the idea. "I have only been exposed to the substance for a minute but I don't see how you could control that kind of attack. The electromagnetic fields associated with shaping the path of the particles as they accelerate would generate a current in the liquid helium well before critical speed. So it would be crushed before that point."

"I think you are right, but it took them a lot longer to figure that out than you just did and they abandoned that approach."

"But they still had all the fluid so..." Bill said.

"Maguambi channels it to the pirates and they use it as a propulsion system for some kind of weapon."

Bill decided he didn't need to inform Parnell of the whale, so he continued. "Thank you. I am sorry it had to come down to all this just for me to get the answers. I'll get Dupré to release you."

As Bill got up, Parnell blurted out, "The Architect."

Bill turned, "Excuse me?"

"It's not over. They abandoned the approach, not the plot."

Bill slowly sat back in the chair and cautiously said, "Go on..."

XXI. WASHINGTON BY DAY

Joey's second day on leave started with a leisurely breakfast and husband and wife banter about all the things in their life that needed attention. From the gutters in the back of the house to the new recycling rules that meant they needed to buy a blue garbage can. An hour later, Joey was on his computer trying to track Parnell Sicard through Interpol when the phone rang.

Phyl came into the room and saw Joey hanging up the phone. "Who called?"

"It was the personnel department of the Executive Branch."

"What did they want?"

"Phyl, I have to go to the office for a while."

"Are you coming home for dinner?"

"I'll be home by four!"

She walked out of the den with him as he stood in the front doorway; she kissed his cheek. "Okay..."

"Want me to pick up something on the way home?"

"Would you like fresh corn?"

"Whatcha makin'?"

"London broil."

"Sounds good. And I'll get some mushrooms too."

"Great, I'll call you if I think of anything else."

"Sure thing."

Joey was amazed that his White House 'A' I.D. hadn't been restricted. Since he was technically still attached to the FBI, he needed to retrieve some of his interagency papers, then go see the HR department.

As he left his office, he was surprised to see the president walking down the hall. He stepped aside out of deference but the Commander-in-Chief stopped to say hello.

"Joey. I thought you were in Paris."

"Got in yesterday morning, sir."

"Really, then why did Bill fly there overnight?"

"He did?"

"Why don't you know that, son?"

"To be honest sir, Bill and I have a difference of opinion."

"Let's go to my office."

"Sir, with all respect, thank you, but you have other things to do. This is not important."

"You don't get to tell the president what is and what isn't important, Joey."

"You know sir, when you put it that way..."

The president laughed and turned to his aide, "Tell Ray to push the Secretary of the Interior for ten minutes."

"Yes, sir."

A minute later, it was Joey and the president in the Oval Office. A Secret Service agent was peering through the peep-hole in the door that led to the secretary's office.

"Joey, Bill works for me and you work for Bill, so you work for me. He's there; you're here. What happened?"

"Can we just say we've reached an ideological impasse?"

"I am not Oprah, and you aren't on the couch, so forget the posturing and tell me what's gotten between the two of you," the president said as he reached for a sour ball and unwrapped it. He tilted the candy dish toward Joey, who demurred.

"No thanks, but what I want you to know, sir, is that I am not comfortable disclosing this to you."

"Duly noted. Joey, the first time I met you, you were risking your career to go up against your boss, the director of the FBI, in defense of Bill. If you didn't do that, Bill would have been sidelined and this country would have suffered millions of dead, under a technical tyranny that would have enslaved us all. So I am damn interested in what you've got to say. So speak, I've got a Cabinet member cooling his jets outside."

Joey enlightened the president as to the disagreement. He tried hard not to cross the constitutional line of accusing the president of a 'high crime or misdemeanor' allowing research on the God Particle to continue.

When he was done, the president sucked on the candy in his mouth a little and then spoke. "You aren't wrong with your concerns; you are, however, wrong about Bill."

"I am afraid that Quarterback has become cheerleader for the research, sir."

"No he hasn't. I asked him to give me the go ahead to support this research. Hell, I sent Professor Landau to his death so that Bill could have every chance to give me the right opinion."

The president opened his desk drawer, pulled out a folder stamped "Eyes Only" and handed it across the desk to Joey. "Read this, then return it to Mrs. Grayson when you are done."

"Thank you, I will sir."

As Joey got up to leave, the president added, "Joey, I had coffee with Agent Burrell the other day."

"Yes, I know sir. That was an extraordinary honor."

"Well, I have to tell you I was surprised, but she's earned her way!"

"Yes, sir." Joey left having no idea what President Mitchell was talking about.

∞§∞

Brooke had left messages for Joey in the office as well as on his cell phone, but Joey didn't get around to them until he sat at his desk. He knew she was on a few days leave, so her call couldn't have been work-related. He sat and read the classified "Report of the Science Advisor to the President on the Safety Issue Concerning Advanced Nuclear Research." The six-page report impacted Joey to his core. In it Bill advised the president that there were not enough safeguards and not enough preventive science known to recommend furthering the experiments at this time. That, added to the fact that the president had told Joey he personally sent Professor Landau to meet Bill at Camp David in one last-ditch effort for him to convince Bill. Even still, Landau failed to change Bill's negative report to the president.

All Joey could say when he finished the report was, "Son of a bitch!" He sat fingering the edges of the top-secret folder, wondering what in the world he would now say to his boss, his friend, his benefactor. His phone rang and interrupted the 'mea culpa' that was forming. "Palumbo, here. Brooke! Sorry I didn't get back to you sooner. Sure, come in now."

Brooke walked the fifty feet from Cheryl's office, where she had been archiving her files, into Joey's office. "Hi."

"First off, I can't tell you how great it was to watch you get your medal. I am only sorry I couldn't be here to shake your hand, so let's remedy that right now." Joey stood and extended his hand.

Brooke self-consciously took his hand and shook it. "Well, thank you for your faith in me, and for allowing me to serve you, Bill, and my country."

"You get a salary for the service, but you got the medal for exemplary action in the face of overwhelming odds. You should save that statement of humility for the future, when they give you the gold watch."

"Well..."

Joey caught the different look in Brooke's eyes. Then the words of Cheryl and the president echoed in his head. He changed his demeanor and casually said, "Hey, you know me and the president, we were just kicking back and chewing the fat, you know just like we always do, and he mentioned something, and you know, my mother having not raised no dummy, I knew that the key to longevity in the White House was not to say to the leader of the free world, 'Hey pal, I don't know what the hell you are talking about.' So why don't you tell me the good news that the president and everyone else around here seems to know already."

"Joey, I have been trying to reach you; I decided to take the package."

Joey was shocked. "Why?"

"Its... it's just time, that's all."

He thought she was going to blurt out that she was pregnant or getting married. He found himself oddly angry. "You are going to dump your career now, for no reason, when you are having corn flakes with the president?"

"I know it doesn't seem to make sense, but Joey, like I told Bill, the events of the last few months have really started me thinking. I don't know, maybe it's also evolution catching up with me, but I don't want it any more. I don't want to be blown off boats or exploding tanker trucks or become shark appetizer or have to make believe a master terrorist doesn't scare the shit out of me while I am working him for information. I am done with the risk, the uncertainty, and the denial of what everyone else takes for granted."

Joey softened, "Those are good reasons. But why wouldn't you consider a leave or sabbatical? Take some time to get your life where you want it and then come back?"

Brooke looked at Joey; she genuinely respected and cared for him. She owed her rise in the Federal Boys Club of Investigation to his guidance and his taking her under his wing. What he was now asking her to do was exactly what he had done. That might work for him, but she was sure it wasn't a life plan for her. Yet she didn't want to attack his choices, so instead she said, "Joey, whatever it was that made me love the job, it's gone! It's not like something else is gnawing at me, something I need to take care of and I'll be right back. No, it's not that. I just don't have the edge anymore or the desire to keep doing this. I want a shot at a normal life. I want to be less of a great guy, and more a happy woman. Can you understand this isn't a phase thing or a whim?"

Joey sighed, "You got me on the happy woman thing; of course you deserve every chance to be happy. You have proven yourself, and the medal the Veep presented you with attests to the fact that you have paid back the Bureau and the U.S. for your training, and we got the better part of that deal. When are you leaving, Brooke?"

"Thanks for hearing me out. I owe you the most. You have become more than just a superior officer in my life. I always want to be able to call you and shoot the shit."

"Sounds like a college break-up."

"In many ways, my relationship with you is one of the longest I've ever had. You see now what a pathetic love life I've had?"

"Thank you, I think. So when are you leaving?"

"The only thing stopping me was talking to you first."

"Well, I appreciate that consideration. Do we at least get to throw you one hell of a retirement bash?"

Brooke then let all caution go to the wind and did something she would have never considered in the past. She opened her arms and hugged Joey.

∞§∞

Bill took over the embassy office that had once been Joey's. A cadre of embassy staff flittered and fluttered in a hubbub of activity that transformed the mid-level diplomatic utility office into that of a cabinet-level official who also had NCA nuclear ranking. It took thirty minutes for Bill to be alone in his new, upgraded office.

The chilling warning from Parnell about the second plot to destroy CERN had no corroboration from any police or intelligence agency in the world. Was Parnell a paranoid or the sharp end of the stick for a group of paranoids, or was he the lone voice yelling about certain Armageddon? Bill could understand the scientific aspect of his allegations, but all the police stuff boggled his mind. He felt like an English lit major dutifully trudging through advanced calculus; he could get the hard facts by rote to pass the test, but he couldn't see the harmonic connections of the bigger picture needed to apply it in the real world. More precisely, should he now commit the considerable resources of the United States of America to alert the world to the threat the of some unknown group against the biggest science endeavor in the history of mankind, on the word of an agent of the Vatican? He looked down at his jotted notes and mind-mapping-style collection of facts that were his way to organize multi-layered problems before him. The more he looked at the cloud of facts on his sideways legal pad, 'Engineer', 'Architect', CERN, Maguambi, U.N., Vatican, Interpol, Dupré, and twenty other words, the more he thought of Joey. He would see this with a cop's eye. See the hidden connections and formulate a practical investigation into this whole murky plot.

The intercom beeped, "Dr. Hiccock, Agent Palumbo on line one."

"Joey, I was just thinking about you. I was..."

"Bill, let me talk."

"Okay..."

"I owe you an apology. Mitchell kind of interceded and proved to me what a knucklehead I have been. I should have never doubted you and I said some things I wish I hadn't. So, there. I think you were right to put me on the beach. Anyway, that's all I wanted to say, 'cept, be careful there in Paris and lean on Dupré if you need anything. He's a good cop."

A wave of relief washed over Bill. The rift between him and Joey had been unwanted and unnecessary baggage he'd been lugging around these last couple days.

"Joey, thanks for that. I was a little pig headed in all this myself. I should have brought you in, but Mitchell was the only one who could clear you for this. I am glad he did."

The moment hung. Bill broke the tie, "So, ready to get back here? I got a whole lot of new stuff that has just come up for you to drill down into. I'll post it on your SCIAD."

"I got to pick up some corn and mushrooms, then I'll be right over."

"Good, cause you know, international crime fighting and thwarting major terrorist plots should never trump going to the market. And tell Phyl you are leaving 'cause of me."

"On the next plane out, boss."

∞§∞

Raffael spent two nights modifying the roulette program on the simulator operating system that he retooled on his home computer. He was about one hundred iterations in when he finally hit the right combination of sensory input and target correlation. He ran it ten more times to make sure he continued to get the same result. He saved the code he had created by compiling it into a file he could load into the system at the LHC. For the first time since the nightmare began, he breathed easier and got six hours of uninterrupted sleep that night. He was ready.

∞§∞

Bill couldn't sleep a wink; his head was spinning with details and scenarios. Parnell Sicard kept coming back as a lynch pin to everything he had learned and was still discovering. He got out of bed and went to the desk in his room and dialed the number he had memorized but never written down.

"Clay, sorry to wake you. I need your opinion on something."

"Hold it, let me take this downstairs."

Bill sat at his desk making circles on his mind-map chart, imagining the super spook treading down the stairs in his PJs and slippers, maybe stubbing his toe on the coffee table as he fumbled for the light switch in the dark.

On cue, Bill heard over Clay's cell phone, "Ow! Damn it!"

"You okay?"

"Damn hassock in the middle of the floor."

Bill tried not to laugh too much.

"What the hell do you want?"

"Clay, I think Percy, er Parnell could be valuable."

"You want to play him? Or bring him in?"

"I think bring him in."

"And you want to know from me if you can trust him?"

"If your crystal ball reaches this far."

Clay sighed the sigh of a man who has just sat down in a big reclining chair. "Well, he is former CIA, so he took an oath once. Of course, you have to be okay with the notion he will probably be playing for his team while he's on your roster."

"I don't think that's an issue. Both teams, it seems, are trying to stop something that could only be the work of a madman."

"Even so, could you shield your sensitive materials from him? Minimize the exposure?"

"Well, that's the thing of it. I've gone over this a hundred times and there is no national security issue here. This is a universal threat. Literally. It supersedes political boundaries."

"Sounds like you already have your answer."

"But tell me, am I being too much the scientist and not enough of a suspicious mission runner?"

"If there is no nat sec vulnerability and you are purely on a quest to identify, isolate, and eliminate a threat, then I say the more the merrier."

"So I should bring him on?"

"You saw his file; he is a first-class operator, good trade craft, and he's gotten you this far. Yeah, I say, put away all your classified materials, lock 'em in your drawer, and let him in on the mission."

"How's the toe?"

"Good night, Doctor. You did good as a spymaster."

Bill smiled and then called Joey to tell him about his decision.

XXII. OFFENSIVE HUDDLE

Joey landed in Paris at 11 p.m and went straight to the Embassy's secure conference area. Upon entering, he went right to Sicard. "Percy, excuse me, Parnell, glad you've decided to join the team. Let's start off again." Joey extended his hand.

Parnell shook his hand; "In the face of a common enemy..." and said nothing more. Joey then acknowledged everyone else. "Inspector Dupré, Marilou, Yardley. Hi ya, Bill."

"Good to have you back, Joey."

"Good to be back, boss. What do we got?"

Everyone took a seat and Bill started. "The big news is that Parnell is on the trail of a new, unknown group, possibly radical extremists or a new breed of black-holers, who have abandoned their primary plot of destroying the Hadron collider, but may still be looking to do this another way. Perc — Parnell was on the trail but it went cold. That's where you come in Joey. I, and more importantly, the president, have made you lead law enforcement officer on this."

"Good. Thank you, Bill. Parnell, would you help me try to pick up the trail again?"

"I would think under the circumstances I really have no choice."

"Come on, show me some love; we didn't burn you to the Vatican."

"And now you want me to be a double agent?"

"No. I want you to work for and be loyal to us and only us. Can you do that?" Bill said.

"You have my word, but only till this is resolved."

"In the face of a common enemy, Parnell," Bill said, then added, "The Inspector and the rest of us here in the Embassy will serve as command and control and communications." Bill then established some pecking order and signed a waiver for Parnell to work under Joey at this high a level of national security.

The others left the room, and just Joey and Parnell were with Bill. "Joey, how do you want to start?"

"Parnell, where were you headed to when you skipped out on us in D.C.?"

"I got a message that the 'Architect' was on the continent. I met with my contact in London and he said either Paris or Geneva, so I took the next flight out."

"To Paris, so what happened?" Joey said.

"I found that Paris was a dead end and I was leaving for Switzerland when Dr. Hiccock and the good inspector interdicted me."

"Why Geneva?" Bill jumped in.

"Besides the obvious since that's where the Hadron is, my British contact had some electronic intel that pointed to Geneva," Parnell said.

"Well then, that's where we start, Bill. Geneva," Joey said.

∞§∞

The first thing she did was open the windows and let the slightly less stagnant New York City night air in. She hadn't been in her apartment for three months. She sat at her kitchen table and leafed through the pile of mail that the widow McGinty on the first floor was nice enough to collect and hold whenever she was away. Ads, flyers, and postcards from every business in the world targeting females, from spas to bottles of skin lotions, diet doctors, and clothes catalogs. *Instant junk,* she thought.

She put aside the letter from the FBI agent's association. It was a testimony to the fact that her status had changed

282 The God Particle

from 'active' to 'retired.' She was too young to be a retired person. Her dad and her uncles were all in their 60s and 70s and only one of her uncles was retired. Although in his case it was at full pension. Since Brooke dropped out of her own volition, her benefits would be based on half of her pay. Though still pretty good, it wasn't enough to live on in New York or Hawaii. Not the way she wanted to live.

Then she found a letter with a Hawaii postmark. The return address was Naval Station Pearl Harbor, HI. Her heart raced as she looked at it. He must have mailed it right before he shoved off. Slowly she slid her finger under the flap, as if it were some prized relic. Inside she found a three-page, handwritten letter. Her heart dropped when she read the first line: "Brooke, I hesitated to write this letter." She put it down as a cold chill suddenly crystallized on her skin. She took a deep breath and looked around the room. On the mantle over the old fireplace, its one-hundred-year old chimney long since bricked over when the brownstone was divided into 'modern' apartments back in the late 40s, was her brother Harley's picture. Although she'd had it for years, it suddenly looked back at her in a questioning expression she had never noticed before. "I love him, Har; for the first time in my life I took the plunge." The picture remained unmoved. "Did I jump the gun?" She looked over at the letter and her eyes caught the word love somewhere in the middle. She took one long look at Harley's photo and then reached over, took the letter and plopped down on the old Barcalounger her dad lugged all the way to her apartment when she first moved in. The worn arms were covered with her mom's crocheted doilies. Even though it was nearly as old as she was, she had welcomed it into her new apartment. She felt warm and at home nestling in it with a good book on long cold nights. She now snuggled up with her feet on the footrest and started to read.

Her mood changed as Mush's explanation for not wanting to send the letter was because he wanted to say these things in person to her. As she read more, she calmed down some.

He wrote of the dilemma he was in. How unfair it was for his love for her — *love for me,* she thought as she beamed — to be couched as a devil's choice between his duty and his heart. How by the time most commanders had earned his grade of responsibility, they were married and more settled. In fact, the only slightly negative notation on his fit-for-duty report was that his status was marked as 'single.' "I guess the Navy was afraid I could be distracted by someone like you :)." She liked his hand drawing of the smiley face. He went on to wonder about her side, if she was facing the same uncomfortable choice. He hoped it was easier for her, because if she decided to spend the rest of her life with him, it might not preclude her job in Washington; that he could probably pull some strings (for the first time in his career) and get re-assigned to the Pentagon. When she finished reading she felt both better and worse. She reread the last few words, 'I don't know how I'll make it through the rest of my patrol. I want things to work out for us more than I have ever wanted anything else in my life, except wishing you were here right now.'

She mulled over everything she had read. Had he already decided to give up his command for her? Could she accept that? Worse, would it fester, rearing its ugly head when the thin times came? Her head stopped spinning when she realized the take-away was, *He loves me, he wants me as much as I want him, and the options are all open for us to find a way to be together, yet still be true to ourselves.*

That thought caused her to squeal and kick her feet on the footrest.

∞§∞

Quietly and unnoticed, Raffey had loaded the many routines he had developed at home into his workstation in the collider's main control room. He masked it as a prototype routine, one of many he was paid to develop, although this one had the ability to end his dilemma in one bright flash.

XXIII. SQUARE PEG

As she walked down Fifth Avenue, a plan was forming: when Mush came back, she'd sell the New York place and they both could move down to D.C. She could probably find work there as a consultant or security analyst.

Brooke had often thought about moving permanently to Washington D.C. after Quarterback had taken her on, but she had a real good deal on her third-story walkup on Forty-Ninth Street, only a few blocks from her old office on Fifty-Seventh Street and Eleventh Avenue. Even though she got to New York only on rare weekends, she had never wanted to give the place up — until now.

Thirty-five more days and he's home. She'd get to Hawaii a few days before, get a little color, and learn her way around a little. At Forty-Seventh Street, she turned west and walked down the street, navigating around the shoppers and gawkers at the windows. Then out of the corner of her eye she saw it: a FedEx truck, one of hundreds in Manhattan on a typical workday. But something red caught her eye, right there by the driver's door. She was torn; the cop in her wanted to see what the substance was, but she also had lunch plans at one o'clock with some agents she used to work with over on West Fifty-Seventh, and she wanted to squeeze in a visit to a jewelry store to see if they still made the kind of ring she had admired on her brother for years. Mush might like a ring like that. Of course, the fact that she turned on to Forty-Seventh Street's Diamond District, with the largest concentration of engagement rings on the planet, never entered into her decision.

Her police instincts took over and she found herself walking toward the truck. She bent down and touched the red; its
stickiness and viscosity between her fingers told her it was
blood. She casually walked in front of the truck to look through
the windshield. No one was inside. She looked over and saw
one of the dozen plainclothes security men who add an extra
layer of protection for the diamond merchants as they shuf-
fle from one building to another, sometimes with millions in
diamonds in little envelopes in their breast pockets. Not used
to being addressed, other than for directions, the man didn't
immediately warm to Brooke's take charge attitude. "Get the
beat cop, now. Tell him to meet me by the truck."

"I'm sorry, what is the problem you are having?"

Brooke recognized the Israeli accent. "Regular Army,
IDF? Or Mossad?"

The man was a little taken aback, but the cold steel of her
eyes told him not to trifle with her. "IDF. My uncle owns a
shop here."

"Brooke Burrell, FBI. Former."

"ID?"

As she fished it out of her bag, he noticed a small-caliber
gun in her purse. He was about to ask her if she had a permit
when she produced her FBI card with the word, RETIRED
stamped through in little holes. "See former. Now get the cop.
I think something is going down with the FedEx truck and it
could be happening right now."

"That truck?"

"Yes."

"The driver went in here." He pointed over his shoulder to
the building behind him.

"When you get the cops, have them search the truck. Tell
'em I am in the building and tell them what I am wearing. I
don't want to get shot." Brooke disappeared into the building, and the man went off down Forty-Seventh looking for the
beat cop.

She approached the building's desk where the guard had everyone sign in. "Do you have the FedEx guys sign in?"

"Everybody signs, lady." The guard said.

"Do you usually see the same guys every day?"

"Yeah, what's this about?"

"Was he the usual guy?"

"No..."

"Where was he going when he signed in?"

"I can't..."

"Look," she read the name from his badge, "Mr. Jackson, in about two minutes the cops are coming." She pulled out her ID again. "What floor, which company?"

"Twelve, Abramowitz and Abramowitz."

She entered the elevator and pressed the twelfth-floor button. On the way up she negotiated with herself: *I am just going to get a handle on the situation; I am not going to get involved. Just surveillance.*

As the door opened, she looked both ways and saw a metal door with a small square window. The sign next to it simply said Abramowitz & Abramowitz. Above the doorframe was a small surveillance camera. She reached into her bag and pulled out a dark scarf. She draped it over her head like a kerchief and approached the door. She looked through the glass square. Immediately behind that door was another door with a slightly larger window and a similar electric lock with an anti-jimmy plate. The two remotely locked doors created a holding cell of sorts. Someone inside needed to ring a person in or out twice. So a potential bad guy could be trapped in the small prison created between the two. Through the window, she saw a woman get slapped hard and Brooke recognized the grey arm of a FedEx uniform as the woman reeled from the impact. The arm swung and she could see the other arm brandishing a gun in a sweeping motion.

Brooke rang the intercom buzzer. No answer. When she rang it again, she could see the sudden freeze in the inner office. She saw the arm of the FedEx guy gesturing with the gun and then a voice came over the box. "We're closed."

"What means, closed? It's Rachel. I got the Goldfarb diamonds for Moishe and I am doubled parked so let me in. I don't want to get a ticket." Brooke did her best Delancy Street fabric-storeowner impersonation. There was no response. She pressed again. "Look, David sent me in with the diamonds in a rush and I got to get back to Brooklyn. Didn't he call Moishe?"

∞§∞

Inside the wholesale jewelry company, Nick Foust was trying to figure out what to do next. He had been planning this robbery for a month. He learned the FedEx schedule. He knew the truck route. He knew that the normally suspicious diamond merchants seldom pay attention to the FedEx guy. He had jacked the truck on west Forty-Third Street. The stupid driver had put up a fight so he had to shoot him right there in the driver's seat. He had thrown the body on the floor, taken his hand scanner thing and badge. He had already lifted the FedEx uniform from a drycleaners, where he had gotten the whole idea when he saw a driver drop it off for cleaning last month.

Now this chick was at the door with more diamonds. If he ignored her she could start trouble, but if he brought her in he'd have more diamonds. Goldfarb diamonds! *Whatever the hell they were.* He waved with the gun to the counter clerk in the small diamond showroom, a woman who was shaking as if she were freezing. "You. Ring her in."

∞§∞

Brooke saw part of the gesture through the bulletproof glass; then the buzzer sounded. She pushed the door and was in the vestibule. The door closed behind her, then the door to

288 *The God Particle*

the showroom buzzed. She walked in. "Thanks. I got to get back to my car, I am double parked." She reached into her bag, "Tell Moishe, I got the diamonds from Goldfarb — who are you?"

"Shut the fuck up, give me the bag." Nick ripped the bag away from Brooke's hand. She already had a grip on her gun and just jutted it into his forehead.

"Don't breathe or I'll blow your brains out. Drop the gun. Do it!" She punctuated the command with a jab over his eyebrow.

Nick was caught off guard. Brooke had turned her body edgeways to him with her arm extended right to his head. "Don't flinch or I'll splatter your brains all over the counter."

Nick said, "Okay. Okay."

"You're not dropping the gun! Drop it. Drop it now or you'll never walk out of here."

"Okay. Okay."

"Fuck the 'okay.' Drop the fucking gun, asshole, or I'll cap your ass!"

That last bit of street lingo registered as the sound of the gun hitting the floor released Brooke's squeeze on the trigger she was a millisecond away from pulling.

"Kick it away, then get face down on the floor. Down!"

Nick looked around, saw he had no options, and one knee at a time got down and then extended his hands and lay down. Immediately, he felt the weight of Brooke's foot on his neck.

"Somebody call the cops and get me something to tie this jerk up with."

As Brooke waited, she noticed something odd. The employees started removing the gems from the display cases and sliding the trays into a huge safe. In thirty seconds, they had all the cases empty and the jewels in the safe. Then the oldest guy there came over to pick up the bag that Nick had been holding.

"Leave those. They're evidence and part of a crime scene," she ordered, standing with one foot on the perp's neck and her gun pointed at his head.

The man looked up at her and obediently nodded as he went back around to his desk in the back room. Brooke had to ask, "Why did you all lock up the stones?"

The old man came back out. "There will be police and others here and sometimes they take souvenirs." He could see the look on Brooke's face as he added with a shrug of his shoulder, "What can I tell you, it happens!"

Twenty minutes later, major case squad detectives and beat cops were crowded into the small showroom with the multi-million-dollar inventory. Detective Crenshaw was trying to understand what had gone down.

"Okay, so you gain entry and he goes for the bag, presumably for the diamonds, and you got a gun and you get the drop on him? Who are you, Annie Oakley?"

"FBI, Special Agent Brooke Burrell, retired."

"No shit! At what? Half pay?" Pay rates and benefits was the currency of cop talk.

Brooke was no different. "Yeah, took the package at twenty-two years in, plus special rate last two years, attached to — a special unit." Brooke almost said, 'attached to the White House.'

"Sweet. Yeah, I was going to pull a federal job, but the wife had the first kid, so moving out of my parents' old paid-for place in Queens and paying D.C. rent wasn't in the cards."

"I hear ya," Brooke said.

"So, you ever see this skell before?"

"No. Like I told the scene commander, I saw the blood on the door of the truck, followed the guy up here, and then kind of improvised from there."

"Look, as a professional courtesy, if you want to come down to the squad later, I'll take your statement."

"Thanks, Detective, cause I was on my way to find a ring for my b — my friend. *That was weird; is Mush my boyfriend?*

"Did you say ring?" Mr. Abramowitz came from the back. "What kind ring?"

"Well, it's a Navy anchor with diamonds." Brooke made a whirly motion around her finger.

"How about an engagement ring?" Abramowitz said as if he were dangling it in front of his favorite niece.

"That could happen."

"You saved my business and who knows, maybe a life or two. When you get engaged, the ring is on me!"

"Really, that's such a nice thing to do."

"What, like stopping a robbery is chopped liver? You'll pick a big beautiful stone, and I'll get my best designer to make a setting you'll plotz from."

"I am ready to plotz then, Mr. Abramowitz."

Detective Crenshaw smiled at Brooke, "Cool!"

∞§∞

Even in Paris, a passerby can easily catch the headlines from the New York Post, especially at the Embassy. The paper is on the desktops of several people who receive the tabloid as one of thirty different U.S. newspapers the ambassador ordered his staff to read every day in order to not lose touch with the tone in America. So Joey was stopped in his tracks when he saw on the cover of the three-day old paper a picture of Brooke next to the headline, 'Familiar Ring' Midtown Jewel Heist Foiled by Alert Ex-FBI Agent. Joey had the paper in Bill's hands in twenty seconds.

"I guess you can't keep a good cop down, Joey."

"I am going to call her later."

"Tell her I said, 'good job.' Now about the Interpol..."

Joey interrupted, "Bill, I was thinking of saying more than that."

"Like what?"

"Like, right now, her Navy boy is somewhere under the North Pole for a few months and obviously she's bored," he tapped the paper in Bill's hand, "so I figured we give the bad guys in New York a break and get her back here on temporary assignment."

"And what would that assignment be, temporarily?"

"I could use Brooke in Geneva with me. Together we could do the whole job and keep it contained — away from the locals and Interpol."

"So Brooke gives us operational security without having to be spread too thin? But what if she's already picking out the china patterns?"

"I bet they have great tableware in Switzerland!"

"It's worth a shot; make the call," Bill said. Then he couldn't help but turn to the sports section to read the hometown view on the Giants' prospects this year.

XXIV. .00000000000000000000000000000 00001

Raffey had not heard from the kidnappers in three days, although he always felt he was being watched. He knew his phones were monitored, and his house was probably under the eye of the monsters. He never knew when he was being followed. He had simply stood next to someone on a tram and almost caused Kirsi to lose her eyes. But here in the lab on his workstation, he was free to upload the files he had pre-pared to stop the madmen in their insane plan. He opened the Unix-compiled roulette program and when it loaded he typed the word 'Simulation' at the password prompt. Although the graphics were rudimentary, the collider and the rings were schematically displayed. Like a marble in a roulette wheel, a small dot started spinning around the col-lider rings on the screen. At the lower right was a time sam-ple number that incremented in powers of ten. That number rose as the speed of the dot orbiting the ring accelerated. The faster the particle went, the higher the sample rate, or as Raffey thought of it, the slice of time narrowed, so that the speed of the dot on the screen remained somewhat the same because the time sample was getting smaller and smaller as the particle accelerated. When the number reached thir-ty-two, the dot seemed to almost freeze, as it now took only a fraction of a pico-second for the dot to make the seven-teen-mile journey; one revolution took only 10^{-32} of a second. Written as a numeral, that's thirty-one zeros after a decimal point before you get to a one. At 10^{-32}, Raffey's narrow slice of time displayed something akin to a slow-motion replay of an event happening at 99.9999 percent of the speed of light.

Only nothing was really happening. The program fooled the giant multi-million dollar, million-ton machine into believing that a sub-atomic particle was actually in its ring. All the ninety-three hundred magnets, sensors, and beam-benders believed this was a real experiment. Only Raffey knew this nuclear gun was loaded with a blank.

∞§∞

Fame is an interesting thing. Brooke recieved a call from her old office. They wanted her to come down and get her mail. She ignored the first call, figuring she'd stop by in a few days and get it. But the next call came from the facilities manager of the New York Office of the Federal Bureau of Investigation; she "needed to remove the mail now."

When Brooke arrived at the office she received the usual razzing any cop who gets a little ink suffers from the rank and file. "Hey, Ring-o!" "Gun Slinger," "Wonder Woman" and more were all respectfully thrown at her as she made her way to the facilities manager's office. On a folding table in the office across from the man's desk was a pile of mail in forty stacks.

Brooke was dumbstruck, "What the...?"

"It started showing up yesterday, all addressed to you," Walter Helfer said.

Brooke started picking up the rubber-banded stacks and flicking the edges with her thumb flipping through the return addresses. Most were from New York, New Jersey and Connecticut, some from as far away as Ohio. One caught her eye; it was from Riyadh, Saudi Arabia. She pulled it from the stack and sat in the chair opposite Helfer's desk. She took his letter opener from his desk to open the handwritten letter. The English was poor but the emotion was clear. It was from the mother of a man who was killed. She was desperate and reached out to the 'hero woman policeman of America.' The authorities in her country gave her no information, no solace and no comfort in the death of her beloved son, Abrim. Her heartbreak was that they accused her son of being less than virtuous and having died in sin. Brooke immediately felt much sympathy for this poor mother who, it seemed, was fighting the Royal Family and government in an effort to resurrect her son's name in the eyes of the followers of Allah. Brooke sighed audibly.

"Tough one?" Helfer asked.

"Saudi Arabia! How shitty must things be over there that his poor woman reaches out to me?"

"How shitty are things here in the U.S. that all these people reached out to you, period!"

Brooke looked at the stacks of envelopes. "Good point! Mind if I go through some of these here?"

"Just so long as you either throw them out or take 'em with you when you leave. I want 'em out of here," Helfer said, as he brought a wastebasket next to Brooke.

Two hours later there were two filled and one half-filled blue recycling barrels next to Brooke, and she was down to her last stack. She had placed nine letters aside, either because they were heartbreakingly eloquent or she thought she'd snoop around a little. For instance, there was a woman who wrote saying that her daughter had been killed by her husband's bookie as a way to get him to repay a gambling debt. Another sought out Brooke to help track family heirlooms that disappeared from a bonded warehouse; the heirlooms were gold coins squirreled away by her grandfather right before the government recalled all the coins in the 30s. The now rare coins were worth millions and she suspected the manager of the warehouse. Brooke didn't know what she would do with these letters. Maybe just write back saying she was retired or maybe offer some advice, but that would probably make her somehow legally responsible, so maybe not.

Maybe with these she could get a P.I. license and make some cash before Mush got back.

Brooke got up to take a bathroom break when her cell phone rang. It was Joey from Paris.

∞§∞

The Boston Seven, as Bill had come to refer to them, were proving to be an isolated group who had two major connections that rattled Bill and the higher-ups in both Justice and Homeland Security. One was a direct pipeline to the militant wing of the Irish Republican Army in America. That was where the surface-to-air shoulder-launched missile had come from. ICE and ATF were raiding and shutting down that arm right now, in raids on docks and airports, and a few diplomats were being uninvited by the State Department to stay in America. The second element, and by far the more worrisome to Bill and the president, was the Knights of the Sepulchre members to whom the Boston Seven had arms-length access. It was they who had forwarded to the seven the instantaneous information on the meeting Bill had with the Landau at Camp David.

What kept the president and all his best people awake every night was that there were spies deep within the American government at the most sensitive levels. Although not Russian, Chinese or Iranian, they were spies who had decided there was a loyalty that surpassed their oath to the United States. Bill knew that all spies share this suborned agenda; however, these individuals were doing it out of religious obedience. The devastating impact of this subtle difference was that a communist spy in the government would never take May fifth, the Russian Day of Independence, off, lest they show their true colors. Yet employees of the United States government openly celebrated Christmas and Easter and Passover and Ramadan. Deciding who was a religious spy was a hornet's nest of conflicting national security and civil liberties tenets. For that reason, the president quickly passed a finding, a secret law, allowing extreme measures to be taken in ferreting out the Knights. Mitchell knew that this kind of treason threatened the sovereignty of the United States at a cardiovascular level compromising the very heart of government. He was out for blood. He didn't have to wait long.

Bill started reading the morning briefing Cheryl had prepared back in Washington on the developments overnight in the Boston Seven investigation. The FBI had broken the IRA connection by arresting the second-level operatives in five states. The FBI, the Diplomatic Security Service, the Secret Service and the CIA were circling around three suspects who might be members of the Knights. Arrests were imminent, one inside the White House itself. Bill knew that one would personally hurt James Mitchell the most. Being the first independent to hold office, and owing no patronage to either party to hand out jobs, he had hand-picked every one of the heads in the administration. This would strike him at his very core. The report was interrupted by a knock on the door.

"Come in."

The janitor of the Paris Embassy entered, "Monsieur, here is the hammer you requested."

"Thank you, er..."

"Henri."

"Yes, Henri, thanks." Bill unlocked his desk drawer and placed the hammer in it.

The report riled up anger in Bill as he read it. He wanted summary public execution in Yankee Stadium for the person whose treason had led to the death of Professor Landau, and to announce to the world, *You can't fuck with America, whether you are a radical Muslim or devoted Catholic.* Bill didn't connect his personal desire for revenge with the fact that he and his son came inches away from being killed by that same treasonous act.

Bill's aide knocked on his door, "Sir, the Papal Nuncio is here."

"Send him in. And no calls." Bill closed the briefing file and put it in his top desk drawer. He stood and shook the hand of the de facto ambassador of one billion Catholics around the world, but principally of the one head Catholic seated in the Holy City in Rome.

"Your Eminence, thank you for coming all this way." Bill gestured to the chair next to the couch, figuring it would be easier for the septuagenarian to sit in than the couch, which swallowed up anyone who sunk into it.

"Coming to Paris is never a burden for the former Cardinal of France," he said with an old man's grunt as he sat.

Bill chided himself for already slipping on a diplomatic banana peel for not knowing that, or knowing the man for that matter. The bishop had been brought up from the French 'farm team.' France being the birthplace of diplomacy, he must have been a shoe-in for the Vatican's chief political officer.

"Will your ambassador be joining us?" the Prince of the Church asked.

"No, no, Your Eminence. I bring a personal message from the president, and he asked that I share it only with you. No disrespect to the American ambassador, but when you hear this sentiment you'll understand why it was better left to me, a non-diplomat."

"Very dramatic introduction, Dr. Hiccock. Before you proceed, may I have some water?"

"Sure." Bill got up, brought the tray with the pitcher and glasses over to the table before them, and poured a glass for the man. "Here you go."

"*Merci beaucoup*. Sorry I interrupted you; go on."

"Yes. Well, the president would like you to convey to the Pope that the sovereignty of the United States will not be compromised by religious zealots and, in the last analysis, downright spies. The Vatican must immediately cease and disband the espionage network through which sensitive U.S. government intelligence is channeled to sects, who then perpetrate atrocities like the assassination of Professor Landau."

"With all due respect, Professor, nothing of the sort has been orchestrated by the Vatican, and frankly, I take deep umbrage at your allegation...No! Your *condemnation,* of the Papacy."

"Bishop, I assure you, we do not make these accusations without overwhelming proof, physical evidence of which is being amassed at this very moment for world exhibition if you fail to comply with the president's wishes."

"Threatening blackmail in the court of public opinion will not serve your end."

"Not the public court sir, but the Supreme Court of the United States, as a prelude to declaring that surveillance of all Catholic churches and other property be considered as necessary to answer a clear and present danger to the United States."

"That's preposterous. American Catholics will not stand for such draconian measures. He will isolate himself and be more of a lame duck than he is already."

"There's more. Every church lease, every retreat, every Catholic university, rectory, and neighborhood bazaar will go right to the top of the IRS audit list. And the Justice Department will sweep through every Catholic archdiocese and very publicly arrest every priest who ever smiled at a kid sideways. Very public! When they're finished, American Catholics will be converting to Protestantism — hell, Judaism, before the next Sunday."

"This is madness, separation of church and state..."

"Don't go there; the separation tradition does not serve as immediate immunity against all crimes or suspicion of illegality. A priest who commits a hit and run with his car is not covered under separation. He is, and will be tried as, a criminal. It's the same for espionage — worse, because your guys really pissed off the president. Off the record?"

"Yes."

"He wants whoever your spy is in the White House executed! His counsel has, of course, objected, but then the old man pushed for and got a mandatory life sentence without possibility of parole for the Vatican mole. Back on the record."

"Doctor, your accusations and the measures you are proposing, are tantamount to a declaration of war. I am afraid I cannot take your word that such a drastic message is truly that of the president and not just your own prejudice as a disenchanted Catholic — a man of science as well."

"I told him you'd say that, and the problem is, if he made this any more official, there would have to be a record of your crimes against America as well as his radical response. So in the interest of giving you and the Pope a way out, he has kept this only between himself and me. But I told him you wouldn't believe me alone, so we came up with this idea."

Bill got up, went to his desk and opened a locked drawer. He returned with a hammer and an iPhone. The old priest watched with curious intent as Bill placed the hammer on the table next to the water tray and moved the pitcher and glasses off the tray.

He touched and slid his finger over the iPhone and held it up for the bishop to see and hear. On the screen was a video of the President of the United States in the Oval Office. The picture was unsteady as it was being held by hand across the president's desk. The bishop watched as the president's eyes looked up and asked, "Is it going, Bill?"

Bill's voice was heard, "Recording, sir."

In the video, the president crossed his hands on the desk, nodded his head, and spoke. "Your Eminence, I have asked Dr. Hiccock to record this message to you because I know what he just told you is hard to imagine; but as God is my witness, this abomination of my country's security and the personal oath and unquestioned loyalty I demand from my immediate staff will not stand."

He pounded the desk as he spoke. "God damn it, I will not have the security of my government eroded by religious subtext. If the Vatican does not destroy this network, I will use everything in my power to put the entire Catholic Church in America on the same status as mosques and radical Muslim groups who enjoy such special attention by the Justice and Treasury departments, which, I may remind you, I run! Make no mistake, Cardinal, don't fuck this up!"

The president then looked up to Bill, behind the camera, and said, "That's all Bill, make sure he sees this," and the video went off.

Bill saw the color drain from the man of God's face; no one had ever spoken to him, much less the Pope, that way. Then Bill broke the stunned silence by saying, "Bishop, it was just the president and me in the room, and the Oval Office recording system was turned off. I made no copy and I recorded it right on this phone, which is, thankfully, not mine." Bill then smashed the phone with repeated blows of the hammer until it was cracked and splintered on the water tray. All the man could do was stare at the carnage of the phone as the weight of the diplomatic dilemma that had fallen on his shoulders became apparent. Bill held up the hammer and admired it. "Plausible deniability, I think you diplomats call it."

Then Bill just couldn't resist, "When can I report to the President of the United States that we have hammered out a deal?"

∞§∞

On the flight over, Brooke reviewed the CIA world book information on Switzerland and found that the Federal Office of Police, or FedPol, as the Swiss called it, coordinated international operations for the twenty-six quasi-independent cantons of police organizations across the Alpine country, so that was their starting point. Brooke met Joey at their headquarters in Geneva. First order of business was a big hug.

"Brooke, glad to have you back, even if only for a little while."

"I found my life in a holding pattern and your call was timed perfectly."

"Nice work, really, back in New York," Joey said as they released each other.

"Before I knew it, I was facing the perpetrator. I didn't stop to think; I just wound up there."

"Instinct. It's hard to suppress. Gee, I guess Mush doesn't know about it, huh?"

"I don't see how he could."

"You going to tell him about the free ring?" Joey asked, pointing his right index finger to the third finger of his left hand.

"If I don't, somebody will, but call me crazy, I think he's the kind of guy who would want to pay for the ring himself. Listen to me, will ya! I mean we haven't even discussed marriage and here I am jumping to conclusions like a school girl in the lunchroom."

"Brooke, love makes teenagers out of all of us!"

Brooke just smiled. He was right; she shouldn't fight it. Risk had always been part of her job. To fall in love and risk that it might not turn out the way she wanted shouldn't be more terrifying than facing bad guys and guns, but it was. "Thanks Joey. How's Phyl?"

"Hates me being here, so the sooner we get going, the sooner I can get home." He escorted her to a conference room.

Parnell was already there with Captain William Lustig, FedPol director. Joey made the introductions and then everybody sat down. Lustig started speaking in accented but flawless English. "Here are the records, cross-indexed to the leads Mr. Sicard was investigating. I have widened the time window on the search to twenty-four hours prior to and after the day Mr. Sicard was to arrive here from France. Each of these twenty-six folders contains the two-day crime reports from each of the cantons translated into English. I suggest that we focus on the cantons of Geneva and the surrounding area first, then increase the scope if we find nothing."

Since the logic was sound, all agreed and the folders were distributed. They started with Geneva and the contents were circulated as each judged it or tried to discern any connection to anything related to the 'Architect' or 'Engineer' that Parnell was hot on the heels of.

After two hours, there were no real hits. Brooke had a thought, "Have we checked with the Security at CERN?"

"They have assured us that all persons coming and going for the month at the facility have been confirmed and identified as who they presented themselves to be both by guard's inspection of their identity papers and, later, facial recognition software from the entrance security cameras."

"It does not rule out the possibility of a turned employee, plant, or mole who is already cleared for work."

"Yes, that keeps the head of security at Hadron alert and he is constantly monitoring the workers and scientists for any suspicious behavior."

"Difficult job; I work for a scientist and quirky doesn't begin to cover it," Joey said before he added, "Ten minute break, everyone?"

All agreed and stepped out of the room to get coffee or relief or both. Brooke made a beeline to the coffee. She had flown through the night and got a little sleep on the plane, but her ass was dragging. As she figured out the buttons on the automatic machine, she looked over at the TV that was on in the office. The news was on, and she noticed there was coverage of a trial or court hearing. Through the standard Swiss German she heard the name 'Abrim.' She glanced up at the screen and saw a file photo of Abrim Walhime, identified as a Saudi national. She grabbed the next person that passed her and asked, "What are they saying?"

"Well, the judge has decided to suspend the investigation into the murder until such time as the woman of interest can be located."

"Thank you." Brooke returned to the room.

They stayed at it for most of the afternoon, and in the end all they had was one possible lead. Parnell thought there was something to a break-in at a computer factory and he went down to the records department to see if it connected.

Brooke took the opportunity to make a special request. "Captain Lustig, I noticed on TV before that there is a case concerning a Saudi national?'

"Yes, the security guard. Most tragic. The victim of a sex scandal."

"I remember reading about that. He goes after a hooker and the pimp kills him," Joey added.

"And both disappeared. There is no case to pursue so the judge has suspended the inquiry pending further developments."

"Why does it interest you, Brooke?" Joey asked.

"After I was in the paper, I got tons of mail. Some were like, 'You go girl,' but most were people writing and asking for help. Oddly enough, I got a letter from Abrim's mom in Saudi Arabia. She also heard about the jewel heist. I felt for her, as apparently the circumstances brought shame on his family so she got double grief. Anyway, her letter really got to me, so I thought since I am here anyway, I'd look into it."

"In your spare time!" Joey said.

"Of course, boss. Spare time." She nodded and opened the next folder from the pile.

They knocked off at seven thirty and Brooke was too tired to take up Joey on his offer to grab a bite, so she went back to her room and crashed. At around eleven, she rolled over and awakened with an urge to pee. She stumbled into the bathroom and upon exiting, she grabbed the remote and popped the TV on. She clicked off the hotel channel and landed on the news. The next story was once again the news that the judge suspended the Saudi case. That gave her an idea. She got out her laptop and signed into the hotel's Wi-Fi network, charging the fee for a twenty-four-hour period to her room, then commenced to search for news about the murder.

Using two different translation programs, she scanned the news reports in Arabic and German. Most of what she read was a rehash of the initial story as retold by other national news agencies, with later reports containing political bents sprinkled in from the Arabs, which was as close as her German-English translation program got her. The Iranian coverage — in Farsi which she was versed in — savaged the Royal Family and charged them with cover-up. As she widened her search, she learned that the men chosen to be security guards for the Royal Family went through rigorous screening and had to prove loyalty before all else to the King. They were selected to be beyond questions of greed, politics, or gambling. She read that many protected persons in the Middle East, or the world for that matter, had been assassinated by their trusted security men.

In an article about the killing of Anwar Sadat of Egypt, she found a kernel of truth to what the woman, who wrote her about her son, had mentioned about her 'chaste' son. Alcohol, gambling, deviant sexuality, love interests, love triangles, and drugs were all leverages an enemy could employ to turn a trusted body guard into an assassin. Under that kind of personal pressure, the loyalty of any human might be swayed. The need for self-preservation of a protector often trumped their oath of allegiance to their protectee. Therefore, men who didn't dabble in these things were the most reliable and less likely to turn their guns on those they had sworn to protect.

In the Hammer of God operation, a trusted Diplomatic Security Service agent had been turned by a Jihadist woman whom he loved. He then engineered the kidnapping of the U.S. Ambassador to Egypt.

At 2 a.m. she finally yawned and closed her computer. Before she nodded off, she made a plan to visit the nightclub tomorrow after work.

XXV. GETTING RELIGION

The aftershock of the president's little video message, delivered by Bill to the Vatican Envoy, had reverberated worldwide throughout the entire Catholic oligarchy. Within 72 hours, three Mitchell administration personnel had quietly resigned, two at low-level positions in the Old Executive Building next door to the executive mansion. The third one was Claire Cunningham, an administrative assistant to the president. Her job in the West Wing was assisting the president with his paperwork and materials, so she was on the inside and privy to almost everything the president was involved in. Her devout Roman Catholic observance, on full display on her smudged forehead every Ash Wednesday, would have been deemed perfectly innocent prior to the emergence of the Knights. Now Claire and other staffers who might wear a cross were suddenly viewed as potential security threats just as surely as if they had a photo of Fidel Castro, Chairman Mao, or Putin on their White House desks.

The president was outraged and inflexible. He was satisfied with the loss of pension and immediate separation of the two members of his administration who were at arms-length from his office, but for Claire he wanted the full weight of his ruling to be brought down on her head. Furious that she would betray the trust of the inner circle, he had her arrested and charged with treason. So deep was his rage and sense of personal violation that even the person who had recommended her for the position and that person's superior were also demoted and lost two levels of pay.

Her arraignment proceedings were cloaked under a national security blackout, in part because it left a diplomatic channel to the Vatican publically intact, but also because neither Mitchell nor Claire wanted it made public that she spied for the Pope. The process stayed under the radar for the first twenty-four hours, until the U.S. marshals found her dead from an overdose of sleeping pills when they came to pick her up for her secret arraignment.

Among the items the marshals logged in as her personal effects was one barbed-wire-type ring. She never wore the ring because it had a tendency to snag fine fabrics; a downside not contemplated by the men who had designed it. In the end, she wore it one final time in honor of her service to the Vatican. That service was indeed rare. She had been specifically approached and allowed to serve as an undercover agent in the normally male-dominated Roman Catholic structure because of her close proximity to the President of the United States. Her comprehensive training in clandestine communications and spy craft, that would make the CIA and KGB proud, were honed on innocent "weekend retreats" which just passed banally as the religious observance of a devout Catholic woman.

Upon Claire's death, the whole thing evaporated into just a human drama. Her death at her own hand was accepted as a personal matter and the indictment was sealed forever by executive order. Not acknowledged, but felt throughout the upper corridors of power, was a collective sigh of relief. It all tied up nicely for everyone: the president, the Pope and the American people. The Papal Nuncio himself had an off-the-record audience with the president in his residence the next day, bringing the assurance of the Pope that the Knights of the Sepulchre were disbanded and dismissed. Then the Nuncio handed over an intelligence file, which detailed the exploits of the Knights over the last fifty years, including their role in foiling the attempted assassination of the Pope in

France. Information that would fill in some blanks in the CIA and FBI's timelines of history.

The president also accepted an invitation to meet with the Pope in Rome and have a joint press conference on efforts to help the world's poor. The president gracefully accepted and sent his appreciation to the Pope in the form of a recently-recovered bottle of brandy from the 1800s found in the safety deposit box of a former communist dictator who secreted it away during World War II. He had the FBI lab run a special analysis of the bottle with a self-sealing needle. It proved to be non-lethal and therefore worth hundreds of thousands to collectors. The president hoped it would heal the rift between him and God's representative on Earth prior to their first face-to-face meeting.

XXVI. RIDE 'EM COWBOY

"It's impossible. The whole thing is totally organic, biological and doesn't have any mechanical parts or metal machinery. So there's nothing to ping or scan to get a return, an echo or signature. According to the plans your Agent Burrell obtained from Disney, even the batteries have minimal hard metals. Dr. Hiccock, it's not a hole in the water; hell, it is no different than water. How can we find it in an ocean?"

Bill sat back in his chair. The head of naval warfare tactics was unloading his frustration at trying to hunt and kill a pirate whale that made less noise and generated less heat than an actual whale. They had calculated that the "whale" displaced approximately two tons of water, but the actual weight of the non-organic, mechanical/propulsion parts, batteries, signal and steering control was probably only ten pounds. That was four hundred times smaller than the faux mammal's total mass. Another way it was described to Bill was like trying to find the insides of a single laptop — just the circuit boards and batteries without the case — floating somewhere in or under the Pacific.

Although Bill felt sympathy for the man and his futile assignment, his job wasn't to commiserate. "Admiral, there has got to be a way, something we are overlooking."

"We've run this up more flagpoles than co-ed underwear on hell night, and no one, not military, not civilian contractor, or even think-tank weenies, has a clue."

"I know this is probably a silly question, but can our current computer-aided sonar be re-calibrated?"

"Re-calibrated to what? Water? Yeah, and you'll get an instant, off-the-charts reading; then where are you?"

"Okay, I admit that was a little elementary, but hey, it was my first shot." Bill tried his proven tactic of adding a smile to his demeanor, but the two-star fleet officer wasn't biting.

"How is the whale piloted? Is it a total remote control weapon or more like a mini-sub with a driver?"

"Look, it could be a pilot whale that swallowed Minnie Driver. She or any human is just as biological as the device. Unless they make a noise like metal on metal, humans are mostly water with the trace amounts of minerals and iron in the body that don't reflect a ping."

Bill was just connecting the actress' name, Minnie Driver, to the admiral's attempt to add a smile to his demeanor.

For some stupid reason, Bill was going to add, "It don't mean a thing if it ain't got that ping!" but the decorum the conversation demanded changed his mind.

The admiral recapped the challenge facing them, "Look, without a bounce or something to bounce off of, there is no return, therefore no range and no firing solution. All we can do is waste a lot of fuel and hope to run the damn thing over."

Bill stared for the longest time at the two five-pointed platinum stars on his desk; the Admiral was right, this was a real tough nut to crack.

∞§∞

Bill was really racking up the Special Air Missions frequent flier's points. He was back in D.C. on a quick thirty-two-hour turn-around and was flying out mid-day tomorrow back to the team in Europe.

Janice had had the day from hell at work and Bill's meeting with the admiral delayed his getting home till after eight, so they decided to go out for dinner. Mimmo's was becoming their favorite place. "Casual and good" was how Bill thought of the bistro where Mimmo's wife, Tina, did all the cooking, while Mimmo worked the dining room. "The no makeup place," was how Janice defined it, in that just a little tinted foundation and lip-gloss and she was at the level of Mimmos. One didn't go there to be seen, just to eat. Figuring that little Richie would probably nod out before they got their entrees, they passed on the sitter and brought the sassy seat.

Mimmo was his usual happy self as he seated the Hiccocks. He attached the sassy seat to the table and even took Richie from Janice and sat him in the contraption. "I got the meatballs tonight!"

"Sold!" said Bill. Tina's meatball dish was a meal in itself. Janice scratched the itch for Shrimp Scampi and then she opened a baggie with skinned apple slices for Richie, since he had already eaten at his usual time. They both took pride in the fact that Richie was always the perfect little kid in restaurants, so they were both shocked when he let out a shriek and then began squirming, throwing apple slices, crying and trying to break free from his sassy little prison. They had never seen him like this, and they were very conscious of the disturbance they were causing in the room. No matter what they did, no matter how they tried to distract him and do the little game things that were usually good for a few minutes of quiet baby time, nothing worked.

"You know it's past his bedtime, so he's a little cranky," Janice volunteered to the couple seated next to them. Their bittersweet smiles in return were of small comfort.

"Maybe we should get it to go," Janice said in the voice that, although it sounded like a suggestion, all husbands know it is not open to discussion. "Gimme the keys, I'll take him out to the car," Janice said as she got up and pulled her son from his seat.

Bill started unhooking it, trying to avoid looks from the other patrons.

Mimmo came over and Bill announced in a voice a little louder than needed, "You know it's past his bedtime and he's a little cranky." Just in case the rest of the diners didn't get it the first time from Janice.

At that moment, Tina emerged from the kitchen, seeing Bill heading out the door with the seat she asked, "Aw, the bambino, he no feel good?"

"Nah, he's just tired."

"No, it's his teeth. You'll see, I raise five kids. I hear him all the way in the kitchen. It-a rattles my own teeth, that's how I know. You'll see, I know."

"You may be right. I'll take this out to the car and come back for our order."

"Its da teeth, I'm-a-tell-a you. It rattles, right here..." She wiggled her fingers in front of her teeth.

Bill got to the car, and of course Richie was now a quiet, happy baby boy banging his stuffed rabbit on the car seat. "Figures; now he's a little gentleman."

Janice was smoothing her son's hair. "He's just tired, Daddy. He didn't want to sit in a stuffy restaurant eating apples while you had meatballs."

"Tina says he starting to teethe. Said she felt it vibrate in her head when he let out that wail." Bill stopped and froze. His last words reverberated in his head.

"He's just getting his second year molars, Daddy — Bill, you okay?" Janice was concerned because he looked as if he had just had a stroke.

Bill snapped out of it, "Yeah, yeah, I'm fine. I've got to call the admiral."

"Why? Is he a naval pediatric dentist?"

"No — what Tina said; she just told me how to catch the whale!"

∞§∞

At four in the morning, Bill's SCIAD network chimed, awakening him from his half sleep with his feet up in front of his desk in the den. He wiped the groggy mask from his

312 *The God Particle*

face with his hand and yawned as he opened the communiqué from element member Thieles. He scanned it and saw
the response he had been waiting for. He looked at his watch
and figured he could catch the last two hours of sleep in his
bed. He banged out a thank you response, closed down the
terminal and went up to bed.

∞§∞

The admiral was in Bill's office at 7:45 a.m.

Bill started right in, "Okay here goes, you were right. There
is no way to get a return off the whale, but that's because our
search is the active component, the whale is passive."

"True, but obvious."

"Piezoelectric effect!"

"I'm listening..."

"We base it on the same principles as ultrasonic time-do-
main reflectometers, only we sweep frequencies from one
hundred kilohertz through one megahertz. At some point the
piezoelectric effect will resonate in the propulsion fluid and
that will be like a high string on a piano, resonating when its
lower octave is played."

"Like long range sonomicrometry."

"Yeah, like that — whatever that is." Bill was beyond his 4
a.m. lesson in piezoelectric resonance. But the admiral had
picked up the ball and was heading for the goal line, so Bill
considered his job was done.

"So we bombard an area of ocean with ultrasonic waves.
If they hit the electro reactive fluid of the whale, at some point
the whole whale starts to vibrate and that becomes an anomaly in the water we can detect."

Bill summed it up, "Like ringing a church bell with a rifle
shot."

∞§∞

Larson Industries had three hundred ultra-high frequency transducers in its San Diego warehouse. Interestingly enough, they were piezoelectric transducer elements that were capable of the megacycle range Bill's idea required. The rest of the circuitry was stupid simple: a two-hundred-dollar frequency generator and a wide-band UHF power amp, the kind right from the hefty end of a radar system. Roughly five thousand dollars worth of cobbled together hardware that could thrive on any ship that had an eighteen thousand watt electric socket, and that was most naval vessels. Soon all three hundred of these units were put on every kind and every style of Navy ship in the Pacific and Indian oceans. Water increases the range and efficiency of sound, so that one unit could cover four hundred square miles of ocean one mile deep. Limiting the search pattern to the areas where the whale had struck the Vera Cruz, the *Nebraska* and the Toyota ship geometrically increased the odds of finding the whale and limited the response area or "box."

What to do when they found it was not as simple. U.S. Naval Intelligence didn't want it sunk, they wanted it captured, either to analyze it and effect counter-measures, but more likely to see if they wanted to replicate the stealthy weapon.

These special missions are normally doled out to the next SEAL team up for assignment. So it was that SEAL Team Nine got the call. Rapid deployment was the key. Once identified, no one could predict how long it was possible to track the still passive machine. Hydro-effects like thermal layers and the salinity of the ocean's water complicated the tracking.

The operational plan was to have half of SEAL Team Nine always in the air, at jump-ready status, working off four Sea Stallion helicopters orbiting the most probable areas. The mission was designed so that one of the teams would always be within twenty minutes flight time to any point within the "box." Each operator wore a wet suit, air-tanks, assault rifle, detonation charges, and one new piece of equipment they called "the knitting needles." It was essentially an underwater Taser, capable of delivering a fifty-thousand-volt jolt, but only at the long end tips of the "needles."

∞§∞

Bill asked for hourly updates on operation Quint, a name the SEALs came up with during the operational brief. Although created as an homage to the Robert Shaw character, Quint, the shark hunter in the movie Jaws, it was close enough to their task that it stuck. Everything about the operation was theory. The sweep might not actually work or not cause the whale to start buzzing and give itself away. To that end there was a two-week time limit put on the entire op so that they wouldn't keep searching with a potentially faulty methodology.

His phone rang. "Dr. Hiccock, the president would like to see you, in the Oval, now."

"Know what it's about, Suzy?"

"No, but the U.N. ambassador, sec nav, and the director of the CIA are in there with him."

Bill hustled down the hall. Usually he had a heads-up on any presidential meeting, even casual ones. To be called in on the spur of the moment was truly a rare event... *Or am I in trouble*, Bill thought. He forgot to take the obligatory deep breath before the agent manning the door swung it open.

"Mr. President, Mr. Secretary, Director, Mr. Ambassador."

"Bill, how did we get here?"

"You mean, Quint?"

"Yes, we were going over our strategy for when we present our case at the U.N., and we noticed we have two hundred eighty ships making circles in the ocean. Some kind of special electronic rig on each and SEALs burning gas in choppers twenty-four/seven."

Bill still didn't know where this was going and responded in a cautious tone, "Yeee-yeah — and your question, sir?"

"How did CERN get us here and do we widen our indictment to include what you are investigating in Europe?"

Bill took that deep breath and sat at the chair opposite the president, "Oh, well, through some diverted funds from the U.N., the Maguambi regime was able to secure the electro-expansive fluid that propels this whale. It was made available to the pirates because the original intention was to add it to the liquid helium cooling systems of the Large Hadron Collider and burst the rings. But the amount of electric charge generated by the rings made that plan impractical because the fluid would expand the instant it came within twenty feet of the rings."

The CIA head chimed in, "So it was on the black market, and Maguambi orchestrated break-ins in America and France to steal and dust off a Disney plan to make animatronic whales for an attraction in their theme parks."

"But the corporation abandoned the development and production due to ecological concerns." Bill chimed in.

The CIA director continued, "Maguambi built it instead and used it for pirate attacks."

"Including the one on the Vera Cruz which our operative was on, sir," Bill said.

The president looked out the window. "So if you find the person or group that stole the initial batch of this super-fluid, they are the ones who are planning to attack CERN?"

"That is the working theory, Mr. President." Bill said.

"Ron, you think Bill's op will succeed?" The president asked the secretary of the navy.

"My head of warfare tactics worked with Bill on it and he's the best, so I approved it."

"Good hunting, Bill. When are you heading back over?"

"I'm wheels up in two hours, sir."

∞§∞

The USS Cayuga, a fleet support vessel that was generally in the rear and well away from any action, was emanating the broadband wavelengths. The sonar man, who also served as radar and satellite communications tech on the small ship was surprised at the return suddenly coming from a spot in the ocean two hundred eighty miles due east of his location. Then it was gone. He placed his hand on the new signal generator that had been installed in his radio shack three days earlier. He switched off the auto-sweep and manually swept the dial that changed the frequency the machine put out. Slowly, he raised and lowered the setting until he got another return. He made note of the setting: one hundred eighty-six megahertz. He then radioed the USS Saipan, the Quint control ship for the sector of the ocean they were patrolling.

∞§∞

SEAL Jump Two was the closest team at ten nautical miles from the spot. The huge twin turbo-shaft engines of the Sea Stallion CH-53D started gulping air as it top ended at 170 knots or 196 miles an hour vectoring to the coordinates they received from the Combat Information Center on the Saipan.

∞§∞

They spotted the whale in the water at two hundred fifty feet altitude. The whale machine was making headway at eight knots. This was a challenge for the frogmen, because they'd have to keep up with the thing as they tried to capture it. They decided to dead drop onto the body, which was luckily just under the surface.

The Stallion hovered to match the speed of the machine at six feet over the waves, its prop wash surely being noticed by anyone inside operating the machine, unless it was a remote-controlled weapon. Operator Number One flattened out to jump and land across the top of the machine, but the whale jerked right and he wound up off the side. Number Two waited as the pilot adjusted his position, then jumped in. He landed on the back of the machine as Number One swam to keep up and Number Three waited on the copter's skid for the disabling of the machine before he jumped.

On the back of the whale, Number Two jammed the needles into the rubber-like skin and pressed the trigger. The entire whale bloated and became rigid, like steel. He felt a tingle, even through his wet suit. The forward propulsion was halted, and it became a rock solid mass due to the high voltage being applied to the fluid, which caused it to solidify and expand, like Bill's electric ice.

It was now Three's turn; he grabbed the winch hook outside the cabin door. The crewman released the cable and he, the cable and the hook dropped into the ocean. Number One was swimming up to the tail and Number Three handed off the cable to him. He submerged and came up on the other side of the whale, then passed the hook back to Three, who locked it around the cable, creating a slip-noose of sorts. He gave the thumbs up, the crewman operated the winch, and the tail of the stiff machine rose.

The whale was estimated to weigh two tons. The Stallion was good for a four-ton payload, but not the winch. So as not to stress the line, they lifted it only a few feet up and then throttled forward at five knots as the Saipan closed in on their location at thirty knots. SEAL Jump One pulled up, recovered the three SEALs in the water, and accompanied the other chopper on its slow drag of the machine across the wave tops.

Then, as if in blasphemy to the gods of Duracell, operator Number One asked, "How long will the knitting needles stay charged?"

Suddenly, the Sea Stallion bucked. The whale's tail started flapping, making huge tugs, straining the winch and with it, the whole copter. It was all the pilot could do to counteract the jolts. He knew he couldn't keep it up much longer. "Cut the line!" he yelled back at his crewman.

The petty officer was about to release the winch when Operator Four interceded. He jumped out of the cabin door and shimmied down the cable as it was whipping from the bucking whale. It was an incredible feat of strength and guts. He slipped the last five feet but had the presence of mind and the dexterity to pull out his knitting needles as he fell and landed jamming them into the tail. Once again the whale stiffened and the bucking stopped. He righted himself and was straddling the tail as the chopper resumed dragging the machine once more. The three SEALs on the other chopper started hooting and hollering and snapped a few shots as Number Four looked like a triumphant broncobuster at a rodeo.

∞§∞

Back on the Saipan, the second chopper landed first and the SEALs watched as Number Four, who rode the thing all the way in, unhooked the slackened cable and attached the harness of the heavy supply crane that swung out off the side of the amphibious assault ship. As the whale machine was being lifted on to the deck, Number Four joined the team and asked the crane op to stop the machine as it hung directly over the deck. They ran beside it with one final mission goal to achieve, as a deckhand handed them a hastily made sign...

∞§∞

At 3:10 p.m. Paris time, Bill's secured smart phone chimed as a terse text message appeared from SUBCOMPAC. It simply read, "Quint got his fish."

Son of a bitch, it worked, was Bill's immediate thought.

XXVII. THROW IN THE TOWEL

Brooke spent the day in the field chasing down a lead in Canton Two on a man who had been taken into custody there. A business card on his person indicated he had recently been in touch with someone called the Architect. After three hours of tedious translations, it turned out his contact had been with the architect of an automobile dealership. A total dead end.

At around seven, Joey called it a day and Brooke left for the club. She had decided the night before to snoop around the nightspot. It was early and the crowd was mostly business people grabbing a drink after work. She walked around a little, then left and went to the hotel down the block where the murder had taken place. It was a fleabag hotel, and while she was standing there a few hookers walked their clientele into the lobby and up the stairs. She had to give the Swiss credit: these girls were less sleazy looking than the New York whores she'd seen as she left her office on the West Side late at night. These working girls had meat on their bones and were not as diseased looking. She went in and asked the sleepy deskman if he spoke English.

"Yes. Very much so," he said.

"Is room 212 empty?"

The desk clerk immediately perked up. "Why are you interested in this particular room, may I inquire?"

"I work with FedPol and I want to see the size and layout of the room." She flashed her new FBI ID.

"Wow. American FBI. I like very much J. Edgar. And Leonardo DiCaprio."

"That's great. Can I see the room now?"

He led her upstairs past many moans, groans and squeaks muffled through the doors of the various rooms. When they reached 212, the clerk opened the lock and added, "The police have told us not to rent the room until they tell us to do so."

Brooke noticed the room was still a crime scene. Chalk, tape and numbered cards populated the area around the massive bloodstain just beyond the front door. She bent down and examined the bloodstain closely, concluding the amount and pattern was consistent with a severed carotid artery of a large man. She walked over to the couch and noted there was some slight blood splatter. She went into the bathroom. The towels were unused, the maid's fold was still the finishing touch on the new toilet paper roll, the soap was unopened, and none of the liquid amenities were touched. Most johns would wash after a tryst with a hooker. She looked one more time and noticed that, although the bath towels were folded and neat, there seemed to be one missing. She walked out and looked around again. She walked to the window and raised the shade but it snapped up all the way and spun on its roller. Outside the window was a fire escape ladder. A spot of blood was on the sill. Since the bed was made, she reasoned that Abrim didn't die after having sex. Therefore, the argument must have happened before, in the negotiation phase. Brooke left the room, shutting the door.

Back at the club she approached the bar. There was a bartender in a Bruce Springsteen shirt, so she figured she could ask in English, "Is the boss in?"

"Are you meaning this boss? Or my boss?"

"Yours."

"Over there by the DJ," the bartender said.

Brooke approached the DJ booth and saw a man in a leather jacket who was barking orders at the DJ. "Excuse me! Do you speak English?"

"A little; how may I satisfy you?"

"Yes, you do only speak a little. I want to see your security tapes from the night of the Saudi murder three weeks ago."

Then a voice came from behind her, "He doesn't have them, we do."

Brooke turned saying, "Who are..." but stopped when she saw Lustig. "Captain, I didn't expect to see you here."

"Yet I fully expected to find you. Let's get out of here."

Back at FedPol H.Q., Captain Lustig had a technician cue up the surveillance tape from the club. The tech looked at the index sheet wrapped around the tape case and fast-forwarded to 11:23 p.m. on the time-code window, then hit play.

Lustig narrated the scene, "The first we see of Abrim is here, when he approaches the woman on the dance floor. It is obvious he is inviting her over to where he is sitting and from the look of it, she declines his invitation." He put his hand on the machine operator's shoulder and instructed, "Now go to the next time."

The tech checked the next time noted on the sheet and shuttled in fast speed to that number.

"Here it's a little hard to see because they are at a table in the upper part of the screen, but he comes to her while she is alone at the table and again she turns him down. Then we never see him again."

The tech stops the tape. It freezes on the woman at the table. Brooke walks over to the screen. "What about her; you think this is the hooker?"

"Can't say for sure. No one knows her; she is not a regular working girl. We think maybe she was the girlfriend of the geeky guy she was dancing with. They may be nothing more than tourists. Maybe when Abrim struck out with her, it was only then that he sought the company of a woman of the evening."

"Maybe. Could you play the tape from here?"

"Abrim is gone. There's nothing more," Lustig said, his voice showing a tint of futility.

"Indulge me." Brooke watched as the woman sat until the geeky guy returned with two drinks. A few seconds later she reached down into his lap and the geek reacted. Then they left.

"Let me see the dancing again."

The tech rewound and ran the part of the tape where the girl and the geek were dancing. Brooke watched intently. She recognized the signs of the game; the geek was trying to impress her. She was ignoring him. To Brooke, the girl's hair hung like a wig. She also noticed the geek's eyes couldn't be pried from the woman's chest. "These two are not a couple; they aren't on a date. This guy is strutting his stuff for her and she is ignoring him. He can't keep his eyes off her chest. That's not a couple who have had sex before. Plus, with the wig, I'm guessing she's a hooker. She may not be our hooker, but she is definitely working this poor schmuck."

"Are there any other angles? Outside the club?"

"No. This is all there is."

"Do you have the testimony of all the witnesses?"

"Yes, transcripts."

"May I see them?"

Lustig's eyes got big. "All of them?"

"I have all night."

Three hours later, Lustig yawned and came into the room where Brooke was poring over the transcripts with a Swiss policewoman, who really didn't want to be there this late, translating.

"Read that back to me again," Brooke said.

"About a minute later the big guy left. He went east on foot."

"Okay and now go back up a few lines. What did the bouncer say about the couple?"

The policewoman yawned and flipped back through the sheets bound across the top. "'Er...I had just let two guys in and then a blonde and a skinny guy walked out.' Then the officer asks, 'Did you see their faces?' The doorman replies, 'No they walked away from me.'"

Brooke slapped the table.

"What?" Lustig asked from the doorway as he was just entering the room.

"She may be our hooker. The way this reads, Abrim followed them out of the club, down the street to the hotel."

"But the bouncer, as you called him, says he didn't see their faces." Lustig pointed at the transcript in the police-woman's hand.

"Last night the doorman had a stanchion with a proof light and stamp pad to the left of the door. If he had just let someone in, he was behind that little podium and facing east with his back to the west like he was last night. So they went east as well, same direction as Abrim did a minute later, and for my money, right to the same hotel."

"Are you saying the geek killed Abrim?"

"That skinny malink? He could never get the drop on a two-hundred-eighty-pound security guard, much less jam a broken bottle into his throat."

"So what you are saying, Agent Burrell, is that Abrim follows them, has sex with both of them? Then doesn't want to pay for the extras, so she calls her pimp, and he and Abrim get into a fight?"

"No that's not it; the bed was untouched. No one had sex. It all came down before anything else happened. Did forensics match the blood on the couch and the blood on the sill?"

Lustig sighed. "Hold on; I can't believe I am not home right now," he muttered as he rifled through the reports looking for the blood-splatter analysis. "Here it is. The blood on the carpet and on the table legs was that of the victim. The blood on the couch was diluted with saliva and was not the victim's, but matched the spot on the sill."

"Okay, last question. Crime scene photos?"

Lustig pulled out the jacket on the bottom of the pile. He spread out the photos from the crime scene. Brooke scanned each one. She tapped the one where the towel was shown on the side of the couch. She then found a different angle from another photo.

"Do you have the towel in evidence?"

"Of course; and yes I have the forensics," he said, anticipating her next request as he rifled through the paperwork and finally found the pages on the towel. "The bath towel was standard from the hotel laundry and was in the room when it was occupied. It was rolled up and did not have any blood on it, so it was deemed not to be crucial to the investigation."

"Can we get that towel to the lab? I want a skin cell analysis."

"First off, you are not a Swiss police officer. Second, it is eleven o'clock, and third, what is your suspicion?"

"The towel ended up behind the couch so it was protected from blood spray, but somehow it got rolled up and into the room. There was no sex, and as far as I can tell there was no use of the sink or bathroom, since it remained as housekeeping left it prior to the occupant's entry, and the murder. So why the rolled towel?"

"What are you hoping to find from skin cells?"

"Tell me what you find, and I'll tell you what I think." With that, she got up, stretched, and headed for the door, "We'll see tomorrow — morning, right?"

"You know, for a retired person you are very demanding."

"You should have seen me when I was on active duty!" She smiled and left.

XXVIII. IT'S THE LITTLE THINGS

With Joey, Brooke and Parnell in Geneva and the Vatican now reluctantly on his side, Bill found no reason to stay in Paris. He was about to make the arrangements to go home when he had a better idea. "Mrs. Hiccock, do you have a free weekend?"

Janice was talking to him from the phone in their kitchen and smiled, "Well, you know I am pretty busy here with my husband away and all."

"So then why don't you call your mom, get her to mind Richie and jump on Air France Flight 891 to Paris leaving Dulles at 6:05 p.m. non-stop to the City of Lights. It's all paid for, just show 'em your passport."

"Well, I haven't a thing to wear!"

"Don't worry mademoiselle, that is why we have French clothes places here... in France."

"Can't stay on the phone much longer, 'cause I got to pack! I love you..."

"Love you too. See ya for breakfast, babe." He hung up and smiled. He had made the right choice.

∞§∞

"Sierra Tango Two in thirty seconds," the chief of the boat called out.

Mush took one more look at the chart. He was navigating through a tricky part of the undersea ice near the Lomonosov Ridge, which divides the Eurasian Basin and the Amerasian Basin into two deep depressions on the sea floor at the top of the world, under the Polar Ice Cap. Training never stops on a submarine. On every patrol, crewmembers constantly have to qualify at watch stations other than their own specific rate. That means they shadow qualified-at-rate crew member to learn that job. Mush was showing a young ensign the basics of under-ice navigation. "Under the ice, with no satellite penetration for GPS, the only way to survive these transits is to use time and distance as you chart your progress." He placed the calipers on the chart where a red line zigged through two under-sea mountain ranges. That gave him the point in the ocean where he needed to make the thirty-eight degree turn to port. It was designated Sierra Tango Two, which by his calculations was now five seconds away.

"And come to port zero-three-eight on my mark. Mark!" Mush ordered.

"What's the next target, Ensign?"

He took the calipers and rolled them point over point to the next zig in the red line that was their safe course thought the range. "I make next target designated as Sierra Tango Three in twenty-two minutes at our present course and twenty-seven knot speed."

"I concur. Keep it up, Will and you'll have your Qual Card filled before the halfway party."

The young ensign smiled, getting his qualifications card filled out in navigation in the first half of the patrol would give him the other half of the trip to qualify in Sonar.

"Exec, you got the boat," Mush said as he left.

"Yes, sir." He took a position at the chart table and announced, "Captain is off the conn."

Mush had time to go back to his compartment and review the promotions list for this patrol. He took off his cap and hung it on the bow of the battleship *Nebraska*, a scale model which was bolted to a shelf over his desk. On his desk was a picture of Brooke. He had snapped it on his cell phone the morning after their walk through D.C. The sun was rising and her hair had the same glow it had when he first noticed how spectacular she was up on the bridge of Big Red in that late afternoon Pacific sun. He sat back, and for the hundredth time since they shoved off, he thought about what he would say when he got his arms around her again. He touched the picture as if to stroke her cheek, then caught himself, shook it off, and opened the folder filled with assessments of his crew.

A yeoman entered the compartment with an iPad. "Sir, I have that encrypted video file downloaded on your pad. Just enter your password."

"Thanks, Bob."

Mush waited until he left the room, then watched a video that had been streamed to the *Nebraska* encoded over the VLF radio link. This process took a few hours, because very low frequency communications were slow but powerful enough to penetrate the earth. This was a video direct from Commander, Submarine Forces U.S. Pacific Fleet. Mush had never gotten anything like this before, and as far as he knew, no other nuclear sub under the ice ever had. The video opened with the logo of COMSUBPAC. Then Mush's face became one big smile as the commander of SEAL Team Nine and his men posed for a picture that sport fisherman live for, proudly standing by a landed blue marlin, swordfish or other game fish catch of the day. Only in this case, the catch was a mechanical whale. One of the SEALs was holding up a hand-made sign that read what the team yelled out in perfect military cadence, "Ahoy, Captain Ahab Morton, we got the whale what got away! Sir!"

∞§∞

As he read the overnight lab report, Lustig was impressed, but had a problem. The crime scene investigation unit that responded to the hotel murder of the Arab was one of the best in Switzerland. This Burrell woman from the U.S. had stuck her nose into the case and hit on something the Swiss detectives missed. For himself, this was not an issue because in the end, the path to justice was the only road he was on, but for the forensic technician, Armend, who stood before him, it was a hit to the pride of the man and his unit. "Would you like to be there when we show her these results, Armend?"

"Yes. I would very much like to…" *See this little bitch,* was the thought behind the smile he hung on his face in the presence of his superior.

The minute Lustig and Armend walked into the conference room, Joey could see it all over their faces, a look of contrition, even resignation. He had no idea what it pertained to and was about to ask something like, 'Hey fellas, why the long faces?' when Brooke walked into the room, after stopping for her morning cup of wake up.

"Madame, the preliminary result of the skin test you wanted is in," Lustig said as he handed the translated form to her.

"Is this about your Arab murder, Brooke?" Joey said.

"Yes, Mr. Palumbo." Lustig answered for her, as she was deep into the report. Somehow he just couldn't warm up to the idea of calling him Joey.

Armend watched her, this slightly built woman, this American heroine, who walked into his crime scene and had the bad manners to question his findings. Yes, there were two different skin cells embedded in the terry cloth material, but what was she getting at? He watched her as she studied the rendering his department had prepared less than an hour ago with the two different color keys on it showing the location and relative amount of different skin residue. She curled her lip while she read. Armend thought it was the mark of a schoolgirl trying to struggle with algebra; perhaps he should explain the results. Then he thought better of it, *Why help her*?

Then she asked for the ladies' locker room. Lustig directed her. A minute later she returned with a towel. Armend scrutinized every step she made. She flattened out the towel on the conference room table and opened her purse. She folded the towel and rolled it long-ways to make it like a rope. She took out an eyeliner pencil and a highlighter and rubbed onto the towel three marks roughly corresponding to the three 'blue-red-blue' marks on the diagram of the towel in evidence as yellow-eyeliner-yellow onto her towel.

Armend looked at the clock; how much longer would this take?

Then she grabbed the towel by the two yellow ends and asked Armend to step over and turn around. As soon as he did so, she swung the towel around his neck and pulled fairly hard. The startled Armend almost fell backwards, but the woman released her grip in time.

"May I?" the bitch asked, as she gently tipped Armend's jaw back showing the smudged eyeliner residue on his neck.

"Now the big money question, did either of the skin types match that of the deceased?" Brooke said.

"No." Armend said, rubbing his throat, but actually his ego instead.

"Gentlemen, somebody other than the deceased was strangled in that room," Brooke said while swallowing her first sip.

"But, mind you, this is just a cursory microscopic examination of bacterial communities and pigmentation levels," Armend pointed out to take some of the sting away.

"But it appears all three do not match..." Lustig said looking over the towel.

"Of course, in a week we will have definitive DNA." Armend said.

"But I got enough for a working theory." Brooke took another sip of her coffee and dabbed at her lips with the demonstration towel.

"Which is what exactly, Brooke?" Joey asked, picking up the lab report and flipping through it.

"Well, it could have gone down like this. The towel was used by a third person to choke someone, probably the geek."

"So you are putting four people in that room?" Joey asked.

"Two's company, three's a crowd, but four's a party!" Brooke said with a wink.

Armend looked down at the towel; how could he have missed that? This American woman had a skill set his entire team lacked. But why would she care about this case?

"Well, Brooke, that's good detective work, but where is this all going to lead you? You are not officially here to investigate this case; you are here to help us find the Architect or Engineer or whomever," Joey said with a shrug.

"I know boss, thanks for these few minutes. I will pursue the rest on my own time."

"Armend, please distribute this new theory to the team. See if they think it has enough meat on its bone for the judge to take a bite and maybe reopen the investigation." He then turned to Joey and Brooke, "Shall we get started on today's progress?"

They both agreed, and Armend took it as his cue to leave.

They spent the rest of the morning looking at priors and travel patterns of train engineers, civil engineers, sanitation engineers, chemical, electrical, software, computer, and mechanical and building engineers whose names were flagged by a crime computer for having any contact with the law. The largest list was that of building engineers, or superintendants as they were called in America, who most frequently called the police or had been called on by them. Nothing they found seemed to fit the kind of profile that Parnell had outlined.

In the afternoon, they dug into a list of 'Architects' with equally disheartening results. After work, Brooke went to the crime lab at FedPol and retrieved a few prints of the video frames from the club's surveillance tape that she had requested during her quick lunch break. She planned to be at the club tomorrow night, Saturday; the murder had happened on a Saturday night.

∞§∞

Janice had arrived at Orly at about 7 a.m., and Bill was there at the airport to greet her. They had a very French breakfast at a little Boulanger Patisserie on the rue Monge. Bill could see she was tired from the all-night trip so he had worked at the embassy while she slept until mid-afternoon. Today, Saturday, they were going to see the town.

Befitting his position in the White House, Bill was afforded a driver/guide from the State Department. He and Janice had a crash course in Paris tourism 101. First the Louvre and then the Eiffel Tower for lunch. In the afternoon, they scooted up to Versailles and took a picture of themselves in a mirror in the hall of mirrors. Bill tried to point out that the Great War, World War One, the war to end all wars, ended in the Armistice drawn up in this room on the eleventh hour of the eleventh day of the eleventh month; which is why Veteran's Day is November 11th, but Janice was more impressed by the chandeliers. As the sun set they headed for dinner at a must-dine spot in the Paris Michelin Guide. Then Bill had a thought. He tapped his driver on the shoulder and said, "You have lived here your whole life. Where would you go tonight?"

"Me? Monsieur, I am not a VIP."

"Hey, Francois, neither are we. I think we did enough of the tourist thing. What would a Saturday night for a Parisian, in Paris, be like?"

"Sadly, the place I recommend would not be in Paris."

"Is the food good there?"

"The best!"

"Then, my good man, take us to your place," Bill said, getting the smile of approval from Janice.

"I will have to call in this change of itinerary," Francois said to make sure his passenger and responsibility for the evening understood that it would become a matter of record.

"Call it in then."

Francois smiled. This VIP, he liked.

The drive outside Paris was both enchanting and surprisingly pedestrian. Many of the little clusters of poor neighborhoods were not the stuff of travel brochures, but the open spaces and quaint villages, now fed by 'off the track' tourism, were maintained to meet the expectations of the pseudo-Francophile and their greedy cameras.

The spur-of-the-moment venue for this evening was a tavern-like restaurant that was not dressed for tourism. The people inside were not tourists and the menus were in French only. Bill took in a deep breath and the aroma of the food told him he had found the true experience. As if on cue, a four-piece band struck up the familiar opening chords of The Beatles, *Day Tripper.* The vocals, in a decidedly French accent, made Bill joke to Janice that at some point the band would launch into the Beatles song, *Michelle,* and the place would probably stand as if it were the national anthem.

Flagrantly in violation of the diplomatic service rules, their guide and driver, Francois, joined them at the table and filled in the blanks in Bill and Janice's hardly passable French. When the waiter came by with the wine list, Bill looked at Janice as if to say, 'Should we?'

Janice just gestured with her palms up at their surroundings and said, "When in France..."

∞§∞

Brooke had persuaded the policewoman from FedPol to tag along with her to the club that night. In civvies, with her hair down, Verena's out-of-uniform appearance turned Brooke's two-woman, ad-hoc investigation team into a female dynamic duo of Saturday night warriors. Between the two of them, they got more invitations to join, offers of drinks and even a few marriage proposals, than all the regulars scored in an evening. To the chagrin of the males, and a few of the females, both these women were focused on the job at hand, namely to find out the 'geek's' name. Here, being two hot blondes helped grease the memories and helpfulness of the club-goers.

Somewhere around eleven, they got a hit. 'The brain,' she called him and said she didn't see him much anymore.

"Much or never again?" Brooke asked the bouncing twenty-something wearing a short skirt and flimsy tank top, which didn't hide the lack of foundation garments beneath.

"Not for a while."

"Do you know his name?" Verena asked in German.

"The brain? I don't know, something like Renny or Rashie."

"Do you know anyone who knows him?"

"No, but I just remembered, he was an engineer or something like that."

Brooke looked to Verena, "Ask her if she knows what kind of work he does or where he works."

"I think he said, Hadron, but all the guys here say that."

"They do?" Brooke said.

"Because that means they got money and they got a good job, but most of them still live with their mothers."

∞§∞

Lustig didn't appreciate being disturbed on a Saturday night. In fact, it was a rare occurrence since he had been elevated to FedPol, where he fought crime in a supervisory capacity, nine to five, as opposed to when he was a Canton cop whose life was ruled by the phone. The fact that it was Brooke, on the scent of the Arab murderer, made it more of an inconvenience, until she said 'engineer' and 'Hadron.'

"I will call the head of security and I'll meet you there at midnight," Lustig said, with a new sense of urgency. He then called and woke up the head of Hadron security, Martin Jenson.

XXIX. DO-GOODER

"I wanna hold your hand, I wanna hold your haa-ah-ah-ah hand." Bill was crooning along with the French Beatles tribute band and Janice was laughing like she hadn't done in a long time. Francois the driver was drumming on the table top with bread sticks. Then the lead singer, the 'John' of the group, made his way over with his boom mike on his head and wireless guitar and leaned over and brought the mike close to Bill as they sang the next verse in unison. The crowd was clapping and laughing and Janice's eyes were tearing up from laughing.

When the song ended, the musician told the waiter to bring this couple more wine. Bill respectfully waved off the waiter, and Janice through her smiles agreed. They stayed for another half-hour, and after everyone did indeed stand for *Michelle*, they asked Francois to drive them back to the embassy.

They entered past security like teenagers sneaking back into the house after curfew. They made their way up to their room and continued the party and the teenager profile for another hour.

∞§∞

"Do you know this man?" Lustig tapped the photo in his hand in front of Jenson.

"No, I don't recognize him," a sleep interrupted Jenson said as he turned to the face-recognition system tech, who had also been roused out of bed for this impromptu late

Saturday night meeting. He scanned the photo and then started a twenty-seven-point feature search. It took all of forty-five seconds and the computer got a hit on a Raffael Juth.

"Raffael. I guess Raffey or Rayphie sounds like Renny?" Brooke said.

"He's a programmer in the measurement and monitoring section. He got an award for a new program that stabilizes sensor output during data lag accumulation," Jenson said, as if he didn't have a clue what that was.

"What is that?" Brooke asked.

"I haven't a clue," Jenson said, "But it was good enough to get him a new Audi A6 as a prize."

"And I assume he has had no run-in with the law?" Lustig asked.

"Yes, he has a very clean past. He was a Fédération internationale des échecs master with a 2639 rating from the World Chess Association."

"Well, that's why he wasn't on our list; we didn't include the chess club," Brooke said.

"Jenson, give us his address and we'll ruin his Saturday night as well," Lustig said.

"I wouldn't do that." Brooke got everyone's attention.

"Look, I know it's a long shot, but I don't make this guy to be a killer, especially the kind to be cool, calm, and collected after ripping opening a guy's throat." Brooke walked over to the file. "How has his attendance been since the murders?"

"Checking," the tech said. "He's not missed a day or been late all year."

"I see your point, Agent Burrell." Lustig chewed it over and then got on Brooke's page. "We know he was there, we know there was violence, we know you can't turn on the TV and not hear about the sex-scandal-murder, yet he, with no record, does not come forward nor run. Why?"

"The blood on the sill!" Brooke snapped her fingers. "This guy got away. And he's hiding something bigger than a murder."

"What could that be?" Jenson asked.

Brooke held up her arms, "This!"

"What do you mean this, you mean here?" Lustig said.

"Yes, he's here at the collider! This is our guy, or the guy who could lead us to our guy. I recommend we do low profile surveillance, because he can be in on it or is being pressured to be in on it. Either way he may have accomplices and they may speed up their time table if we spook 'em."

Jenson went into hysterics. "Wait. You come in here, at midnight, on the weekend and tell me you have been investigating my facility — for what? Sabotage! And this is the first I am hearing of it! And now I am supposed to not act to remove this cancer from my system? On what or whose authority do you make such a request?"

"Jenson, I am sorry my friend, but this is bigger than FedPol. The Americans are running this show by the invitation of our government. This is a most sensitive matter and I am going to have to ask you and your man here to come along with me to our offices."

"You are arresting us?" Jenson's indignation was punctuated with his foot slamming the floor.

"No, I am simply asking you both to come down and be apprised of the situation so that you will not pose a security risk to the investigation. I assure you that you will be back here, at your post, on Monday."

"Captain Lustig, we are going to need to ramp up surveillance and intelligence on Raffael. I am going to call Agent Palumbo and have him meet us here," Brooke said.

∞§∞

By noon Sunday, every aspect of Raffael Juth's life was on the conference table. Unmarked police cars were staking out his home, which he shared with his sister and her daughter. A new employee appeared at the Hadron Monitoring Division, an undercover policewoman who was subtly learning what she could about Raffey.

"Brooke, what's your take on what we are dealing with here?" Bill asked over the secure teleconference from the Paris Embassy to FedPol.

"Bill, since no one has seen his sister or her little girl lately and we have no visa or passport records of them leaving the country, they may be hostages. In which case he is possibly a pawn in all this."

"Or he's a pathological maniac and they are stuffed in a freezer in the basement," Bill said.

"Could be, but I agree with Brooke's theory. Someone is pulling the strings on this kid and he's toeing the line," Joey added.

"Okay then, I'll take your recommendation. Tell me what you need and I'll get it going immediately."

"We're still pulling together our operational plan; as soon as we have it we'll get back to you, Bill."

"I'll be waiting. Oh, how did we get here? How did this guy come on to our radar?" Bill asked.

"Blame Brooke. She was freelancing as a do-gooder; and she stumbled on the kid while investigating a murder here in Switzerland."

"That's sounds like a long story over a tall drink. I can't wait."

∞§∞

Two FedPol officers moved into the house across the street from Raffey's and set up laser listening devices and a piece of equipment from America, an infrared camera that can see through walls. Down the block, taps were placed on the phone wires, and a small device, which sensed and transmitted electromagnetic spectrum emissions from the house, was thrown over the back fence. When washed through a computer program, they could read the key clicks and screen

raster from his computer, and even the time and cook set-
tings on his microwave. Three of Switzerland's best teams
trailed Mr. Juth every time he went to work or the store and
home again. By opening his phone records through a special
warrant from the Swiss court, his IMEI (International Mobile
Station Equipment Identity) and ICCID (Integrated Circuit
Card Identifier) codes were obtained and his phone cloned.
All incoming and outgoing calls were now monitored and
recorded; except there were none.

∞§∞

By the third day, Brooke was frustrated. Mr. Juth did
nothing different in his routine every day. He never changed
the route he drove to work, never spoke with anybody, never
made any contact with another human. Brooke could not
fathom how 'Mr. Leather Pants,' the not so wild and crazy guy
from the disco, could all of a sudden live such a monastic life.
He made and received no phone calls. He only worked on
local files from the hard drive on his computer, no Internet,
no e-mails, Facebook, or messaging. She reached out to
Kronos when she saw that he had no social network presence.
That was unfortunate, because nowadays a ton of potentially
incriminating or exculpatory evidence was available, volun-
tarily offered up by the eight hundred million citizens of the
virtual nations of Facebook, Twitter, Four Square, Tumblr,
Instagram and the like as social data, just waiting to be
scraped by police agencies around the globe. Kronos assured
her that once something is posted online it never goes away.

Except in the case of Raffael Juth; even Kronos couldn't
figure how he did it. Not a trace of him. Even the founder of
Facebook had his personal pictures hacked, yet Raffey was off
the grid. Kronos, not one for complimenting another genius,
said, "This guy is good!"

To Brooke the total impression of all Raffey's inactivity was almost as if he knew he was being — *watched*, she thought.

∞§∞

"Okay, where are we?" Bill asked in the conference room of FedPol. After a great four days in Paris together, they flew to Geneva now that the lead Brooke, Joey and Parnell Sicard were following was getting hotter.

Sicard started first, "It's very nice to meet you, Mrs. Hiccock."

"Nice to meet you too, Mr. Sicard." Janice looked over to Bill as if to say, "He's not only good looking, he's got manners as well." Bill gave a sour look as he stuck his tongue out.

Sicard continued, "Our man, Juth, is a mid-level programmer at the Hadron Collider; he has distinguished himself and received awards. He is an exemplary employee and never absent a day's work."

Joey clicked a mouse, which brought up two side-by-side photos on the eighty-inch plasma screen at the end of the table. "The security camera, which scans the entrance he uses every day, shows a bruise under his left eye, and a day or so old, bloody fat lip, the Monday after the murder. It is not there on the tape from the Friday before."

"How do you know it's a day old?" Janice asked.

"I used to box on the FBI team," Joey said.

"So he's our Arab's killer?" Bill looked at the two candid photos on the screen.

"If that were the case, we would have simply turned him over to the Swiss. But there's more here." Brooke took the mouse and brought up two other files. "These photos were taken of his desk in the office. In the picture frame there, that's his sister and her daughter; they live with him, or lived with him. In the four days since we began watching him, they haven't been home."

Sicard referred to a folder. "There are no out of country passports scanned or stamped, no visa or other travel records that Captain Lustig here at FedPol could find, so they are still somewhere in Switzerland. Or the continent if they drove across the border off road."

"There is only one family member outside the country; we had local constabulary check them out and the mother and daughter weren't staying with them. Of the four relatives in country, they have not seen or talked to the brother, the sister or the little girl since before the murder," Joey added.

"I know I have asked this before, but could he have killed them?" Bill flipped back the mouse and brought up Raffey's photos again.

"Bill, since she accompanied you on this trip, I took the liberty of asking Janice to profile our Raffey. Janice, will you share with us your thoughts." Brooke gestured to her.

Janice read the puzzled expression on Sicard's face, "Parnell, I run the Behavioral Sciences Department at George Washington University Hospital, and I have worked with and been a part of this team in the past."

"In fact," Bill jumped in, "Janice has personally briefed the President of the United States and was dead-on accurate in her assessment of the threat matrix we faced at that time," Bill said like a proud dad bragging about his son's touchdown. "So her analysis of who we are up against is something you could take to the bank." He turned to his wife, "Janice."

"Well, it's quick and preliminary; I just got all of the information this morning, but outside the slim chance of total schizophrenia, he's no killer. His actions are defensive, not offensive, and from his lifestyle to his chosen profession, he is a thinker, not a person who acts. His seemingly sudden shutting out of the outside world is more an act of isolation or self-imprisonment."

"Janice, could that self-detachment be a result of extreme guilt of getting his family out of the way?" Bill asked.

"You mean like he locked himself up in his own jail for killing his family? Not likely, Bill, because the rest of his pattern is wholly unaffected. It would be quite rare that his self-imposed sentence would be that surgically exact. Remorse or conscience would have a widening effect on the mode of behavior, which is not evident from what I have reviewed."

"Janice, could we be looking at a bi-current... er, whatever it was that we dealt with during the Eighth Day affair?" Joey asked.

"You mean, induced bi-stable concurrent schizophrenia?" Janice said.

"Yeah, that," Joey said.

"To be sure, we should also have Kronos run a scan on his computer just to check for the interstitial images that triggered those individuals, but that only affected those perpetrators when they were seeking or were close to their particular targets. In his case, he is living this reality twenty-four/seven. That fact alone doesn't rule subliminal programming out, but it's just not in keeping with what I have observed before."

Bill thought for a second, then closed his briefing book. "Brooke, get Kronos to take a look, but I am going to go with the notion that we left that brain-scrambling hardware and software twenty thousand feet below the Pacific Ocean in a deep trench. Thanks Janice, glad you are here." He smiled at her and placed his hand over hers on the tabletop.

"Nice to be back with the team again," Janice said with a genuine smile.

"Bill, I heard they captured the whale. Any leads?" Joey said.

"Naval Warfare and Tactics has it, and a team from NCIS is processing it for any traces or prints. The unfortunate thing, and who could have known this, is that when the SEALS took the machine they used high-voltage, which expanded the fluid to the degree that the one, sole pilot who was driving the thing was crushed to death.

"How did the pilot breathe?" Joey said.

"Blowhole, just like a real whale. Two bladders in the compartment expanded and contracted forcing bad air out and pulling in 20 minutes or so of new air whenever it was running on the surface. It was those bladders that over-expanded under the high voltage, crushing him to death."

"Do we know who he is?" Brooke said.

He had no ID on him. They are doing a workup on his bio-metrics now, but no clues as to who was behind it."

"Shame, those tests are going to take time we don't have." Joey said.

"So absent any evidence from that end, what's your operating theory, Brooke?" Bill asked.

"Well, Joey and I concur on most of this. The murder took place three days before the day Parnell was coming to Geneva. So this crime happened 24 hours prior to our two day crime computer search on each side of that date."

"That's why it wasn't listed in our printouts." Joey said.

"We agree that Raffey was set up and the Arab security guard tripped over the attempted abduction and was killed for his trouble. Juth then escaped his kidnappers so they counter-moved, or were planning all along to take his sister and niece, who are in all likelihood being held by someone who wants Raffey to do something at the collider." Brooke paused to see if Bill had any questions.

"Seems like it fits the facts; go on," Bill said.

"Now, here's where Joey and I part opinions. I think they are going to get him to do something major against the facility."

"And I think, and Janice touched on this, he's not an action player; they may just be using him to gain access or let in the real perpetrators who will wreak havoc," Joey said.

"Either way, both of you are saying the collider is the target and whether it's Raffey pulling the trigger or unlocking the door, this is your plot. So who's pulling his strings? The Architect? The Engineer? What do you think, Parnell?" Bill sat back to hear his answer.

"I turn it around but it comes out the same, I have it as the Arab was an enforcer in the plot, probably emanating out of a Wahabi Saudi sect. Raffey gets lucky and kills Abrim. They counter and take his family so it's all for naught and he settles down into the pattern."

Bill stopped listening when he heard the word 'Wahabi.' If this was an extremist Muslim plot, then there was not necessarily a rationale to the attack. In that, it would not be an attack to leverage against another country or a statement made to cower the world. Fanatics of any religion, who believe that they are doing their God's work, have no limits. This whole plan could be to trigger Armageddon.

"Bill. Bill?" Joey tapped the table. "Where did you go, buddy?"

"Parnell, why were the Knights so interested in this?"

"We protect the rings, the ring or crown of thorns. And by extension all first class artifacts of Christianity," Sicard said.

"No, Parnell, why does the Vatican and, by extension, you, have an interest in these rings, the rings of science, in your cross hairs?"

"You don't know?" Sicard said.

"I am afraid that I do know. In fact, I am scared out of my wits that I know," Bill said.

"Wanna clue the rest of us in?" Joey held his palms up.

"Dead-enders, of the extremist variety."

"Okay, so what is their end game?" Brooke asked.

"The end is their game. The end of everything," Parnell added.

"So it isn't blow up the rings to strike a blow against modernism or European Society. It's 'get the rings to trigger a black hole,'" Joey reasoned out. He looked over to Bill, his best friend since second grade. The emotions that passed between them at that moment suspended time. The look was a mixture of 'I told you so!' mixed with 'Oh God, what do we do?'

For Bill's part, his expression was one of extreme intensity; his mind working it's hardest to crunch the problem down to its basic components. Then, in an instant, he looked at his wife, but what he saw was his son in her arms, and the reasoned calculus of the previous second dissolved into a primal need to ward off the predator that endangered them.

So pronounced was the impact of Bill's deliberation that it mesmerized everyone in the room. All fell to silence as the downward force from the weight of what they now faced compressed their spines and increased their blood pressure.

After a few moments, Joey broke the stillness. "If Raffey is the key, we take him out of the equation. They lose their operational ability."

"If we move on Juth, we may spook them back under their rocks; we'll never find them," Parnell said.

"I think through a massive police effort we could smoke 'em out, but removing Raffey may not end this," Brooke said.

"How so?" Bill asked.

"What if Raffey is just one of many?"

"Good point; once we alert them, if they have redundant capability, all we may accomplish is accelerating their time line," Bill said.

"Yet, this isn't a fish that you give a lot of line to, and if you lose him, all you have is a 'one that got away' story. I say shutting them down is paramount to the world's survival. If we try to accomplish too much police work, we increase our chances of miscalculation, with the most unthinkable consequences," Parnell said.

"But what if he isn't a pawn and we are reading these tea leaves wrong? What if he's the chess master; he's the total threat? He dispatches his family because everyone's going to die anyway, and having them around could only betray his plans. What if he is the one and only bad guy here?" Joey said.

"In that case, every minute we delay allows him more time to act," Parnell added.

Bill considered the arguments before him. He encouraged out-of-the-box thinking; it had been the cornerstone of his strategy in defeating every major terror event he and his team had faced. But here, all the theories were just different paths within the same box. The outcome was the same for each connection of facts and intuition. *Maybe I should call the president?* But that would only delay everything.

Besides, when compared to the extinguishing of the known universe and every life form in it, the president's mere U.S. constitutionally defined authority was so parochial as to make it a non-issue. The leader of the free world would have no better handle on this than that of any other human who was facing extinction. And Bill had a room full of humans right now. He doubted the president would add anything new. No, he was going to have to make this call. Raffey could be counting down to turning the universe into a null void as they spoke. On the other hand, if he was just a cog in the plan, his handlers might have protected against losing him by having others in a similar position, as Brooke had pointed out. That would be the military or intelligence communities' way of mounting such an operation. He looked one more time to Janice. He was deciding for her and Richie as well.

He tried to elevate his thinking to a higher perspective so as not to be emotionally swayed, but in the end, it was all about them. At that moment, the actual weight of history was on his shoulders. Then a thought snapped all into alignment and he had his way through the maze of the known and unknown.

"Okay, here's how I see it; if you disagree, now is the time. There is no reason for Raffey or his controllers to delay his plan if it is to detonate the collider. The optimum time would be when the machine goes operational at the sub-sub atomic level running the Landau Protocols in two days."

"The search for the God Particle!" Parnell said.

"Or the splitting of it." Joey said.

"Exactly. Our government is lobbying the council at CERN to delay this line of research, in no small part because of my recommendation to the president that there aren't enough safeguards as yet to avoid exactly what we are fearing now."

"Although the notion of sabotage certainly bodes well to shut it down," Brooke said.

"The council meets to consider our proposal at ten. I am going to them and bringing what we know; maybe we can make this a non-event," Bill said.

"What about, Raffey's family? What if they are hostages? Do we sacrifice them?" Brooke was emphatic.

Bill looked to Joey and jutted his chin toward him, "Your call Joey."

"Brooke, you'll continue electronic and human surveillance; if you get any actionable intelligence, we'll move to rescue."

XXX. WORLDWIDE CONCERN

"Swiss authorities are using the word 'calm' at the moment in the aftermath of clashes with riot police in the normally quiet city of Geneva. These protests turned violent when a small group of protestors tried to storm the gate here at the CERN facility that houses the Large Hadron Super Collider. There were over a thousand arrests, and the Swiss police have doubled their forces and have drawn a line in the sand, so to speak. For now the protesters are gathering more and more in strength every hour. Nils Macintyre, BBC World Service." Macintyre waited for the follow-up question from the anchor in London. Behind him were protestors holding signs, only one of them stated simply, 'No LP at LHC.' Thankfully, Nils didn't ask what LP stood for lest he find a whole new angle to the story about the dead Dr. Landau and his Protocol being the reason behind the protest.

The anchor was now addressing the large studio monitor in front of him with the video of the reporter. "Nils, there are similar spontaneous outbursts all across the globe. Is there any indication from where you are that there is some organization to these eruptions?"

"Bryan, the level of this 'movement,' if you will, seems to be totally grass roots. There are no prepared brochures or even quickly printed or copied press releases one usually finds at less spontaneous gatherings. There are American TV crews here, and they are pretty much asking the same question, wondering if these folks here are part of the protest in New York, Washington, Chicago, and a dozen major cities across that country. And aside from the social media activity that accompanies any large group, we haven't found any pre-organization or build up to these now-turned-violent, events of the last hours. Back to you Bryan."

"Thank you, Nils." Anchor Bryan Diggs turned from the monitor and settled on Camera One as a graphic appeared in the screen behind him reading, 'Collision at the Collider.' "But what do the protesters want? Joining us now for some more analysis, from his home in Cheshire, is Professor Ward Sessions director of the Daresbury Laboratory. Dr. Sessions, what is this all about?"

"The LHC is about to perform their greatest and most ambitious experiment yet, the extreme agitation or splitting of the smallest known entity in the universe."

"Is this the fabled God Particle we've heard spoken about?"

"Well, no. Actually, the God Particle, which is a popular, Hollywood-type term that I don't particularly subscribe to, is what they are hoping to verify. It is in fact a clarification of Higgs Boson. As your viewers probably don't know, decades back, Peter Higgs theorized about a smaller than small particle, which he named a Boson. It exists in the grey area between matter and energy. He concluded this speck of creation was the weak force of attraction, or the glue of all matter."

"Well, I think some of us have followed you, but didn't they find this particle in July of 2012?"

"They found a particle that fit the profile of the Higgs Boson, in that it's actions under extreme forces were Higgs Boson 'like', but this new initiative, the Landau Protocols, is to again agitate or split what ever that particle is in to revealing it's true makeup and origin to us."

Luckily the host was not well versed and didn't focus on what the Landau Protocol was; instead, he jumped on what he thought the headline was. "Wait, so it could or could not be the God Particle that they are attempting to split?

The show went on, doing more to confuse the average viewer than enlighten.

∞§∞

It was the constant whimpering that made it so unbear-
able. *Why can't we just kill the kid now!* Maya thought. The
endless sniffles and wails were driving her mad. She had
slapped the kid silly, but that only made it worse. Luckily,
soon it would all be over. The Architect would get this Raffey
jerk to do whatever it was he wanted him to do, then they
could kill these witnesses and she could get on with her new
life in Egypt with a new identity and new bank account. Just
thirty-six more hours. Her patience and boiling point reaching critical, she rapped on the door to the room the kid and
her mother were chained up in. "Shut up in there or I'll come
in there and really give you something to cry about."

∞§∞

"Shhh. Shhh. Kirsi, it will be okay. It will be okay," Leena
said for the thousandth time since they had been thrown
into this room with only two meals a day and shackled to just
enough chain to reach the toilet and the wash sink where
they drank water from the faucet. Their ankles were red and
bleeding with welts from the chain's irons clasped around
their legs. She had no idea why someone would do this to
them. She kept her mind from dwelling on their ultimate fate
by protecting her daughter and trying to ease her fears minute by minute. Her blouse was wet from her daughter's tears
and her sleeves crusted with mucus from wiping Kirsi's nose.
She sat silently in the room, which was pitch-black save for
a crack of sunlight coming through the seam of a tarp nailed
over the window, gently rocking her whimpering little girl.

∞§∞

More and more, Brooke was convinced that Raffey was
a manipulated pawn rather than the brains of the outfit. She

knew in her bones that his sister, Leena, and his niece, Kirsi, were the control elements. Her dilemma was that she was in a foreign country, investigating a kidnapping/blackmail/terrorist plot that had been put into motion before she landed in Switzerland six days ago. And how did Abrim's death play into all of this? Luck, instinct, and drilling into police reports had gotten her so close, yet in many ways she could still be back on the East Coast, and no closer to the answers, while time was running out. She needed to get into Raffey's house, his life. The tea kettle on the stove whistled and broke her chain of thought. As she took it off the burner and turned off the gas, it hit her!

∞§∞

"Mercaptan?" Bill said, as much impressed with Brooke's research as blindsided by the randomness of her plan.

"You want to do what?" Joey asked.

"I want to get into Raffey's house while he's at work. There have to be some clues there. Also my idea takes away any surveillance teams that maybe have eyes on the house."

"What if they are using electronics, cameras and such?" Captain Lustig said.

"I've been told I look good in a head-to-toe hazmat suit."

"You know, I can't find a thing wrong with it!" And so, with that statement, Bill effectively greenlighted Brooke's out-of-the-box scheme.

XXXI. IT'S A GAS

It took about an hour for the techs at SIG, the Swiss gas company, to rig a fuel oil truck with two pressurized tanks of pure T-butyl mercaptan, the foul smelling additive to normally odorless natural gas that allows immediate detection of gas leaks or extinguished pilot lights. They also wired up a remote aerosol nozzle to dissipate the chemical safely. Their fluid dynamics engineers gave the final approval by judging that the colorless cloud of dissipated mercaptan would stink up the whole neighborhood without any toxicity to the residents. Although, one added, some people might vomit.

At 10:30 a.m., an innocuous tank truck turned down the street that Raffey's house was on. Ten minutes later, the calls started coming in to SIG, local police, and the firehouses. Brooke was briefly instructed on the gas mask and ventilator that kept her hazmat suit cool and waited for the organic progression of police or fire to call on the gas company to investigate the leak. Their first plan was to order the immediate evacuation of the entire neighborhood. Bill had added a great touch by suggesting that the leak was so severe that the air space above the leak be cleared lest a possible static discharge from the rotors of a copter ignite the very air itself.

Brooke rolled in the first SIG truck on the scene. The engineer who rigged the tank truck was first out with a handheld monitor and declared the leak at five hundred parts per million, which was the trip wire for mass evacuations. The police and fire companies went to work, and by 11: 45 a.m. a three-block square area surrounding Raffey's house was a ghost town; even pets were brought to the temporary shelters set up at two local high schools. SIG released a statement saying the residents should only be inconvenienced for three to four hours.

Only the gas company engineer and Brooke knew this was a false alarm. All the other gas, police, and fire personnel took it as seriously as they had been trained to do, which included insuring that the citizens didn't lock their doors, so that the gas crew could have acces to find the leak. One added plus was that the procedure for gas leaks mandated that the power to the affected blocks be cut. This was done to protect against accidental ignition by electrical spark from timers, heaters, and other automatic electric appliances that could trigger a gas cloud into an explosive force.

Still, for appearances, and any battery powered cameras or monitoring devices, Brooke first went into the house next to Raffey's, as over fifty crewmembers went into every other house on the street. She dallied for a few minutes and then went to Raffey's. The door was locked, and she had to fumble a little working the lock pick and tension bar through hazmat gloves.

Once inside, she removed her hazmat helmet and took a big flashlight out of her tool bag. She opened the hall closet and saw the M-16 and the box of ammo on the shelf. She rifled through the clothes hanging in the hall closet. She found women's and little girl's coats, hats, and gloves. She went into the kitchen. This morning Raffey had had breakfast for one, left dishes in the sink and should have taken out the garbage. She went into the den, reached in her bag, and placed a small disk device under his keyboard. She also rested a similar device over his cable modem. Brooke found the power strip to the computer, unplugged it from the wall, and plugged it into the ten-pound uninterruptable power supply in the canvas sack she had lugged in. The UPS had a lead-acid battery that could power a computer for up to twenty minutes if the wall power went out. She would only need ten. She put a five-terabyte hard drive into the fire wire port, turned it on, and hoped there wasn't a password on his home computer. The pre-programmed hard drive dug right in and started cloning Raffey's entire computer and drives. She went down into the basement looking for Bill's gory freezer stuffed-with-dismembered-family-members, but all she found was a mouse in a humane trap. She released the little creature and then went upstairs to the second floor and found Kirsi's room. The drawers were full, her closet full, and her hamper smelled like it hadn't been cleared in weeks. She found Leena's room to be the same. The bathroom cabinet showed no prescription medicines for any of them. She noticed Raffey used a hair dryer this morning. Leena's heated curlers, which were the kind you could take with you, were on the shelf with the cord wrapped around them. In fact, Leena's makeup case was untouched and could have easily been grabbed if she had left on a planned trip.

She took out her camera and went back to take a picture of Raffey's desk and his papers as she rifled through his notes and doodlings. She checked the drive, it had two more minutes to go. She looked around and then had an idea. She ran upstairs, took the teddy bear pillow pet from Kirsi's bed and shoved it in her kit. In the kitchen, she opened the cabinet below the counter and attached a magnetic box to the underside of the sink.

When the drive finished its copying routine, she wrapped it up and placed it back in her kit. She shut down Raffey's computer and re-plugged it into the wall. She tried to replace the notes and other items on his desk exactly as they were, using as a guide the first picture she took on her digital camera before she moved everything. One last look and she left. Again, for appearance's sake, she entered to the house across the street.

By two thirty, the all clear was given and the gas company released a statement that the source of the leak was a separated main trunk line that led to the house three down from Raffey's. They thanked the residents and the emergency services personnel for a quick, orderly, efficient evacuation, which ensured minimal disruption to everyone's lifestyle.

∞§∞

"Most disturbing." The Engineer took a drag from his skinny cigarette and blew out the smoke with an exasperated sigh. He turned to the Architect, "Do you believe in coincidences?"

"According to the gas company, the leak was on the same street. I would have been more suspicious if it had happened when Juth was home. As it is, if they did plan this, they were inept in not securing him in one of the shelters. I'd say whether actual or induced, the gas leak has not damaged us."

"Yes, but they shut down the power; our cameras were blind. And Klaus and his team were moved out with the other evacuees. We have no way of knowing if they went into the house or even near it." Maya pointed this out as she shut off the TV news, which only had a shot taken from a camera at the police line five blocks away.

"Well, Architect, how do you wish to proceed?" The Engineer said.

After a long moment's contemplation, he looked at Maya. "Maya, did Kraus report smelling any gas?"

"Yes, he said the odor was quite strong."

"That would seem to support the coincidence theory, but just as a precaution, do you think we need to reinforce our position with Juth?"

"It couldn't hurt. Just in case the authorities did try something, he'll know that we know, and that should make him resist any thought of going along with them." Maya said.

"What would you suggest?" The Engineer was agreeing.

"Let's send him a body part," Maya suggested as if she were sending flowers.

"I would not suggest any physical connection right now. We don't know if the police have wired the block. Any attempt to reach him with anything physical may expose us with only one day remaining before the Landau experiment," the Architect countered.

Maya actually was deflated. But she understood the risk.

In the end, they decided on a phone call.

∞§∞

In a small town newsroom in Maryland, cub reporter Juan Gonzales was pitching a story to his editor. "So what I am saying is this Landau guy dies in a copter accident, he's got some kind of connection with the government in some forward looking initiative for science, and in Europe they are about to run something, my source tells me, is called the Landau protocol. It's the reason people are gathering and planning to protest.

"Conspiracy theories don't win Pulitzers, there is no second source on this. There's nothing on the web anywhere."

"Maybe they erased it from the web?"

"You can't do that. There's always a trace and besides no one in the government is that smart, only in the movies. Until you get a second source, your story is spiked."

∞§∞

"Dis is friggin' easy," Kronos said as he dove into the contents of the hard drive that Brooke had downloaded from Raffey's computer. He was a little punchy after flying all through the night, but seven cups of coffee later his digital skill was as sharp as ever.

"Kronos, look closely for any communication that could tell us where the kidnappers are holding the family," Bill stressed as he reviewed the photo prints of Raffey's notes that were part of the treasure trove that Brooke's fake gas emergency diversion had provided.

"What was he doing, thinking about gambling?" Brooke asked as she studied one picture of a page from his yellow pad that showed a doodle of a roulette wheel.

"Let me see." Joey took the photo and looked closely. "What's this next to it — university?"

"That's what I thought, but it's an abbreviation. Maybe University of Xenia, Ohio?" Brooke said.

"Right, it is U-N-I-X, not V."

"Roulette dot unix," Kronos said.

"How do you figure that?" Joey asked as he moved the photo closer and farther to try and make out the chicken scratch.

"Because it's right here on the friggin' drive. It's a unix operating program. I'm opening it now."

"So our boy Raffey had dreams of the big wheel at Monte Carlo?" Joey said.

"My cousin, Mathilde, lives a few miles away from there. I can swing on down in one of your SAM flights, check the casino cameras ,and be back by dinner!"

"Let's see what brain boy comes up with first, shall we?" Bill said.

"It's a super-collider simulation program. It is just one module, but it has open loops to another program. This is interesting — "

"What's happening now is our techno-sapien, as I like to call him, has latched onto a digital clue. At times like this, our whole plan can change...wait for it...wait for it," Bill said.

"Leather Pants was planning to do something; he was running a lot of permutations of different acceleration possibilities and some sort of malfunction."

"And there it is," Bill said.

"Okay, help me here, Kronos. Was he trying to figure out how to make the thing go boom or trying to stop it from going all blooey?" Brooke asked as she stood behind him looking at the lines of code, which meant nothing to her, but was clear as day to the human robot.

"That I can't tell without the master program at the Hadron that he was tied into," Kronos said.

"And there it's not," Bill said, surprised for the first time that Kronos didn't know everything.

"But he was playing with destroying the rings, right?" Brooke said.

"He ran a program in which various paths to destroying it were simulated. But again, you'd do the exact same thing whether you're trying to destroy them or stop their destruction," Kronos said.

"So you can't tell intent? Is that what you are telling me, Kronos?" Bill said.

"That's pretty much the story, Hick."

"Keep digging, see what else you could find," Bill said, more as an order than a suggestion. Then he turned to Brooke, "University of Xenia? Ohio?"

"Sorry, it was just the first thing that came to my head," Brooke said. She grabbed a set of the note photos, and flopped down on the couch in the conference room. She was up again like a jackrabbit in one second. "Wait a minute. Kronos, he has made no connection to the Internet for weeks. So how could he interface with the computers at Hadron?"

"Here it is, it's a whole compiled routine under another program called Wedgestone. Hey, this is brilliant work. Didn't you say this guy got an award or some shit?"

"Yes. He received a new car for a program he wrote," Captain Lustig chimed in as he flipped his notes. "Here it is, stabilization of accumulated data during sensor input lag."

"Sure, that explains these polynomials and all the variable fractals this bad boy draws on. Saaweet hunk of code here, Billy boy."

"So, now can you determine what he was doing with this program?" Bill asked.

"I can try, but his ultimate reason for doing this may not be apparent just from this one program."

"What does that mean..." Bill's question was interrupted by a loud signal emanating from the clone phone system that the FedPol techs had set up. It had been silent since its establishment a week ago. Everybody froze. The tech held up his hand as he hit record, but nothing happened.

"False alarm?" Kronos asked.

"Pocket call or wrong number maybe," Brooke said.

Then it rang a second time. This time they heard Raffey pick up.

"Hello?" It was Juth, tentative and cautious as he spoke.

"The authorities were in your house today." The voice on the other end said flatly.

Bill shot a glance to Brooke, who closed her eyes; her ruse didn't work.

"What? No. There was no one in this house. When?"

"Today, during the gas leak."

"What gas leak? I don't know what you are talking about."

"Do we need to send you Kirsi's left foot?"

"No, no. Don't do that. I'm sorry, I'm sorry I didn't know. But my door was locked and nothing here has been touched. Are you sure they were in this house?"

"It does not matter. If you even think of going to them, your sister will regret ever bringing her daughter into this world. Do you understand?"

"Yes, of course, I've done everything you've said, please just don't hurt them. Please."

"You will perform your task tomorrow during the first test. Do you understand?"

"Yes. During the first experiment. Then you'll let them go?"

"If you perform well, yes."

"May I speak to them? Please, I beg you, let me just know..." The connection was ended but Raffey continued, "No...No! Just let me know they are okay, damn you!" Then he sobbed and eventually hung up.

"Did we get a location?" Joey ran to the tech. He held up his hand as he was in communication with the signal tracers on another floor. "We got the cell tower. North of the city. That's as close as we got."

"I want a map now! And start scrubbing the audio, I want voice print, background amplification and any other electronic test that can lead us to a twenty on these people, er — location." Joey used the common American radio code 'twenty' from the ten-twenty signal used almost universally by cops and later Civilian Band radio code used by truckers as a request for or statement of one's location.

"Boss, I want in on this. I want to get those people back safe," Brooke said.

Bill looked to Joey. "Joey's call."

"Brooke, get 'em back alive, girl."

Brooke ran from the room, headed down to the ready room to suit up for battle.

"Kronos, anything else?"

"I think he's planning to do something with the power frequency."

"Why do you say that?"

"All the simulations I have found seem to deal with over-heated magnets in the rings. As far as I know, the only way to get them to heat up would be to throw them out of their efficiency peak."

"Couldn't that also happen with a surge?" Bill said.

"Harder to do because the circuit breaker would trip. But amperage-or wattage-based breakers would be impervious to frequency shift. In fact, the result of the counter-EMF inductive forces within the magnet would actually decrease the draw."

"Because the hysteresis curve starts trading frequency for I squared R losses very rapidly," Bill reasoned as he looked over Kronos' shoulder at the screen.

"Whoa! Hey, English only here..." Joey protested with his hands up.

"Or at least German," Captain Lustig said.

"Let's just say he can melt the rings in a few milliseconds."

"So that sounds like he breaks the thing. How is that a black hole event?" Joey said.

"It depends when he does it. If he does it before the collision, it's just a broken machine. If he does it at the point of collision, then no safe-guards."

"One more time for the slow of thinking, please?"

"Magnetic bubble or jar. The whole Landau experiment depends on the suspension of the collided matter floating or suspended in a magnetic field, not touching any other matter."

"That's why inside the rings it's a vacuum that equals deep space. The acceleration is done with the magnetism created by 9,300 super-cooled and superconducting magnets, and so is the containment of the mini big bang."

"So if you disable the magnetic containment and the explosion starts to interact with the matter that makes up the rings and the supports and eventually the support concrete..."

"Then the earth it's seated into, then the dark matter that surrounds us and eventually sucking in all the planets, galaxies, and then the entire universe till it's all so compressed it becomes another big bang."

∞§∞

Brooke had strapped on a Kevlar vest and had an MP-5 submachine gun, two Mark 7 concussive flares (stun grenades), a night vision goggle headset, her Glock model 17 tactical weapon 9 on her hip, and a Seecamp .32 caliber semi-auto in her ankle holster. She was driven by a Swiss SWAT sergeant in his civilian car to be less conspicuous. They cruised the streets in the area north of the city where the cell tower was, looking for a strategic rationale with which to spot a potential safe house. She didn't know what she was looking for, but had to try to spot a place she would select if she were a bad guy.

∞§∞

Raffey started the day with the thought that this was the day he and his family would die in sacrifice for the continuance of all mankind and every other planet in the galaxy. Either that or his last-minute gambit would work. He prayed all night and into the day that his plan would work, and if it did not, that the death of his family would be swift and painless.

The first attempt at the collision was computer-timed and accurately set for 3:00:01:000000001 p.m., that is, one billionth of a second past one second after 3 p.m. Geneva time. He'd make his call at 1 p.m. in order to give the kidnappers two hours. As a mid-level-ranked chess master, he had played out all the gambits, moves, and countermoves. It was his riskiest play ever, but he knew that in the end, he had to risk it all.

∞§∞

Brooke had narrowed her mental list down to four structures which were the most favorable if you wanted to hide out with hostages, yet not be totally incapacitated as to means of escape or blindness to any approach. Of course, it didn't mean the bad guys read the same tactical books she had studied at Quantico, but there was no other way to whittle down a list. She checked her watch: *10:32 a.m.* Bill's meeting at the Hadron should be starting.

∞§∞

"Dr. Hiccock, the claims you have made here this morning are fantastic, to say the least," the head of the Large Hadron Collider proclaimed as he turned to his colleagues, who nodded in support.

"Sir, your own head of security concurs," Bill said.

"Is this true, Jenson?"

"Yes, I am afraid the confidence is high that Mr. Juth may have an ulterior purpose."

"Well, have we talked to him?"

Bill resisted the urge to say, *it isn't that simple*; instead he tried to use a scientific rationale. "Sir, it is a matter of cause and effect. While Mr. Juth may be committed to this path, we don't know what the effect would be of confronting him. It could be disastrous. Instead, I believe our plan to isolate and contain him will yield the greatest amount of actionable data which we can then use to get all the facts as to complicity and accomplices."

"I see. Of course this means our entire Landau Protocol's-worth of experiments, our most ambitious effort yet will be derailed. The delay could cost us weeks."

"I am aware of your schedule and the incredible cost that disengaging from your schedule will bear. But erring on the side of safety, not only for you, but for the facility as well as the machine, is in the final analysis the best, and may I dare say, the only course of action."

The men around the table, all multi-PhDs and esteemed men of science, held an eyes-only conference and wound up all nodding. "Dr. Hiccock, we will follow your directive. We will take Mr. Juth out of the equation by not actually running today's centerpiece experiment."

"Thank you, gentlemen. May I stress how essential it is that he not know that this is not a real experiment? If at any time he senses we are aware of him, I fear we will lose any hope of eliminating this threat and all its components."

One of the men at the table, who had not spoken previously, stood. "His console will be disarmed at the hub, but I can have nominal critical feedback routed to his station so that up to the moment he deviates from his tasks he won't suspect a thing."

"Thank you. That is precisely what we need."

Then the head of the LHC spoke again. "Of course Dr. Hiccock, what if his means of destruction isn't digital? What if there is some other attack, a physical one in the works?"

"We have taken steps. As soon as Mr. Juth signed in, army forces secured the facility from the outside, so if he is merely going to open the door for others who would do the deed, they will be stopped by the security." Bill motioned for Jenson to continue.

"Also we have physical examination of every part of the collider and its support systems being checked by hand and electronic surveillance, including bomb sniffing dogs and experts in detonation all along the seventeen-mile ring," Jenson said.

∞§∞

The immense size of the collider facility and the hundreds of staff meant there was much distance between Juth's desk and any of the security measures being put in place. No one in his section was aware of any army personnel or search dogs, those elements being at least a quarter-mile away and above ground.

The "spin up" procedure was progressing normally toward the fraction-of-a-second-past-3:00:01 p.m. collision. Raffey's part in the scientific drama had been rehearsed to be easily performed on the actual day of a collision, so he had time to go over in his mind his ultimatum to the bad guys and to pray to the ultimate good guy a few times.

At 12:57 p.m., Raffey left his station and headed for the employee smoking area. Most people in Europe had not read the American papers on the evils of smoking, so the place was packed. He decided to find a quieter place. There was an exit door in the hallway that afforded him quiet and seclusion to set forth his master plan.

He punched in the number that he had detangled from encrypted data strings he monitored at home when the

364 *The God Particle*

kidnappers called. The phone rang three times. Raffey imagined them in shock, looking at the phone which they were sure was a secure one-way line.

The call was answered, but no one on the other side spoke. Raffey took a deep breath and read from the prepared speech he had written, rewritten, scrapped, and written again dozens of times since his plan emerged. "In two hours I will become an unnecessary appendage, and as such will be of no further use to you. Since I am the only one who can achieve your goal, you must comply with my demand. I want proof that my sister and her daughter are safe at a police station, or I will not carry out your plan. You can no longer pressure me. I know you will kill them as soon as I do what you ask, if they are not dead already. You have one hour and fifty-eight minutes to prove to me they are alive and safe. There will be no further communications."

His hand was shaking, as he ended the call and crumpled the paper.

∞§∞

"Brooke, Kronos got a twenty! Juth just made contact with the bad guys. We got the address." Joey said over the phone. "It seems like Juth has given them an ultimatum."

Brooke immediately tightened the straps on her vest and seated a magazine in the machine gun on her lap as her driver headed to the address.

∞§∞

"How do we respond to this?" The Engineer asked.

"We must maintain our control over him. He cannot feel that he has any choice in the matter," the Architect said.

Maya grabbed the cell phone and turned on the video camera.

"He wants proof of life; let's send him proof of death."

"How would that work to our goals?" The Engineer said dismissively.

"We only kill one!"

∞§∞

The hideout was an abandoned tire factory that had been one of the possible targets on Brooke's quick list. From a safe distance, she used extreme-powered binoculars and spotted a lookout on the eastern end of the roof. She estimated the shot at about six hundred yards. "Get your sharpshooter team up here on the double," she ordered the Swiss SWAT commander.

"As soon as the lookout is neutralized we go right through the front gate. On the way we'll use the radar imagery scope and locate the outlines." She took out of her breast pocket a copy of the picture from Juth's desk. Even though every cop on the case had a copy and memorized the faces and body types, she held it up, tapping it, "Remember we got two hostages, an adult female and a little girl." Three more SWAT members appeared. "You three, you are responsible for any opposition on the first floor. We are weapons-free, but somewhere in there is a person who can be a high-valued intelligence target. He is known as The Engineer or Architect, or it could be two targets. We'd like them alive if possible, but take no chances. Everybody gets to go home tonight, right?"

The eight SWAT guys and the commander answered verbally in unison, "Right!"

Thirty seconds later, the Swiss kill team was on the roof of a nearby building and drawing a bead on the lookout at the factory. A few seconds later, as Brooke was closing the door on the SWAT van that would ram the front gate, her radio crackled, "Target acquired."

"Take 'em out," she said into the radio mic, then turned to the driver, "Gun it."

Through the scope of the GM6 sniper rifle, the police sharpshooter could see the lookout scanning the terrain. He saw the man stop his right-to-left panning of the area that lay before him and swing his glass back to the sniper's own position, where he surely thought he saw a glint. If he did, it was the last thing he saw, as the 50-caliber slug punched a hole in his forehead and blew the back of his skull halfway across the rooftop.

As soon as the spotter radioed, "Confirm one kill," the van smashed through the rickety cyclone fence and darted to the entrance of the factory.

Brooke jumped out of the vehicle before it came to a full stop, shouting, "Go, go, go, go!"

In the hallway of the dilapidated factory one of The Engineer's goons saw the van lurch. He ran to the front door and trained his weapon on the first person exiting the truck.

He squeezed the trigger, but was spun around as his shoulder exploded from another .50 caliber sniper round that made him grunt.

Upon hearing the grunt, Brooke raised her silenced Glock Model 17 and fired. The goon hit the floor dead. She was in full run and jumped over his body as she hit the lobby. She glanced at her phone, which was getting the video signal from the radar scanner, which finds warm bodies through concrete walls. It showed five targets on the second floor, then two in the corner of a room on the other side of the second floor. But what caught her eye was the outline of a lone figure headed toward the two distant outlines nestled in the corner of the distant room. The stillness of the other figures told her that the presence of her team was not yet known to the remainder of bad guys in the building.

∞§∞

At the Large Hadron Collider, Bill had taken up a position fifty feet from Juth in a room that was just off his area. The big clock on the wall read 2:57:08 p.m. He hoped Brooke was seconds away from rescuing the reason Raffey was following their unthinkable orders. That was the pivot point the whole operation rested on; namely Bill's assessment that Juth was not the mastermind of the plan and was being pressured. Just in case, a Swiss army commando was seated next to Bill. If Brooke was unsuccessful, or Juth proved to be the real threat, hell bent on blowing up the LHC, the military man's orders were to put a bullet into Juth's prodigious brain. Bill was okay with this back-up plan because, in the end, he felt the universe was protected whichever way this turned out.

∞§∞

Brooke found the main staircase and was joined by the first floor team, who now headed up to the second floor and to the cluster of bad guys. Brooke headed toward the two figures in the far off room. She was convinced they were the hostages and, with the clock ticking, the figure heading toward them was their executioner. She took the stairs two at a time and before going through the door waved on a SWAT guy with a fiber optic camera. He bent the flexible lens around the corner and saw that the way was clear. She pointed to the five-man kill team and directed them to the room down the hall, and she ran off in the other direction with one cop in tow.

The main body of the SWAT team reached the room, which held the five figures. A flash bang would have been the recommended way of storming the room, thus temporarily blinding and deafening the men inside, however, with the hostages' whereabouts not confirmed, the noise could signal their hasty execution. So they hit the room in force and acquired targets, shooting to kill those with weapons and to wound those who were unarmed. As they had practiced for hundreds of hours, they swept in, two right, two left and one center, each responsible for his own field of fire. Their instincts took over from there; two men in the room with weapons in their hands were immediate kills, one from team right and one from team left. The center SWAT man shot the legs out from under one of two older men and placed the muzzle of his gun on the temple of the other, who was scrambling across the table to get a pistol. The man saw the logic in freezing and retracting his hand. Given the muzzle suppressors of their guns, the sound didn't go much farther than the immediate hallway around the room, and since no bad guy got a shot off, their presence was still a secret.

The center man suddenly realized something. "Confirm, I count four targets?"

"Confirm four," came the response that caused him to say, "Shit, one got away!"

Three from the team immediately hurried to get the one who was now running toward the other end of the building.

∞§∞

Checking her phone quickly, Brooke saw her own outline and that of the figure just ahead, but there was no one in the corridor in front of her. She immediately reckoned there was a parallel hallway. Then her phone lost its signal in the steel of factory structure. She was flying blind now, but knew she had just seconds to save the mother and child.

As she reached a crossing corridor, she cautiously approached the corner. The SWAT guy looked with the fiber optic gooseneck lens and gave her the clear sign. She ran as lightly as she could in order to not give her position away. She knew the figure headed toward her might not have passed this corridor yet, and at any second she could stumble across the person, so she had her weapon up and was ready to kill anything coming at her. First she peeked around the corner in the direction someone would come from. It was clear; a quick turn of the head allowed her to catch a glimpse of a woman entering the room at the end of the hall.

Brooke padded quickly to the end of the hall and flattened up against the door jamb. She pivoted in and saw a woman standing five feet from Leena and her daughter. Then the woman's cell phone's bright video light went on and

Brooke could see the image of the two hostages cowering in the screen.

The woman spoke, "You want to play games?" She cocked the gun and pointed it at Leena. Brooke raised her weapon and squeezed the trigger, but at that instant her body was racked to one side by a concussion in her left shoulder bade. The impact made Brooke stumble as she fired and missed the center mass of the woman, instead hitting her in the arm. She then heard two shots behind her.

The trooper down the hall reacted immediately when a man unexpectedly came out of the stairwell door right next to the room at the end of the hall. The man got off the shot that hit Brooke in the back of her vest, but before he could fire again, the SWAT man double-tapped the intruder in the head and he was down.

Brooke had a searing pain in her left shoulder and was on one knee trying to raise her weapon. She saw the face of the woman as she was also struggling to raise her own weapon. Brooke managed to flop her almost-dead hand onto her knee, adjusted her aim from her hip, and hit the woman dead-center. The woman fell back as her gun fired, the bullet perforating the ceiling. The SWAT guy jumped over Brooke, ran to the downed woman, and kicked the gun away from her lifeless hands. In short gasps, Brooke demanded the phone from the woman's hand. When she got it she told the SWAT man to squat next to the hostages. Brooke fumbled with her good hand and pressed the FaceTime icon. She had the camera pointed at herself and could see her own image on the screen. The call was answered by Raffey. Through short labored breaths she said, "Mr. Juth...your family is safe... with the Swiss...police." She turned the camera around and showed him the two of them with the Swiss SWAT guy as she reiterated, "Again, they...are safe this...is real time, they have been...rescued." Then the camera hit the floor as Brooke collapsed.

∞§∞

Watching all this on the cloned phone one room away was Bill, who looked at the clock as it clicked under five seconds to the collision, '2:59:55:54.' "Let's go!" he said to his military guy, and they entered the room where Juth was seated at his workstation holding the phone. Immediately, Bill had a bad feeling about what he saw.

∞§∞

The screen showed the video that proved his family was safe and there were tears in his eyes, yet he busily typed away. Three seconds.

"Raffael Juth! It's over! Your family is safe — step away from the console," Bill barked as he approached.

The soldier drew a bead on Raffey. "Put your hands in the air, now!"

One second.

Juth looked to Bill; there was a small smile of satisfaction breaking as he pushed the enter key. The blood from his head wound splattered over the workstation and the keyboard before the alarms started sounding.

Bill grabbed a supervisor who stood nearby, stunned by the gore, and snapped him out of it. "What did he do? Can you reverse it? Hey! What did he do?"

Cautiously, the supervisor looked at the blood-spattered screen. All he could say was, "Oh, my God."

Bill pushed him aside to see if he could reverse whatever Juth had just done when everything started shaking and a low rumbling growl enveloped the room. It was like an earthquake. Every screen and meter flashed and pinned against the maximum range.

A moment of extreme terror froze Bill's mind and body as he looked at Juth's lifeless body and realized that he had been wrong — it had been Juth all along.

A technician three positions over yelled, "Ring temperature critical and rising...off the scale."

The supervisor, now engaged in the drama, looked over Bill's shoulder and flatly and without emotion said in a small voice, "He overrode our simulation with his own; he's melting the machine."

Bill's mind raced, it didn't go off! Everything is still here. Everything should have been atomically disrupted, a cloud of plasma to dissipate into nothingness. Yet we are all still here. Then he got it. Juth made his own play, a master's gambit to rob from anybody else the opportunity to destroy eternity. Bill looked down at Juth's lifeless body and was caught by the now frozen smile of satisfaction on his face. "Well played, Raffey. Sorry you didn't get to call 'Checkmate!'"

XXXII. GIFTS BOTH BIG AND SMALL

Brooke returned to consciousness on a gurney outside the factory, her shoulder bandaged. On a gurney to her right were Leena and Kirsi. She called a SWAT guy over and whispered something into his ear, and he trotted off. Leena was crying — her ordeal was over and her emotions flowed. Through her sobs she saw the cop come back carrying something. She wiped her teary eyes and saw that it was Kirsi's 'beebeebear.' The mother started heaving deeper sobs as the magnanimity of the gesture released even more torrents of emotion. She looked to Brooke and said, "Vielen Dank, Vielen Dank."

Brooke managed a half smile, but the strain of holding her head up took over and she lay back down. She rolled her head sideways and saw the little girl squeal with delight as she hugged the worn, ratty stuffed toy almost as tightly as her mother was hugging her. Brooke closed her eyes as the IV of painkillers kicked in, her last thought being that this was the best way to end her career and start her new life with Mush.

∞§∞

"Seventeen years!" was what Bill told President Mitchell over his secure phone when he asked how long the collider would be out of commission.

"So we all dodged a bullet then?" the president said, not hiding his relief.

"It seems that Juth outsmarted everyone. He paid for it with his life, but he took away the biggest target any terror group could hope for, and maybe saved the known universe as well."

"How's Brooke? I heard she was shot."

"She's good; the bullet was slowed by the back of her vest and lodged in her muscle. She'll be sore for a while but the docs here say no permanent damage but she'll know when it's going to rain without a forecast."

"Thank God."

"What do we know about who was behind this?"

"We've got The Engineer and The Architect. So far they seem like our worst nightmare: brilliant, insane, and bent on a religious belief that if they destroy everything, their God will be able to rebuild a perfect new universe — without infidels."

"So detonating the collider was the only way they could have ever even dreamed of achieving that madness."

"Again, Juth has made sure that no one else in the fore- seeable future could ever get that close."

"The man gave his life to see to it; to some he will be a hero."

"I can live with that, sir," He smiled at Janice as she walked over to him. His attention returned to the phone as the presi- dent's tone changed.

"Bill, you and your team performed above and beyond any expectations a commander-in-chief could wish for. Hell, you've already got lots of medals you can never show anyone. Is there something else our nation could do for you?"

"Two things, sir."

"Name 'em."

"Can Janice, Joey, Phyllis, Brooke, Mush Morton, Kronos, and whatever he is dating these days book in for a weekend at Camp David? That was awesome."

"That's easy. Done. Next?"

"A full scholarship and the full death benefits befitting a staff officer for the family of Corporal Deon Bradley; a good man, a patriot-warrior and loving father who died too soon, sir."

"Great idea Bill. In fact, I'll cover the scholarship myself and Congress will enact the annuity to his wife and kid."

"Then I'd say we are even, sir."

Bill slipped the phone in his pocket.

Janice was beaming at him. "That was the best thing you could've asked for. And you, my dear husband, are the best thing I could ever ask for."

She turned and leaned back against Bill. He put his arms around her as they enjoyed the silence and the exquisite storybook beauty of the lake. It seemed unreal that five hundred feet below, the rings had melted and collapsed. Thankfully, the machine's demise did not mar the beauty of Lake Geneva and this picture-perfect setting... or the universe.

"Mmmm, beautiful isn't it." Janice said as she sighed.

"Yes, you are." Bill nuzzled and kissed her neck.

"Okay, I've had enough of this place, lets grab some chocolate and go home."

"I'm right there with ya."

∞§∞

Ten hours later, they were standing by the lake behind their Great Falls, Virginia house. The morning sun was burning off the mist.

"Ours is pretty too," Janice said, again leaning against Bill with his arms around her as they both appreciated the panorama of God's creation in a new light.

"Yes, you are."

She turned in his arms, "Bill, that line's getting a little o..."

He kissed her. She threw her arms up over his shoulders and pulled him in tighter.

They continued to kiss like that until little Richie started running around them with his toy helicopter and saying, "Boom. Boom. Boom."

XXXIII. THE HOMECOMING

A month and five days after the collider was disabled and the universe was safe, Brooke stood on the wharf looking out over the warm, tranquil waters of Pearl Harbor. For forty minutes, she had watched the USS *Nebraska*, from when it was a dot on the horizon until she steamed past the Arizona Memorial with all hands manning the rails in tribute and salute to the fallen men and ships of December 1941. The SSBN 739, the USS *Nebraska*, Mush's boat, was built to deter any future nation from even contemplating a similar attack.

From the bridge of the boomer, Mush let his exec dock the boat. His total concentration was on the blonde standing on the pier with her arm in a sling. At that second he patted the cold, titanium edge of the conning tower as he whispered "goodbye, old girl" to his first wife.

- — - — - —

Acknowledgments

I am blessed to have a mastermind group of individuals who guide me through the specifics of lives that I have not lived. They freely lend their experience, knowledge, and achievements to me so that I may tell you a better story. In no particular order (because they would all be first on the list) they are:

Colonel Michael T. Miklos, US Army Retired, who provides a dash of warrior spirit in my story recipe that makes all things military in my work very tasty and, more importantly, correct.

Len Watson, my science soulmate, who places no limits on his contributions and encouragement of me when I am deep in the insecurity of building a story.

Anthony Lombardo, Retired First Grade Detective NYPD, who keeps all those "gotcha" e-mails from gun enthusiasts at a minimum as he makes my weapon choices and police procedure... bulletproof.

My cousin, author George Cannistraro, whose brilliant analysis always points me to golden nuggets of plot and character that I didn't see.

Editor Sue Rasmussen, who was with me brick by brick as I built the book. Sue's ability to decode what I thought was English into words and sentences that now read exactly like I meant them to was a luxury that I had the good fortune to enjoy.

Monta, who shares my life and shares me with the writing process. Without a complaint, she allows me to work at times when we should be at play.

To MHC who, with a few choice words, reached across the great divide that separated my aspiration from her tremendous fame and achievement. She steeled my confidence by giving me a glimpse of what was possible.

And my publisher, Lou Aronica of The Story Plant, who is a Zen master at compelling me to be a better novelist. He has potent "mojo," which puts me under the illusion that no challenge is too big, no rewrite insurmountable.

And finally to you, the reader. I have been thinking about you since I wrote the first sentence. And unless you jumped right to the acknowledgments before reading the book, I assume you stayed with me to the last line. Thank you, for without you I am writing to myself.

A Word about Mush and Subs

Which is also to say a word about courage, honor and sacrifice. I met Dudley "Mush" Morton posthumously through the excellent work of William Tuohy. His book, *The Bravest Man*, affected me like a rocket's red glare over Ft.McHenry. Everything I thought knew of war and human commitment to a cause was crystallized between the pages of that book. My invention of a third generation Morton to embody the best traditions of the service is my feeble attempt to encapsulate the tremendous respect, reverence and awe that arises in me whenever I read or hear of bravery in the face of adversity. My efforts in this book are a mere penny toward the trillions in the debt-of-honor we owe those who fought, fight, and will fight again to preserve our way of life.

In the writing of this story, I used many reference books, two in particular: *Stealth Boat: Fighting the Cold War in a Fast-Attack Submarine* by Gannon Mchale and *Silent Steel: The Mysterious Death of the Nuclear Attack Sub USS* Scorpion by Steven Johnson. I developed the deep-water intelligence plot in this book from tendrils of the accounts in those and other books. However, it wasn't until after *The God Particle* was in editorial that, amazingly, a veteran submariner who served on the USS *Growler* said, "Oh, like Blind Man's Bluff!" Ten seconds later, I was feeling foolish. Coming at subs from the land, I only knew what I read. Obviously, I never heard of or read *Blind Man's Bluff: The Untold Story of American Submarine Espionage* by Sherry Sontag, which is, as I found out, a very popular and well known nonfiction book. If you loved the sequence under the sea to retrieve the crucibles, you will love *Blind Man's Bluff*. But read my next book, *The Devil's Quota*, first.

About the Author

TOM AVITABILE, a Senior VP/Creative Director at a New York advertising firm, is a writer, director, and producer with numerous film and television credits. He has an extensive background in engineering and computers, including work on projects for the House Committee on Science and Technology, which helped lay the foundation for *The Eighth Day*, his first novel. In his spare time, Tom is a professional musician and an amateur woodworker. He recently completed his fourth novel, *The Devil's Quota*.